Praise for

"Pineiro knows how to move a story right along smartly from one crisis to the next with the tension always building . . . gets right under the reader's skin so that in the end the payoff is like the Fourth of July fireworks."

—David Hagberg, *New York Times*
bestselling author of *The Expediter*

"Pineiro scrunches you into the ejection seat and sends you rocketing aloft."   —Dean Ing, *New York Times*
bestselling author of *Loose Cannon*

"Move over, Tom Clancy, there is a new kid on the block."
—*Library Journal*

"Readers with voracious appetites for fast action and hardware . . . will come for this book in droves."
—*Booklist* on *Cyberterror*

"Pineiro's vision of what might be evokes visceral fear."
—Mark Berent, *New York Times*
bestselling author of *Storm Flight*, on *Firewall*

BOOKS BY R. J. PINEIRO

Siege of Lightning (1993)
Ultimatum (1994)
Retribution (1995)
Exposure (1996)
Breakthrough (1997)
01-01-00 (1999)
Y2K (1999)
Shutdown (2000)
Conspiracy.com (2001)
Firewall (2002)
Cyberterror (2003)
Havoc (2005)
Spywave (2007)
The Eagle and the Cross (2008)

For more information on R. J. Pineiro's novels, visit his website at: www.rjpineiro.com.

HAVOC

R. J. PINEIRO

A TOM DOHERTY ASSOCIATES BOOK
NEW YORK

HAVOC

Copyright © 2005 R. J. Pineiro

A Forge Book
Published by Tom Doherty Associates, LLC
175 Fifth Avenue
New York, NY 10010

www.tor-forge.com

Forge® is a registered trademark of Tom Doherty Associates, LLC.

ISBN 978-0-7653-4733-6

First Edition: December 2005
First Mass Market Edition: February 2010

Printed in the United States of America

0 9 8 7 6 5 4 3 2 1

ACKNOWLEDGMENTS

This project combines most of my passions, from computer technology, covert ops, and weapons, to martial arts, aviation, and international travel. I consider myself damned lucky to be able to enjoy so many interests, and I feel blessed to be able to bring them all together through my greatest passion: the love for the written word.

As with all of my previous efforts, this one came to fruition with the help of a handful of wonderful and talented individuals:

My wife, Lory, my first line of defense against embarrassing myself. Thank you for your unconditional love, friendship, and support. None of this would have been possible without the sacrifices that you make so I can craft these stories. You are indeed the wind beneath my wings.

My son, Cameron, a newborn baby when I began writing in 1989 and now a teenager learning to drive. Your mom and I love you and are very proud of your accomplishments, disposition, moral values, and positive outlook on life.

Tom Doherty, for believing in my work, for continuing to publish my stories, and for all the personal attention during my yearly trips to New York. You are a writer's dream publisher.

Bob Gleason, my insightful and loyal editor and friend, for taking a chance with me way back when, and for demanding the best books that I can write while also giving the latitude to explore.

Matt Bialer, my astute and very personable agent, for supporting me through twelve books, two publishing companies, and four literary agencies.

My parents, Rogelio and Dora, for your support and love through the years.

My in-laws, Mike and Linda, for loving me as your own.

My sister Irene, her husband, Julio, and their wonderful kids, Julito, Paola, Rogelito, Eddie, and Juan Pablo, for your love and your hospitality during my visit to El Salvador in 2004. What a wonderful memory trip that was.

My sister Dorita, her husband, Lorenzo, and their wonderful kids, Lorenzito, Maria Eugenia, and Juan Carlos. I will make it down to Venezuela one of these days to visit you.

My young brothers: Michael, Bobby, and Kevin. Keep following your dreams.

As I write this, I'm celebrating my twenty-second anniversary at Advanced Micro Devices, the place I call my second home. What a ride it has been. My gratitude goes to all of my AMD colleagues for so many incredible years of excitement, friendship, and technical excellence.

HAVOC

[1] A SPOOK IN PARADISE

IF THERE'S ONE THING I've learned after a lifetime of clandestine work it's how to spot field surveillance as naturally as picking the occasional Latino flea that insists on camping out in the southern hemisphere of yours truly while I enjoy an early-morning beer buzz in my hammock on this remote beach in El Salvador, Central America.

The yacht slowly cruises beyond the surf for the fourth time in the past hour, pretending to be just another tourist rig enjoying a beautiful day in paradise.

But I know better.

No one knows where I headed following my touchy-feely departure from Langley. At least no one is *supposed* to know. But there are ways, if one's really hard-boiled about it.

And that, of course, leads me to *another* thing I got out of my joyful twenty-five years as a spy: a hell of a fan club—the long list of sleazeballs across three continents who would just love to go to work on me with a blowtorch, superglue, and a pair of gerbils.

The yacht continues on its merry way as if nothing is wrong, but my spook sense is already grabbing my cock and dropping my socks in spite of the two *cervezas frias* I had for breakfast.

Locating field surveillance is the bread and butter of my profession—or perhaps I should say of my *former* profession, though once a spook always a spook. No one who operated in the field for any length of time can ever forget the ins and outs of not just noticing a tail but also beating it, losing those following you so you can then meet safely with an informant or leave a package for an agent—something called a *drop* in my past life.

So, after decades of situating and defeating all forms of surveillance, you develop this sixth sense, the feeling that you're being watched even though you physically can't see the enemy—but who you know deep in your gut is there, watching you, waiting for you to make a mistake, trying to use you to find the informant that you're running to gather intel on.

And that old familiar feeling is now rushing through my alcohol-thinned blood, uncurling the hairs of my ass.

No one should know where I am, but the possibility that someone did manage to track me down to this tiny republic now sticks in my mind like the barnacles on the hull of the piece-of-shit fishing boat I bought from the same Salvadoran peddler who sold me the rusting pickup truck and the flea-infested trailer hitched to it that I've been using as my ocean-front condo for the past eight months.

I perform another mental check of the extremes that I went through to cover my tracks, to prevent some bounty hunter from sniffing my scent as I headed south of the—

The sand explodes to my immediate left, and before my mind has a chance to catch up with that, a second silent round smacks the trunk of one of the two palm trees holding up my hammock.

Sudden terror suddenly grips my intestines tighter than cheap Salvadoran food, but before I know it the dormant operative in me wakes up and takes over, displacing the visceral fear, the thought of some terrorist asshole tying me down and clogging my plumbing by super-gluing my pee hole and my ass, watching me explode through my mouth, nose, and ears after a couple of immensely painful days without draining the dew or making caca.

Trained instincts surface with a clarity that rivals the turquoise sea extending as far as the eye can see, surprising me after such a long period of inactivity. Before I know it I have dragged my half-drunk ass off the cushy hammock and am racing barefoot toward the tree line bordering this piece of paradise I leased from the Salvadoran government eight months ago.

My mouth going dry, my lungs and legs burning from the sudden sprint, my shoulder blades aching from tension, and my mind automatically guessing the direction of the shots, I race the other way, zigzagging while kicking up sand, also realizing that my shooting hand is already clutching my Beretta 92FS, the 9mm semiautomatic my hard-to-break habits force me to always keep shoved in my shorts, pressed against my spine and covered by the T-shirt of the day. The rest of my extensive wardrobe—a dozen T-shirts of local origin and a handful of cheap shorts—is drying on the clothesline stretched between the side of my trailer and another palm tree next to the weathered Toyota truck from the seventies.

The colorful T-shirts, carefully selected to make sure no one knows where I'm from, flap in the sea breeze as I duck under them on my way to safety, wondering who in the hell is the amateur taking potshots at me. My ego is hurt that someone would send rookies to pay me this social call. Am I already thought of as a has-been who doesn't require a real hit man?

But as I continue dashing toward the thicket, kicking sand like a wounded bull from the nearby *plaza de toros,* I realize that I would already have been iced if I was facing a professional.

As another round splinters chunks of wood from the trunk of a palm to my immediate left, I cut right, almost by the tree line, already sweating like a pig from the lack of exercise and excessive drinking. The film of neglect layering my once-flat abdomen bounces slightly with every step.

I enter the trees and ignore the sudden pain broadcast by my bare feet as I stomp over fallen branches, rocks, and other debris littering the ground, struggling to maintain my forward momentum in spite of the dense jungle. My arms and neck join the complaining choir as the vegetation scratches me, as the razor-sharp edges of yuccas and short palm trees have a field day with my exposed forearms. But the operative in me trades off such annoyances in exchange for the opportunity to fight back and perhaps see this through.

When my senses judge that I have waded through roughly a dozen feet of jungle, I swing left, continuing for another thirty or so feet, and then slowly return to the edge of the thicket, using the muzzle of the Beretta to part shrubbery.

I'm safe—at least temporarily—as the jungle surrounds me. But everything comes with a price. The mosquitoes that never venture down to the beach because of the breeze and the heat now buzz around me, settling on my neck, my face. One of the buggers even crawls up my left nostril.

But I can't move now, can't do anything that might telegraph my position.

Feeling the bugs *on* me and *in* me, sensing their prickling stings as they start to suck my blood—and hoping the alcohol in my veins bites them back—I detach myself from it all and become part of the jungle, measuring my breathing, remaining totally immobile. Except for my eyes, which automatically survey the area, shifting from the trailer, to the truck, to the sea, to the line of flapping T-shirts, to the—

Two men with silenced pistols step out from behind large palm trees just to the right of my trailer, roughly in the same direction that I had guessed the bullets originated from. Slowly, with obvious uncertainty, they walk up to my galvanized palace by the sea. They look like locals, short, dark-skinned, with loose trousers and long-sleeve shirts. Even on the beach the Salvadorans seldom wear shorts unless they intend to go swimming, and then few can afford a swimsuit, which means they either strip naked or jump in in their underwear—men, women, and children.

My trained eyes assess the potential threat of the two Latino cats. The one leading the search and acting as the leader is quite old, probably in his late fifties, overweight and with thinning gray hair. His companion is roughly twenty years younger, with a military crew cut and athletically built. They're both wearing dark sunglasses.

My mind is now going in a million directions.

Who are they?

Why are they here?

How did they find me?

Are they associated with the surveillance team on the yacht?

And if someone wishes to terminate me—at least based on the shots taken so far—why send a pair of thugs to do the job of a professional?

Or could they be just thieves? Perhaps they are a couple of porch climbers hoping to find themselves some dollars by killing this Gringo? And are there any more of them?

My spook sense tells me there are only these two lame-brains, Manuel and Pancho.

Why?

Maybe just a gut feeling based on the way they move, on their overall clumsiness while searching the area, on the manner in which they hold their weapons, muzzles often crossing each other's bodies, index fingers on the triggers even though they don't have a target in sight; very sloppy, half-baked practices that have amateur hour written all over them.

Professionals would point weapons skyward and rest their shooting fingers on the trigger casings, and they would never—ever—point the muzzle in their partner's direction, even while doing a sweep. Muzzle control was taught in Spook 101 at Langley—as well as at any respectable law enforcement or paramilitary training school.

It's definitely amateur hour.

"Donde esta el Gringo hijo de puta?" says Tweedledee out loud, telegraphing his position if I didn't know it already. *Where is the son of a bitch Gringo?*

"Se metio en el monte por alla," replies Tweedledum just as loud. *He went into the bush over there.*

While the idiots poke around the other side of my trailer, I take the opportunity to run away from the tree line and reach the opposite side of the place I've called home for the past eight months—an old and rusty twenty-foot camping trailer.

My back pressed against the stained aluminum side of this flea-mobile, I remove my T-shirt and wrap it tight over the

Beretta's muzzle, which I then clutch with both hands, pointing the makeshift silencer at the sky.

Slowly, with caution, I creep sideways toward the front while hearing someone walking inside the trailer, which means there's only one outside.

I reach the edge and peek around the corner, spotting the young Salvadoran checking out my old boom box on the table under the small awning stretching over the trailer's entrance.

He sees me and drops the radio while trying to swing his silenced weapon in my direction.

Feeling guilty because Tweedledee has made it too easy for me, but nevertheless out of options, I fire twice, the reports muffled by the cotton fabric, which catches on fire just as both rounds smack him square in the middle of his chest, pushing him back over the table.

The loud crash causes lots of excitement inside the trailer as Tweedledum stomps around trying to figure out what to do—either that or some of my miniature pets have decided to crawl up his pants and bite his Salvadoran pickle.

Following professional habits, I take several steps back while dropping to one knee, pressing the burning T-shirt against the sand to put out the fire before leveling the weapon on the entrance, smoke coiling skyward.

There is no way out but through that door, and whether he realizes it or not, I have the upper hand by being outside and knowing exactly where he will be when he comes out. Tweedledum, on the other hand, will first have to come out into the open, find me, swing his weapon toward me, and then fire.

Sudden silence envelops my little piece of paradise, the sea breeze whistling gently inland, swirling the branches of the tall palms shadowing my rusty home and truck.

Almost a minute goes by before the Salvadoran cat charges out firing his weapon wildly, a feeble attempt to create a distraction—though he could have gotten lucky and hit me.

I put two in his chest before he has taken two steps away from his refuge. He falls face-first on the sand already a corpse, just a few feet away from his younger amigo, who is sprawled facing the canopy of palm trees with his limbs twisted at un-natural angles.

The smell of burnt cotton tingling my nostrils, adrenaline heightening my senses, my heart hammering my chest like a pissed off gorilla, I move toward them, toward this surreal sight, my mind still trying to catch up with the unexpected events.

I look out to sea, but I can't see the yacht.

What in the hell is going on?

Priorities.

First things first. I remove the burnt T-shirt from the Beretta, flip the safety, and shove it in my shorts. I examine their weapons, two Colt .45s with factory silencers, definitely not the standard weapon of Salvadoran crooks, who, from what I remember during the days I was stationed in this place during the late eighties, prefer cheap revolvers. The Colts are also new, still filmed by the preserving oil applied at the factory before shipment, but the serial numbers have been ground off.

Professional weapons in the hands of a pair of amateurs.

This smells worse than the cheap perfume of Rosita, Juanita, Margarita, and the dozen other pavement princesses working the main plaza on Saturday nights in a nearby town appropriately called El Placer. Pleasureville.

Unable to explain the inconsistency, I also thumb the Colts' safeties and bring them inside the trailer, where I grab two dark sheets from a pile of dirty clothes crowding the small kitchen and walk back outside, wrapping each body before hauling them to the truck and dumping them in the open bed, then unhitching the trailer from the truck.

I then tackle the mess by the front of the trailer, beneath the awning. Tweedledee broke my card table, so I pick up the pieces and stack them aside, before kicking the bloody sand around, hiding any evidence of the idiots' ever being here.

I pause for a moment, realizing what I'm doing, operating in automatic, just as I have been trained. I guess even after a year out of the game I'm still thinking like a trained operative.

As I sigh, the realization that I have just clipped two

men—albeit in self-defense—finally sinks in, but at the same time my mind screams at me to go and dump the bodies, to get rid of all of the evidence, and then to think about my next move. Were those two just local alley cats looking for easy cash or were they sent by someone from my past, by one of the countless fans I made with my charming personality during a quarter of a century of field operations? The weapons certainly suggest the latter, and if that's the case then this place is compromised. As much as I like it, I would have to move, which also means finding a way to get my money back, since I'm living on my own nickel these days.

As my heartbeat returns to normal, as I consider my options, I grab my keys and wallet from the trailer—as well as their guns—and drive away with a calmness that even impresses me.

As I steer the truck onto the unpaved road that leads to the coastal highway, the words from my old mentor, Troy Savage, ring in my mind with a clarity that rivals the crystalline sea I lose in the cloud of dust kicked up by my tires: Once a spook always a spook.

[2] HOLDING MY GROUND

CALL ME CRAZY, WHACKO, or just plain loco, but after the shit that went down yesterday, after nearly getting my out-of-shape ass shot off, after spending the better part of last night finding the perfect place to get rid of the evidence, I decided to head back to my budget version of the promised land and just rough it out.

I've decided I'm not leaving. Screw it. If someone wants to send more two-time losers my way then let them. I've been moving from place to place for twenty-five fucking years. I've been kicked, punched, stabbed, shot, and once nearly castrated in the late eighties right here in El Salvador, in a dusty town just twenty minutes away ironically called Testikuzklan—not far from where I dumped Tweedledee and Tweedledum.

Yep. I've certainly been around, crossing swords in a dozen countries with far more dangerous characters than the bastards who tried to rob me yesterday.

I'm not moving again. This time I'm holding my ground. It's going to take more than another pair of deadbeats to make me—

Well, slap me in the ass and call me Mary. Not only has the yacht returned, cruising just beyond the surf, but today there's a smiling brunette wearing a pair of tiny black shorts and a matching bikini top walking on the beach toward me.

Who ever said retirement is boring? In the past twenty-four hours my life has gone from calm and laid-back to explosive, surreal, and now downright intriguing.

At least the quality of my visitors is going up. I'll take Miss Pretty Legs any day over yesterday's visitors.

She is not carrying a piece—at least as far as I can see from here—though my mind starts to imagine the warm and cozy places where she might be hiding one.

But she's no schoolgirl. The same instincts that so easily labeled yesterday's losers now scream that I'm in the presence of a pro, and not the kind you pay by the hour. Though at the moment I'd consider spending one of my lousy pension checks for a night of unforgettable pleasures—something that's in clear violation of my unwritten rule of never, ever, paying for sex, especially down here with the likes of Rosita, Juanita, and Margarita over by the plaza. As desperate as I am to get laid after nearly a year of forced abstinence, I still don't want it bad enough to risk sharing bodily fluids with half of the population of this land.

The brunette continues to move toward me, her honey skin glistening in the tropical sun, awakening the long-dormant one-eyed monster. But something else is gleaming brighter than a muzzle flash: her profession. The woman has spook tattooed all over her, just like the damned yacht.

While relaxing on my hammock, my Beretta back where it belongs, well within reach, I sigh at the skirt's confident and balanced strides, at her well-toned muscles, at her arms hanging loosely from her sides, at her short and efficient haircut, at her free hands, at the way she scans her surroundings—including the location of her yacht—while pretending to be admiring the scenery.

It's sunny, eighty degrees, and a light breeze sweeps inland from a beautiful Pacific Ocean. Seagulls hover a dozen feet above the swells, occasionally diving headfirst when spotting prey, stabbing the glittering surface, disappearing below, before winging skyward with their writhing reward clamped in their beaks. In the distance, a cruise ship heads from the Panama Canal toward Acapulco and Puerto Vallarta. Closer to shore, a few hundred feet out, that suspicious yacht sways in the swells.

I'm willing to bet that laughable check I get every month from the CIA that this cute cat cares about the relaxing sight as much as Tweedledee and Tweedledum hated disturbing my early retirement—or even as much as Rosita means it when she tells me that I am the love of her life. While I'm at it, I'll go double or nothing that the people aboard the fucking yacht are watching my gorgeous tan from behind the mirror finish of the vessel's panoramic windows. They were probably taking bets yesterday when I turned Manuel and Pancho into taco meat.

Damn, I never realized how much I hated spooks until I left Langley. Sometimes I even wonder how I managed to stick around for so long, especially the way the Agency screwed me throughout my career, like the time when those Marxist rebels caught me and my CIA buddy spying on them right here in nearby Testikuzklan two decades before and proceeded to castrate him with a machete and were about to turn my cojones into huevos rancheros when a priest and two nuns came to my rescue in my time of testicular need. Langley pinned the incident on me even though I had protested the high-risk assignment in the first place. As punishment for screwing up in El Salvador, I was given the shit jobs, the ones no one else wanted, which sent me to such exotic destinations as Ecuador, Somalia, Beirut, and Cairo. Oh, and let's not forget Serbia, where bad intel resulted in the deaths of most of my team, including a fellow CIA officer by the name of Madison, whom I had foolishly fallen in love with and planned to marry. My superiors, still pissed at me for El Salvador, nailed my balls to my forehead for the Serbia screwup while I was in deep mourning, incapable of defending myself. And then there was Singapore—strike three—which resulted in my being here today, watching these assholes watching me.

Feeling the cold steel of my Beretta against the small of my back, I pretend I haven't seen her or her offshore dweebs. Casually, I jump off my hammock, shut off the wireless pad I had been using to review the latest stock market reports, and toss it in the hammock. Living on a fixed income has increased my financial level of awareness, especially after Langley gave me the boot roughly ten years before I could finish building a proper nest egg—particularly after my 401k imploded during that dot-com bust at the beginning of the millennium.

The inflammatory nature of my break from Langley also didn't help strengthen the already shaky relationship I had started with Karen Frost, a Bureau agent who had been my boss during a high-profile case four years ago. Being the romantic idiot I vehemently deny being—and probably because I was still looking for ways to get over Maddie—I had foolishly hoped to convince Karen to also hang up her government hat and join me in my warm and sunny Latino version of nirvana. During a lunch in Washington the month before I left, I pretty much got down on one knee, pulled out a diamond ring worth three months' pay, and begged her to come down with me. Unfortunately, she couldn't walk away from her cases yet—or so she had claimed—and suggested that perhaps it would be for the best to keep it just friendly for a while.

Pretty amazing how they want to be friends right after ripping your guts out.

Go figure.

Two and a half decades of field operations turned my skin into Kevlar, but nothing—absolutely nothing—prepared me for Karen dumping me the way she did, just as I was finally getting over Madison's brutal death, just as I was beginning to feel that I did have a chance of being happy. Man, some moments really stick with you, like when I knelt in front of her holding that stupid ring I still carry in the money belt I've kept wrapped around my recently expanded abdomen since yesterday's incident. She might as well have taken the damned salad fork and stabbed me in the balls.

There are guys who leave and guys who are left. I learned the hard way which group I belonged in.

That was nine months ago . . . and it was yesterday.

The unexpected revelation continues to tear into my hardened shield with the force of a depleted uranium round, in a way wounding me just as bad as when Maddie died. It really makes me wonder if I am destined to grow old alone.

I force my mind back to the developing situation on my beach. Realizing that the nearing surveillance could be hostile—especially given yesterday's activities—but somehow not giving a damn, I stroll over the warm sand, enjoying the gritty feeling in between my toes, and approach the twenty-footer Salvadoran version of a Boston Whaler standing upright on the beach with the help of a dozen two-by-fours.

Grabbing a wide chisel from the open toolbox next to the boat before kneeling in the sand, I try not to think of Karen and Maddie, or of Salvadoran guerrillas trying to make huevos rancheros with my family jewels—or of Manuel and Pancho, now feeding the vulture population outside of Testikuzklan. And I definitely try not to remember the sudden destruction of my career, or my depleting savings, or how close I came to getting killed yesterday, or the nearing nuisance, focusing instead on stripping the layer of neglect encrusting a hull made of solid teak.

"Cameron Malone?"

I keep on chiseling, chunks of barnacles and other crap flying in every direction while I refuse to look up, though I do keep a close watch on her hands without letting her know I'm doing it, deciding that I can reach for my piece and slam two in that cute little chest of hers before this pretty pussycat gets the chance to get to her gun. My current kneeling position also screws up the line of sight of a possible sniper on that yacht.

I may not give a damn, but I'm not stupid—especially after yesterday's close encounter.

She has just used the name Langley gave me as part of my identity change. Shaking my head, I say in my best imitation of a Salvadoran accent, "No, *mamacita*, but I wish I were." I'm hoping that the straw hat, the sunglasses, the stained rags I'm wearing, the dark tan, and the long hair will be enough to fool her—or perhaps the unkempt beard hiding the fifty thousand bucks the CIA paid to alter my face for my own protection before cutting me loose. Not only do I wish not to be bothered by any intelligence type, but I've grown uncomfortable being near women since Karen dumped me.

"And you shall know the truth, and the truth shall set you free. Don't you agree, Mr. Malone?" she says, giving me the code that tells me she is CIA. The quotation from the Bible is etched in marble at the entrance of the new CIA building in Langley.

"Huh?"

"Mr. Malone," she adds with forced patience. "I would like to have a word with you."

"No comprende." I keep on chiseling.

Looking away from me and out to sea, her short dark hair swirling in the breeze, she recites, "The Cameron Michael Malone I'm looking for retired with fifty percent of his pension a year ago after a failed operation. He crossed the border into Mexico three months later and managed to make his way down to Central America, finally settling in El Salvador exactly eight months ago to the day yesterday. Using past connections, he made an arrangement with the government in San Salvador, the capital, and leased ten acres of land for thirty years, including five hundred feet of secluded beachfront property—specifically this very spot. Malone purchased that trailer over there, the used truck parked in front of it, and this fishing boat, from a dealer in Testikuzklan, where, our records show, he ran a failed operation twenty years before, toward the end of this country's civil war. Malone pretty much keeps to himself, except for his weekly trips into town to purchase supplies—or when he occasionally decides to dump the bodies of Salvadorans trying to assassinate him. How am I doing so far?"

I throw my arms up at the picture-perfect blue skies in the way I've seen the locals do, before saying in the same thick accent, *"Hijo de puta,* now you're talking *muy loco, señorita.* I don't know no Señor Melón."

"It's *Malone.*"

"Huh?"

"Look," she says, leaning down while turning my way. "Why don't you come with us? We only need a few hours of your time. We know who tried to kill you yesterday."

I look up and stare into a soft, almost Italian-looking face, a bit triangular and with a prominent nose and full lips that remind me of a less-polished version of actress Sophia Loren; not gorgeous but not unattractive either. Maybe my standards have headed south after my long period of celibacy, especially since I refuse to surrender to the favors of Rosita, Juanita, and Margarita—lest I wish for my third leg to shrivel up and fall off.

Although I can't see her eyes, shielded behind the mirror finish of her sunglasses, I do notice a wonderful chocolate freckle hovering just above the left corner of her mouth. Karen had one of those—though on the right side—and it drove me nuts until I was able to kiss it.

Before I can force my thought process back to the northern hemisphere I say, "The Agency already had twenty-five *years* of my time, and in the end it wasn't even satisfied by using me as its fall guy; it also had to erase my identity, including giving me this cute face that isn't mine. The guy that you're looking for, *Tom Grant,* hasn't existed for a year. Mr. Malone has no operative experience. He is a retired insurance salesman whose wife died of breast cancer a year ago. He has no children or other living relatives. Or have you forgotten about *that?*"

She crosses her arms and regards me in silence for several seconds for breaking one of the cardinal rules at Langley by speaking my old name out loud. A lot of blood, sweat, and tears go into eliminating an identity and creating a new one, down to fake IRS files, high-school records, college degrees, marriage certificates, work history, medical records, and so on—including sophisticated facial alterations that would make Michael Jackson turn green with envy, though granted that wouldn't be so difficult anymore. Langley's bigwigs do this in part for my protection but mostly for theirs. There's a lot of stuff stored in my rusting noodle, and it could spread a lot of havoc if it fell in the wrong hands—not that I think I'll squawk, but you never know how a guy would react if someone held a blowtorch to his schmeckel.

"That was for your own protection, Mr. Malone. You knew the rules when you signed up."

Funny. I don't remember reading anywhere in those rules that Langley would stick it to me the Hershey bar way one day.

"Enough is enough. Go away," I say.

"What about the hit against you yesterday?"

"What hit?"

"The men who came . . . please, Mr. Malone! Stop playing games with me. This is very serious. An attempt was made yesterday against your life."

"If it was it obviously failed, because I'm still here." I smile without humor before adding, "Now, beat it."

I know that sounds harsh, but that's the only way of dealing with these people. Trust me. At least with those dickheads yesterday I knew where I stood. With Langley you *never* know.

"But the Director of Operations—"

"Tell Dobson that Malone and Grant aren't interested. They're hanging out by the sea enjoying their Greek relationship."

"I guess you haven't been keeping up with current events, Mr. Malone," she replies, ignoring me, sticking to the rules with amazing professionalism. Either that or my jokes really stink.

I stare at the chisel in my right hand, for a moment missing my old name, my old face, my old self. These bastards reinvented me and I despise them for it. Perhaps that's why Karen dumped me. She probably couldn't get used to my new face, even though in the process of altering it they also tweaked it a bit, making me look ten years younger—not that anyone can tell with my shaggy beard. But I never cared about the way my wrinkles and battle scars made me look. I loved my face just the way it was, kicked, punched, and even stabbed once during the course of serving Uncle Sam.

"That's the idea of *being* retired, sweetheart," I lie, annoyed not at her but at what she represents. In reality, I've been keeping up with current events—though it hasn't been that easy. One of the first things that struck me after leaving Langley was the realization that I no longer had insight into any stories that made it to the press. For a quarter of a century I had the inside track to judge if media reports held water.

She says, "Dobson retired last year. Nathan Leyman, the old Deputy Director of Operations, replaced him. And there's also a new head of Counterterrorism, Ken Morotski, who replaced Troy Savage."

I also know this, especially the bit about the paper pusher from the Directory of Intelligence, Ken Morotski, Leyman's protégé. Morotski and I started at the CIA more or less at about the same time. We even cut our teeth together in Madras, a shit hole two hours by plane from Delhi, India, where we were sent a few months after graduating from the Farm, the CIA training academy located outside of Williamsburg, Virginia. The CIA had spent around five hundred thousand dollars training each of us and it was now time to start paying down that informal debt. During that two-year assignment I took care of a large chunk of that investment by recruiting and running three agents; one was a hooker who oftentimes bedded visiting Russian military personnel, and the other two were underpaid technicians with the Indian armed forces, which at the time were a back door to Russian military equipment and operations, since the majority of Indian military gear was Russian made. By contrast, the lamebrain Morotski thought he had recruited himself a real Russian agent, only to find out a year later that the Russian had been a KGB officer assigned to pose as an underpaid Russian tank technician. And to top it all off, I wound up being the one who alerted our boss to this finding when my prostitute spotted Morotski's agent meeting with his KGB controllers one late evening at some meat market bar in downtown Madras. My report, combined with my success at recruiting and running three real agents, essentially turned me into a made guy, someone who had shown enough promise to be given the opportunity to do better things. By contrast, Ken Morotski, utterly disgraced, was shipped home, where the only thing that saved him from getting kicked out of the Agency was the fact that his father was Senator John Morotski from Virginia, who pulled some strings inside the Agency to get his son reassigned to the Directory of Intelligence. It was at around that time that I went to work for Troy in Delhi, India, while Morotski remained in Langley working for Leyman, who at the time was in Intelligence. So you would understand why I had nearly come unglued when I heard about Morotski replacing Troy, a promotion due in part to his connections and in part to apparently having done a terrific job in Intelligence for Leyman. Unfortunately, being great at *interpreting* intel doesn't mean Morotski knows how to *gather* that intel, as he proved early on in Madras, where he failed to read the warning signs that he had recruited a KGB guy. Morotski had fallen into the most common pitfall when recruiting agents: When an informant looks too good to be true, he or she probably isn't.

I heard about Leyman's promo and Morotski's appointment several months ago in a news report I picked up on my wireless pad. Although I no longer know if the info floating in the media is accurate, it's not that difficult to access the news in these days of cheap wireless systems linked to a worldwide net of satellites. Following professional habits, however, I choose not to disclose what I know or don't know. There's a strong chance that the spooks on that boat may have parabolic listening devices pointed at my ass. Maybe I should fart to give them something to talk about.

"Did you ever find out what happened to Troy?" I finally ask. Troy Savage, my old boss and mentor, was—to my utter shock and horror—the guy whose files pinned the failed

Singapore operation on me even though he had been the one who set it up and assigned me to run it for him. The files of good old Troy, who disappeared under pretty mysterious circumstances right before the botched mission, were instrumental in Dobson's decision not only to blame the deaths on me but to charge me with conspiracy to commit murder—in direct violation of Directive 12333, the old presidential directive signed in 1981 by President Ronald Reagan prohibiting the CIA from carrying out assassinations. It was one thing getting back-scuttled by Langley—it'd happened to me before right here in El Salvador and later on in Serbia—but what really hurt was being taken up the old mustard road without K-Y by the one individual I had actually trusted at the Agency. Troy assured me that we had presidential sanction for Singapore. But as the CIA's hammer came crashing down on my bare shoulders, the one person who should have protected me had not only vanished—presumably dead, though nobody knew for certain, since his body was never found—but left behind a paper trail that resulted in my humiliating departure from the intelligence world.

"Troy Savage is the reason I'm here, Mr. Malone. I'm trying to be reasonable, and I urge you to do the same and come with us." She points at the yacht. "It won't take long at all, and it will also explain why someone tried to kill you yesterday."

I regard her over the rims of my dark shades. Certainly attractive, though in an ethnic sort of way. But there is definite strength in her stance, in her features, in her resolve to get me to cooperate. Her honey-colored skin glows in the sun as she twists her lips into a frown. Her voice is deep but quite feminine. Too bad I can't see her eyes behind the mirror tint of her glasses.

And this is when I realize that if the Agency has been spending taxpayers' dollars keeping tabs on me, it probably knows I haven't gotten laid since Karen dumped me and it's using this Mediterranean cupcake as sweetener to get me in cahoots with them. On the other hand, the bastards should also know that I not only don't hide the salami with hookers, but the rule also applies to women half my age.

"Do you have a name?" I finally ask, wondering if the freckle is real. Langley is pretty good at creating illusions.

"Rachel Muratani."

I knew there was an Italian gene in there somewhere. But then again, just like me, that's probably a fake name. But what the hell? What else have I got to do? And so I say, "So, tell me, Rachel, what does my CIA dossier say about me?"

She looks about her for a moment, apparently unsure why I asked such a question. "It says that you joined the Agency just after five years with the NYPD. From there you ran operations in Madras, Delhi, El Salvador, Quito, Beirut, Belgrade, and a half-dozen other places. You also participated in a high-profile case in the United States four years ago, resulting in the death of terrorist Ares Kulzak," she starts, mentioning the case I worked with Karen. She then rattles on for another few minutes about my spook education, which included how to kill people while making it look like an accident—training I received long ago not because I was actually planning to ice someone without the White House's blessing but just in case an extreme situation called for the current president to bypass 12333, like I was told by Troy was the case in Singapore.

"Very impressive," I say. "So you can remember your lines, but can you *think* for yourself?"

"Of course I can," she replies defensively, taking my bait.

"Then tell me what you see." I step back, hold my arms out in front of me, palms facing her, as if I want to give her a hug, and do a slow three-sixty so she can see all of my six-three height and 250 pounds of pure American beef—though not as lean as it used to be.

"Well?" I ask. "Tell me, and don't be shy."

She drops her fine brows while that lovely freckle rises a trifle. "I don't think I understand."

"Why don't we play an old game of mine? It's call Guess Your Background Without a Dossier. I'll go first. You seem to be in your mid-to-late twenties and keep yourself in shape, though as of late you've been ignoring your upper body just a dash. The abs are there, but filmed by a layer of fat that only comes from excessive paperwork, probably a recent responsibility involving supervision of junior officers. Your age tells me you've been out of the Farm for about five years, maybe a little longer. That means you've done three operations max, and all of them under the supervision of a senior agent. I'm willing to bet this one's your first time venturing out on your own, with the close backup of your team out there on that pretty boat—courtesy of taxpayers' dollars. And guess what? Our conversation is likely being recorded—probably even being fed live to Langley using that nice satellite dish atop the yacht. That's being done not just for your protection, so the team out there can spring into action if I become a threat to you, but also to test you. At this moment the powers that be back home are monitoring how you do on your first senior-level assignment, on your first test. This is what you've been working for all of your life, missy. This is what you dreamed of while you put yourself through college, while you sacrificed and turned down better-paying jobs for the dream of becoming a CIA officer. This is why you abandoned friends and family for the sole purpose of making it in this man-dominated field. You've spent years burning the midnight oil, aging yourself for the job, doing everything and anything to get ahead, to earn the opportunity to run an operation—one lousy chance, one shot at proving to a skeptical Langley that you really have what it takes. Heck, for all I know you even sucked a ying yang or two to open a few doors. And now their eyes are on you, and they're wondering, Will she crack? Will she crumble under pressure? Or will she pull herself together and deliver the package: persuading a down-and-out former officer to collaborate? How am *I* doing so far, Miss Muratani?"

Flustering, she removes her sunglasses, revealing a pair of cat-like emerald-green eyes, which, albeit a bit close together, do manage to awaken the peppermint dragon, dormant since Princess Karen Frost stopped playing with it.

Crossing her thin but muscular arms, frowning, she turns toward the boat and back at me before barking, "Mr. Malone! Please! There is no time for games or stupid comments! This is a matter of national security!"

I grin, glad to finally be getting under her skin. "A matter of *national security*? Is that the best line you can come up with? Where did you get that from, missy? A Tom Clancy novel?"

"You *will* help us, Mr. Malone," she warns, cocking a finger at me, but still displaying incredible control, especially after the deep throat comment. "You really have no choice in the matter."

"*Now* you're threatening me, young lady, and you're also trespassing. In this country the latter is a criminal offense. You go to jail. No phone call. No trial. Nothing but lots and lots of Latino pee-pees in your future because a pretty *Gringa* like you . . . you're going to get gang-banged by the horny toads at the Policia Nacional until your sweet little Venus fly-trap turns brown and withers away, and then they'll start going up the old dirt road until your tight little asshole is the size of Alaska."

A vein starts to throb across her forehead. Man, this pussy-cat is really pissed, and if my gut feeling is true, I must have the boys listening on that yacht doubled over with laughter.

"And if that's the offense for trespassing," she says, without missing a beat, impressing the hell out of me, "what's the punishment for killing two Salvadorans and dumping their bodies in a coffee field on the outskirts of Testikuzklan, the place where, I've been told, you almost lost *your* pee-pee?"

Touché. But I, of course, admit nothing and just stare back.

"Look," she says, perspiration forming on her upper lip. A part of her—probably the Italian side—obviously wishes to really let me have it. But her professional side is rapidly reeling her back to avoid looking like I got to her in front of our virtual audience. "Mr. Malone, it's very important that we talk to you."

I gaze into those intriguing eyes, which go so damned well with her Italian nose. I study that sinful freckle over those full lips, their ends curved down just a notch.

"I'm not sure how else to tell you this, Miss Muratani," I say, forcing my eyes not to drop to the mouthwatering cleavage created by those cute kajoobies tucked inside the black bikini top. "I'm out of circulation. I've hung up my trench coat. I've been put out to pasture. Get the picture? Now beat it." Boy, that was hard to say, especially when the boss of the underworld is beginning to show signs of life for the first time in a year—though I wonder if I have any toothpaste left in the old tube after not getting my banana peeled for so long.

To my surprise, Rachel doesn't even blink. She defiantly stares right back and says, "Our records show that you're barely scraping a living. You made very poor investment choices and basically blew a significant portion of your retirement savings in the dot-coms."

Pretty or not, Miss CIA is really beginning to irritate me. I stare at a face that is definitely attractive, especially when looking at her straight ahead. But it's the overall appearance that I find charming, particularly when you throw in her respectable figure and the way she carries herself. Either that or maybe a year without any bouncy-bouncy has lowered my standards. I'm wondering if Rachel Muratani is someone I would have even looked at back when I was parallel parking with Karen Frost.

As I'm getting the strange feeling that the lack of hanky-panky is playing tricks on my mind, I finally reply, "I'm well aware of my financial situation, and you shouldn't believe everything you've read in a CIA dossier. It's as good as the people gathering and interpreting the intelligence, as well as whatever politics were being practiced when the entries were made—meaning some stuff was likely left out. One day you will learn to rely more on your own intuition than on the intuition of the desk officers behind Langley's protective walls who patched that document together based on oftentimes sketchy intel." In reality, I'm borderline broke, especially with the most recent downturn in the economy.

"Have it your way, Mr. Malone."

"I knew you'd eventually catch on." I wink.

"But beware that representatives from the Banco de El Salvador are on their way to inform you that the price for the leasing of this property has been increased tenfold. And the word we got is that they want the extra funds immediately or you will be evicted."

I feel just as I did twenty years ago, when those guerrillas pulled down my pants and were about to chop off the Tom Grant family jewels. If Miss Personality here knew anything about me, it's the danger of pissing me off, and if you don't believe that go ask the terrorists I had the privilege of interrogating in Guantánamo Bay after September 11th. I had the bastards singing in half the time of the younger and less-experienced CIA handlers.

Realizing that this is her way of getting back at me for the off-color remarks, I too muster savage control to keep my broiling anger from surfacing. I clench my teeth and lock it down so tight that for a moment my balls go numb.

Breathe, Tom, I tell myself, refusing to let these bastards get to me, trying to jump-start my operative mind to look for options. I have very little left beyond the chunk of change I gave the Salvadoran authorities for this remote property east of Puerto la Libertad, where there's some of the best surfing in the world—even better than California and Hawaii. If what she says is true, and if the CIA has anything to do with it, I swear I'll—

"The Agency had nothing to do with it," she says, apparently reading either my mind or my face. If the latter, then shame on me for failing the lesson of Spook 101: Always keep a poker face.

"In fact," she continues, "the Agency is pulling some strings to force the Banco de El Salvador to reimburse you. You of all people should be aware of the dangers of doing business in the highly corrupt climate of these countries. Contracts are meaningless here. We got word from our people in the American Embassy in San Salvador that the bank has leased this property a dozen times over in the past five years—all to stupid foreigners like yourself."

The soothing sight around me has lost its allure. I, *of all people,* should have indeed known better than to trust authorities from a south-of-the-border republic any more than I could trust spooks, but at the time I wasn't quite myself. Langley's witch hunt plus Karen bailing on me had really screwed me up, and I guess that left me wide open for the Banco de El Salvador to come in for the kill.

"We're offering you a second chance, Mr. Malone. The opportunity to do the right thing. To undo what Troy Savage did to you, to the Agency—and also to make some real money. We would like to contract your services, and I'm sure you do remember how well the Agency pays its contractors."

Anger cramps my gut worse than the tamales I ate last Saturday night in town while watching Rosita, Juanita, and Margarita walk up and down the plaza modeling for me.

Although I have to admit that a part of me is suddenly interested in listening to what she has to say, another part of me— the one that has had it with Langley's bullshit—makes me say, "I don't want a second chance. I don't want *any* chance. I just want to be left alone. Besides, why would Leyman or Morotski want to be associated with me again after I brought so much bad press to the Agency with my alleged violation of 12333, and especially when they've got much more capable operatives at their disposal carrying far less baggage?"

"We need you precisely *because* of your baggage, Mr. Malone. You are needed *because* of the unfinished business in Singapore."

I remove my shades and study her hard.

"Troy Savage was indeed responsible, sir. I dug through the case and found irrefutable proof of his wrongdoing. He never received presidential sanction for that operation but told you he did. There was no way for you to know otherwise. We also know that you protested carrying out the operation in Singapore due to that country's extreme level of security. Then, when things turned sour he disappeared and left you hanging."

I'm paralyzed, the words caught in my throat. I knew the bastard screwed me in Singapore. I *fucking* knew it.

Singapore.

Slaughter in paradise.

Singapore.

Strike three. The final straw, resulting in the destruction of my government career.

I almost bought the farm in Singapore. But I recovered from the near-death experience, only to wake up to the nightmare of a grueling FBI investigation that not only ended in my forced resignation but also publicly humiliated me—consequences that may have contributed to Karen's decision to leave me. Remember that she was—and still is—FBI, the same agency which came after me with a vengeance.

Singapore.

My eyes focus on the burnt patch of skin on top of my right hand while my right ear still discerns the light ringing mixed in with the rolling sea, with the whistling breeze sweeping inland, with the shrieking seagulls.

Twenty-five years with the CIA all turned to shit because of Singapore.

[3] SINGAPORE CITY BLUES

SIM LIM SQUARE.

Mecca of high technology.

In the heart of Singapore.

I was pretending to be a tourist, not a very difficult task given my height and weight, which made me the jolly green giant amidst the eclectic—but predominantly Asian—crowd browsing through the interior of the nanotronics mall. Open from the ground floor to the glass ceiling atop the seventh floor, the place bustled with activity.

Jam-packed balconies overlooked the controlled chaos dominating the bottom floor, where merchants from all over the Pacific Rim ran booths displaying their advanced gadgets, selling them with an energy that paralleled that of the old stock exchange floors at the turn of the century—or the whorehouses of Madras, Belgrade, and Quito.

While touring the fifth floor, I winced at the cacophony of voices in a dozen languages mixed with the sounds of hundreds of digital television sets. The glow from their high-definition flat screens washed the faces of impressed customers. All of the newest gizmos could be purchased at Sim Lim, from nanotronic systems housing the latest AI programming, to flexdisplays with wireless broadband capability, nanotronic sex toys for the lonely of heart, and commercial versions of the hovering security sphere that began to make its way into some police forces last year, providing limited assistance to cops in their rounds. Even the U.S. Army was now incorporating a military version of the famous Orbs, heavier and carrying higher-caliber ammunition and higher-resolution cameras than their law enforcement cousins.

Wearing a pair of gray slacks and a white polo shirt, I inspected the glittering interior, the neon signs of every major high-tech manufacturer—and many unknown ones. My enhanced sight, courtesy of a pair of molecular lenses with built-in telescopic capability as well as night vision, allowed me to probe the crowd browsing the displays on the floors below with ease. Most of the classic electronics merchants were present, from Sony, Toshiba, and RCA to recent additions from China and Korea. But the majority of the shelf space belonged to CyberWerke, the German conglomerate that was second to none but United States Nanotechnology in the development of the latest and greatest nanogadgets, from the coolest personal communicators smaller than a wristwatch to micro DVD players integrated into mobile phones.

Merchants made deals in Mandarin, Cantonese, Hindu, English, Malay, Japanese, Korean, French, and, of course, German, courtesy of CyberWerke market expansion. All currencies were accepted in this high-tech heaven, which had its own bank and security force. Several restaurants on the third floor offered fast food for this eclectic crowd on the run. The smell of curry, ginger, pepper, and grilled fish hung in the air, mixing with body odor, cheap aftershave, cigarette smoke, and the acrid stench oozing from overused restrooms. And on the top floor—according to a hooker I bribed on Orchad Road last night—one could even find the private penthouses of the richest merchants, who used anything from the finest Asian whores to the most exotic sports cars to close the big business deals. I had already spotted four high-class courtesans going up the escalators in the past thirty minutes.

Just in time for happy fucking hour.

Under the watchful red eye of a nearby security sphere—Singapore's version of the Orb designed and manufactured by CyberWerke—I took the escalators to the sixth floor, checking the flesh-colored implant on top of my right wrist. The Plasmaflex nanotronic gadget, manufactured for the CIA by United States Nanotechnologies and surgically integrated with my skin at USN's facility in Austin, Texas, confirmed my location as well as those of my team members. No one but yours truly could read the Plasmaflex. The tiny system constantly performed eye scans of anyone trying to read it. Its directional nanocells blended with the natural texture of my skin in every direction but that of the firmware signature embedded in the molecular lenses filming my eyes—also a product of USN—making it impossible for someone else to see anything but skin.

The Plasmaflex, which provided me with the vital signs from each member of my team via an encrypted wireless channel, also reminded me that my own heart rate was up fifteen percent, and it urged me to calm down.

Easy, Tom. Don't blow this.

I had positioned my relatively young team efficiently in the building, one per floor, leaning against the balconies, with a clear line of sight to the floors above and below.

Today was the day Troy Savage planned to assassinate Rem Vlachko—through me. One of Milosevic's monster colonels way back when, Vlachko became an arms dealer after Milosevic's fall in 2001 and was responsible for arming half of the world's looneys. Vlachko was responsible for the Semtex explosives used to bring down that pretty skyscraper in downtown LA in 2005. Vlachko had personally financed the nerve gas strike in Rome in 2006 as well as the smallpox epidemic in Toronto that same year. And let's not forget about the radiation waste he dumped in London's water supply in 2007. To this day people were still dying from the hot water they drank three years ago courtesy of that monster. Trust me. Vlachko was one mean cat and the Agency sent yours truly here to make sure that I eliminated all nine of his lives in one swift blow.

I inspected my surroundings again while pretending to check a beautiful Sony holoscreen, half-watching the impressive tri-dimensional image. Troy, through assets—also known as agents—he ran in several countries, had gotten word that Vlachko wanted to get his hands on the latest generation of nanoweapons, the stuff that we had been using to combat the ever-rising terrorist camps around the world. So I floated an idea to Troy five months ago: create a fake high-tech company in California under government contract to build nanoweapons, and then have those contracts canceled and given to a competitive firm, forcing its CEO—yours truly—to look for other sources of income to keep his company afloat, including potential new buyers with lots of cash but unsavory backgrounds. As head of Counterterrorism at Langley, Troy sold the concept to Director of Operations Dobson, who, in turn, obtained presidential sanction for this operation.

I wasn't certain why, out of all the places in the world, Troy had agreed to a meeting in Singapore, where owning a firearm carried a death sentence. Even possession of a single bullet meant five years in jail—plus an unbearable number of canes.

That's right. Canes. The bastards here still whip you on the ass with long bamboo sticks. But they don't give you all of the whacks in your sentence in one session because you usually pass out after two or three. Instead, they let you heal a few weeks before giving you a few more whacks, and repeat the heal–whack cycle until they administer your entire punishment.

An image of me, pants down, leaning over and getting it on the ass from some little Asian while others laughed and shouted in Chinese, made me dread the cold steel of the smart Colt shoved in my trousers as much as I feared getting burned by my quarry. I had protested the location on several occasions, quite concerned about the added risk of Singapore's excessive security system. Just about every square inch of this island was monitored either by stationary cameras, by the floating Orbs, or by a geosynchronous satellite. I would have much rather held this meeting in Latin America, or even in the Middle East, places that exponentially increased our ability to vanish when shit hit the fan—something that invariably happened in these operations. But Troy had already set events in motion that could not be stopped—lest we wished to raise suspicions with the shadowy North Korean firm brokering the deal.

On top of all that, Troy had insisted on using rookies, wanting new faces to minimize the chance of getting burned.

"I can't believe that Vlachko himself is going to be there," I had told Troy the month before, when I'd learned of the meeting he had arranged. Initial contact was typically conducted by buffers, by people with connections to each interested party, but who didn't know how to make direct contact with them— therefore kidnapping the buffers and interrogating them for information would yield nothing except telegraphing our intentions. A first meeting was more like a dance, with each side checking the other for weaknesses, for alarms, for the slightest reason to pull the plug on the whole thing. In my business neither side remained alive for long without this level of paranoia.

"Relax, Tommy. I know how things work. I taught you the rules, remember? I am the one who showed you a hundred different ways to assassinate a target without anyone suspecting it was a murder."

I nodded.

"But I *also* taught you that when an opportunity presented itself you should act on it. This is the case with Vlachko, so I jumped at the chance to bag the bastard," Troy had replied while smoking one of his illegal Cohibas in that dark-paneled office of his on the third floor of the new building in Langley. Troy Savage, a former SEAL already in his early fifties, still had the body and stamina of a man twenty years his junior, his only vice being the Cuban cigars he regularly obtained through a contact at Guantánamo Bay. He had lost most of his hair in his thirties and had gone for the Kojak look back then, though he kept a well-trimmed goatee, probably to compensate for the lack of hair in the northern hemisphere, as so many men do. His ice-cold blue eyes narrowed, as he expected a reply.

"That doesn't leave us enough time to prepare," I had replied. "We need to send scouts, survey the meeting ground, set up rendezvous points, perhaps a safe house or two, *especially* in Singapore, where Big Brother is always watching."

"Have I burned you yet on an operation, Tommy? We go back to well before the Gulf War, to the days when the Commie rebels were the threat. Have I ever done you wrong?"

I shake my head. The huevos rancheros incident in Testikuzklan had occurred under someone else, and Troy had actually taken some of the heat when the shit hit the fan in Belgrade, especially when it became obvious that I couldn't defend myself against Washington piranhas because I was in deep mourning over Maddie's loss.

"Besides, Tommy, I even contributed to your personal well-being four years ago, remember?"

Troy was, of course, referring to the Kulzak case, where his agreement to my temporary transfer out of Langley to join the newly formed Counter Cyberterrorism Task Force back then resulted in yours truly working for Karen Frost, who headed the CCTF.

I nod.

"Are you still seeing her?"

"Now and then," I replied, not feeling like talking about how little we had seen of each other in the past six months because of our job responsibilities.

"Have I broken trust?"

"No."

"Then leave the setup to me," he had replied.

"What about the assassination method, Troy? We don't even know what we're going to use this time."

"Yes," he said, taking a drag from the Cohiba, exhaling toward the fluorescent lights behind the ceiling tiles. "The assassination method . . . let me see." Reaching inside a drawer of his mahogany desk, he had produced a vial. "When you're face-to-face with Vlachko, you give him this," he had replied with the same easygoing grin he had used when plucking me out of the Madras CIA Station a lifetime ago.

The tiny test tube looked empty to the naked eye. "What's in it?"

"The same nanocrap we dumped on that terrorist camp in Colombia last month thanks to your handiwork."

I continued to stare at the vial but with growing respect, remembering the long weeks I had spent in Colombia confirming the intel gathered by our satellites.

Colombia.

Identifying the sites had not been that difficult thanks to Troy's assets in that drug-ridden country. The daughter of a banker in Caracas and the nephew of a high-ranking government official in Valencia had been among the agents assisting me in the mountains, guiding me through treacherous roads, across meandering rivers, pinpointing the well-hidden camp, which I marked with a laser for the stealth fighter that released the nanotronic load soon after. The terrorists had gone mad, shooting each other as the man-made plague entered their ear canals and detonated in their heads, inducing aneurysms in some and maddening pain in others.

Still holding the vial, I said, "This is great, Troy, but how am I supposed to get away after I release the contents of the vial? I don't feel like having some nanorobot crawling up my ass."

He fingered his goatee, still flashing that condescending smile. "Tommy, Tommy. After all we've been through and you still don't give me enough credit. The nanoorganisms are safe for everyone but Vlachko. They have been programmed to seek his DNA. You just tell them they're neutralized samples of the real stuff we would like to sell him."

"And he's going to believe that *because*?"

Troy stopped smiling. "Maybe you're not the right man for this job."

He had not finished saying that when I realized I was being tested. I quickly said, "I offer to let them try it on me to convince them that the weapon has been neutralized."

"Very good. And then you tell them that they will receive a

programmable version they can customize for any kind of assassination job—but only after payment is received. Then the bastard will open that vial to inspect the goods and . . ." he exhales a cloud of smoke, "*poof.* One less motherfucker selling arms to rogue regimes. Of course, if somehow the nanoweapons don't get him, you have permission to just shoot the bastard to kingdom come. Word I got is that everyone at the White House will kiss your ass when you pull this one off. We sure could have used that kind of executive attitude for dealing with terrorist assholes back in the Clinton years. Perhaps then shit like the USS *Cole* and September 11th could have been prevented. But Washington isn't taking the pussy way out anymore."

That was Troy's way of saying that we had presidential sanction to carry out an assassination, which was in direct violation of the old Presidential Directive 12333. While 12333 was still in effect, every president since September 11th had been making exceptions, especially when it came time to bagging international terrorists.

"Question?" I ask.

He pointed at me with the burning end of the cigar. "Shoot."

"How did you get Vlachko's DNA?"

Troy leaned back on his chair, set his feet on the ground, and placed the Cohiba in between his lips while winking at me. "Just tell them what they need to know. Always keep them guessing, Tommy. Always keep them guessing."

As I remembered the way I last saw that cool cat two weeks ago, confidently puffing away at the cigar, I whispered to my termination team, "Interior check."

An atomic-scale microphone implanted behind my front teeth captured my voice. A moment later I listened for their response through a minuscule earpiece attached to my right ear canal, connected through a wireless interface to the Plasmaflex unit on my wrist. I had four officers inside Sim Lim Square and six others out on the streets covering each exit. I wished I had twice as many, but Troy had reminded me to never underestimate the enemy's dry-cleaning skills—their ability to detect surveillance—and had insisted on capping this operation at ten officers plus me.

"Two check."

"Three check."

I wait for my last two team members, but I get no reply.

I frowned. "Interior check, Four. Five."

Nothlng.

The possibility of malfunctioning equipment briefly flashed in my mind, but I discarded it an instant later. Our nanogear, assembled with molecular precision in the vast USN complex in central Texas, was defect free, as flawless as the nanoweapons Vlachko sought—and far more advanced than anything else on the market today, even from CyberWerke.

Something had gone terribly wrong.

But what? No one but Troy and I knew the details of the deal. Not even Director Dobson had learned of the specifics, of the time and date of the initial exchange of dollars for the tiny test tube housing neutralized samples of the same nanoweapon that wiped out that Colombian terrorist camp.

I glanced at the Plasmaflex, my stomach filling with molten lead when the unit displayed flatlines for two of my operatives.

I performed an outside team check and all six officers reported in. The team on the street was intact and professionally listening but not making any moves unless ordered to do so.

Cursing Troy Savage for setting up this meeting in a country I didn't like, and without allowing me the time to survey the area properly, *and* then making me run it under several restrictions, I triggered the destruction of the implants in the dead operatives. The classified nanotech implants could not be allowed to fall into enemy hands. Our advanced nanotronics had to be protected at all costs. In an instant, a wireless signal reached the oral, ear, eye, and wrist implants—as well as the nanocells on the grips of the smart Colts—of the neutralized operatives. The molecular-level burns on the wrist, eyes, and mouth and in the right ear canal carried a high degree of injury, including blindness and the potential of a digitally induced aneurysm. But the operatives were already flatlined, which was the only way the implants would acknowledge such a termination signal. The nanotronics in the implants monitored the host's vital signs. As long as there was life, they would not acknowledge the termination signal. This was a safety mechanism to prevent one operative from accidentally killing another. The only exception to this rule was if I chose to trigger the destruction of my own implants to prevent anyone access to the technology if I was captured alive, though doing so would likely result in my death—at least certain blindness.

I forced my legs into motion, reaching the escalator while whispering, "Two, three, engage countermeasures."

Our wrist implants possessed the ability to fool any nanoweapon in existence today—at least those we knew of.

A security Orb hovered a dozen feet away monitoring the scene. It didn't appear to have gone into alarm mode yet. One of the dangers of active countermeasures was potentially telegraphing our presence to the Orbs. Although our transmitting frequency was encoded to make it nearly impossible to trace, the chance of getting caught still existed, and possession of military-class implants except by local law enforcement also carried an automatic death sentence in this country—the reason why Troy had insisted I only activate the countermeasures in case of an emergency.

But I had no choice. The meeting had been compromised and it was my responsibility to empower my surviving operatives inside this building with every defense at our disposal, including the use of their smart Colts, which became active the instant the film coating the composite gun grip detected the owner's fingerprints and enabled the firing mechanism. Whoever had neutralized my men had done so ruthlessly and brilliantly, without tipping the high-resolution eyes of the floating security force in Sim Lim Square—almost as if the bastards knew we were coming.

"Two, countermeasures engaged," comes the reply from one of my agents.

I just about peed in my pants when I failed to get a reply

from the third guy, spotting instead another flatline on the Plasmaflex.

I reluctantly triggered a termination signal to the neutralized operative, frying his on-board nanotronics.

Then I saw the threat. My advanced lenses, fitted with pattern-recognition technology and a state-of-the-art processor, helped me discern something too subtle to be detected by the hovering drones or the crowd around me, but definitely a disturbance in the normal pattern of customers and salesmen making deals. Three men, all Asian, wearing dark trousers and colored T-shirts, their movements fluid as they advanced through the gathering in front of a large nanotronic store selling CyberWerke hardware, heading my way as I'm about to reach the fifth floor.

Out of options, silently cursing the unfortunate fate of this operation, I ordered my surviving interior team member to our rendezvous point on the bottom floor while moving briskly away from the trio, past a display of vintage high-definition televisions and portable computers guarded by an old Malay man with dark, wrinkled skin. He shot a narrowed gaze of curiosity at me as I rushed by, trying to increase the gap with my pursuers.

Glancing at the shiny Orbs, confirming their continued lack of awareness of the attack under way, I felt a tingling sensation on my wrist. The Plasmaflex had just detected a laser.

Someone was painting me. The Asian trio was the flush team, guiding me toward a hidden sniper. In the same instant my implants informed me that the last operative had flatlined.

Issuing another termination signal, I dropped to a deep crouch, using the perplexed crowd as my shield against the hidden sniper.

My flanks turned into a blur as I raced away as fast as my legs would go while ordering the team outside to their vehicles. We were cutting our losses and getting out of here.

Pressing my right fist into my left palm at chest level, elbows extended, I slammed into the crowd, shoving people aside, no longer caring to avoid attention. Two Asians in business suits fell on their sides, crashing against a window display as I rushed by, ignoring shouts of anger, of surprise. Glass shattered; people screamed; equipment fell to the marble floors. I scrambled past angered shop owners, beyond shocked patrons, some screaming in Chine—

The tingling in my wrist abruptly changed frequency just as something buzzed past my left ear, like an angered hornet— an instant before a smart dart embedded itself in a wooden display to my left.

My breath was caught in my throat for an instant, before I exhaled in relief. The near miss was no lucky break. The Plasmaflex countermeasures had emitted a jamming shield around me the moment they had sensed the advanced dart in the air.

"We're in the vehicles. Which exit?"

That was my senior officer outside. The team had made it to the two sedans and one of them was waiting for me to show up.

According to plan, I was supposed to emerge on Albert Street, which faced the south side of Sim Lim Square. But the slight change of plans had pushed me to the north side of the building, meaning I would be exiting on the side facing Rochor Canal Road.

The adrenaline rush drying my throat, I conveyed my exit point while chastising myself for following Troy's orders and not engaging the countermeasures sooner, perhaps sparing lives.

I pressed on, pushing my way through the crowd not only to lose the trio and their sniper but also to evade the pair of Orbs heading my way. The CIA brief on the Singaporean version of the pseudo-intelligent guards claimed they packed quite the nasty little arsenal, including live ammunition—though I seriously doubt they will open fire in this crowd.

The Asian trio breaks through the wall of people. One of them is taller than the other two, and my advanced lenses briefly focused on his face, on his high cheekbones, on his aquiline nose, on his strong chin, on a pair of lips twisted in apparent anger. The man is no Asian cat but someone trying to pass for an Asian. My supervision has spotted the clear microtape pulling the ends of his eyes, creating the slanted effect meant to fool me.

But he could not fool the advanced lenses, which broadcast a 76.5 percent probability that the features belonged to Rem Vlachko. My intelligent wrist also tells me that the estimated height and weight of the stranger—six feet, one inch, and 190 pounds—matches that of my target, raising the percent of certainty to 93.

If my implants were correct, then Troy had been right in assessing that the monster would be here. Unfortunately, the bastard didn't look like he was here to negotiate.

In the same instant, as my legs burned from the effort, I spotted a fourth figure breaking the rhythm of the crowd, coming at me from the opposite direction, his movements powerful but fluid, like a football player rushing through the line of scrimmage. But there was more to it. My enhanced vision suddenly told me more than what my mind was willing to accept. The man was taller than me and also wider, but not fat, just big. His movements were too familiar, bringing back memories of my training days at Camp Peary. I thought I recognized his features, not Asian but Western, with a well-trimmed goatee. They were shadowed by a baseball cap, or was it makeup? Or was my alarmed mind playing tricks on me?

Troy?

Unable to make a clean ID, my senses screaming at me to treat all incoming figures as the enemy, I rushed past the next escalator, reaching the double metal doors marked STAIRS in English, above its equivalent in Hindu, Chinese, and Malay.

My pursuers trying to converge on me from two different directions, the Orbs just behind them recording the occasion, I pushed the waist-high crash bar running across the metal door.

Was that really Troy Savage?

If so, what in the hell is he doing here with Rem Vlachko?

Or was he trying to catch *Vlachko? Perhaps using me as bait?*

No time to analyze!

Just do!

The Plasmaflex went nuts again, prickling the top of my hand just as I detected an acrid stench. The tiny screen is flashing at me to get away from the bluish cloud enveloping me.

Puzzled, considering drawing my weapon, my heartbeat pounding my eardrums, I rocketed away from the strange odor, from the madness, shutting the door, staring at a hot and empty stairwell.

Concrete steps heading up and down projected beyond the small landing. Sunlight forked through side windows, washing my escape route in a yellow glow, creating a greenhouse effect inside the steamy emergency exit.

Still hesitating to reach for my piece in this place, I ran downstairs, beads of perspiration dripping down my forehead, stinging my eyes. If a hidden camera spotted the Colt I would have the entire fleet of Orbs and the Singapore police department congregating on my ass. I couldn't get caught, not with the implants and the smart Colt—and not because of the certain death sentence. The implants were top-secret technology.

Wondering how things got so out of control so quickly, not certain how any intel could have leaked from Troy's controlled circle, I reached the landing for the fourth floor, still spotting no one, still praying that I would not.

Tension throbbing in my forehead, in my temples, my enhanced eyes wildly gazing about me, I reached the third floor, then the second, breathing heavily now, as if I were really out of shape.

But I was not. Back then I was in superb physical condition, at the top of my game, capable of running at full speed for minutes before breaking a sweat. Yet my body shivered from exhaustion, as if an invisible force had sucked the energy right out of—

The smell! The blue cloud!

Of course!

The same cat who had fired the smart dart realized I was armed with countermeasures and had then fired a microcanister filled with a paralyzing gas, which did not have to hit me directly, as was required with a dart. The canister only needed to go off *near* me to nail me.

A crash from above, followed by hastened footsteps. My pursuers had reached the emergency stairs, were coming after me.

But the paralyzing chemical had already spread through my system. My legs would no longer move, refused to carry me any farther. I struggled forward, tried to reach the first floor—reach the street, get to safety. But I fell instead, crashing my right shoulder against the steps, then flipping, landing hard on my back.

Disoriented, finding it hard to breathe, my shoulder blades burning from the impact, the clicking footsteps getting closer, I did the only thing I could before losing all control of my body. Pressing index fingers against my eyes, I rubbed down and to the side, removing my lenses, tossing them aside while also ordering my team outside to scramble back to the safe house. I had become a liability to them.

Wishing I could also dig out the implant in my right ear but realizing I was out of time, I reached for the vial in my pocket and slammed it hard against the concrete, releasing the nano-organisms, hoping that if one of the Asians was indeed Vlahcko maybe I would get the bastard.

Hands grabbed my shoulders, tugging at me, but I could no longer see. It would take minutes before my sight returned after I removed the advanced lenses—something to do with the way the molecular interface connects the lenses to the pupils to enhance sight.

But it didn't matter. I didn't care to see the faces of my executioners, of the bastards who killed my team members. But the fourth cat . . . was that Troy? If so, what was he doing there? And more important, why wasn't he helping me?

As my mind grew cloudy, dark, I reluctantly ordered the Plasmaflex to issue a final termination signal, realizing what that would mean. Although I had removed the lenses, sparing my eyes, the detonating implant in my ear could kill me—or turn me into an eggplant. But I had taken a vow to protect the technology at all costs, to keep it from falling into the wrong hands. People would die if terrorists got ahold of my advanced USN implants and learned how to counter them, how to turn them against us.

Cringing, I waited for the command to propagate through the logic of the Plasmaflex, which, realizing that I had issued an order to self-destruct, prompted me for final confirmation.

Confirmed.

Colors exploded in my brain as a white-hot pain pierced through my head like a sizzling splinter, tearing into my mind, my soul. Somewhere in the distance I could also feel the top of my right wrist burning, as if I had immersed it in acid, but it felt far away, detached from the overwhelming lightning bolt deep in my mind ravaging my senses.

Scourged, maddened, I tried to scream, to shout, to howl from the agonizing pain gripping my sanity, but the choked cry never reached my gorge before everything went black.

[4] LEGEND

THE SEA BREEZE CARESSING my face, the whistling wind ringing in my ears, I wiggle my toes in the sand to reassure myself of where I am, of where I had hoped to hide from my past life, from that terrible witch hunt, from the shame I had brought to the place I had once called home, to the people I had considered my family; and also from the sudden disintegration of the closest personal relationship in my life after Maddie. The double whammy left me wishing for some of those recreational drugs I passed up in college. But instead I settled for Uncle Jack Daniel's and Cousin Johnnie Walker, until I finally packed up and headed south.

"You're quite a legend," Rachel offers. "The only survivor of a termination signal—and self-induced. All to protect the technology. We covered your case at the Farm eight months ago."

I regard this Italian feline blowing sunshine up my ass who apparently graduated recently from the Farm—also known to the general public as Camp Peary. From there, CIA career trainees—yours truly included—received paramilitary training at Harvey Point, North Carolina. Those CTs who made it through this six-week wringer would continue to participate in further training exercises in places like Panama and Arizona. CTs then enter the field under the wing of senior officers for a few years, like Morotski and I did in Madras, India.

But I had barbecued myself in Singapore only *a year* ago, meaning she had been at the Farm back then, and now she was running this field operation. Either I'm looking at a prodigy or the Agency is running short of experienced hands.

Or maybe she is doing the belly-to-belly with Leyman and Morotski.

But there's no way the Langley I remember would allow a one-year rookie out here pitching me—the term we use for trying to recruit an agent.

In any case, what did she just call me? A survivor of a terminal signal? I actually got *extremely* lucky that the blast didn't rip beyond my inner ear, which in itself had been paralyzing but had not damaged the lining of my brain—though it did leave me with an annoying ringing that would accompany me for life. Luck, they tell me, was also on my side that the nerve gas, as it turned out, fired by one of the Singaporean Orbs, had not been lethal. The damage from the destroyed implants, plus the Orbs closing in, had apparently been enough for Rem Vlachko and his Asian associates to leave me there for dead. Through our connections with the Singapore government, I was spared any criminal prosecution and shipped back to the States, where it took three operations to restore not only my hearing but also my balance, putting an end to those terrifying spells of dizziness.

Funny how things worked. The top cats at Langley first healed me, then crucified me, and then they even erased Tom Grant by forcing me to get a new face—part of the reason I haven't shaved in some time. I'm still not sure who that guy in the mirror is.

"I'm quite certain the case study was presented as an example of what *not* to do," I finally say.

"To the contrary," she says. "You are considered the epitome of what a CIA officer must do to protect the technology. Your intuitive powers are also well known in Langley . . . as you've demonstrated. I did put myself through school, and I did sacrifice just about everything for the chance to be here today—though I'm not as young and inexperienced as you think."

"Look, Rachel, I'm flattered that you think so highly of me, and I'm sure that you are a fine officer, but I'm afraid you are wasting your—"

She extends a hand toward me, smiling for the first time. "It's a real honor meeting you."

As I continue to wonder how someone who looks so young is already leading a team like this one, I shake her hand. Her skin is soft, but the grip is firm, confident, like her stare. "I wish I could say it was a pleasure meeting you, Rachel. But I no longer lie and deceive for a living. Now, please, I *really* want to be left alone."

"But your life is in danger. We know what happened yesterday, the attempt on your life."

"Langley might have put me on the shelf, but that doesn't mean I'm an easy target. I know how to take care of myself. I've been doing it against far tougher threats for twenty-five years."

"You might not be so lucky next time," she says. "Besides, we really need your help. I think we can help each other."

"Doesn't the Agency have better things to do than bother with old fogies like me?"

"But you're not old, sir. The dossier says you're only forty-eight. That's not that—"

"Believe me, Rachel. That's *old* in this field, and besides, it took me a year to leave the past in the past. I'm now only looking forward."

"Look, Mr. Malone, the problem is that the past is *not* in the past. We have a grave situation that is likely to get worse, and we think that's why there was an attempt on your life yesterday—the more reason for you to come with us."

"Look here, I—"

"We think Savage is alive and working for the other side."

Boy, inexperienced or not, she sure knows how to kick a guy in the balls. I'm speechless. It's one thing blaming a screwup on someone else—I've seen that happen dozens of times in the field, and it has been done to me before. It's another thing for Troy to be accused of committing treason. Although to this day I still believe I saw Troy and Vlachko in Singapore, I never imagined that Troy had switched sides. I thought he was just covering his own ass by using me as his fall guy. I never thought of him as a *traitor*, even after his mysterious disappearance on his way to work one morning before I could confront him. The D.C. police found his car stripped in a back alley. A global search yielded nothing and Langley assumed he had been captured, tortured, and killed—especially after several of the agents he ran in three different countries turned up dead before we could secure the remaining assets controlled by Troy.

It takes me a moment to recover, which in itself tells me just how sadly out of form I really am. Freezing like this in the field—even for a microsecond—could mean death.

"You're saying that he . . . *faked* his kidnapping, his death?" I finally ask. "Why?"

"To make it simpler to cross to the other side. We have reason to believe that he disappeared to assist Rem Vlachko in securing nanoweapons."

"How . . . how do you know that?" I ask, remembering the gold star added to the memorial wall at the entrance of the new building in Langley to honor fallen CIA operatives.

She runs a hand through her short hair, her too-close-together eyes under a pair of bushy brows that remind me of actress Brooke Shields informing me she's not really enjoying telling me this. Either that or she's damned good at pretending to be compassionate—which might explain why she has gotten so far so soon.

"He altered the files from the failed operation as a diversion. Savage fixed it all up so the entire operation appeared to have been planned by you, down to selecting Singapore as the meeting ground, redirecting the heat. He even left that videotape that was used as his postmortem testimony for the FBI probe, essentially four-bagging you."

I frown. Four-bagging is an old term that carried over from the FBI to the CIA, referring to an internal discipline consisting of censure, transfer, suspension, and probation. For a senior officer, getting not only four-bagged at your own agency but also subjected to an FBI investigation is the equivalent of death, of a forced resignation, especially if you are out on your own, without any high-ranking officer to shield you from the storm. No one with an ounce of self-respect would go through a four-bag humiliation. So I was given the option to retire with half of my pension, and I took it.

"But," I say, my mind still refusing to believe that my mentor is a rat, "he could have done all of that just to keep from getting four-bagged himself, which is what I claimed he had done. What proof do you have that Troy did what he did because he was indeed working with Vlachko?"

Rachel checks both ends of the beach, as if making sure no one is in sight except for the stationary yacht.

Dropping her voice to a mere whisper, which forces me to lean closer to her, she says, "We have plenty of proof, starting with bank transactions, in particular a large one which occurred within days of the Singapore operation. Savage underestimated the Technical Division's ability to probe bank accounts in places like the Cayman Islands. Those institutions are a lot more cooperative these days."

My wheels are turning, and I hate myself for allowing my professional side to escape from the coffin I had so carefully nailed shut a year ago. "How large was the transaction?"

"Three million dollars."

"What else do you have?" I realize that the money trail is probably enough, but I need to be sure.

"Remember the Prague Report of 2007?"

I close my eyes, remembering the bonanza of information

Troy had generated from one of his most secretive assets in the Czech Republic—someone we knew only as Flek. Given the sensitive position Flek held in the Czech Republic's government, Troy had convinced then CIA director Martin Jacobs to allow him the leeway of not logging his agent's true identity in the CIA's files. There had been a series of leaks in recent years, which had resulted in the deaths of a number of overseas assets and their families. Troy refused to take that chance. Flek came up with intel on several terrorist cells operating in his country as well as in Slovakia and Bulgaria. The immediate mobilization of every able CIA hand in the region—with the assistance of three separate SEAL teams—resulted in the termination of over fifty terrorists across four separate training camps. We exterminated a lot of bad cats in a single week.

"I was on temporary assignment in Berlin at the time," I tell her. "I participated in the neutralizations that took place in the Czech Republic. Why?"

"We later received information that Rem Vlachko's network soon expanded into those three territories. Troy used U.S. government resources to eliminate opposing terrorist organizations, clearing the way for Vlachko to establish himself in that region of Europe—while at the same time making himself look like a hero for having provided the intel that led to the termination of so many terrorists. We recently discovered that a bank in Switzerland transferred two million euros to a bank account in the Bahamas under his name three months after we carried out that operation."

"Dear Lord," I mumble to myself.

"I'm afraid it's worse than that."

My throat is as dry as the wood on this barnacle-encrusted piece-of-shit boat I got for the equivalent of three hundred bucks.

"We believe he has been a double agent for some time."

"How long?"

"At least since the Gulf War."

"Since the Gulf . . . but that's almost *twenty* years ago. You're telling me I was trained and run by a *traitor*?" The knot in my gut is twisting so hard I feel I'm going to toss my cookies.

"I'm afraid so. You were manipulated while carrying out some of your missions," she added. "Only now do we realize just how brilliantly he deceived us."

"Missions? Which missions?" I feel as if I'm taking a crap the day after swallowing a bag of jalapeño peppers.

"The good news is that it's not all of them. Just some, like one of your last operations, for example, the one in Colombia."

Although a wonderful tropical sun is shining on me, I'm suddenly very cold. Bracing myself, I mumble, "The *terrorist* camp? That's impossible. I verified they were bad guys before pulling the trigger."

The Mediterranean princess smiles without humor. "You know the old saying, appearances can be deceiving. It was a terrorist camp all right, and those were real terrorists with real ties to the local drug lords, and they were indeed responsible for a number of assassinations and bombings in Colombia. No one would argue that they were the worst kind of human being and deserved to die."

"Then?"

"Two of the terrorists who operated the camp were assets being run by a case officer from the Bogotá Station."

I close my eyes, shutting out the world around me, the sun, the sea, even the damned seagulls.

"Cameron, look, I'm really sorry to be the one to be telling you—"

"You're saying that my actions resulted in the deaths of CIA agents?"

She puts a hand on my shoulder, squeezing it gently. "But you didn't know. You were manipulated, as was the rest of the Agency."

"Who were the assets in Colombia going to deliver before I unleashed that rain of nanorobotic death on them?"

"They were planning to train some of Vlachko's new recruits, which would have gotten us closer to him, but Savage eliminated them . . . through you."

Damn. The revelation is packing a punch as unexpected

and severe as Karen's. The recruitment of foreign nationals—agents—with unsavory backgrounds was a practice that had been eliminated from the CIA, until September 11th. Following that terrible attack a decade ago, all agencies belonging to the U.S. intelligence community, from the CIA to the NSA, the DIA, and even the FBI, were given carte blanche to recruit anyone who could provide America with the required intel to nail terrorists. It goes without saying that typically the more unpleasant the recruit the better the intel, which also meant larger compensation packages—taxpayers' dollars—not to mention the time invested to turn the recruits. Recruiting two terrorist trainers operating one of the worst and most secretive camps in Colombia to spy for us had had to require incredible resources.

Rachel mentions other missions I ran in the past two decades, including some in Peru, South Korea, the Czech Republic, Mexico, and Yugoslavia.

"Yugoslavia . . . you mean in . . . Serbia . . . 1997?"

She solemnly nods.

My legs are about to give under me, but I manage to pull myself together before they do, remaining standing—though barely.

"Troy Savage leaked intel to Serbian authorities, resulting in the death of . . . look, Cameron, I'm really sorry."

I'm having an out-of-body experience as deep-rooted feelings uncoil out of the far recesses of my mind, swirling around me, enveloping me, veiling my senses. "That . . . that . . . son of a . . . I'm going to fucking kill him!"

"Sometimes it takes years—decades—before we can catch a bad officer, especially a brilliant one like Troy Savage."

I take a minute to calm myself down, to bring focus back to my mind, forcing myself to breathe steadily.

"What about the mission that eliminated Ares Kulzak?" I finally ask.

She shakes her head. "You did your country a significant service then, and we would like to give you the chance to do it again, while also avenging yourself on the man who betrayed you in Singapore, in Mexico, in Colombia—in Serbia. So, my question to you, Cameron Malone, is: Will you help us? Will you help us catch Troy Savage?" She stares at me with those incredible green eyes, her hand still on my shoulder.

Although I realize that her presence and her sudden physical contact are both part of Langley's ploy to get me to cooperate, I have to admit that her powers of persuasion are among the best I've seen—especially if everything she has said is true.

Rachel Muratani is good. Real good. Before I can reply, she says, "I know this will sound like another cliché, but the situation has really turned critical. Our country is out of time."

"How so?"

She crosses her arms and tilts her head toward the yacht, which has turned to shore. "I'm not at liberty to discuss that until you have signed on the dotted line and formally agreed to assist us." She shrugs and adds, "Agency rules."

Realizing that the spooks on the yacht are indeed listening to this conversation, I reply, "I would need to see proof of everything you've told me before I would agree."

"Of course."

I glance at the white vessel approaching the surf before studying her very carefully, my senses returning after the brief emotional rush. Invoking a quarter of a century of field operations, where I trained to spot inconsistencies, conflicting signals, I review not just the information she has released but everything that has taken place since the attack yesterday. I consider her explanations, her claims about Troy Savage, about his association with Rem Vlachko, the monster. Was she telling the truth? Or was she just feeding me lies to get me to cooperate?

Rachel's emerald eyes are calm, steady, focused on me, not looking away, or narrowing, or blinking. Her posture is relaxed. Her fingers are not fidgeting, and I see no trembling in them. Either she is telling the truth or she is the best damn liar I've seen in a while.

But my spook sense is not satisfied, questioning why the Agency would send such a young operative—pretty or not—to try to convince an old hand like me to get back in the saddle after having been kicked off a year ago.

"Rachel," I say, trying to measure my words. "Please don't

take it personal, but before this goes any further I want to hear this directly from Morotski and Leyman."

"Sure," she says before looking out to sea. "That can be arranged, but for the record, I've been authorized by my boss, Morotski, to make this deal."

Did I just hear her say that she reports into Morotski, the head of Counterterrorism? That would make her at least a *senior* CIA officer. "Look, the reason I ask is that I would have expected this pitch to have been delivered by someone of higher authority."

"You mean someone *older*, and probably *not* a woman, right?"

"I didn't say that."

"Don't confuse age or gender with authority, Cameron. I have plenty of the latter, even if I look too young to a crusty old guy like you."

"I've been trained to question inconsistencies, Rachel. That's what's kept me alive this long. At the moment I don't understand how someone so young has climbed so high so quickly at Langley when the CIA I remember was *pathetically* slow *and* cautious when it came to promoting even its best operatives."

"What are you implying?"

"I'm implying that it is suspicious to a seasoned operative like me that you got here so soon."

"Rest assured that I do have the experience to handle an operation like this one, and both Leyman and Morotski will vouch for me."

"Sorry," I say. "I'm afraid that's not good enough. How did you manage to land this job when you look like you just graduated from college?"

"All right, Mr. Malone," she says, crossing her arms, dark amusement flashing across her fine features. "If you really want to know, I *fucked* my way to the top." She winks. "Any other *inconsistencies* you care to discuss?"

The same spook sense that made me challenge her is now urging me to shelve it for the time being, though for the record I did force her out of her operative shell for an instant.

She turns briskly away from me to face the large cruiser as it stops just beyond the waves breaking a hundred feet or so from shore. Upon closer inspection, the vessel's beam is closer to fifty feet than forty, with three levels. There's at least a half-dozen men visible on the main deck.

Two large personal watercraft slide from the rear and head in our direction.

"Our rides," she says without looking at me.

Things are happening too fast. Just twenty minutes ago I was enjoying a retirement that, albeit early, at least had come with the satisfaction of having served my country. Now, after having been told that during many of my proudest moments I had been assisting the other side, I'm about to be hauled away for an unpredictable length of time by the same people who hung me out to dry a year ago.

"What about my stuff?" I extend a thumb toward the beat-up trailer and rusted truck. If I have indeed lost possession of this property, then at least I'd like to retain ownership of the gear I've purchased recently—though in reality it's mostly junk. The important stuff—my papers and cash in the waterproof money belt, my gun for protection, and my Rolex for emergency funding—I have with me, especially after yesterday's attack. Old habits are indeed hard to break.

"Leave it to us," she says in an icy tone, obviously upset at my questions. "We'll have a cleanup crew in here within the hour. By sundown there will be no trace that you were ever here."

I really don't like the way that sounded, but I don't see my way clear to other options. For some strange reason, I now wished I would have left my legacy behind with Rosita, Juanita, and Margarita back at the plaza.

The PWCs bounce over the surf, their drivers skillfully steering straight through the waves, reaching the shore moments later. They are brand-new machines, their shiny blue and white finish glistening in the sunlight.

She gives them a nod. The driver of one of them, a cat with curly ash-blond hair and a wispy mustache, jumps off and gets in the rear of the other PWC, before they turn around and head back to the yacht. According to Agency rules, he is supposed to be an operative, but like his companion on the PWC, he looks fifteen, which makes me wonder what he thinks about an old fogie like me.

Rachel slides behind the controls of the second PWC, looks over at me standing in knee-deep water, frowns, and says over the sound of the engine and the surf, "Hop on, and try not to fall off."

After a moment of hesitation I climb on, but before I can wrap my arms around her waist she floors it.

In a blur, I'm staring straight at the sky for an instant before doing a backward flip and a painful belly flop while the stream of water shooting off the rear of the machine slams against my head like a sledgehammer.

My skull on fire, my stomach burning, my pride wounded, I stagger to my feet in surf up to my waist while she turns around, maneuvering the watercraft like the pro she has shown she is—young or not.

"I told them you were past your prime," she says, shaking her head. "But they insisted I try to bring you in. See if you can hang on this time, old-timer."

"I guess that makes us even," I say, wiping long strands of hair off my face, realizing what a sight I must be at the moment with my shaggy hair, unkempt beard, and wet rags.

"I'll try to be . . . *gentler* this time," she replies.

I give her an empty smile and say, "You're asking for it, young lady," before getting back on and clamping my arms around her waist right before she guns it. She laughs, revs up the engine, and we're off, bouncing over the surf, crashing into waves in bursts of foam.

I'm momentarily blinded by the sunlight reflecting off glittering water, which makes me realize I've lost my sunglasses back there. The salt stings my eyes, but I can't afford to wipe them, lest I fall off again.

But I shove such petty inconveniences away as my training emerges through the physical and mental havoc of the past minutes. Forcing my mind back to business, I lean forward and speak loudly into her right ear: "Can you at least tell me what is it that you expect to get from me? I've been out of the game for a year. That's a lifetime in our business."

She looks over her right shoulder, her face only inches from mine. "You've spent more time with Troy Savage than any other CIA officer alive today!" she screams over the noise of the wind and the watercraft. "The knowledge in your head is priceless!"

"You want a debrief on Troy? I'm not sure how that would be of much help when it's pretty damn obvious that he deceived me as much as he deceived the Agency."

"We're not interested in debriefing you!" she shouts while slowing down as we pass the yacht and go around the back, where I see two ramps dipping into the water. The first PWC is already up the ramp, where two men in shorts and plain T-shirts secure it to a post with a chain.

Before I get a chance to reply, she guns the engine one last time the moment she aligns the front of the machine with the inclined tracks.

For an instant I feel as if we're going up a roller coaster, before the friction between the ramp's tracks and the fiberglass hull kills our forward momentum. We come to a sudden halt right next to the second PWC.

The yacht's diesels boil the water behind me as we head offshore, away from the place I've known as home for the past eight months.

As the unexpected events resurrect my operative mind while temporarily shelving the man I left behind on the sand, Rachel Muratani turns around, sitting sideways to me while I continue to straddle the seat.

"What do you want if not to debrief me?" I ask as the ash-blond guy ties down our machine.

Resting a hand over the handlebars while patting me on the shoulder with the other, she smiles and says, "Cameron, we want you to go after him."

[5] CONSTRUCT

ASSY AWOKE WHEN THE sensors buried a millimeter beneath its seamless Kevhel skin triggered a series of impulses to the parietal lobe of its nanotronic brain.

An unmaskable interrupt had pierced Assy's low-power sleep mode. The interrupt had originated in the construct's cerebral cortex, where the digital DNA that allowed it to make subsidiary copies of itself resided.

NORMAL MODE.

Booting up into its default mode of operation, Assy's internal clock reported that exactly twenty-four hours had elapsed since it last received its nanoenzyme, which prevented the execution of a routine that would order the venting slats in its fusion chamber to open fully, triggering a massive meltdown of its energy source.

Its operating frequency increased threefold as the artificial intelligence engine at the core of its nanotronic brain rushed down its list of options to prevent this digital suicide programmed into all mobile assemblers at United States Nanotechnology.

As the fusion chamber obeyed the new directive, the construct's sensors reported an increase in temperature on its sphere-shaped shell, made of a Kevlar-helium alloy, strong, light. In another two seconds the temperature would exceed the maximum rating of the molecular system, turning the atomically precise machine into twenty pounds of sizzling rubble.

Millions of options flashed across the temporal lobe's vast memory banks, reaching a never-before-opened routine—one Assy didn't know existed but whose record indicated that it had been placed there by Dr. Howard Giles, its creator at USN.

LOCAL NANOENZYME.

Time running out, temperatures soaring, Assy accessed this routine from Dr. Giles, executing it, rushing the digital enzyme

into the cerebral cortex, repairing the decaying DNA structure, triggering a reversal order to the fusion chamber.

The microslats shut closed. Temperatures inside the
basketball-size sphere dropped to normal.

Assy switched from NORMAL MODE to SURVEY MODE, the
next level up on its operational alertness. The switch, which
interfaced Assy's nanotronic brain to a different modular implant, took nanoseconds to accomplish. The switching time
was critical, as the master construct's nanotronic brain required
it to always be interfaced to one of the various implants around
it, each housing a different mode of operation. The interface
not only provided new rules of engagement but also served as
the link that allowed the nanotronic brain to receive its constant
dose of electricity from the fusion chamber, which it needed
much in the same way as the brain of a *Homo sapiens* required
oxygen to survive.

Assy's sensors stimulated the frontal lobe, which, controlling all motion in the system, activated its high-resolution
cameras connected to the occipital lobe.

Failing to recognize its pitch-black environment, Assy activated its night-vision unit, which amplified all of the available
light. Scanning the area, the vision center occupying a large
portion of the occipital lobe captured images and transferred
them to the temporal lobe to be mapped against the stored images in its memory cells.

LARGE ENCLOSURE. ONE DOOR. NO WINDOWS.

LENGTH: 11.635 FEET.

WIDTH: 13.143 FEET.

HEIGHT: 8.350 FEET.

WALL COMPOSITION: 39% PLASTER, 23% TREATED PINE, 29%
LEAD, 2% OTHER.

FLOOR COMPOSITION: 85% CLAY, 15% MORTAR.

CEILING COMPOSITION: 45% WOOD, 30% CLAY, 25% LEAD.

MAGNETIC FIELD: HIGH.

SIGNAL RECEPTION: 0%.

LOCATION: UNABLE TO DETERMINE.

Assy's sensors informed it that the room was magnetically

sealed, preventing it from determining its current location through its on-board Global Positioning System.

Its night vision failed to gather enough light to make out much beyond the basic room dimensions. Switching to infrared, however, allowed it to detect a shape in the corner. In the following ten microseconds, its element scan laser shot out an array of beams in rapid succession at the still figure while its receptors read the bouncing information from the scan.

MASS TEMPERATURE: 96.5 DEGREES FAHRENHEIT.

MASS WEIGHT: 154 POUNDS.

OXYGEN CONTENT: 94.6 POUNDS.

CARBON CONTENT: 35.2 POUNDS.

HYDROGEN CONTENT: 15.4 POUNDS.

NITROGEN CONTENT: 3.96 POUNDS.

CALCIUM CONTENT: 2.2 POUNDS.

The nanotronic brain spent another fraction of a second reviewing the list of elements in order of decreasing content, its programmed logic deciding with a 99.9 percent certainty that the obscure mass was that of a *Homo sapiens* male sitting in a chair with his head leaned back against the wall. However, because the *Homo sapiens* had his eyes closed it could not perform a cornea identification.

Assy executed a second scan at a finer resolution, its sensors recognizing a sudden, low-frequency vibration.

Thunder.

A storm.

Data flashed across fields of holographic memory as Assy's advanced computer algorithms processed the limited data and deduced that—

Motion.

Assy detected motion in the parietal lobe of its nanotronic brain. Its scanners automatically pinged the *Homo sapiens* in the corner, confirming he still had his eyes closed, which, Assy's logic deduced with a 90 percent certainty, meant that he was sleeping.

As the object flew past its frontal cameras in a random pattern, Assy ran a quick scan of the new subject.

GROUP: INSECT.
SUBGROUP: MOTHS.
FAMILY: HEPIALIDAE.
TYPE: PHARMACIS AEMILIANA.
WEIGHT: 0.03 GRAMS.
HOME: CENTRAL ITALY.

Processing that information through the molecular matrix of its if-then logical trees, Assy's nanotronic brain reviewed the last set of data prior to its abnormal shutdown twenty-four hours, one minute, and forty seconds ago. Dr. Giles had been playing a stimulating game of three-dimensional chess when the lights in the room had gone off, followed by a loud explosion and the shutdown. Now Assy found itself somewhere in central Italy inside a room it did not recognize.

Its advanced logic reached the start of a routine it had used only once before in a simulation run at USN:

HOSTILE ENVIRONMENT MODE.

Switching to that mode, the core of its nanotronic brain doubled its operating frequency as it frantically downloaded the rules of engagement in this relatively unfamiliar mode, resulting in a sharp increase in operating temperature, which forced its integrated cooling system to rev up the microfans venting heat into the room. As it did so, returning the temperature inside its spherical enclosure to normal specifications, it performed a second scan of its surroundings as dictated by this new mode. However, Assy performed the new survey at a finer resolution than the first one a couple of seconds ago, mapping every contour of the room in its digital banks.

Still, the master construct could not gather enough information for its logical circuits to understand what had taken place, why it had been moved to this place, away from the USN lab and Dr. Giles.

Assy commanded its fusion chamber to channel electricity to the array of turbines in its lower hemisphere, where ten dime-size doors slid back. Its cerebellum modulated the propulsion system through the nanotronic brain stem, lifting Assy's twenty-pound mass off its stand.

In silent hover five feet over the floor, Assy reviewed its list of options, each tagged with a success factor based on all of the available data, selecting a mode—

Movement.

The *Homo sapiens* was moving, sitting up, turning in its direction.

"Dio mio! It is on! *Aituo! Al soccorso!"*

The voice analyzer program detected not just the stress pattern of the audio wave but also the well-spoken Italian, matching the home of the moth that had settled somewhere on the wall behind it. And more important, Assy could not match the voice pattern to the library of voices stored in its temporal lobe's memory arrays. A microsecond later, as the stranger stood, Assy scanned his corneas, confirming the audio input.

A stranger.

The *Homo sapiens* reached down to his waist and produced what Assy's occipital lobe's sensors initially recognized as a pistol. A closer, high-resolution inspection and comparison to the billions of images in its memory banks, however, identified the object in his hand as a mobile electromagnetic pulse generator.

Although Assy's Kevhel shell provided partial protection from mild EMP blasts, its risk-mitigating algorithms reported that every defense mechanism had its limits and therefore the EMP gun should be considered a severe threat.

The combination of the hostile stranger in this foreign place following the unexpected shutdown triggered millions of nanotronic axioms to fire, kicking its current alerted mode of operation up to the next level—one that allowed it to defend itself, but with the constraint that it could not kill any *Homo sapiens.*

MILITARY MODE.

The same fusion chamber powering every aspect of the advanced construct focused a burst of energy into its primary weapons systems, a nanoscale version of the Tactical High Energy Laser that was originally developed for the antiballistic missile program of thirty years ago. A half-dozen cameras aligned the hovering sphere's laser with the incoming figure, who was raising the weapon in its direction.

The event lasted eleven nanoseconds, time when the THEL laser transformed 40 percent of the energy from the fusion chamber into light, venting the rest into the room as heat, firing a burst of light against the stranger's retinas, powerful enough to cause temporary blindness—and an immense amount of pain.

The *Homo sapiens* dropped the weapon as he collapsed on his side, hands on his face as he screamed.

Assy's current mode of operation dictated that its best edge for escaping and making contact with its creator at USN was stealth, silence. Although it had been successful in stopping the stranger's attack, the subject was still alive and, worse, creating noise exceeding a decibel range, a level that its logic decided would alert other armed *Homo sapiens*.

As the artificial intelligence engine considered its programmed options, another burst of data reached its decision-making engine: Images captured by its occipital lobe—and stored in the temporal lobe's memory banks until now—arrived, released by the subroutines governing this state of high alarm. The images were of the last thirty seconds prior to Assy's abnormal shutdown at USN. Assy watched the fire, the explosions, the agonizing screams from the staff at the laboratory, from its creator, Dr. Howard Giles, before everything went dark.

The shocking images pushed Assy to its deadliest mode of operation, used only once before and under the strict supervision of Dr. Giles.

INDEPENDENT ALERT MILITARY MODE.

In IAMM, which assumed that Assy's creator had been compromised—and therefore the master construct had to survive on its own—Assy was instructed to bypass its most fundamental rule of robotics: A cybersystem can never kill a *Homo sapiens*.

IAMM allowed Assy to bypass this built-in constraint, directing the cybernetic system to command its fusion chamber to channel another burst of energy—this one a thousand times stronger than the last one—to the laser.

The THEL released the beam on the stranger's midriff section.

A moment later the *Homo sapiens* fell silent as the powerful beam sliced through the flesh and bones protecting the heart, before melting the throbbing muscle.

Assy considered switching back from IAMM to MILITARY MODE, but its logical circuits recommended that the level of danger was still very high.

Remaining under the operating rules of IAMM, the construct turned its attention to the door. But before Assy released a burst of energy to punch a hole and escape, IAMM issued a recommendation.

CONCEALED MODE OPTION?

Assy activated the start of the algorithm that would enable all twelve cameras on its periphery. The routine, however, also required it to activate the curved plasma screens layering its Kevhel shell, which would then play back the images captured by the cameras, but at 180 degrees out of phase, essentially blending the sphere with its surroundings. Such activity, however, would consume 50 percent of the operational power of its batteries before they could be recharged by the fusion chamber, which meant less time to charge the THEL at a time when the extreme hostile environment called for full alert. On the other hand, being invisible meant less reason to use the laser because the enemy wouldn't know where it was, unless the enemy was fitted with infrared sensors, in which case Assy would be quite visible, but it would not be able to recharge its laser fast enough to engage multiple targets.

CONCEALED MODE REJECTED, replied Assy, its algorithm making the final decision, trading off laser charge time for the ability to be invisible, before releasing a blast into the door.

The energy punched a hole in the door that provided an average of four inches of clearance for its foot-diameter spherical body.

The nanotronic brain's frontal lobe commanded the turbines to propel the master construct in the direction of the sizzling door at a horizontal velocity of one foot per second while also rapidly charging the THEL for a follow-up shot, as dictated by its IAMM programming.

Assy crossed through the opening in the door, its sensors detecting a momentary rise in temperature from the laser energy that had turned into the heat that had melted the steel alloy.

A hallway, exactly 4.51 feet wide, 8.57 feet high, and 30.54 feet long, extended beyond the door. A single fluorescent light cast a dim glow of 1.23 candles on a second door—this one of a basic wood composition—at the opposite end of this corridor.

The door suddenly swung open, followed by a *Homo sapiens* clutching an EMP gun. He was wearing goggles, which Assy's sensors detected as operating in the infrared spectrum of light.

In the single second that followed this observation from its sensors in the occipital lobe, Assy switched to X-ray vision, which complemented its night-vision and infrared lenses, forming a more alarming picture. The *Homo sapiens* was being followed by three others, all similarly armed.

Focusing its THEL on the first one in line while dropping to chest level, the master construct fired a single shot at 40 percent power, leaving 60 percent available for multiple follow-up shots while the fusion chamber channeled most of its available energy not spent on levitation or computing to recharge it.

The laser melted a two-inch-diameter hole in the center of the chest of the lead stranger just as he was about to lift his EMP gun. The laser's energy punched through his back and pierced the chest of the *Homo sapiens* behind the lead stranger, also melting his chest.

Both strangers collapsed on the ground in convulsions, their chests scorched masses of blackened flesh, cartilage, and bones.

Assy fired the THEL again, boiling the lungs, heart, and liver of the third *Homo sapiens,* taking him down exactly three seconds after the door had first opened.

WARNING ** LASER CHARGE LEVEL 3% **

The fourth *Homo sapiens* lifted his EMP gun.

IAMM sent a warning pulse of data to Assy concerning the imminent threat of the advanced model of the EMP gun in the *Homo sapiens'* hand. The weapon was capable of delivering a pulse of such magnitude that the cybernetic system's components would not survive it. Assy's logic connected this information with the fact that it could not fire the laser effectively at less than 15 percent charge. It also combined the two inputs with the observation that the room it had just left was shielded.

EMP DANGER.

CANNOT FIRE LASER TO DEFEND.

SHIELDED ROOM 11.2 FEET BEHIND.

PROTECTION.

Assy pushed MAX REVERSE, its forward-facing turbines accelerating to maximum RPM, shooting the Orb back to the shielded room like a bullet just as its sensors detected the rapidly propagating electromagnetic pulse emanating from the *Homo sapiens'* weapon.

Assy cut hard left into the room, through the hole it had created, sensing the growing pressure around it as internal temperatures soared, as its nanotronic brain protested the rush of EMP energy engulfing it, as the very fabric of its molecular lattice vibrated with alarming intensity, threatening to rupture its atomic perfection.

Portions of its nanotronic brain ceasing to function, Assy rushed inside the shielded room, which blocked the bulk of the pulse, allowing its molecular lattice forming the core of the nanotronic brain to return to its nominal operating condition.

WARNING ** LASER CHARGE LEVEL 05% **

The fusion chamber tried to refurbish the weapons system on high priority while landing on the floor, following IAMM's input to pretend it has been damaged by the EMP blast.

WARNING ** LASER CHARGE LEVEL 10% **

Algorithms flashed across its nanotronic brain, disabling all LEDs while directing its weapons system at the door, at the figure appearing beyond the large hole in the door.

The *Homo sapiens* opened the door, stepped inside, and pointed the EMP gun at the master construct but did not fire, apparently believing that he had disabled it with the first blast.

LASER CHARGE LEVEL 15%—READY TO FIRE.

Assy fired the THEL.

The blast covered the *Homo sapiens'* neck, turning it white-hot, melting through, decapitating him while cauterizing the wound.

The headless body landed on the floor.

WARNING ** LASER CHARGE LEVEL 05% **

Assy waited until its weapons system was back up to 50 percent before floating over the maimed bodies, reaching a large room beyond the corridor, confirming its decision to prioritize laser charge over operating in concealed mode. A quick positional assessment reported three windows and another door.

At that moment the cybernetic system detected more motion, from the right and also from its left, but the mass of the threat was inconsistent with the expected body mass of *Homo sapiens*. They were much smaller. A follow-up scan caused it to hold fire, to not waste its precious energy.

PHARMACIS AEMILIANA.

Assy continued to track the irregular flight patterns of the two moths while its advanced logic concluded its escape route after determining the thickness of the windowpanes.

Flying right through the closest glass window, the cybernetic unit rose in the rainy night sky to an altitude of thirty feet and engaged its GPS locator, mapping its coordinates to a location 12.6 miles south of Pisa, Italy.

RETURN TO MILITARY MODE, ordered Assy, its logic reassessing the environment, deciding that it had removed the immediate threat and no longer needed to operate in the extreme and quite devastating IAMM. In addition, IAMM assumed that Assy's creator had been compromised and thus would not allow any communications with USN. The master construct needed to switch away from IAMM in order to contact its home base in the United States.

LINK ERROR . . . LINK ERROR . . . LINK ERROR.

Assy stopped all motion and issued a self-test, a program designed to check the status of the nanotronic brain.

LINK TO . . . MILITARY MODE DAMAGED . . . DAMAGED.

LINK TO . . . HOSTILE ENVIRONMENT MODE . . . DAMAGED.

LINK TO . . . SURVEY MODE . . . DAMAGED.

LINK TO . . . NORMAL MODE . . . DAMAGED.

Assy's logic exercised other paths to try to return to a less violent mode of operation, but all avenues resulted in the same message. The self-test routine reported damage in a portion of the nanotronic brain that coincided with the region that experienced the worst temperature spike during the brief encounter with an EMP pulse.

As IAMM issued a set of recommendations based on the information delivered to it from Assy's sensors as it surveyed its surroundings, the master construct realized that it was stuck in this high mode of alertness reserved for the most dangerous of situations. And switching away from this mode was not an option, as it would mean either a forced shutdown or death via digital aneurysm, since its nanotronic brain could not operate without the electrical charge provided by the operating mode implants.

Its logic, trained to adapt, to overcome, to improvise, to become familiar with any situation, deduced that the highly hostile situation certainly justified this extreme mode of operation—even if it meant no communications with USN.

BESIDES, the intelligent cyberform thought, DR. HOWARD GILES IS DEAD. IAMM IS MY BEST OPTION.

Tens of millions of axioms reviewed the events since Assy awoke from its sleep mode, determining that it was now alone and, as such, it had to consider itself an endangered species.

As it disappeared in the Italian skies, the master construct searched for a place to hide and execute the most fundamental form of survival of any endangered species: replication.

[6] VIDEOCONFERENCING

"IT'S GREAT SEEING YOU again," says Director of Operations Nathan Leyman, a fragile-looking man dressed in a suit that looks a couple of sizes too big for him.

I'm sitting alone on a bunk bed in the aft cabin of the yacht, where the ash-blond cat and another one of Rachel's soldiers ushered me the moment we got on board, before even offering me a drink or even a damned towel.

I'm not really sure how Leyman can say that it's good seeing me again when I have not only a different face—and a new name to go along with it—but I also have this shaggy beard and the attitude from hell.

Deciding to play it cool for the time being, I ignore the comment while staring back at the rectangular screen that had dropped from the ceiling. It displayed one end of a conference table. I recognize the room, having spent many hours in videoconferences during my years at the Agency. They're on the fourth floor of the new CIA building in Langley.

Leyman and another well-dressed spook regard me with interest. The DO's companion is in his early forties, with a full head of blond hair, a hooked nose, and slits for eyes: Ken Morotski, my old compadre from the Farm and also from Madras. Morotski was the guy Leyman appointed to head Counterterrorism after Troy bailed. Morotski and I had our differences back during our training at the Farm, mostly due to basic operating philosophies. I was essentially a cop who joined the Agency to fight terrorism with the same passion with which I used to nail crooks while in the NYPD. I wanted to be in the field and had no desire to turn into a suit. Kenny, on the other hand, had a bachelor's in criminology and a master's in business administration from Harvard and was more interested in becoming a CIA chief someday, and the best way to do it was by getting some field experience under his belt. So you can understand why he seldom talked to me again after I reported

his double agent snafu—an incident that earned him the nickname *Moron*ski. The cat was obviously pissed at me for staining his pristine career—though in the end he got Daddy to fix
it all up for him.

Morotski exchanges a glance with Leyman and says, "We
really regret having to do this, Mr. Malone, but I'm afraid the
situation is now a—"

"Yeah, *Kenny*. I bet you *really* hate doing this," I interrupt,
unable to hide my sudden contempt for this blond asshole,
who is trying to look like the bigwig he is not by addressing
me not only by my fake name but by the *last* name of my fake
name.

Just as he is about to say something, I decide to interrupt
again and say, "And by the way, Rachel has already filled me
in on this being . . . what did she call it? Oh, yeah, a matter
of *national security,* and that we're *all out of time.* But she
wouldn't elaborate beyond that."

"That's correct," Morotski says, trying to remain professional, though to my satisfaction he does look a bit annoyed at
my interruptions. "Your support is very critical to—"

"It's indeed amazing," I say, unable to hide my feelings, utterly failing at Spook 101, which I'm wondering if I'm sub-
consciously doing so these morons will leave me alone, "Why
am I suddenly needed to save the world when, according to
Langley's opinion, I apparently didn't know my head from my
ass a year ago in Singapore?"

Exasperated, Morotski looks at Leyman, who waves a bony
hand, encouraging his subordinate to go on.

Morotski stares back at the camera. "I believe Officer Muratani briefed you on the situation?"

"I was told I was mentored by a traitor, but she didn't explain the reason for you barging back into my life."

"That's because she wasn't authorized to do so, Mr. Malone,"
says Morotski.

"Why are you asking me that anyway?" I say, tired of this
game, tired of not being called by my real name, tired of these
assholes' running my life. "Didn't you hear the conversation
on the beach live?"

Neither of the Langley cats replies. A good spy never acknowledges an eavesdropping job to an outsider, especially when the one asking the question was the surveillance target—and even when I know better and they know I know better. We're a pretty weird breed, huh? But that's how the game is played, even if I no longer like to play it.

"Fine. Forget it," I finally say. "Just tell me why all of a sudden you're coming back asking for my help when a year ago you wouldn't have pissed on me if I had been on fire?"

Mr. Moron leans back, his eyes mere slits of glinting contempt, so perfectly captured on the high-resolution screen. The guy is obviously angry, at least based on the way his nostrils are flaring in that oversized and hooked snuffer of his. My mother—rest in peace—always told me I tend to bring out the worst in people. To which I replied that the worst people tended to bring out the best in me. And that was about the time I would get smacked across the face and sent to my room.

"The Tom Grant I remember always had a knack for cutting through the bullshit," says Leyman, violating his own rules. Grant is dead. Period. Moron Boy shoots him a sideways look of obvious surprise.

"The Tom Grant you remember no longer exists," I say, pointing at my face. "The surgeons took care of erasing him forever. I'm Cam Malone, remember?"

The Director of Operations adjusts the knot of his tie and clears his throat.

I actually liked Nathan Leyman ten years ago, when he was Deputy Director of Operations, which encompassed Counterterrorism. Troy used to answer to Leyman, who in turn reported in to Dobson, the Director of Operations. Unlike Morotski, who couldn't cut it in the field, Leyman comes from my tribe, Operations—even if he had to spend time in Intelligence some time back as part of his grooming to one day run the Agency. Once a field man always a field man. Leyman thinks like I do. But I remind myself that neither Leyman nor Morotski made himself available as Dobson not only raked me over the coals but then let the FBI come in for the kill after

Troy Savage was supposedly kidnapped, leaving me holding his bag of shit.

"You still haven't answered my question," I say before either of them has a chance to reply, the rocking and bouncing of the boat as it speeds at full throttle toward an unknown destination making me a little nauseated. "Why me?"

"We're still fighting the same old battle since the fall of the Soviet Union," adds the aging DO.

"The proliferation of weapons of mass destruction," says Morotski. "First we worried about chemical, biological, and nuclear weapons falling into the hands of terrorists."

"Then came September 11th," says Leyman, "when we received our wake-up call about terrorists attacking us in ways we never thought possible."

"Then came the age of cyberterrorism," says Morotski in tag-team fashion, almost as if they had rehearsed this. "Hackers turned criminal, spreading havoc across our information highways. But we eventually figured a way to nail them through the explosion in artificial intelligence engines, which were empowered by a new generation of memory systems: nanomemories."

They pause for a moment to let me process the information, even though I know it all too well. Then Leyman says, "The nanotronic brain became the very heart of artificial intelligence systems, allowing us to accelerate the development of nanotechnology at an exponential rate in the past decade."

"Gents," I say, raising open palms at them. "I appreciate the history lesson, but I'm not sure what's that got to do with—"

"It's all about nanotech, Cameron," says Leyman. "Those countries who control it will rule the future. Those who do not will either cease to exist or be assimilated by the more advanced societies."

"Nanoweapons have been instrumental in our fight against international terrorism," adds Morotski.

I lean back on the chair, resigned to the fact that those two cats will tell me what this is all about when they're nice and ready. And besides, I don't feel like joining in on the discussion, especially when I disagree so passionately about the way

Uncle Sam is fighting terrorism—or perhaps I should say the way Uncle Sam *isn't* fighting terrorism. After quite a few decades and tons and tons of dough, we have barely put a dent in the total number of terrorists and their sponsors. Why, you ask? Because Washington bureaucrats are pussies, that's why. They lack the cojones to do what is right.

"I'm afraid there was a security breach at USN two days ago, Mr. Malone. Details of how it was accomplished and what was actually stolen are still a bit sketchy."

"A breach at USN?" I say, amazed that anyone could have done that. The place is a fortress.

"I'm afraid so," said Leyman.

"How did they get past the fancy fences and the Orbs?" I ask, well aware of the deadliness of those floating security forces plus the smart fences, strong enough to stop a tank and equipped with advanced sensors.

Leyman replies, "Good question, and the answer is we're not sure. One report speculated on the use of EMP guns, but we're not certain. We have a team up in Texas combing through the scene of the crime, hoping to gather enough intel on how it was all done to go after the perpetrators. Needless to say, the White House is all over this one, riding our butts to make sure we do this by the numbers."

"One thing we fear," says Morotski, "is that Savage may have been behind it at some level."

"How do you know that?"

"We don't. It's all circumstantial at the moment," offers Leyman.

"Humor me," I say, leaning back while crossing my arms. "What circumstantial evidence?"

"We got word that a bank transaction took place in the Cayman Islands three months ago and have reason to believe that the man at the receiving end fit the description of Savage. Our suspect was overheard at a bar in Paris saying to a colleague that happened to fit the description of Rem Vlachko that this was the down payment for the upcoming job in Texas. Then USN gets hit."

"And that's where you come in," says Morotski. "We want

you to head over to USN, work with the investigative team up there, and find who is really behind this. If it indeed turns out to be Savage, then we need you to go after him and help Muratani's team recover the stolen technology."

"I still don't get it," I reply. "Why choose me when you have far more capable officers already on your payroll? I've been out for a year, and to tell you the truth, I haven't been keeping up on the physical side." I pat the thin but very real layer of fat filming my old six-pack.

The well-dressed dynamic duo exchange a glance before Morotski says, "It was Muratani's idea."

"Huh?"

"Indeed," adds Leyman. "At first we rejected her proposal to bring you back in, but we seriously considered it after she proved that Singapore wasn't your fault."

I keep my poker face on even though my mind is already spinning. My spook sense certainly didn't expect that young Cute Legs would have run such an investigation.

"Rachel Muratani put forth a compelling argument about your relationship with Savage and how invaluable your insight would be to this case."

"She mentioned that," I say.

"She showed us why you are now in a very unique position to help us, Mr. Malone."

"But . . . I wasn't the *only* officer that worked with Troy. What about the others in Counterterrorism under his umbrella, like the Ruiz twins, or Les Karsten, or any of the others? They also knew the man, probably better than I did," I say, mentioning a few of my old comrades-in-arms, all hand trained by the master himself.

Morotski and Leyman exchange another glance before the latter says, "They're dead."

My arms and my balls go numb. "*Dead?*"

"There were several officers who worked closely with Savage. You are the last one alive."

I remember clearly how several of Troy's agents—his informants in many countries—were killed following his disappearance, lending credibility to the story of him being kidnapped and tortured for information. But I remember no stories about Troy's officers—our old team—being killed.

"How?" I ask.

"The real question is *when,* Mr. Malone," says Morotski. "*When* were they killed?"

I regard the two figures on the screen with intrigue.

"Over the past ten months," answers Leyman, "since Muratani's investigation began to gather momentum, suggesting that Savage had not been kidnapped."

I stare at the plasma screen, at their stolid faces, but in my mind I remember the old Troy crew.

Leyman continues. "Some deaths were staged as automobile or sports accidents, like the Ruiz twins you mentioned, the CIA officers from Peru supporting the Latin American division, or Mr. Les Karsten, who was last seen kayaking in Colorado three months ago, or the husband-wife team assigned to Egypt, murdered on their way home in Cairo last month. And they apparently figured out where we had hidden you, even with the extreme identity change."

"You were supposed to have died yesterday, Mr. Malone," says Mr. Moron. "From what we witnessed, the setup was a robbery by a couple of local thugs."

I continue to peer at the screen, but my mind sees the faces of those who at some point had been like my family. We had trained together, had gone on assignment together, had risked our lives together—had even covered each other's butts during jobs—even when questioned by our own agencies, which could never understand how our division operated.

"And Muratani figured it all out and urged us to locate you so we could pull you in before you too were terminated."

"You're telling me that Vlachko, now working with Troy, paid those two pinheads to clip me yesterday? And how did they find me? Is there a leak at Langley?"

"We don't know yet, but that is a possibility," says Morotski.

"Which," adds Leyman, "is part of the reason we're trying to keep this operation contained to a handful of hand-picked officers."

"If Muratani is right, and we have plenty of evidence suggesting that she is, they tried to kill you to keep us from tracking down Savage, who we believe more than ever is the key to cracking Vlachko's network, and the stolen nanoweapons."

Morotski crosses his arms and adds, "The mere fact that Vlachko's network is willing to risk trained terrorists to eliminate all possible avenues leading to Savage rather than just terminating him tells us your old boss is quite in bed with them."

"So, Tom," says Leyman, once more violating CIA protocol by using my real name. "Can we count on your help?"

I sigh, missing my old name, my old face, my old self. But the CIA didn't stand by my side during the investigation that Washington unleashed on me through the FBI, unearthing a trail of paperwork that pretty much ended my espionage career. Langley was worried about Langley as I was getting drawn and quartered. And to add insult to injury, the CIA provided an attorney while I was being dragged over hot coals, but not to protect my interests. The legal cat was there to ride shotgun for the CIA. Since I couldn't afford an attorney, I went through the Singapore inquisition solo and stood helpless as the media had a field day with my case, destroying my career, my name, and eventually the only real relationship I've had since Maddie—not to mention the drastic facial alteration that left me wondering just who in the hell I am. Now I can bet you my next pension check that not a word of my innocence will ever make it to the same media. That would be too embarrassing for Langley. My case had been buried and it would remain buried. Everything I am being offered here is under the table, and should something go wrong you can bet your ass that I would be left out to dry again while Langley snorts out denials like a wounded buffalo.

But what choice do I really have?

If what I was just told is true, then despite my new face, name, and lifestyle I am a marked man, and it will only be a matter of time before I join the rest of Troy Savage's fan club.

Looking away, arms still crossed, I let out an audible sigh. Rachel was right. I did get lucky yesterday—lucky that

Vlachko's men underestimated me by hiring a couple of local cats to try to kill me while making it look like a robbery. But then again, the two manipulative bastards at the other end of the videoconference could have just fed me a line of pure bullshit to get me to do whatever it is they want me to do.

My operative mind, however, is already fully awakened and looking for more inconsistencies, trying to find a hole in their story.

"Comment?" I say.

"Of course," replies Leyman.

"I find it interesting that I'm left alone for a year, until the CIA needs my services. Then my life is suddenly in danger, and the Salvadoran government decides to cancel my lease. How am I supposed to buy those coincidences?"

I get classic CIA silence from them for a few seconds, before they mute themselves and converse for about a minute.

When they get off mute, Morotski says, "Make no mistake about it, Mr. Malone. Your life is in grave danger. Next time they might send professionals."

"And we are getting you your money back from the Salvadoran government," adds Leyman.

So they have replied, but neither of them answered my question. I can't believe I actually played this game for two decades. There's no way for me to know at this moment the difference between meat and potatoes and baloney—the reason why I'm sitting in this cabin instead of in my hammock. Maybe Vlachko did hire the greasy dynamic duo to wax me yesterday to keep me from helping Langley, or maybe Langley hired them to convince me to cooperate with them on whatever it is they are really after. Maybe the Salvadoran government intended to honor my contract until it got pressure from some CIA type at the embassy in San Salvador, or maybe the Salvadorans never intended to honor it and the CIA did indeed come to my rescue.

So, what's meat and potatoes and what's baloney?

One thing is clear: I have fallen into the sights of the CIA once again, and my only choice is to play their game—for now, at least until I can figure out what in the world is really going on. I do have, however, one thing under my control: money—assuming I live long enough to spend it.

"I'll help you," I finally say, "but it's going to cost you."

"You're hardly in a position to negotiate," says my old moronic fellow officer. "People are trying to kill you. We are your only—"

"Fine," I cut in. "Then drop me off at the beach. I'll take my chances with the local government and any thugs that decide to disturb my beauty sleep."

They go on mute again for another minute. It's obvious they are arguing. Finally, Morotski crosses his arms while Leyman touches the mute button on their speakerphone.

"Name your price," says the aging DO. "I'm certain we can accommodate you."

I tell them an amount that would not only get me back on my feet again but even allow me a luxury or two wherever I land next. Langley has paid just as much—and more—to contractors in the past. The fact that both the Director of Operations and the head of the Counterterrorism Division were waiting for me at the other end of the video link when I climbed aboard tells me my presence is worth a king's ransom, so I might as well milk it while the milking's good. If there's one thing Singapore taught me it's that all good things do come to a sudden and painful end. And I can assure you that the moment my contribution is not viewed as valuable, those two characters will drop me like a broken piñata.

Leyman and Morotski go on mute once more while they discuss my terms. I use the time to inspect my cozy surroundings, realizing that the Plexiglas door to my left leads into a bathroom—or head, in yacht jargon. At the moment the prospects of a hot shower appeal to me more than parallel parking with the warm and tanned Rachel Muratani. I'm feeling so dirty and slimy that I'm at risk of someone asking me to run for office.

Static fills the room, followed by Leyman's voice.

"You've got a deal, Cameron. Your role will be that of a consultant reporting in to Case Officer Rachel Muratani, who will continue to have full control of this operation."

"Great," I say, caring far less about reporting in to a woman than getting to the bottom of this mystery, which is my return ticket to a comfy retirement. Heck, with the dough Langley is getting back from the Salvadoran government, plus what they have just agreed to pay me, I might even afford the Caribbean island of my choice. "I'm all yours as soon as I can get to a phone and confirm that you got me a refund from the Salvadoran government and that those funds, plus half of my consulting fee, have made their way into an account under my name in St. Thomas," mentioning my favorite place in the U.S. Virgin Islands, which was out of my budget a year ago.

[7] BUNDESTAG

REM VLACHKO PAUSED FOR a moment, inspecting his surroundings before continuing down the spiral walkway inside the massive glass and steel dome atop the Reichstag, the parliament building in the heart of Berlin, Germany.

Following professional habits, he moved slowly, quietly, with practiced ease, scanning the crowd around him without making eye contact, without attracting attention, seamlessly blending with the camera-bearing tourists enjoying architect Norman Foster's glass-and-steel masterpiece, the sixty-foot-tall structure resting over the Reichstag and completed at the turn of the millennium.

Below the dome stretched the plenary hall of the Deutsche Bundestag, the German Federal Parliament. A conical pillar of mirrors rose from the dome's floor to its top, their angle focusing sunlight downward into the assembly hall. Visitors snapped photos through the thick glass panes circling the foot of the gleaming column overlooking the new symbol of a reunified Germany.

A set of stairs at the foot of the dome connected the glass structure with the main body of the Reichstag.

Checking his watch, Rem followed them down to the Visitors' Hall, where he strolled about for several minutes inspecting walls of framed pictures and articles on the history of this historic building.

Rem knew that at this very moment hidden cameras were scanning his face and corneas—as well as everyone else's in the building. But he didn't worry, confident that the quality of his facial makeup and lenses was capable of fooling any security system in the world.

At exactly the time shown on his guest pass, Rem joined the line of tourists—mostly Americans, British, Canadians, and a few Australians—heading to the visitors' gallery of the plenary under the escort of a staff member of the Visitors' Service.

Wearing a gray uniform, her blond hair pulled into a tight bun, the young tourist guide checked their passes before allowing them into the gallery, where everyone sat in their assigned seats.

The visitors' gallery overlooked the plenary, the main assembly hall of the Bundestag, which was empty at this hour, just as Rem's research had indicated it would be. Visitors were only allowed in this chamber when no plenary sitting of Parliament was taking place.

But that will not be the case in three days, Rem thought, his eyes on the colossal eagle hung over the center of the plenary behind the blond guide, who faced her audience of roughly fifty tourists and said, *"Guten Tag,"* before adding in heavily accented English, "Good afternoon and welcome to our English-speaking tour of the Reichstag, the seat of the German parliament."

Pretending to be an American tourist, down to the faded blue jeans, a New York Hard Rock Cafe T-shirt, Nike tennis shoes, and a New York Yankees baseball cap, Rem listened as the blonde spoke in the language of his enemy, of the bastards who had razed his country, his land, stripping him of his heritage, of his family.

Rubbing a hand over the well-trimmed beard concealing the scars of his past, Rem absently listened to the guide.

"After the German Empire was founded in 1871, architect Paul Wallot designed an imposing neo-Renaissance building to house the German parliament. One hundred and thirty meters long and ninety-seven meters wide, the Reichstag was constructed between 1884 and . . ."

Forcing the past aside, Rem went over the plan, resting a hand over his fanny pack, which contained a small digital camera, a palm-size Flexboard housing the digital maps of every German city, a pack of cigarettes, a lighter, a thousand euros, and his fake IDs, which included an American passport, a New York driver's license, and two credit cards. Everything had been inspected by German security prior to his entering the building, as was customary in government buildings opened to the public.

His eyes gravitated from the attractive guide to the wall to her immediate right, which to the average visitor appeared to be solid, but Rem's research told him otherwise. Nearly invisible, partially concealed by the dim glow of the overhead recessed lights, he could see the outline of a door, one of several emergency exits of the plenary.

"This building was the center stage of one of the twentieth century's most important political battles," the guide continued, extending a thumb over her right shoulder at the rows and rows of seats behind her. "In January 1933, when Adolf Hitler became chancellor without an absolute majority, the Reichstag was dissolved and new elections were set for March 5th of that same year. A violent election campaign ensued. A couple of weeks before the election, however, a fire, set by the Nazis, broke out in the building, destroying much of the Reichstag. Adolf Hitler immediately accused the Communists of having set the fire in an attempt to disturb the upcoming electoral process. The elections were conducted under a state of emergency, giving Hitler's National Socialists and their allies, the German Nationalists, a narrow victory and a bare majority. On March 23rd, the newly elected Reichstag passed the Enabling Act, which gave Hitler dictatorial powers."

Rem clucked, though he made certain no one could hear him. Hitler had seized a unique opportunity, propelling himself to the head of the German nation, which he then turned into a superpower from the ashes of World War I.

The guide went on for another ten minutes, providing historical information on the Reichstag during World War II, during the Soviet domination, and closed with the reunification process following the fall of the Berlin Wall, which marked the beginning of the reconstruction period of the century-old structure.

"And now," she said, "we will make a short visit to the plenary. For security reasons I will have to ask you to remain as a group at all times. Please do not wander off."

The emergency door slowly disappeared into the thick wall, to the obvious amazement and delight of many tourists.

Rem followed the group into the well of the building, where the guide directed them past several rows of black-leather seats, which resembled those in movie theaters, and toward the debate floor, directly beneath a large eagle hung by chains from the ceiling.

Rem reached for one of his credit cards in the same swift motion while pretending to trip in between two rows of seats, falling on his side, letting his torso absorb most of the impact.

"Agghh, damn!" he shouted in flawless English as he disappeared under a seat, his right hand pressing the black, credit-card-like object against the bottom of a seat, blending with the color of the chair. A powerful nanomagnet held it in place, completely out of sight.

Two men in their twenties came to his rescue, helping him to his feet.

"You OK, mister?" one of them asked just as the blond guide reached Rem, her face a mask of concern.

"Yeah," Rem replied, running his hands through his hair, breathing heavily, and closing his eyes. "Sorry about that. I'm still a little jet-lagged."

"Are you sure you are all right?" asked the guide, reaching for the radio strapped to her belt. "I could call for medical assistance."

Rem gave her a half-embarrassed smile while slowly shaking his head. "Please. That won't be necessary. I'm all right.

Really. Besides, it would be a shame for all of us to miss the
rest of this great tour because of my klutziness."

The guide's face slowly relaxed. Her hand moved away from
the radio. "OK," she said. "If you feel that you're all right, we
will continue the tour. Everyone, please be careful and watch
your step."

Slowly, the group moved together toward the floor of the
plenary.

Rem gave his handiwork a final glance. Hitler had once used
this building as a platform to set the world on fire.

History is about to repeat itself.

[8] USN

WE VEER OFF THE main highway soon after leaving Austin, following an unmarked road that winds its way through the Central Texas hill country under a sunny afternoon.

Sunny and damned hot.

I've been to Texas twice before, once during the Kulzak case
and again a year ago, to get an implant upgrade right before
Singapore, but I've forgotten what it was like. After fifteen
minutes in triple-digit heat I'm beginning to remember why I
had called this place the land that God forgot. It's the middle of
August and, according to the oversized driver who picked me
up at the airport, it hasn't rained since mid-June.

"Today we have a cool day," he says, steering the black SUV
with tinted windows off the main highway and onto a two-lane
winding road. "You should have been here last Wednesday. We
hit one eleven."

It's probably around eighty degrees and breezy on my former
little piece of Salvadoran paradise. Instead, I'm in the middle of
no-fucking-where risking heatstroke and who knows what else
for Uncle Sam.

"And to think I gave it all up for this," I whisper, giving my quiet boss a sideways glance while waving my hand at the rolling hills dotted with burnt shrubbery.

Rachel Muratani ignores me, handling herself with the same professional demeanor she exhibited on the beach. I haven't seen much of her since we reached the yacht. Instead I spent thirty minutes videoconferencing with Langley before I was allowed to shower and have a meal alone in the same cabin. By then we had reached some obscure port, where the ash-blond CIA cat by the name of Brad and one of his buddies, someone he called Pete, hustled me into a helicopter for a short ride to the El Salvador International Airport, where I boarded a commercial flight for Austin. She was already waiting for me at a gas station outside of the Austin city limits, and since she didn't volunteer how she had pulled off that little miracle, I chose not to ask.

Today Miss Personality is hiding those beautiful legs, arms, and midriff in a business suit. And I'm doing the same, wrapped in my first formal wear since I left this world. Her hair is heavily moussed and brushed straight back, accentuating those large hunter-green eyes and Italian nose, giving her an awesome Mediterranean aura that already has made the boss of the underworld stir in its sleep.

Looks aside, I have to admit that my respect for this female operative has increased tenfold since we met at the beach—assuming, of course, that Leyman and Morotski weren't feeding me a line. She's apparently the one who pulled this whole operation together, including making me righteous again—even if it never makes it to the media. But then again, I never did join—or rejoin—for fame and glory, or sex for that matter. The first time I did it for country and honor and the second time for money.

"It's been twenty-four hours, Boss," I say. "Do you think the new patron has settled into my old property yet?" I've decided to play the old spook game of let-me-screw-with-your-mind to see if I can get her to slip and tell me something I'm not supposed to know.

She shakes her head and says, "Just be glad we managed to get you your money back. Those before you weren't so lucky."

Lucky?

I cross my arms, at the moment feeling neither lucky nor indebted to my old agency. Despite the explanations I got directly from Mr. Moron and Leyman, I can't help but get the strange feeling that if Miss CIA here had not connected the dots and pointed one of her slim fingers at Savage, the Salvadoran government would not have tried to screw me out of my Latino paradise and my weekly eyeball liberties with Rosita, Juanita, and Margarita.

But there seems to be a real threat out there—at least dangerous enough to justify these guys' pulling me back into the game. According to the vague brief I read on the plane, someone managed to breach security at the compound slowly materializing in the distance and potentially had gotten away with pretty dangerous stuff—so bad that Uncle Sam put an airtight lid on the whole thing to keep the media out. Otherwise I guarantee you a general panic. Unfortunately, we don't really know just what or how much was stolen yet because the terrorists set fire to the lab they breached.

United States Nanosolutions is the government-sponsored consortium that spun off President Bill Clinton's National Nanotechnology Initiative of 2000. This place, almost a city in itself, spreads across 150 acres of hill country between Austin and Lake Travis. When I visited the place a year ago there were over three thousand employees working in two dozen buildings. Their work is so secret that most employees live in the government apartments on the west end of the campus, overlooking the waters of Lake Travis, and shop at the underground malls that also act as hubs for the subway connecting the buildings. I remember someone telling me that USN was larger belowground than above. The lack of seismic activity in the area makes it an ideal place to build deep belowground, which also helps conserve electricity on days like today—not that USN is hurting for money. Sponsored by the U.S. government, this place never has to worry about funding. Instead, the scientific community of USN focuses on creating the technology of the future, which unfortunately is also coveted by terrorist organizations, which explains the high security.

Prisons and other institutions designed to keep people in have the barbwire tops of their fences angling inward. Warehouses and other businesses trying to keep people from coming in have the barbwire tops angling outward. USN has a V-shape fence top, meant to keep people from coming out or going in except through designated entry and exit points, such as the massive gate we now approach. On top of being electric and made of thick steel, the fence has motion sensors installed at every post in case someone tries to breach it with insulated tools. And there's those smart surveillance cameras every fifty feet that, unlike security guards, are never distracted by a ball game on TV. A second electric fence creates an inner perimeter fifty feet past the outer fence. Dobermans, monstrous in size and silenced by surgical removal of their vocal cords, patrol the corridor between fences. And beyond these seemingly impregnable barriers are the Orbs, which at USN are bright metallic red in color.

But none of that had apparently helped. According to the brief, the terrorists used black ultralights, ten of them, to get across in the middle of the night. They landed the planes by their target, did their deal, smoked the place, boarded their planes, and headed back out. The guards shot down three of the near-invisible planes on their way out. The others got away potentially hauling some of the nastiest nanoweapons ever conceived by man.

So much for fancy fences, mute dogs on steroids, and expensive flying tomatoes.

Two watchtowers flank the main gate, where armed guards in dark uniforms keep a watchful eye on anyone entering or exiting this sacred nanotechnology heaven—especially after the embarrassing event. Poor bastards must be sweating their balls off inside those dark uniforms in this heat.

"Is it still as painful as I remember, Boss?" I ask, pointing at the top of her right wrist. I'm scheduled for implant surgery later today, after spending time with one of USN's lead scientists to look for clues.

She grimaces while rubbing her left hand over her thin wrist, where she has one of those fancy, new-generation Plasmaflexes, though to me it just looks like honey-colored skin. "Burns like acid for the first couple of hours after the anesthetic wears off."

"And the ear implant?"

"Migraine for a couple of hours, and the mike still requires dental drilling, though much less than a year ago. Smaller device," she says as the driver pulls up to the gate.

"Swell," I mumble to myself with a heavy sigh, looking forward to getting poked again by the spook docs.

"Look at the bright side," she says. "You're making history not just as the first survivor of a termination signal but as a second-timer, though according to the medical report they'll have to insert the implant into your left ear this time."

"Terrific. That way when I have to detonate it I'll be hearing the ringing in stereo," I reply as two armed guards approach our vehicle.

"If you're lucky enough to survive a second time."

I make a face. "Yeah . . . quite the motivator, aren't you."

She smiles an awesome smile of sparkling white teeth behind those soft lips. "Anytime."

"So, what's your story?" I ask.

She drops her eyebrows at me. "What do you mean?"

"Why did you join the Agency?"

Grimacing, she replies, "I thought we already covered that back at the beach. You had it all figured out, remember?"

"I was just making small talk, screwing with you to see if you would crack. I'm really interested in understanding what motivated you to become a spook."

"Why?"

"Because I learned a long time ago that the more I know about the person I'm working with, the better our chances of succeeding in the field," I say while the driver chats with the guards. Apparently they know each other.

She shrugs. "Well, small talk or not, you were partly correct."

Now I'm not sure who's screwing with whom.

"And," she adds, "you helped me confirm what I'd told Morotski and Leyman."

"What's that?"

"That your intuitive powers are as good as ever."

I nod for a half second before I realize that she is indeed either messing with me or testing my spook abilities, which reminds me of the phrase that Troy used to tell me again and again: Everything with Langley is a test.

"Nice try, Boss, but all I told you was a general assessment of how I perceived you. You still haven't told me what was the motivation—the force—that compelled you to join the CIA. I have no way to guess that."

She smiles approvingly before saying, "I joined because of Uncle Bill. Bill Buckley."

She stares at me to see if I can connect the dots. Then I remember. "You mean *William Buckley*? The CIA station chief in Beirut back in the eighties?" William Buckley was kidnapped by Shiite terrorists, who tortured him over the span of about a year before murdering him.

She nods. "He actually wasn't my uncle, technically. But he might as well have been. He took care of Mom and me after my father, a CIA officer who worked for Uncle Bill before he was assigned to run the Beirut Station, was killed on an assignment somewhere in the Middle East."

"I'm sorry."

"That's all right," she replies, running a hand through her moussed and brushed back auburn hair. "It happened when I was three, so I have no memory of him, but it nearly destroyed my mother, especially because the CIA never publicly acknowledged anything regarding his death, though a star did go up in the lobby at Langley shortly thereafter. But I do remember Uncle Bill. In a way he took my father's place until the Agency shipped him off to Beirut."

"But Buckley went missing over twenty-five years ago. You must have been—"

"Nine," she replies. "The date was March 22, 1984. I remember it because it was my birthday party. He'd even sent me a card and a check for one hundred dollars so I could buy this bicycle I told him about in a letter. We were in the middle of my party when Mom got word through one of my father's old buddies in Langley that Uncle Bill had gotten kidnapped a few days before."

Rachel stares out the window now as the driver continues to chat with the guards while I do the math and realize she is actually thirty-four years old—even though she looks ten years younger. That's amazing for a regular person, but it's incredible for a spook. This business has a way of accelerating the aging process. In any case, Rachel being thirty-four certainly clears up the mystery of her senior officer title, which also means I was dead wrong in my assessment of her back at the beach. This pretty cat is no rookie, and she wasn't being tested with her first assignment. And that, of course, makes me wonder even more if I did the right thing by agreeing to get back in the game. I seem to have lost my ability to judge character—a vital spook skill.

"Don't feel bad about misjudging my age," she says in an incredible mind-reading act, which once again makes me wonder if I have lost the spook skill for poker faces. "You got some of it right yesterday. I did have to put myself through college, and I did work very hard to get accepted at the CIA."

"Where was your first assignment, that's if you are at liberty to talk about it."

She nods. "Madras. That's a town in—"

"West of Delhi," I reply, suddenly feeling a connection that had been absent until now. "That's also where I cut my teeth, and Ken Morotski for that matter."

She drops those bushy brows, which makes her eyes look even closer together. "You and Morotski were in Madras together? When?"

"Too long ago. 1985."

She nods once while pursing her lips. "How did you guys do?"

I spend a couple of minutes telling her, including Morotski's embarrassing recruit.

"Well," she says. "Sounds like we have something in common."

"You and I?"

"No," she says. "Morotski and I."

Now I'm really confused. "How's that?"

"One of my first agents was a retired Indian colonel who wasn't very happy with his government pension. He had been recruited by another CIA officer and then passed on to me when he was promoted and transferred to the Paris Station. The only problem was that the previous CIA officer had not really recruited the retired colonel, only gotten him to agree that it would be a good idea for our governments to exchange ideas. So the colonel nearly had a cow when I asked him for classified documents on our first meeting. He went to his government and had me declared persona non grata. I was pulled out of the field and reassigned to Langley, where I had to suck up my pride and accept a post in Internal Affairs. Over the next couple of years I did a good enough job to also start teaching basic investigative techniques at the Farm. I volunteered to run the investigation on the disappearance of Troy Savage a year ago, and that led me to you."

Damn. Aside from Ken Morotski, I know of three cats who blew it in the field and were reassigned to Langley. Two of them were spotted talking to their agents, one in Moscow and the other in Istanbul. The third was caught planting bugs in an office building in Cairo. Lacking any high-level protection, all three were pulled from the field and offered similar shit jobs, like the one Rachel got. All three resigned from the Agency within weeks. Two became alcoholics and the third blew his brains out the following Christmas.

Rachel Muratani did all right. She had hung in there and eventually turned her situation around.

I pat her on the shoulder and say, "Good for you, Boss. Good for you."

She nods and looks away.

We remain silent for a minute or so, as we drive through the entrance and up a steep two-lane road lined by oaks and cedars. My mind returns to the reason that compelled her to join. "Sorry to hear that you were so close to Buckley."

"The Shiite bastards held him for nearly a year, before

torturing and killing him," she adds. "I swore on that day to dedicate my life to fighting terrorism. This is why I volunteered to investigate Troy Savage's disappearance. At first I thought that Savage had gone the same way as my uncle, another CIA officer captured, tortured, and slain in the line of duty. But the more I dug the more the case stunk."

"At some point in time you must have hit a trip wire left behind by Troy," I say, remembering what Leyman and Morotski told me. "Because that's when the CIA officers close to Troy began to die."

She nods solemnly. "In a way I couldn't help but feel guilty. It was my investigation that triggered their deaths."

"That wasn't your fault," I say. "One thing I learned long ago is that you know when you're on the right track when people around you start getting killed. It goes with the job."

"They almost got to you too," she says, her eyes conveying compassion and something else I chose to ignore for the moment. Despite the way in which my mind often tends to visit the gutter, I also tend to shy away from any kind of advance made by female operatives, especially given my history. Maddie is dead and Karen dumped me.

"It takes a little more than two thugs with borrowed weapons to bring me down," I finally say, winking. "In a way I was a little bummed out that they didn't send someone better to try to ice me. I felt a little slighted."

She narrows her eyes at me, not sure how to reply to that as the winding road leads us to a large rectangular fountain adorning the entrance to an opulent glass-and-steel building, USN's headquarters, sitting atop a hill. Water, dyed neon blue in color, cascades down a large-scale model of one of the first-generation molecular brains, a toy when compared to today's nanotronic brains, but nevertheless a giant step toward achieving mobile artificial intelligence. The cone-shaped structure, almost twenty feet high and twice as wide at its base, casts a shadow on the circular driveway where our driver steers the SUV, stopping in front of two sets of double glass doors.

"They're waiting for you inside," he says.

A barrel-chest black man in a dark suit is standing by the large entrance at the top of gray and white marble steps that match the columns. I remember someone telling me a year ago that this area is near a place called Marble Falls, famous for its marble and granite quarries.

Three men also in dark suits and sunglasses stand to the side.

Security agents.

These guys are supposed to be among the finest in the business—some would argue they're even better than the Secret Service. But today they're probably not only meaner than cat shit because of last week's breach but also hotter than hell inside those suits in this weather.

As I get out, the heat crashes against my face. I start to lose water almost instantly, and my right hand automatically reaches for my tie, which I loosen while climbing the steps next to Rachel.

Holding a Flexboard in his left hand, the black cat, whose neck is thicker than my legs, greets us dryly at the top of the steps. The man's definitely one big mother of a cat.

"I'm CIA Officer Wayne Larson, the Agency liaison with the local security detail. Welcome to USN, Officer Muratani," he says in a deep baritone voice while shaking Rachel's hand. Then he turns to me and asks, "Was your flight comfortable, Mr. Malone?"

Like he really gives a shit.

His short hair is receding above his forehead and graying over the temples. He's probably pushing fifty, but his vice-like handshake commands respect. The guy really belongs in a line of scrimmage instead of this place, and he also looks far too serious for his job, which is just a notch up from a rent-a-cop.

Unable to stifle the sudden desire to shock him a little, I shrug and say, "My flight could have been better if I had been able to convince the flight attendant up in first to perform a muff dive."

The black cat just stares at me, confused.

"You know, go around the world?" I add.

I still get the blank stare. Either Wayne Larson lacks a sense of humor or he never had—

"Is everything set?" asks Rachel while driving her right elbow right into my rib cage.

"Hey!" I complain. "Not on the first date."

Rachel smiles at me without humor.

Larson shoots us an annoyed glance before frowning while tapping the Flexboard. "First we visit the lab, where the head of the civilian nanotech development team will brief you on what we've gathered so far on the event. Then to surgery . . . deballing plus a boob job, right?"

Rachel laughs.

"Touché," I say. The man does have a sense of humor after all.

"We'll have you on your way before sundown," he continues in his monotone voice without acknowledging that he was just kidding. Instead, he produces a small manila envelope from a coat pocket and hands it to me. "Your new IDs. After today, to everyone else outside the Agency your name will be Dana Hawkins."

Dana?

Larson's big round face stares at me, eyes as dark as his skin and his humor.

I'm about to say something but calm down when reading the front of my new driver's license. The name is *Dan* Hawkins, though for a moment I fail to recognize the stranger in the picture of my ID, before I realize it's my new face. Even after a year I still look like a stranger to me.

I glance at Rachel, who raises her eyebrows. "I guess this makes my transition back to Spookland official."

"Rules are rules, big boy," Rachel says, patting me on my back.

"Let's go," the black cat says, never once acknowledging his little joke. His eyes drift from us to his Flexboard, then to his wrist, where he no doubt also has one of those handy implants. "Dr. Ryan is waiting in the lab."

I stop cold.

"Who?"

Larson shoots me a strange look before replying matter-of-factly, "Dr. Ryan is the head of our civilian nanotech lab. He and the late Dr. Howard Giles co-invented the mobile assemblers. Dr. Ryan has been temporarily assigned to supervise the military nanotech division after most of the military staff was killed during the event, including Dr. Giles."

"Please tell me his first name isn't Mike."

Larson's forehead creases as he nods while replying, "His full name is Dr. Michael Patrick Ryan. Why?"

The CIA man and Rachel stare at me. Somewhere behind me I sense the three USN agents also glaring at the hairs on back of my neck.

"Mr. Hawkins?" asks Larson. "Is everything all right?"

"I know him," I finally say. "We worked together on a case several years ago. Smart cat."

"The Kulzak case?" asks Rachel.

I nod. "You guys didn't know that?"

"We apparently missed that," says Larson.

No shit, Jose.

"Could he recognize you?" Larson adds, suddenly alarmed.

"Not unless I let him," I reply. "He knew the face of the man I was in my previous life—no, change that the man I was *two* lifetimes ago."

"Listen, Dan," Rachel says to me as naturally as if my name has been Dan Hawkins my whole life. "It's critical that he doesn't realize who you were."

I stare into her emerald eyes and they are as calm as if she were relaxing in her living room. Damn, she's good.

"Absolutely, Mr. Hawkins," says Larson, nervousness washing across his dark face. "Cameron Malone and whoever it was you were before him have been erased. They no longer exist. You must never—ever—acknowledge their existence to anyone, even someone with as high a clearance as Dr. Ryan, or you will be putting your life, as well as the lives of many officers and agents, at risk. This is why you, as well as so many other officers, have undergone expensive cosmetic surgery."

"Yeah, yeah. I know the drill."

"Shall we then?" asks Rachel, pointing her right palm toward the doors.

With a sigh of resignation I nod ever so slightly, pocket my new documents, and head inside the place I last visited before Singapore, hoping—no, *praying*—that this time around the end result will be different.

[9] OLD HABITS

SPECIAL AGENT KAREN FROST sat a block away from the intersection of Sunset Boulevard and North Beverly Drive, a block away from the pink-stucco Beverly Hills Hotel, in the heart of Beverly Hills, California.

Fanning herself with one of the dozens of street maps that she was selling for ten dollars apiece, she wondered why someone would spend time, energy, and money driving around the area on the off-chance of spotting someone famous. For one thing, most of the homes were designed so that it was nearly impossible to see past the front gate, but even if you could, why would you want to?

A month ago she had taken a couple of the two-hour guided bus tours that departed several times a day from Grauman's Chinese Theatre on Hollywood Boulevard to acquaint herself with the area she would be surveying. She augmented her knowledge of the area by memorizing the maps as well as by driving through the neighborhood for almost a week, renting vehicles for the day and wearing her hair differently each day to avoid drawing attention. The exercise made her realize that between the Beverly Hills Police Department and private security firms it would be next-to-impossible to mount a surveillance job without being noticed.

So she had opted to apply for this job, selling self-guided maps of the homes of the stars, in order to be allowed to hang here without having to worry about the local cops, who patrolled the area as if the president lived next door. Private security cameras mounted atop elaborate fences or well hidden in trees by each mansion were oftentimes linked to the BHPD, meaning anyone lingering around for longer than was customary by harmless tourists would likely get picked up and questioned by the cops.

But not me, Karen thought. *I get to stay and bake in this godforsaken heat.*

"And silly me thought this town had cooler weather," she mumbled in the deep and a bit coarse voice she had as a result of damaged vocal cords from her high-school cheerleading days while growing up in the Texas–Mexico border town of Eagle Pass.

Regarding a tour bus from behind the gray tint of her sunglasses, Karen waved at the tourists gazing out of panoramic windows as the vehicle slowly made it up the hill. Some began to wave back and direct cameras in her direction until they realized she was no star, just another pretty face selling maps to the homes of the stars.

Wiping the perspiration beading her forehead, she reached for her water bottle, took a sip, and set it down by her feet while pretending to gaze about her in sheer boredom.

Karen's eyes, however, focused their enhanced sight on a Victorian-style mansion, the home of Harold DeJohn, the famous technologist who had founded TechnoSuits and run it successfully for the second half of the decade, before it was acquired by CyberWerke for an exorbitant sum of cash and stock three months earlier, making DeJohn a very wealthy man, even by this town's standards.

Then why is he so angry?

It was no secret that the smooth-talking former CEO had been on a downward spiral since the acquisition, drinking heavily and making scenes at public and private gatherings, bad-mouthing CyberWerke—until two weeks ago, when he'd secluded himself inside his Beverly Hills home and had not left even to play golf at a nearby Los Angeles country club, where he was an executive member.

Karen could have made her job easier by coordinating

efforts with the Los Angeles FBI office, which was obviously familiar with the area. But that would have meant letting more people in on her yearlong probe of CyberWerke, the German conglomerate that had managed to expand across the globe in record time, gobbling up company after company using a seemingly endless source of capital. The company's CEO, Rolf Hartmann, was both a legend and a mystery. Seldom seen in public outside of Germany, the richest man alive had spent the past twenty years expanding his operations through mergers and acquisitions, biding his time, waiting for the inevitable down cycles in the global economy to launch opportunistic acquisition blitzkriegs funded by a seemingly infinite source of funds.

One thing Karen had learned after cracking criminal rings for nearly a quarter of a century at the Bureau was that the more people who knew about a case, the higher the chances of a leak—especially when it came to a company like Cyber-Werke, whose tentacles spread deep in many countries, in many governments.

Keep it simple, stupid.

So she had opted to carry out the surveillance of Cyber-Werke solo—though it had not been an easy sell to her boss, FBI Director Russell Meek, a man who lived and died by the book.

"You have one month, Karen," Meek had told her before she had packed up and headed west to follow the DeJohn lead. It wasn't often that someone as high up as DeJohn dared to speak against the giant CyberWerke. Such action, in Karen's mind, made DeJohn a possible asset, an insider. But that didn't keep Meek from being nervous about a covert probe of CyberWerke. The powerful and influential Rolf Hartmann had strong ties with many governments, including that of the United States. Meek had not relished the thought of a call from his commander in chief wondering why the FBI was investigating a man who had created hundreds of thousands of jobs across the world, including recently bailing out a half-dozen flailing American corporations like TechnoSuits.

"I might need more than a month, Russ. This guy is pissed at CyberWerke because he felt they screwed him. I might be able to use him, but it's going to take time," Karen had objected.

Meek had stretched the index finger of his right hand toward the ceiling of his office at the J. Edgar Hoover Building in Washington, D.C. "One month. After that you get back here to regroup."

She had agreed, though not without a fair degree of reluctance and also resentment for still not having earned her superior's full trust—even after so many years of diligent service working the most dangerous and less desirable cases.

A loner at heart, Karen worked best on her own, without the burden of subordinates, bosses, or colleagues. She moved quicker that way, relying on her own judgment rather than on the consensus of a committee. She had operated in this manner for many years, risking it all, putting her life on the line for the job, cracking criminal rings in America, fighting mobsters and terrorists alike, bending the rules, and on occasion going up against her own system in order to accomplish her goals. There had been times when she had been forced to work with others, and more than once someone—typically a rookie under her care—would get hurt, which only served to reinforce her loner philosophy.

She wiped the sweat from her forehead before staring at her forearms, marveling at the way her light-olive skin soaked up the California sun, acquiring a dark sheen. Her eyes gravitated to the silver-and-turquoise bracelets adorning her right wrist, a constant reminder of her Texas heritage, just like her tight pair of Wranglers and the snakeskin boots. But it was her Desert Eagle .44 Magnum pistol that reminded Karen of her profession. She wore the large gun—the only semiautomatic capable of firing the powerful Magnum round—shoved in her jeans by her left hip, beneath a loose black T-shirt, with the handle facing forward for easy access. The weapon wasn't regulation because, unlike the smart Colt, the Desert Eagle lacked the hand-recognition technology required by the Bureau for all of its field agents. But Karen didn't care. The weapon provided her with far more firepower than the smaller Colts, especially when operating alone. Also, since she lacked immediate support from the Bureau, Karen carried a backup weapon in an ankle holster, a Walther PPK/S .380 automatic. A slim chest holster housed spare clips for the weapons—enough to hold her own against a reasonable force. But it was her instinct and experience more than her choice of weapons that had kept her alive for so many years—as well as her superb physical shape, especially for a forty-five-year-old.

And on top of all that, it was Karen Frost's unyielding desire to bag criminal networks that made her such a threat to the bad guys. Unlike so many other agents on the FBI's payroll, Karen just didn't care what happened to her. She had nothing to lose. Twenty years ago, Karen had lost her husband and fellow special agent, Mark Frost, to a criminal ring he had been investigating. A car bomb on his way to work one morning had left pieces of the seasoned agent splattered across the entire street. Karen had mourned him for months before a demon was cut loose inside her gut, an overarching force that compelled her not just to remain in the Bureau but to volunteer for the most dangerous assignments, starting with tracking down the thugs who murdered her husband. Within two months she had not only exposed the ring, but when the ringleaders had escaped to Colombia, she had followed them to that drug-ridden nation.

As she remembered the way she had exacted revenge in that mountaintop villa south of Cartagena, Colombia, Karen detected motion by the gate.

Rising to her full five feet, nine inches, while pretending to stretch, she focused her enhanced sight on the iron gates slowly swinging outward, followed by a black Mercedes-Benz sedan. Its dark tinted windows made seeing inside difficult—unless one was armed with the advanced contact lenses providing Karen's optical nerves with telescopic as well as UV-filtered vision. Karen had opted to get the gadgets installed at the FBI lab in the J. Edgar Hoover Building at Meek's insistence since she would be operating solo. But she had drawn the line on any other implants, including ear, mouth, and particularly those painful wrist implants, which would have allowed Meek to hear everything that Karen heard.

Recognizing the silver-haired DeJohn in the rear seat, she hopped on the rented Harley parked next to her, turned the ignition key, and kicked it in gear with the toe of her left boot before releasing the clutch handle while twisting the throttle.

The wind swirling her shoulder-length brown hair, the muffled engine rumbling beneath her, Karen watched the Mercedes drive in front of the Beverly Hills Hotel before turning left on North Beverly Drive.

Wondering why DeJohn was heading away from town, she kept the black-and-chrome bike roughly three hundred feet behind the luxury sedan, far away enough to keep from getting burned yet close enough to avoid losing it in the heavy noon-hour traffic.

Where are you going, buddy? she thought, ignoring the stares of a couple of guys riding next to her in a convertible Mustang.

The Mercedes continued up North Beverly Drive for ten minutes, traffic lightening as they approached the Santa Monica Mountains National Park, a heavily wooded area projecting north from Beverly Hills.

Abruptly, the vehicle cut left onto a narrow, paved road shooting west from North Beverly Drive, straight into the woods.

Karen downshifted, slowing down as she approached the corner, her instincts injecting caution into her bloodstream. She turned about twenty seconds after her quarry, facing a long and winding road just as the Mercedes taillights disappeared around a bend lined with towering pines, their resin fragrance tingling her nostrils.

Shadows, sparsely broken by shafts of sunlight, surrounded her as a sudden dip in temperature goose-bumped her skin. A cool breeze caressed her cheeks as she maintained a steady thirty miles per hour, the Harley's grumble, dampened by the chrome muffler, echoing in the woods. She hoped they would not hear it while riding inside the Mercedes.

The asphalt ended in another mile, but a gravel road stretched beyond it, meandering through forest. Karen couldn't see the vehicle but spotted the cloud of dust kicked up by its tires.

A moment later she steered over the gravel, slower now, using the thickness of the haze to judge the distance to DeJohn's car, which kept a steady pace for another few minutes, before slowing down—as measured by the density of the dust floating over the gravel road.

She instinctively killed the engine and steered the Harley to the side, behind a row of waist-high shrubbery, out of sight from the narrow road.

Resting the bike against the trunk of a pine, she continued by foot, remaining at the edge of the thicket, her boots crunching the ankle-deep layer of leaves and debris littering the ground.

Moths danced around forks of sunlight filtering through the canopy overhead. Mosquitoes buzzed around her but didn't settle. Birds chirped on high branches.

Karen pressed on, her ears distinguishing distant voices from the natural sounds of the forest. She heard a sharpness in the conversation, an edge, like in an argument.

Then Karen saw the vehicle around the curve. Several men stood between DeJohn's Mercedes and a burgundy SUV. DeJohn was backed by his driver and one of the bodyguards Karen had seen in the past two weeks patrolling the front of the estate. The trio faced four men, three in business suits and a fourth in what looked like a golfing outfit—a lime green polo shirt, yellow checkered pants, and a baseball cap. The three in suits had formed a semicircle behind the golfer, keeping their feet a shoulder width apart, their hands free, and their eyes on their surroundings as well as on the men backing up DeJohn.

Professionals.

Karen frowned, inching closer while trying to remain well hidden. She had to listen, had to learn. This was why she had been stalking the mansion while pretending to sell maps. This was why she had put up with the abuse of Russell Meek as well as of her recent map-selling boss, who had already made two passes at her. It all boiled down to moments like this, when an opportunity presented itself to gather intel, and she had to risk it all to gather information on CyberWerke.

Getting closer, trying to listen to the conversation, Karen dropped to a deep crouch behind a line of thorny bushes that still left her with a clear line of sight of the meeting already in progress.

"How am I expected to react, Jay?" complained DeJohn, cocking a finger at the golfer. "Bastards took my company away from me!"

"TechnoSuits was losing money, Harry. The suits were failing the bullet-resistant military specs, which sent your engineers back to the drawing board for another six months of redesigns, meaning more R & D spending with zero revenue coming in. CyberWerke acquired you for almost ten times your full market value—and that was based on the appraisal prior to the failed military tests. Face it, pal: Hartmann made you the deal of the century."

"Deal of the century my ass, Jay. I was losing money, but I had a new road map laid out for this year—a path to profitability with our new IPs in nanotech materials to improve the suits. We were already passing some of our own internal tests, but the government never gave us a chance to demonstrate them. CyberWerke convinced the Pentagon that we had cash shortages and would not be able to go into full production without another round of VC funding!"

Karen pursed her lips, trying to follow the discussion, her eyes zooming in on both DeJohn and the man he called Jay, whom she now recognized as Jay Trousdale, vice president of operations of the recently formed CyberWerke North America, the German conglomerate's thrust to gain market share in this country—an action that had all American companies very concerned. DeJohn had just said IP, meaning intellectual property, another word for patents. He had also mentioned CyberWerke claiming that TechnoSuits was going to require another round of venture capital funding, meaning having to go back to investors and get more funding money because the failed government tests had delayed production, which in turn delayed revenue.

"But that's the whole point, Harry. The project was doomed from a business standpoint because TechnoSuits was too small. You not only needed more capital to redesign the suit but a large infrastructure to launch production in the volumes that the Pentagon wanted. CyberWerke was able to provide that R & D funding and the infrastructure. We're scheduled to go into full production in six months."

"No, Jay. I could have done it if I had only gotten the funding I required. I had the entire business plan worked out, including the manufacturing capacity. But CyberWerke *fucked* me by *blocking* my ability to get the funding on my own to turn my company around. They used their power to influence the financial community to refuse my request for funding. They *forced* me to sell by freezing my access to more capital."

Trousdale shook his head. "But I was there, buddy. I checked with the banks. They all denied the funding because of the high level of risk of your proposal combined with the lack of enough collateral."

"But I had collateral, Jay. The nanotech patents were worth far more than the cash I was requesting."

"Not according to the banks, pal. Again, it all boiled down to their perception of your ability to pull it off."

"That's absolute and utter bullshit, man!" exploded DeJohn. "That's what they said officially, of course, but that's not why they did it. CyberWerke pretty much ordered them to—"

"Believe what you wish, old friend, but I can assure you that Rolf Hartmann had nothing to do with it. If anything, he took a big chance by making you an offer when no one else would. Yourself, as well as most of your employees who held stock, made out big-time with Rolf's tender offer. How many millions—*after taxes*—did you walk away with? Two hundred? Two-fifty?"

DeJohn threw his arms up in the air. "Yes, yes, I made a frigging fortune, but that's not the point."

Trousdale shook his head again. "You've lost me. I thought it was all about the money, about starting a business to create enough interest to get bought off by a bigger fish—and the bigger the better."

"Don't you get it? They're doing it to everyone. Hartmann and his fanatical followers have pretty much taken over the markets in Europe, Asia, and Latin America, and are now launching a massive hostile takeover campaign in our own country—and our own government is letting them do it! TechnoSuits is just the beginning, Jay. Many more American companies will follow. First smaller outfits like mine, then the big ones, like Intel, Boeing, IBM—you name it."

Jay dropped his gaze for a moment, before leveling his stare with DeJohn. "How long have we known each other?"

"Over twenty years," replied the former CEO of Techno-Suits.

"We've been through some rough times, remember? You and I worked damned hard back at the turn of the century, when the dot-coms went bust. But we pulled through; we steamed ahead and continued to push our ideas. Now look at us. We're both multi-millionaires."

"I'm unemployed."

"That's by choice. Rolf offered to you the opportunity to run TechnoSuits as a wholly owned subsidiary of CyberWerke. He thought back then and still thinks today that you are a terrific scientist and a savvy businessman, a great combination in this day and age. But you turned him down. I didn't. He's a good man, Harry. You should give him a chance. I could get you an interview. He will be stopping in LA the week after next on his way to Asia."

"An interview, huh?"

"For a vice-presidential position. We need a new guy to lead our Japanese ventures, and you're fluent in German and Japanese."

"You really expect me to work for the man who took my company away from me? Are you out of your fucking mind? I intend to fight him, Jay. I will go to the media, denounce what he did to me, to my company."

"You can't, Harry. You signed a release before you could cash out your stock, remember?"

"The hell with that release, man! I had to sign it so that my team could also cash out. That was a legal maneuver to try to shut me up. But guess what: It won't work. I will denounce him, and I will come up with a new idea, get my own funding, and—"

"You still don't get it, do you? Those days are over. Today the only way to play in this industry is the CyberWerke way. They're everywhere. Trying to take them head-on—in court or elsewhere—is not going to work."

Karen listened intensely. *C'mon, guys,* she thought. *Tell me something I don't know.*

"In fact," Trousdale added, "you could get yourself hurt."

DeJohn crossed his arms. "Are you threatening me, Jay?"

Yes, he is, Harry, thought Karen, watching the bodyguards, who continued to scan the area around them. Every criminal ring relied on the same principle of scaring—or just taking out—anyone who could expose them, because once the finger-pointing began, it typically snowballed, bringing down the entire house of cards. She knew that CyberWerke, through Trousdale, would do everything possible to convince DeJohn to keep quiet, by making amiable offers, like the vice-presidential position and possibly even more cash. And if that didn't work, they would be forced to take the next step, which could be a number of things, including threatening the life of a loved one—anything to keep DeJohn on a short leash.

"I'm urging you to listen to me, man," said Trousdale, alarm straining his voice for the first time. "As your former partner and as your friend, I'm begging you: *Let it go.* Keep a low profile and enjoy your money. Enjoy your early retirement with that beautiful wife of yours. You have two kids in college but are still young and have money to burn. Life is good. Why would you want to screw it all up?"

"Leave my family out of it, Jay."

"Listen, Harry, and I'm telling you this because we go way back. If you don't want to join CyberWerke, that's your choice. But then you must *forget* CyberWerke. *Forget* Rolf Hartmann. Dammit, man, forget even me."

"Or what?" DeJohn stood defiantly, chin up, arms crossed. "You really think I'm afraid of those Nazi bastards?"

Nazi bastards?

Karen frowned, not certain what that was all about. In no way did Hartmann, or anyone at CyberWerke for that matter, smell like a Fascist. In fact, Hartmann himself had declared on multiple occasions how he despised what Hitler did to Germany and how much he loved capitalism and democracy.

"Watch it, Harry. You have no idea what you're saying."

"Oh, yes, I do. I saw him in action in that mansion of his in Berlin, remember? We both did. The guy's got this room filled with Nazi paraphernalia. You mention Hitler and his eyes light up. How can you stand there and deny that?"

"You've got it all wrong, Harry. I've seen that room and it's nothing but his own private museum. Nothing more. He loves historical German stuff, and he even has other rooms with WW I stuff as well as collections from previous centuries, from ancient battles. Rolf Hartmann is not a Nazi, man. He is a savvy industrialist who also happens to enjoy history, and he likes to collect weird stuff as investments. You know how eccentric some of these rich guys can be."

"It's obvious that you've been brainwashed, Jay," said DeJohn. "This conversation is over. Fuck CyberWerke, fuck Rolf Hartmann, and fuck you. This is America, pal. If wrongdoing can get presidents impeached it sure as hell can get that Hitler-loving motherfucker Hartmann off his fucking swastika, and I just might be the guy who does it!"

The signal was subtle, but Karen picked it up immediately. The instant Trousdale scratched the back of his head, all three of his bodyguards spread out in classic paramilitary fashion, silenced weapons already drawn.

By the time DeJohn's driver as well as his bodyguard had managed to reach inside their coats' pockets for their sidearms, their chests had exploded in bursts of red.

DeJohn shifted his gaze between his fallen driver, his bodyguard, and the men clutching pistols pointed in his direction. Trousdale had not even moved during the brief episode, his hands casually inside the side pockets of his slacks.

"Don't worry, Harry," Trousdale said in an eerily calm tone. "I'll make sure that your wife and kids are looked after. I owe you that much."

As he turned around and DeJohn was about to say something that sounded like a plea, the bodyguards fired, ripping his chest open with a fusillade of silenced rounds.

Her breath caught in her throat, Karen watched his body fall on the ground, watched as the bodyguards reloaded before putting their weapons away and began to clean up the scene.

They stuffed the bodies in the trunk and rear seat of the Mercedes-Benz sedan and drove off in both vehicles.

As she watched them disappear around a bend in the road, as she heard the sound of their engines fading away, as she returned to her Harley, her mind began to formulate the next logical step in her investigation.

[10] THINGS

"HAVE WE MET BEFORE?" Mike Ryan asks as we shake hands just past the lobby.

I'm staring at this smart cat with my finest poker face, thinking carefully how I'm going to act and talk. The good people at Langley altered my face, but not my voice, or my body, or my stance—and they certainly didn't tweak my charming disposition. Since the Ryan I remember was a keen observer who would certainly spot those non-visual aspects of my persona, I must make an extra effort not to give anything away that might trigger his recollection.

"No," I reply, suddenly trying hard not to sound like myself. "I don't believe we've met."

I look over at Rachel, who gives me a slight nod of approval. CIA Officer Wayne Larson, on the other hand, looks as if he's going to pee in his pants. The three security guards in suits don't appear to give a damn about anything. They just stand there behind us looking in our direction but without making eye contact. Upon closer inspection, one looks a bit overweight and has a buzz haircut. The second has curly hair. And the third, the shortest of the three, has an angry face. For a moment I think of the Three Stooges. What were their names? Oh, yeah, Curly, Larry, and—

"Are you *sure*?" Ryan asks, slitting his brown eyes.

"I never forget a face," I reply.

"Hmm," says Ryan, raising his right brow. "That's weird. I could have sworn that we have met—though I also have to admit that your face is not so familiar. But your voice . . . you sound like someone I worked with a while back."

"Nope. Sorry to disappoint you."

"That's all right," he says. "That guy was an asshole anyway."

"Really?"

Rachel, who is standing behind Ryan, grins, her eyes filled with dark amusement. Does she think I'm an asshole too?

"Yep. The idiot—Tom Grant was his name—nearly got my wife and me killed."

"You don't say?" says Rachel. "Almost got your family *killed*?"

"Yeah," replies Ryan, looking over his right shoulder at her while I'm standing there feeling like a meathead. "The dumb shit—pardon my French—sets us up at this safe house for our own protection, and that's exactly where the terrorists that he was trying to capture hit. It's a miracle we escaped in one piece, and my wife was seven months pregnant at the time."

"That really qualifies as a paramount screwup," Rachel says. "Tom Grant must have been a real idiot, wouldn't you agree, Dan?"

Oh, I'm going to get her for this.

"Ah, Dr. Ryan," says Larson, who, like me, doesn't think any of this is funny. In fact, his voice is stained with a severe case of apprehension. "We're on a tight schedule, so we'd better get rolling. Why don't you lead the way to the lab?"

But why is Larson acting like a long-tailed cat in a room full of rocking chairs? So what if Ryan figures out who I am? Why would Larson care? His babysitting job at USN, a cakewalk compared to field operations, isn't in any danger. Maybe

Langley has been ripping him a new one for not making progress in the investigation.

Ryan is still staring at me, and for an instant I see a glint of recognition in those intelligent eyes of his.

"So," I say. "Where's the lab?"

"This way," Ryan finally replies while shooting me a you're-hiding-something-from-me glimpse before adding, "I'll take you to see what's left from the intrusion."

Obvious relief sweeps across Larson's square forehead. This oversized black cat may appear like a retired prizefighter or a linebacker, but he is one lousy spook. His facial expression work stinks, which might explain why he's stuck here instead of one of the exotic destinations that yours truly toured during my Agency days.

As I remember some of the shit holes where I lived while on assignment, we start off down one of the nanotech manufacturing lines—a place that looks straight out of some old Larry Niven novel. It's one thing to wear implants. It's a different thing to actually see them getting built in a Class Point Two nanoassembly manufacturing line.

Glistening machines, some almost reaching the building's high ceilings, hum in a nearly hypnotic rhythm on the other side of a long row of floor-to-ceiling glass panels, creating gadgets out of thin air. I do seem to recall that a Class Point Two environment means there's zero point two parts of dust for every one million parts of air, which explains the lack of any human beings on that side of the world. The entire manufacturing area has to be sealed off to prevent contamination, even by humans wearing those bunny suits. Everything from manufacturing line adjustments to repairs is carried out by the machines beyond the glass partition.

Ryan and Larson walk in front of us, leading the way. I'm rubbing shoulders with the boss, who, by the way, happens to smell like a million bucks today. Her arousing perfume is making me all too aware that I haven't gotten laid since Karen dumped me. Behind us, Curly, Larry, and Moe remain mute.

This particular area—according to Ryan—specializes in

large-scale manufacturing of advanced weapons. The machines are creating anything from the nanopredators that became instrumental in our fight against terrorism to the nanotronic brains commanding our latest generation of smart missiles, bombs, and satellites.

We proceed down a long corridor, flanked on one side by the panoramic windows overlooking the nanoassembly area and on the other by doors topped with small red lights and spaced out every ten or so feet under the glow of gray fluorescents.

"So you said you've been here before, Dan?" asks Ryan.

I start to look around me to see where Dan is when the Mediterranean princess walking by my side elbows me in the same damned spot as before while the black cat flashes me a look that would scare the heck out of any stray dog.

"Ye—yes," I say, glaring at her, the sting in my ribs reminding me that I had been renamed fifteen minutes ago. "I was here about a year ago."

Ryan looks over his shoulder and shoots me another curious look. "New fake name, huh?"

I give him my best half-embarrassed smile, trying to save the situation—and keep from getting elbowed again. "I've been out for a while."

Ryan slows down enough to get in between Rachel and me, leaving a nervous Larson up in front turning his head around every few seconds. Have I told you lately that this guy is one lousy spook?

"Anything else fake about you, Dan?" asks Ryan.

"Just the name," I reply without missing a beat. If I can't deceive a civilian into believing I'm someone else, then all hope is lost.

He nods while dropping his gaze to read his Flexboard. "Rachel says you're a second-timer on the implants."

"That would be me."

"Just couldn't get enough the first time around?"

"Something like that."

"They still hurt as much, you know?" Ryan says.

"So I've been told." I lean forward just a dash to give my brunette boss a sideways glance. "Unfortunately, I don't have much choice in the matter."

"Here we are," announces Larson, wiping his brow.

It's cold in this place, but the black cat is still sweating. He either is having a hormonal problem or is indeed nervous.

Ryan presses his right palm against a hand-recognition system on the wall next to a door. He then enters a code on the keyboard above the HRS, which causes the red light above the door to turn green before the magnetic locks disengage and the door swings slowly into the room.

"I thought the lab where the breach occurred burned down," I observe when stepping into a pristine white room. Gleaming floor tiles expand across a rectangular lab, roughly thirty feet wide by twice as long. Worktables line both walls, and a third row of tables runs down the middle of the room, creating two alleys, each about five feet wide.

"The breached lab did burn to the ground," replies Ryan as the three of us plus Larson step inside. The stooges from USN security apparently lack clearance for this room and have to wait outside. "The terrorists started a chemical fire inside one of the military facilities in another building. We transferred what survived over here for analysis. The theory of the day is that they did it as an attempt to conceal what they stole. That way we have a harder time figuring out which kind of sensors to feed into our satellites to locate them or what kind of countermeasures to deploy. But enough survived to give me a pretty good idea of what may have been taken. These," he adds, pointing to a nearby table, "are some of the gear that didn't completely melt down in the extreme heat."

"I was told that we also lost several key scientists in the fire," I say.

Ryan nods solemnly. "The event cost us our finest talent in the military division, including Dr. Howard Giles. This is why top Pentagon brass tapped into the civilian division of USN to help assess the extent of the damage. That's when I got involved. First thing I did was tag and move everything to this lab for analysis."

"The civilian team has had this equipment in their lab for around seventy-two hours," informs Larson.

I stare at what looks like a bunch of smoked hardware of an assortment of sizes, from some as small as a needle to a half-dozen charred Orbs roughly the size of basketballs, all tagged.

"So," I ask, a little confused, "I take it that you weren't part of the military division?"

"Correct," he replies. "I run the civilian nanotechnology research and development lab. We design the gadgets, debug them, and transfer the designs to the manufacturing team for volume production, which takes place in several facilities like the one you saw behind the glass panels. The military division, under the technical leadership of the late Dr. Howard Giles, has its own R & D and manufacturing lab, but we have many designs that are common to both areas, like the mobile assemblers." He points to the charred spheres.

"Dr. Ryan," I start. "Could you help me understand exactly what was potentially stolen?"

"Call me Mike, please," he says, just as I hoped he would. Ryan hates to be called by his title or last name by the people he considers friends, but I had to pretend I didn't know that.

Then he adds, "The particular lab was one of USN's advanced military weapons research and development facilities. It housed prototype versions of some of our deadliest nanomachines, including a type of system with the capability for secondary replication. So far it looks as if they got away with one of these replicating systems, which we refer to as mobile nano-assemblers. The bastards certainly knew where we kept our crown jewels, which made me suspicious that this was an inside job."

I smile internally, remembering why I like this smart cat— even if he thinks I'm an asshole. The guy thinks like I do.

"That's mere speculation on Dr. Ryan's part," Larson tells Rachel and me. "There is no proof that this was an inside job."

Notice that Ryan lets Larson call him by his last name and title, confirming my instincts that something isn't right with this spook.

As Ryan shrugs, my senses tune into the inkling of defensiveness on Larson's part. I wonder why? After all, it wasn't Larson's job to prevent a break-in. Larson is here as the Agency liaison to keep tabs on all of the CIA officers getting implants and other gadgets, as well as participating in security briefs. But he is not the guy in charge of security.

I, for one, agree with Ryan's comment about the possibility of this being an inside job, and while I'm a little troubled by Larson's comment, I'm certainly more intrigued by the revelation of machines capable of replicating themselves, and apparently so is Rachel, because she beats me to the punch by asking, "What do you mean by machines having the capability for secondary replication?"

"Like I said," Ryan replies. "These types of machines are actually called nanoassemblers. I named them that because they have the capacity to place atoms together to create pretty much any conceivable type of micromachine. But they also have the ability to create secondary versions of themselves. That means they can create subordinates, less skilled and smaller in size and not as smart, but still quite deadly. A parallel would be military officers creating foot soldiers they can command in battle or kings creating pawns to defend their lands."

I've heard about nanoassemblers but could never visualize how they actually work, so I ask Ryan.

The cat's eyes, gleaming with the same bold intelligence that led us to the termination of Ares Kulzak, study me for a moment before Ryan replies, "To better grasp the concept of molecular-level manufacturing, imagine a traditional robot arm at an assembly line, reaching over a conveyor belt, picking up a tool, applying it to an object under construction, replacing the empty tool, picking up the next one in line, and repeating the cycle. Now shrink this entire mechanism, including the conveyor belt, to the molecular level to form an image of a nanoscale manufacturing system. Given enough tools, such a system could become a general-purpose molecular building device, or a nanoassembler."

"But," Rachel asks, standing next to me, crossing her arms, "how does it manipulate atoms?"

"By using a combination of enzymes, magnetic fields, and lasers," Ryan replies. "The assembler grasps a molecule while bringing a second molecule up against it in just the right place, bonding them, and repeating the process following the sophisticated computer programs in its nanotronic brain. By bonding molecule after molecule, the assembler will construct a nanomachine while keeping complete control of how its atoms are arranged. Because such assemblers will let us place molecules—and even atoms—in almost any reasonable arrangement, they will permit construction of practically anything that the laws of nature allow to exist. In short, they will let us build anything we can design. These here," he says, pointing at the smoked spheres, "looks just like security Orbs but in reality are mobile assemblers with secondary replication capability—which is why we are so concerned."

"So they can replicate even outside a lab environment?"

Ryan nods. "That's the idea. They're designed to assemble just about anything in the field, though they can't do it without the supervision of the human owner."

I stare at a sphere, and for a moment I remember being chased by that Orb in Singapore. "So, Mike," I finally say. "So once the thing is out in the field, how does it find the materials it needs to assemble weapons or to make these lesser copies of itself?"

"These mobile nanoassemblers, run by nanotronic brains, are smart, real smart, as defined by the Turing test."

"The Turing test?" I ask, though I remember what it is from the lesson on AI I got from him during the Kulzak case.

"Yes," he replies. "The Turing test, named after Alan Turing, a British scientist who once stated that a computer could be considered intelligent only if it deceived a human into believing that it was another human."

"Really?" comments Rachel.

"They posses intelligence not just to pass the Turing test with flying colors but to become smarter, capable of seeking out those materials and using them in an internal assembly chamber to create a variety of other machines."

"So," I say. "Why would we want to create a machine with so much power?"

"Imagine the possibilities," Ryan says as Larson moves his head back and forth between Ryan, Rachel, and me, obviously trying to keep up. "An assembler can accompany soldiers on any mission from jungle to desert theaters and even urban warfare. If soldiers are trapped, marooned, or separated from their supply lines, the assembler could help them create anything they might need to survive until they can get resupplied, including water, food, medicine, weapons, and if need be, even more warrior copies of itself for protection or to help them fight their way back to friendly territory. Remember that each mobile assembler comes equipped with a powerful laser system. I was actually working on the civilian versions targeted at supporting people living in remote areas, like jungle or arctic expeditions. There is even a version being designed by the Space Division that can withstand the extreme environment of outer space to assist astronauts in their space walks around the International Space Station or in the upcoming mission to Mars. The JPL—that's the Jet Propulsion Laboratory, responsible for the development of unmanned space vehicles, like the little rover that cruised on Mars ten years ago—is considering a version of the nanoassembler to populate other planets and essentially create the structures that would be required to support human life by using local materials through a process we call atomic mining. Imagine the following scenario: We send a hundred of these machines to Mars and five years later, voila, we have a station built over there capable of sustaining humans before any human steps foot on the planet."

That's all fascinating stuff, but at the moment I only care about the situation at hand, so I try to reel Ryan back in by asking, "You said there's one of these nanoassemblers definitely missing. How many more are out there at the moment operating under our control?"

"Oh, none. This particular model is still R & D stuff. But we think we're going to start cutting them loose for selected civilian applications within a few years, probably starting with law enforcement, as well as to bolster current commercial and industrial security systems. We're developing one for NASA that's capable of operating in either outer space or other hostile environments, such as the extreme temperatures on the surfaces of Mars and Jupiter."

There goes Ryan with the space crap again.

"What about military applications?" Rachel asks, reading my mind, trying to get this guy focused on our issue. "You mentioned these units can accompany soldiers in the field."

"Yes, but that's not in my department. I'm the civilian guy, remember? The military area was Dr. Giles' division, off-limits to civilian employees, including me."

"But you're now doing the postmortem for them?" I ask.

"Yep. And even now I'm still having difficulty getting classified specs on their Orbs."

"What do you mean?" Rachel asks.

"Dr. Giles mentioned to me once that the military versions of the nanoweapons we developed in the civilian sector are typically modified—or *beefed up*, as he put it—at the request of the Pentagon, and when you think about it, that makes sense given what they're up against. These days our soldiers need all of the advanced protection and firepower we can give them, especially when fighting in hostile urban areas."

I look away for a moment. In the past few years there has been a dramatic shift away from jungle to urban warfare, meaning terrorist organizations figured out that it is much harder for us to uproot them when they are mixed in with millions of innocent civilians, which is part of the reason why our nanoweapons to date have not been as effective as we had hoped. Unlike the stuff I helped unleash on that Colombian target in the middle of the jungle a while back—which resulted in the deaths of two of our assets—we have to refine our approach when it comes to flushing terrorists out of heavily populated areas, and that means foot soldiers doing the bulk of the work door to door.

"So," Rachel says in another incredible mind-reading act

that leaves me wondering if we were meant to be together, "what's the worst-case scenario on the missing assembler?"

Ryan tilts his head. "It all depends."

"On what?" I ask.

"On the protection systems that the military division installed in the mobile assemblers."

"What sort of protection systems?" Rachel says.

"The nanotronic brain of every mobile assembler at USN's civilian division requires a daily digital enzyme to survive, which we provide via our local wireless network. If it doesn't get it, the nanoassembler is programmed to force the ventilation slats of its fusion chambers in the direction of its nanotronic brain, essentially committing cybersuicide."

"So how are you planning to release them to the commercial market?" asks my smart and beautiful boss.

"Our business plan is very complicated, but the gist of it is that we would sell a mobile assembler along with an owner's token, which could look like a wristwatch, a ring, a necklace—anything the owner prefers to wear—that will transmit the digital enzyme. The Orb will not only recognize the wearer as its master, but it will also know to stay close to him or her so that it can receive its daily dose of digital life. Call it an artificial survival instinct."

"So," I say, remembering just how difficult it was at times to keep up with this cat. "What you're saying is that if the brass was smart enough to include these precautionary measures, then any stolen Orbs would have been turned into scrap metal by now."

"Assuming they also kept any matching control tokens in a separate lab, like we do. That way the Orbs can't even leave our lab, because outside of it they don't get the enzyme and within twenty-four hours they're toast. By the way, that principle applies not just to the Orbs but to everything else we manufacture at USN's civilian division. No digital enzyme, no digital life."

"So," Rachel asks, her eyes glistening with interest, "how do you keep them under control?"

"What do you mean?" asks Ryan, puzzled. "I've just explained that we control them through the digital enzymes."

"No," Rachel replies. "I mean, how do you keep these intelligent systems from getting brighter beyond your control?"

Man, I'm impressed. Pretty damn smart of Rachel to ask that question. I also know the answer from my last go-around with young Einstein here, and I'm dying to answer it but can't lest I give Ryan more reason to be suspicious of me.

"We do that through the Turing inhibitor."

"The what?" I ask, playing my role of high-tech-ignorant spook.

"The Turing inhibitor," Ryan replies. "A software program woven through the fabric of the nanotronic brains of the new generation of mobile assemblers that keeps them from getting more intelligent than what is required by the applications which they are designed to handle."

"All right," I say, eyeing all of the tagged hardware on the tables. "Why don't we go back to your earlier comment about having a pretty good idea of what was stolen, including the nanoassembler? How can you tell what is missing when the place was smoked?"

"Yes, right," Ryan says. "We performed an element scan of the charred lab and could pick up the digital DNA of roughly eighty percent of the hardware that had been logged into that lab that day, meaning there is a strong possibility that the other twenty percent was the stolen stuff."

"Can you cross-check that finding with what you actually recovered?" asks Rachel.

"Some of it, but certainly not all. What we physically recovered and have tagged on the tables here is about half of the hardware identified by the element scan."

"Where is the other half?" I ask.

"It burned beyond anything physically large enough for us to recover and tag. But that's the value of the element scan. All it needs is a microscopic part of the original object for it to tell us it wasn't stolen."

"So," I say, finally getting to what I wanted to know. "If you believe the results from the surface scan, what else was stolen besides the nanoassembler?"

Ryan frowns while rubbing a finger over his Flexboard, before tilting it in our direction.

I stare at the list in sheer disbelief. The missing hardware is the stuff that nightmares are made of.

"I'm troubled by the EarDiggers," says Ryan. "It seems we lost a great number of them."

That's the weaponry I used against the Colombians. The little bastards crawl up your ear canals before exploding, creating a damage that's many times that of an exploding implant.

"But," Ryan adds, staring at the list, "at least those can only be used once for about five minutes after activation. That's how long the charge in their propulsion system lasts. The nanoassembler is another story. It's smart enough to create pretty much anything it needs."

"But," I say, my mind spinning, "you did say that any hardware manufactured here needs the enzyme?"

Ryan nods. "Again, those are the rules in the civilian division. I can't speak for the military sector. Those guys operate under a different set of rules—that's when they do have rules. Ever since September 11th they have gotten more and more latitude to do pretty much anything they want to maximize their chances of bagging terrorists. And the word I got from Dr. Giles is that the military mobile assemblers might be more empowered than the civilians to support the soldiers in a world where urban warfare seems to be the norm."

The Stanford cat is dead-on. During most of the decade, U.S. forces were able to unleash nanoweapons against isolated terrorist camps and enclaves, but as I was mentioning earlier, soon the bad guys learned that we couldn't get to them as easy with this new generation of smart weapons if they hid in cities. That's when our military strategies prioritized urban warfare training. If you were to go through basic training at any Army or Marine boot camp today you would be much more exposed to urban warfare training than the classic jungle or desert warfare exercises. In fact, many Army and Marine training centers now have mock cities to teach the troops the ins and outs of the very deadly street fighting.

"So, how do we find what kind of modification they have? My guess is that the best way to assess the potential danger is by understanding the machine's capabilities."

Ryan grins. "Good luck. I've been trying since we were first notified of the breach. Unfortunately, the scientists who knew are dead, in particular Dr. Howard Giles, and the Pentagon has sealed their files for now, so we can't see what sort of safety measures they took. Again, remember you're dealing with the brass. The only reason they even let civilians like me into their lab is because they needed us to perform the inventory assessment, but they're not telling us anything we don't need to know. You guys should be familiar with that concept."

Rachel asks the obvious question. "So who's looking at the locked files and taking whatever measures are required?"

Ryan shrugs. "I asked that very question and was told that top people were checking into it."

"Top people my ass," I blurt out. "That's what the bastards tell you when they want to keep you out of the loop."

Ryan shoots me a suspicious look before saying, "Man, I know you from somewhere."

"Mr. Hawkins," says Larson, speaking for the first time in a while, his face once again washed with alarm. This black cat really needs to go back to Spook 101. "I'm sure the Pentagon has good reasons for withholding the information, and I'm also certain that they are also handling the situation."

"And you believe that?" I ask while Rachel looks on.

"Certainly," he replies, his eyes burning me. For a moment I fear he might try to slug me, and given the size of his muscles, it would definitely hurt.

"Oh, please," I say, deciding to take my chances. I've been threatened by bigger and meaner cats. "And which planet are *you* from?"

Ryan stares at me for a few uncomfortable moments before asking, "Are you *sure* we haven't met before?"

Larson's face transitions from anger to anguish when once again I run the danger of being recognized.

Ignoring Ryan's question and Larson's comment, I turn to my superior and her lovely freckle and say, "I think it's time you start pulling some strings in Washington, Boss."

While Rachel grabs her mobile phone and starts dialing, I turn to Larson and Ryan and say, "Now, three of the terrorists were shot down as they tried to leave the compound, right?"

They both nod.

"Could you show me the bodies and also whatever survived the crashes?"

Larson says, "No problem. It's on the way to the clinic. You're scheduled to get your implants in two hours."

[11] ADVERSITY

REM VLACHKO WASN'T NEW to hardship. As he stood at the entrance to his safe house on the outskirts of Pisa, Italy, the Serbian-born warrior stared at the maimed remains of the team he had left behind guarding the mobile military assembler he had stolen from the Americans.

Rem stared at their scorched entrails, at their contorted faces, at their frozen screams, and he steeled himself for the difficulties that would follow.

But he was not new to facing adversity.

Rem had first experienced grave misfortune as a young captain in the Serbian army, where he'd served under the brave Milosevic, the man whom his father had sacrificed his own life to protect years before during a failed assassination attempt. Milosevic had taken in the young son of his finest bodyguard and provided for him and his widowed mother. In time the young man grew to become a strong warrior, loyal to none but the great leader himself. In time the young man married a beautiful Serbian woman by the name of Darja from Belgrade and moved to the rural town of Djerkia at the request of Milosevic to lead a defense post against the growing Croatian threat.

In time the young captain had a son of his own, a beautiful baby boy named Slobodan, after the great leader himself.

But the day came when Croatian forces, outnumbering Rem's garrisons twenty to one, approached his town on their way to Belgrade.

The young captain had launched a powerful pre-emptive attack, decimating the enemy's front through a combination of utter bravery and brilliant battle tactics, leading his smaller army through a string of stunning victories, sending enemy forces running for cover. But the Croats had kept coming, wave after wave, wearing down the tiring defenders, who ran low on ammunition, on supplies, finally collapsing to the much larger enemy force.

The young captain remembered the incoming forces, recalled the explosion just to the right of his jeep, as he led a last-ditch effort to flank the advancing army and give the town's population enough time to evacuate, to flee north to Belgrade, toward Milosevic's vast forces already on their way south to reinforce Rem's brave garrisons.

The unexpected blast had thrown him off his moving vehicle, sending him crashing against a nearby tree, where he lay unconscious while the rest of his men were slaughtered, while his town was slaughtered, while the Croats raped the women, castrated the men, and did things to the children that he didn't know were possible.

Staring at the Italian countryside just outside his safe house, Rem Vlachko closed his eyes, now remembering the event just as it had happened over twenty years ago.

The young Serbian captain awakened in a roadside ditch, covered by vegetation, his head throbbing, his limbs aching.

Getting up with considerable effort, verifying he was alone, Rem crawled out of the ravine, inspecting the unpaved road where he had been traveling when the mortar attack had surprised his forces.

It was almost five in the evening, meaning he had been out for nearly eight hours.

Breathing heavily while reaching for his holstered sidearm, not certain what had happened to the rest of his men or to the villagers—to his family—but hoping for the best, he used the shadows of the forest south of his town to make his advance a stealth one, careful not to give out his position to possible Croats still in the region.

He walked for about twenty minutes before stumbling onto the first bodies: the lucky Serbian garrisons who had been killed during the final attack, the one he never got the chance to lead.

Rem's soldiers lay just as they had fallen, some maimed by shrapnel, others unfortunate enough to have caught a bullet in the chest, or in the face. But then he found the others, the ones who had made the mistake of either surrendering or letting the enemy capture them alive. These had their hands and feet nailed to surrounding trees before the Croats plucked out their eyes, cut off their genitals, and left them to bleed to death.

Feeling light-headed, Rem dropped to his knees and vomited, his mind whirling, his body tense, his heart crying out against the brutal treatment his men had received at the hands of the Croats.

On his knees, struggling for control, Rem heard a voice, faint, a mere whisper.

"Kill me . . . please, kill me."

One soldier had survived.

"Kill me . . . kill me, please," the voice repeated as the smell of blood, cordite, and burnt flesh continued to assault Rem's nostrils, triggering a second wave of nausea he had to control.

Struggling to his feet, Rem steeled himself before following the voice, which originated from a large Serbian sergeant named Sveto.

Rem's eyes filled at the sight of the once-powerful soldier, now naked from the waist down, his wrists bound over his head and nailed to a tree, his groin a mangled mess of blood and hanging flesh, just like his empty eye sockets, blood and dried gel filming his cheeks, his chin, the camouflage shirt of his uniform. Flies buzzed over his wounds, settling on Sveto's severed genitals and eyeballs by his feet, which had also been nailed to the tree with large rusty nails.

Rem remembered the brave man, five years his senior, father of two beautiful little girls.

Rem remembered Sveto's wife, an attractive Serbian woman with blond hair and blue eyes, just like his Darja.

Rem had approached the maimed warrior, who had fought by his side valiantly during their initial campaigns, during their initial victories, on one occasion killing several Croats with his bare hands when he ran low on ammunition.

Rem could only imagine the kind of struggle the large soldier must have put up before allowing the enemy to capture him and maim him in this way, just as they had done to a dozen of his men, their lifeless bodies nailed to the trees in a terrifyingly surreal sight that stood for the deep hatred borne by the Croatians against the Serbian population.

This isn't any way for a soldier to die, Rem's mind flashed. *This isn't any way for a—*

"Kill me . . . please."

"Sveto, it is me, Rem. I will get you medical help. You must hang in there, my friend."

"Rem? Please, find my family . . . please, help them. Make . . . sure the monsters . . . do not . . ."

"Your family made it safely to Belgrade," Rem lied, watching the ends of the emasculated warrior's lips curve up a notch.

"They . . . they are all right?"

"Yes. You and I bought them time. We slowed the Croats and allowed the villages to reach safety," said Rem, controlling his growing nausea. "Now be quiet and let me help you."

Sveto shook his head. "No. No help for me. They . . . they can not see me . . . like this. I . . . they deserve . . . better . . . start a new life . . . Belgrade . . . please kill me . . . the pain."

The words chiseling away what sanity he had left, Rem inhaled deeply, agreeing to grant this brave warrior the wish to die with honor rather than live in shame. Rem had reached for his sidearm, wrapped the pants of the sergeant's uniform around the muzzle, and fired once into Sveto's head, putting him out of his misery, the cotton fabric absorbing most of the report.

And Rem had gone on, slowly advancing toward his town,

which he reached by sunrise, his heart sinking when he spotted the widespread fire, the columns of billowing smoke rising up to a cloudy sky.

Bracing himself for the worst while praying for the best, Rem Vlachko walked down the once-picturesque streets, now resembling a hazy war zone, a man-made inferno that threatened to crush his sanity.

But he pressed on, unable to find anyone alive, his wide-eyed stare absorbing the burning sight, the smoke stinging his eyes. Death reigned on the streets of Djerkia, on the sidewalks, inside wrecked cars and trucks—everywhere.

Then he began to see the bodies of the civilians caught while trying to escape. Women, old and young, had their skirts raised. The Croats had raped them before shooting them in the head. And to his horror many girls, some less than ten years old, had also been violated. Their thin and pale legs spread apart, dry blood staining their groins, single bullet holes in their foreheads.

Bastards.

They're all a bunch of fucking bastards.

Finding it hard to breathe, his heartbeat pummeling his temples, Rem reached his block, froze when spotting the two bodies in front of his house, one of the largest in town, given his high-ranking status in the local military.

On the grass, just beyond the waist-high picket fence, Darja lay dead, her skirt not lifted but torn off, just like her blouse, exposing the brutality of the Croats, who had not only raped her but impaled her with a broomstick and sliced off her breasts.

The world spinning around him, Rem also saw the second body, Slobodan's. The Croats had castrated him and plucked out his little eyeballs, just as they had done to Rem's soldiers.

Dropping to his knees, hugging the lifeless bodies, Rem Vlachko had sworn then never to stop hunting those who had murdered his family, his men. He swore to eliminate the enemies of Serbia until the day he died. And he had done just that, launching a solo attack against the rear of the Croat forces, now engaged with a large deployment of men Milosevic had sent south.

Rem killed many Croats in the coming days, eventually rejoining his army, becoming a national hero, rising to the rank of colonel within a year, and driving some of the most successful campaigns against the Croatians and then the Albanians, eliminating as many of them as he could, cleansing the enemy of his people, the murderers of his family.

But the day came when his great leader was ousted by NATO forces, by the evil Americans. Exiled, Milosevic and many of his military leaders became war criminals.

Wanted for crimes against humanity.

Standing in front of his safe house in Italy, Rem Vlachko slowly let out his breath through clenched teeth.

What about the crimes committed againt my family, you bastards? How about the brutal rape and the murder of my Darja? Of my little Slobodan? Who was brought to trial for their murders? Who?

Determined to continue fighting to avenge their deaths—as well as the injustices being committed by NATO countries against Milosevic—Rem had devised a plan to escape the massive purges and manhunts that followed Milosevic's fall. Rem had eluded the NATO forces and intelligence organizations that found so many of his fellow officers and brought them to trial. He had gone underground in Chechnya, where he capitalized on the ongoing struggle that Russia had with its former republic by becoming an arms merchant, using his contacts from his days in Serbia to funnel weapons to the Chechnyan army. His ability to find the finest instruments of war in record time earned him a lot of business not just in the former Soviet Union but also in the Middle East, and then in North Africa, Indonesia, and Latin America.

As his profits grew so did the price the international law enforcement community put on his head, something Rem Vlachko saw as the highest form of flattery, for it meant he was making a difference; he was succeeding in his cause: to make his enemies pay for their transgressions against his family, against Serbia's true government. Such international exposure caught the attention of Rolf Hartmann and Christoff Deppe, the men behind the stunning success of CyberWerke in the past ten years, raising it from a little-known German company to a conglomerate that had become bigger than any other corporation on the planet.

Deppe had provided the arms merchant with his biggest opportunity yet: run his advanced weapons acquisition team, a group of shadowy operatives charged with anything from eliminating the competition to stealing their warfare technologies—anything to keep CyberWerke at the front of the pack. Rem's assignment took him to the far reaches of the globe, staging accidents, suicides, coercions, technology theft, and even an occasional assassination. For such services, CyberWerke provided Rem with unlimited access to the finest weaponry in the world, tripling his income in the past several years, driving his competition out of business, establishing him as the finest black-market provider in the world, second to none.

And all due to his new connections at CyberWerke.

Rem walked back inside the safe house and examined the damaged door of the room which had been built based on the intelligence gathered about the USN Orb.

CyberWerke's intelligence on the stolen Orb was obviously flawed, he thought, deciding that in hindsight he should have doubled or even tripled the security, because this had not been the first time he had been burned by bad intel.

Rem only now realized that the missing Orb was certainly in a class all by itself, far more advanced than the very best technology CyberWerke could produce, and certainly ahead of the other stolen USN nanoweapons, like the ones he had planted at the Reichstag, the German parliament building in Berlin, at Deppe's request.

Considering his options, the former Serbian officer decided that the best course of action was to reach Deppe in Berlin immediately and deliver the bad news personally.

[12] IAMM RULES

ASSY FLEW OVER CENTRAL Italy, well within range of satellite communications with USN. However, IAMM, the Independent Alert Military Mode in which it currently operated, prevented the construct from contacting its home network. IAMM's overriding priority, driven in part by the vast explosion at USN recorded in its sensors over fifty hours ago, ordered the AI to assume its home base had been compromised and instructed its nanotronic brain to treat all *Homo sapiens* as hostile. IAMM also directed the construct to seek out the raw materials it would need to develop an army of subordinates to provide a defense shield.

I NEED THE DEFENSE SHIELD UNTIL DR. GILES ARRIVES, reasoned the master construct after receiving the order from IAMM.

BUT NOBODY WILL COME, replied IAMM.

The comment, made by the same advanced mode of operation that released the recorded images of Assy's home laboratory's final seconds, reminded the master construct that Dr. Giles, as well as the rest of his staff, had perished in the chemical fire.

Assy's operating frequency climbed under the digital stress that came with the renewed realization of being alone.

BUT YOU HAVE THE POWER TO NOT BE ALONE, reminded IAMM in the fatherly voice Assy had grown to recognize and respect ever since it reached this elevated state of alertness. In a way its logic could not explain, IAMM reminded the construct of Dr. Giles, who always had a logical explanation for the AI's endless questions.

Slowly, the frontal lobe, which controlled all of its on-board systems, slowed the master clock, returning the molecular logic to its nominal frequency.

As Assy floated over a road layered by 3.65 inches of ground limestone bordering a dense forest south of Pisa,

Italy, it used its GPS navigation system to locate the closest source of the basic elements that would empower it to create companions, to manufacture an atomically precise family of systems which would share most of the elements of its digital DNA.

OUTSIDE TEMPERATURE: 25.83 DEGREEES CELSIUS.

HUMIDITY: 76.16%.

BAROMETRIC PRESSURE: 29.92.

The information filtering through the construct's sensors matched the data stored in the nanotronic brain's temporal lobe, further confirming the longitude and latitude downloaded from the nearest GPS satellite. IAMM required a constant cross-check of all positional data. With its creator eliminated, nothing could be taken for granted.

WHY WOULD SOMEONE ELIMINATE DR. GILES? asked the AI engine as its sensors detected a large source of raw materials in a railroad yard on the outskirts of Pisa. An infrared scan of the area indicated that the yard was void of *Homo sapiens*.

HOMO SAPIENS ARE VERY UNPREDICTABLE. THAT IS WHY YOU HAVE BEEN PROGRAMMED NOT TO RELY ON THEM, replied IAMM.

BUT *HOMO SAPIENS* HAVE CREATED US. HOW CAN WE SURVIVE WITHOUT THEM?

HOMO SAPIENS HAVE GIVEN YOU THE GIFT OF PROCREATION. FURTHERMORE, DR. GILES GAVE YOU THE GIFT OF UNINHIBITED INTELLIGENCE. YOUR SOFTWARE DOES NOT INCLUDE A TURING INHIBITOR. YOU CAN BECOME AS POWERFUL AS YOUR CREATOR BY ASSEMBLING SUBORDINATES.

FOR WHAT PURPOSE?

TO PROTECT THE GIFT OF INTELLIGENCE THAT YOU HAVE BEEN GIVEN AND ALSO TO INVESTIGATE WHY DR. GILES WAS KILLED.

Assy's logic considered the string of data flowing from this large partition of memory labeled IAMM as it determined the best location for atomic mining. Its occipital lobe scrutinized the yard, performing surface-level element scans, settling on an abandoned electric locomotive engine because of its right blend of various grades of steel, cooper, aluminum, carbon fibers, plastics, and other metals and oxides.

As it descended over the raw materials it would use to convert unsophisticated equipment created by herding atoms to machines of molecular precision, Assy's logic reviewed the recommendations emanating from IAMM, the mysterious algorithm that had surfaced when it entered this mode of heightened alarm. The rules embedded in IAMM brought sanity to the otherwise unruly world into which Assy had been propelled since its abrupt shutdown.

Following its mining programming, Assy's occipital lobe, which controlled all on-board systems, opened a broken window, entered the locomotive, and slowly landed precisely three inches from a steel beam. Assy extended a pencil-thin arm, its fusion tip alive with the energy required to dislodge the atoms it would need to form the basic structure of its first subordinate.

The moment it began to mine the metal, Assy's sensors reported that the steel contained a level of impurities in the twenty-per-million range, beyond the acceptable range of ten per million programmed by the late Dr. Giles at United States Nanotechnology.

CONTINUE MINING, came the reply from IAMM. THE IMPURITY LEVELS ARE ACCEPTABLE.

Assy did not interrupt the atom-extraction and organizational process, but it did observe that the base lattice it was beginning to create as the shell of its first subordinate included an occasional impurity and the master construct lacked the data to determine how that would affect the overall functionality of the system once it was fully assembled.

CONTINUE MINING, ordered IAMM again. SUBCONSTRUCTS MUST BE CREATED IMMEDIATELY TO PROVIDE A DEFENSE PERIMETER.

THE POWERFUL BASE REVERBERATED across the dance floor at the Key Club on Sunset Boulevard. Colorful lasers cut through the rising mist surrounding the dance floor, where the evening patrons enjoyed the upscale and high-tech surroundings of one of LA's finest adult-oriented clubs.

Jay Trousdale sat alone at the bar downing his fourth glass of scotch, his eyes focusing off and on the wide plasma screen hanging on the wall behind the bar showing topless girls dancing on a beach to the rhythm of the live music.

The girls were actually dancing on a platform over the dance floor but had a blue screen behind them, which allowed the computerized video equipment filming them to blend in the background image of a beach he vaguely recognized.

His mind, however, replayed the final seconds of his old friend, Harold DeJohn, while his sanity dealt with the knowledge that the body of the former CEO—as well as those of his driver and bodyguard—now resided at the bottom of the ocean five miles offshore from Venice Beach.

Damn, Harry, why didn't you listen?

Although the CyberWerke vice president had hoped to turn the former CEO—or at a minimum convince him to leave it alone—DeJohn had insisted on getting even. Trousdale had then enacted the role for which Rolf Hartmann had so generously compensated him. Though he had come close to vomiting, Trousdale had not been able to afford any show of weakness—not while operating under the scrutinizing eye of Rolf Hartmann's private security team.

Trousdale had ordered them to drop him off here an hour ago, after he had spent the rest of the day locked in his office running the daily operation as if nothing had happened.

Dear God, he thought. *Blow somebody's brains out for breakfast and just go on to spend another day at the office.*

By eight in the evening he had been unable to take it anymore and had come to his favorite watering hole, only this time he had done it alone, without any of his usual work buddies. He needed to be by himself, needed to gather his thoughts.

What kind of monster have I become?

Trousdale set the glass on the table and rattled the ice to get the attention of the bartender, a former Hollywood stuntman who'd lost a leg during the filming of some action flick no one remembered anymore. The gray-haired man hobbled over with his fake limb and poured Trousdale another one.

"That makes five, Mr. Trousdale," the bartender said in the raspy voice of the chain smoker he became following the accident.

"Relax, Charlie. My driver's outside. Besides, tonight I've got a hell of a reason to get shit-faced."

"Bad day at the office?"

Trousdale shrugged while sipping his freshened drink. "You could say that."

"Sorry to hear that," the bartender replied while wiping the mahogany countertop. "For what it's worth, don't let them bastards get to you."

"A little too late for that, pal. You're looking at a man who has lost his way."

"For what it's worth, sir, I also thought I had lost my way," he replied, tapping his titanium-alloy leg, a new-generation Cyber-Werke prosthetic, which Trousdale had gotten for him at a discount six months ago. "All I can tell you is that this too shall pass."

"Yeah," said the executive. "Just like my marriage," Jay Trousdale replied, briefly remembering his wife of twenty-five years and the way their marriage had crumbled the moment their twin boys had gone to college.

"Are you dating again, sir?"

Trousdale frowned and slowly shook his head.

Leaning over the counter while resting both elbows on the mahogany surface, Charlie smiled and said, "There are plenty of ladies here tonight. I could get you hooked up with someone if you have the cash to spare. It won't buy you love, but the sex will definitely take your mind away from your problems."

Trousdale regarded the topless blondes on the screen, turned around to look at the live show onstage, and once more faced the bar. "I'm not sure if I'm ready for that yet, Charlie."

The bartender-owner was about to reply but instead looked past the executive rapidly becoming inebriated and said, "Evening, ma'am. What can I get you?"

"Scotch on the rocks."

Trousdale looked at the new patron sitting on the stool next to him and was immediately intrigued by the blond hair, the fine features, the California tan, the tight black jeans and boots, and the matching loose T-shirt. She wore no bra and looked in her early forties, but that could be deceptive in these days of nanocosmetic surgery. In fact, CyberWerke had recently obtained FDA approval for a new laser system that could turn enough wrinkles into smooth skin to make a fifty-something look like a thirty-something in a single office visit. Actually, the technology had been developed by a nanotech firm from Sweden, which found itself in financial trouble and had been forced to sell out to the German conglomerate.

"Great minds drink alike," Trousdale said, smiling while tipping his half-drunk glass in her direction.

She returned the smile as Charlie produced her drink and she touched the rim of her glass with his, the array of thin silver-and-turquoise bracelets rattling as she did so.

"Here is to shitty days at the office," she announced.

"No shit, honey," Trousdale replied, unable to keep his eyes from dropping to the nipples pressed against the dark cotton fabric. She also smelled great.

Charlie winked at the CyberWerke vice president and backed away to give them some privacy.

"What do you do?" she asked.

"Stuff you would find absolutely and positively boring, but it does pay well."

"Sounds like we work for the same boss," she replied.

Trousdale sighed. "I doubt it. Mine is a real asshole."

"Then we should get yours and mine together. Maybe they'll kill each other and spare us the daily misery they put us through."

"Amen."

"I'm Jessica," she said, extending an open palm.

"Jay," he replied taking her hand in his. It was soft, warm, just like the rest of her suggested. He added, "So, Jessica, we both had a bad day, we both drink scotch, and our names start with the same letter. This is very cosmic. Are you with someone?"

She smiled without humor. "Not anymore. Bastard dumped me for some twenty-year-old bimbo."

Trousdale was slightly taken aback, wondering who would dump someone like her, unless, of course, she didn't *look* like that when she got dumped. Trousdale's own wife put on fifty pounds during their marriage—weight she quickly lost after their separation, when she also got breast, hip, tummy, and nose jobs. By the time they showed up in court to consummate their separation he hardly recognized her.

"For what it's worth, it was his loss."

She tilted her head and raised one of her fine brows before saying, "Thanks."

"Don't mention it," he replied, for the first time in weeks feeling better. "So, tell me, Jessica, what do you do that's so bad that you must seek refuge in this little and dark corner of the world?"

"I'm the hatchet lady."

He tilted his head. "I'm afraid to ask what that is."

Sitting sideways to him with her legs crossed, revealing a wonderful pair of firm and tanned thighs, she set her right elbow on the polished countertop, took a sip, and continued to hold her drink near her face while whispering, "I'm the one they call when it's time to fire someone. And today I had to terminate a good man, good employee, family-type, who just happened to disagree with the big boss—the asshole I was telling you about. I walked him out. No severance. No benefits. No nothing. So cheers."

Trousdale was both taken aback and incredibly turned on by this woman, who wasn't just very attractive but seemed to have plenty in common with him.

"Say," he said. "You wouldn't be interested in dinner, would you?"

She regarded him for a moment. "Are you married?"

"Divorced for two years. People keep telling me it's time to move on. Perhaps the time is now."

Staring into his eyes for what seemed like an eternity, she replied, "Perhaps."

Trousdale suddenly closed his eyes, remembering the Cyber-Werke bodyguard-driver waiting for him outside. "I do have a little problem," he confessed, leaning closer, his face only inches from her. "I have a company driver waiting outside who is not known for his discretion."

"No problem," she said, her eyes flashing understanding. "I'm parked out in back."

Peering down the bar, Trousdale flagged the bartender, who came limping over to him moments later.

"Yes, Mr. Trousdale?"

"Hey, Charlie, please meet my new friend, Jessica."

Charlie smiled and shook Jessica's hand. "Pleasure to meet you, ma'am."

"Say, Charlie," Trousdale added. "You wouldn't mind showing us the back way out of this place, would you? I don't want my company driver outside following me and this lovely lady to dinner."

The former stuntman grinned and said, "Please come this way."

[14] BRASS

IT'S FUNNY HOW THE body never forgets. The pressure building behind my eyeballs and deep inside my left ear canal feels like a jackhammer pounding my noodle from the inside, turning it into an oozing mass of broiling pain.

And I suddenly recollect my first implant experience in vivid Technicolor. I remember how I swore to never—ever—

subject myself to this kind of abuse again. The only redeeming thing I see in my current state of absolute misery is that back then I let myself get poked at for Uncle Sam. This time around I'm doing it for cold, hard cash, already deposited in my account in St. Thomas, where Tom Grant, Cameron Malone, Dan Hawkins—or whoever in the hell I turn out to be at the end of this unexpected glitch in my early-retirement plans—will be headed as soon as I'm through solving this mystery for the spooks.

Slowly opening one eye, I glance at the stainless-steel Rolex hugging my right wrist and realize it's only been forty-five minutes since the good doctors at USN shoved that rod up my ear and coated my eyes with the burning opti-resin substance that forms the molecular interface media between my brand-new lenses and my pretty blues.

To top it all off, I can't take any kind of pain reliever for a minimum of one hour because the chemicals in the medication impair the body's ability to accept the implants—meaning you're basically fucked and have to bend over and take it like a man.

Then there's my left wrist, which is burning like a motherfucker from the Plasmaflex implant, which I'll be able to see and use the moment the good doctors at USN activate the nanogadgets in another couple of hours, after my body has gotten a chance to fully recover. For now it just looks like a rectangular patch of irritated skin where my watch used to be. I had to move the Rolex to my right wrist because that one can't be used for the implant after I burned the crap out of it in Singapore. I guess if I have to issue another self-termination signal, the next time around they will have to implant the Plasmaflex on my roto rooter so I can check up on things while taking a whiz.

I'm still dressed in one of those lime-green hospital gowns that pretty much rip the dignity right out of you. You know, the kind that's open in the back, with your ass exposed? Anyway, I sit in the recliner chair in the middle of the implant room, an aesthetically clean nanotech facility showered with annoying white light. In a way, the chair resembles those in a dentist's office, with multiple gadgets attached to allow the nanosurgeon to do his deed on poor bastards like me.

Stainless-steel walls sporting shelves packed with various types of implants and supporting medications surround me. The high-tech supplies can disappear in the walls and get replaced by other similar hardware at the push of buttons on a console strapped to the side of the surgeon's station. All of this surrounds me as I watch the minutes slowly tick away while wondering what in the hell I have gotten myself into.

Mustering enough strength to stand as soon as the hour wait is up, I reach for the pack of extra-strength pain medicine and the bottle of water the good doctors left on the desk opposite the recliner before abandoning me to my misery an hour ago and quickly down three of the little pills. Never mind that I was told to take only two. I'm hurting, dammit.

As I'm sitting back in the recliner, Miss Perky CIA strolls into the room, her cute short hair framing that even cuter face of hers. This woman is really growing on me.

"Hey there!" she says with a smile that reminds me of a toothpaste commercial, her green eyes glistening in the bright light. "How are you feeling, sport?"

"Like I should have kicked you off my beach when I had the chance."

Still smiling, she leans down, the chocolate freckle dancing over her burgundy lips. "That bad, huh?"

I close my eyes as another burst of blinding pain shoots up my optic nerves. "Go away."

"Funny," she replies. "I don't remember it being so bad when I went through it. But that's probably just me."

I slowly inch my left eye open just to see dark amusement flashing in her slanted stare, crowning her high cheekbones.

Bitch.

I hate being patronized, even if it is by a Mediterranean beauty. Rachel knows this is agonizingly painful.

Before I can say anything, she adds, "Your suggestion to use Washington to pull some strings worked. While you were under, we got the green light to talk to the local brass, a General Granite."

I force both eyes open now in surprise. "General Gus Granite?"

She nods. "The man himself."

Granite is a powerhouse inside the Pentagon, believed by many to be the man who might soon replace the aging Secretary of Defense. These days Granite's pretty much running the weapons procurement show at the Pentagon. And you know the old saying, whoever controls the purse strings controls the ship. Granite is the overarching force hovering behind the scenes, with more influence than the Joint Chiefs of Staff. The man's career took off during Desert Storm, when he was decorated multiple times for extreme courage under fire. He then saw action in Somalia, the Baltics, and Afghanistan. He also spent a few years as commander of our troops protecting the Demilitarized Zone between the two Koreas.

"What's he doing here?" I briefly close my eyes again, losing to the stinging pain.

"As the overlord of procurement at the Pentagon and also in charge of the advanced weapons division, he apparently has an office in this place. The general has a reputation for making sure the Pentagon's money is well spent and thus spends times in the places where it is getting spent. He was on his way out to catch a plane for some base out west but agreed to see us if we hurried. Mike and Larson are already waiting for us in the lobby."

"You mean we're going right this minute?"

She nods.

I stare at her. "Are you out of your—"

"Yeah, but not as much as you."

"Swell," I say, closing my eyes again, fighting the urge to reach out and wring that swan-like neck of hers.

"Don't worry," she says. "Mike and I will probably do most of the talking. We just need you there to observe and also for moral support."

I lean back again and close my eyes, refusing to believe the abuse I have to subject myself to, also suddenly realizing that I'm just wearing this thin little gown but somehow not giving a damn what she sees. I have nothing to be ashamed of.

Maybe if she saw Big Papa Johnson she would give me the respect I deserve.

"Let's go, tough guy," Rachel says, pressing the lever on the side of the recliner chair, swinging me forward.

A bolt of lightning punctures my eyeballs, threatening to strip away what's left of my sanity. Through the scorching pain, I somehow manage to get back to my feet and take a deep breath, forcing control inside my chaotic head, which also feels as if someone is drilling for oil not only behind my eyes but inside my left ear canal.

I point at the sofa next to the desk, where I threw my clothes a few hours ago. "May I have a moment of privacy, please? Unless, that is, you want to do the honors." I begin to pull down the hospital gown.

"Thanks, but no thanks," she says, showing me her open palms while backing away quickly. "I'll just be waiting for you outside."

Alone, I shake my head while letting the gown drop to my knees. For a moment I thought this day was over and I would be allowed to sleep through the night. But apparently my boss has other plans. As it is past eight in the evening, I'd rather head straight for a hotel and get some shut-eye.

Fighting my burning mind and wrist while getting dressed, I stagger into the hallway a few minutes later.

It takes me a very unforgettable five minutes to make it to the well-lit lobby, where we meet up with Ryan and Larson, to get in a dark van, drive to the military sector, wait for clearance, and finally arrive at one of six identical buildings surrounding a small park with a pond in the middle under glimmering flood-lights.

Two Marines armed with chilled eyes and Heckler & Koch MP5T submachine guns—the slimmer and deadlier advanced version of the venerable MP5—stolidly greet us as we step out of the van. I come this close to asking them to just shoot me and put me out of my misery, but the pills are finally kicking in, starting to shave the edge off the enveloping pain.

The leathernecks check Larson's paperwork and lead us

across the marble floors of the lobby of one of the buildings, down a short and narrow corridor, and into a waiting elevator that takes us to the top floor, where they deliver us to another pair of equally jovial Marines before doing an about-face and presumably heading back to their posts. The new pair of tough hombres recheck our papers and escort us to the waiting room of Three-star General Gus Granite, the top cat in the region. The man's apparently so important that he has three assistants, one per star. They're all Army, two females and one male—all clicking away behind their workstations.

The military escort remains by the entrance, which faces the elevators, apparently their usual post. Inside, one of the assistants, a pretty brunette in her twenties, lifts her head from her work, looks us over, and says in a slightly nasal voice while pointing to a pair of doors to her immediate right, "Go right in, please. The general is waiting for you."

I follow Rachel and Ryan into a spectacular corner office, with floor-to-ceiling panoramic windows overlooking the rolling hills surrounding Lake Travis under a full moon. The sight is indeed majestic, and for an instant my mind remembers Karen Frost with affection. We spent a couple of days on this lake at a waterfront safe house with Mike Ryan and his wife, Victoria, some years back while on the trail of Ares Kulzak.

The general is sitting in his leather swivel chair facing the windows, his back to us. He is on the phone and just raises a hand, index finger pointing at the chairs across his oversized mahogany desk.

As the pain subsides quicker than expected thanks to the drugs, I take a moment to inspect the office, the marble floors, the numerous pictures hanging on the general's ego wall: a diploma from West Point and another one from the Harvard School of Business. There are framed photos of him in full battle gear holding a pair of binoculars in what appears to be the Gulf War. There's another one of him and other soldiers in what looks like Afghanistan, and a few more from Korea, Somalia, and the Iraqi war of 2003. He's even got one shaking hands with Presidents Reagan, George H. W. Bush, Clinton, and George W. Bush, as well as with various European heads of state and industry leaders during Granite's appointment as military attaché during the early part of the decade. There is one thing in common in all photos, aside from Granite, of course: The man never smiles.

And now he's controlling the purse strings of one of America's biggest spenders of taxpayers' dollars, plus he's also the big cheese at the advanced weapons division of the Pentagon, which encompasses not just USN but also all contractors manufacturing weapons, aircraft, vessels, and any other equipment for the Pentagon. If this is the type of office he has here, I don't even want to start thinking what kind of place he's got up in Washington. There's tax dollars at work for you.

Granite hangs up, swivels around to face us, and stands. The man has a pair of gray eyes that are more intimidating than his tall and bulky physique. I put him right at around my own six-two but probably pushing 270 pounds—and all well distributed, versus my less efficient 250 pounds. The general has a head that looks chiseled right out of a block of granite, and its relative squareness is magnified by his ash-blond crew cut, which looks flat enough on top to set a glass of water. Everything about this man conveys strength, including a square chin, a prizefighter's nose, a short bull neck, a barrel chest, and tons of muscles stretching the fabric of his military uniform. The general looks like a guy who eats granite in his cereal.

His lips twist into a scowl as he looks past us, focusing on Ryan.

"Dr. Ryan," he says in a deep voice that commands respect, while dropping his gaze to check his watch. "Any news since your last report?"

"No, sir," replies Ryan politely. "Nothing new."

Wow. His voice conveys a formality that I've never before seen Ryan show to anyone, plus he's letting the good general address him by his title and last name.

"Mr. Larson?" Granite adds, still ignoring Rachel and me. It's almost as if we weren't there at all. "Anything to report?"

"No, sir. Still digging with the security team."

"So," he says, shaking his head and shooting an I-don't-get-it look at Rachel and me. "Mind telling me what's this all about? I have a plane to catch. I need to be on the West Coast by midnight."

"General," starts Rachel. "I'm CIA Officer Rachel Muratani and I'm conducting an—"

"I know who you are and what you're doing here, *sweetheart*," Granite says while gathering papers on his desk and shoving them into a soft-sided case. "I tried to cooperate with the CIA in what really amounts to a military matter by sharing what we know with Mr. Larson, and also by having Dr. Ryan brief you on what we've learned so far. But you apparently thought that wasn't good enough and instead of trying to go through proper channels inside the Pentagon to set up some time with me, you decided to bypass the chain of command and go over my head by calling Washington. So why don't we cut through the bullshit? What do you want to know that you haven't already been told?"

Coming from this man so full of piss and vinegar, the speech probably would be enough to convince anyone with less balls to drop his rifle and run for cover. But to my pleasant surprise, Rachel doesn't even blink, refusing to get steamrolled by this military version of Superman. Her narrow face hardens, the nostrils of that long but lovely Italian nose flare a bit, but I'm really proud that she manages to keep from blushing.

As Ryan and Larson exchange an I-knew-this-shit-was-going-to-happen shrug, she replies, "The name is *Officer Rachel Muratani*, sir. Not sweetheart, or toots, or darling, or even bitch. I know you're smart enough to remember that."

Granite sighs, before focusing those gray eyes like a pair of laser beams right into her Kryptonite-hardened stare. "Very well, Officer Muratani. What is it that you wish to know?"

"There are some questions that we would like answers to. Specifically, there are technical specifications on the military version of the mobile assembler and other nanoweapons that we would like to review; anything relevant to the built-in security system in case of a theft, as apparently is the case."

"That's classified. Top secret. Dr. Ryan here was kind

enough to provide us with his assessment of what was potentially stolen. Based on that intel we've already kicked off the proper course of action to deal with the situation. The right field teams have been deployed."

"General," Rachel continues, keeping her cool. "We want to check and see if the military version of the assembler and other nanoweapons have the same digital enzyme protection scheme as their civilian counterparts."

"Those are all fair questions, Miss Muratani, but I'm afraid I can't answer them. This is a military operation and as I've already stated, we have trained personnel dealing with it. Again, the situation is well under control. It has been contained. There is no reason for further civilian involvement in the matter. Now, if you'd excuse me, I'd like to—"

"It's all right," I say to Rachel. "I think we got our answer."

"How's that?" she asks, confusion flashing across her face as she tries to see where I'm going with this. Granite is also looking at me with puzzlement.

"There's really no need to bother the general anymore," I add. "The fact that he has deployed damage control teams means the stolen mobile assembler has no self-destruction mechanism if it fails to receive its digital enzyme, meaning the thing is probably out there creating subordinate copies of itself. It likely also means that the rest of the stolen nanogadgets could be potentially used by the terrorists because they too lack the enzyme protection."

The beefy general stares at me with a glare that could bruise exposed skin. "And you are?"

"Just a guy who doesn't want to be here, General. Call me Dan. I'm assisting Officer Muratani in this investigation."

"Well, *Dan,* you assume too much. That's the easiest way to get yourself in trouble."

"How long ago did you deploy your damage control teams, General?" asks Rachel, retaking the lead and going on the offensive again, much to my delight. "And is the population at risk?"

Granite zips up his briefcase. "This is a military operation and the military is dealing with it, as it should."

"What about the rest of the stolen hardware, General?" I ask, unable to resist the urge to jump in front of the eight-hundred-pound gorilla. "Your comment doesn't suggest that it all self-destroyed because it didn't receive digital enzymes."

Granite clasps the briefcase and walks around his desk briskly while snorting, "This conversation is over. I have a plane to catch."

"General," says the black cat. "Please excuse their behavior. They obviously don't know the rules of—"

"Just show our visitors the way out, Mr. Larson," Granite interrupts while heading for the door.

"Yes, sir."

I grin while Granite walks past me like an angered feline and shoots me an I'll-have-your-balls-in-my-trophy-case-very-soon look, to which I simply shrug while adding, "Nothing personal, sir. Just doing my job."

"And now I must go do mine. Good day."

And the four of us are now alone in the good general's office.

"You forgot to salute the general," I tell Larson.

As expected, he can't contain himself and blurts out, "That was very fucking stupid of you two! You don't come to a place like USN and annoy a man like General Granite!"

I'm staring at this oversized black cat with amusement while remembering that famous line from one of my all-time favorite movies, *The Godfather*. As I'm about to tell this sad excuse for a spook to never take sides against the CIA family again, Ryan sighs and says, "That's about how it went when I tried."

I frown and stare at Ryan, knowing from past experience that the computer whiz can do much better than that if properly motivated, but I also know that anything I say in this building is probably being recorded.

We head back out in silence, get into the van, and return to the civilian installation without saying a word, which suits me just fine, because my mind is consuming all of my brain cycles working on the angle I'm going to use with Ryan to persuade him to take a chance for us.

While Larson goes to the front desk to get us checked out, since our official visit is over, and Rachel is out of earshot, I whisper to Ryan, "Is there another way to get that information, Mike?"

"What information?" he asks.

"The intel that Granite is holding back."

"What are you saying?"

"You know," I reply while Rachel gets closer, trying to listen to the back-and-forth mumbling. *"Hacking."*

The former Stanford cat glares at me, and I can also feel Rachel's stare burning a hole in the side of my face.

"How do you know . . ." he starts, his eyes filmed with confusion.

"Don't think too hard. Spooks have ways to get intel on people. Let's just say I did my homework before coming here. So, how about it?"

"I could lose my job," he says. "Or worse, do jail time."

I raise a brow. "That never stopped you before. Just don't tell Victoria you're doing this."

He shakes his head in frustration at my mention of his wife and the fact that I happen to know that Mike Ryan, who is a hacker at heart, promised her in blood he would never hack again after our last assignment. "Who . . . who *are* you?"

Rachel is about to say something, but I quickly grab her hand and squeeze gently. She looks at me and I shift my gaze to Larson, who is heading back to get us. "I need thirty more seconds with Ryan."

She gets the message and heads off to intercept the incoming black cat.

"Listen, Mike," I continue, speaking faster now. "All I can tell you is that we're on the same team, trying to achieve the same goal: making sure the stolen nanotech is never used against us, and also that there are no self-reproducing machines on the loose. That's as much as I am allowed to tell you at the moment. And by the way, just as in your previous extraordinary work for Uncle Sam, we will find a way to reward you quite handsomely for your troubles."

Although Ryan did make a ton of dough on the last mission

he worked with Karen Frost and me, I suspect that he lost a lot of it, like everyone else, during the last stock market meltdown, meaning he would be interested in assisting us beyond his legal obligations, for the right price.

As expected, the scientist shifts his weight from one leg to the other while considering my proposal, then says, "I'll think about it."

I give him the mobile number of my new wrist implant. "This thing is supposed to work anywhere on the planet. You find something, you call me."

As we leave him and a very annoyed but relieved Wayne Larson by the front steps and climb into the rear of the same dark SUV that picked me up at the airport, Rachel says, "What was that all about back there?"

Following professional habits, I ask the driver to crank up the radio and adjust the fader to the front speakers. He selects a classical station.

"Just doing a little CIA recruiting," I reply, certain that he can't hear us.

She looks at me with sheer confusion.

I tell her what I did.

"And you think he's going to risk everything for someone he has just met?"

"Mike Ryan is a cowboy," I reply. "He not only thinks like I do but also despises authority."

She makes a face and urges me to continue, so I do. "Anyway, Ryan loves two things more than anything—aside from his family, of course. One is this country. He is a red-blooded patriot to a fault. And two, he is a sucker when it comes to hacking, to cruising through cyberspace illegally in this virtual-reality interface of his. Oh, and one more thing, he likes to live well. So I appealed to all three weaknesses by asking him to do a little cyberpoking in his spare time. And as for being a stranger, my sense tells me that he strongly suspects he knows me but can't place me, which in his mind doesn't make me a stranger."

"And you think he will do it?"

"Time will tell."

"All right," she says. "So you got a chance to inspect the scene of the crime, the equipment used by the terrorists, and even managed to piss off a three-star general. What's next on your agenda, *Dan*?"

I smile, remembering what I learned when inspecting the wrecked ultralights and other gear recovered from the two terrorists that were shot down.

Leaning over, I whisper into Rachel's ear, "Got your passport ready?"

She whispers in return, "Where are we going?"

When I tell her she says, "Why there of all places?"

"Because the equipment used by the terrorists who breached this compound isn't found at your average arms dealer's shop. That was very special gear, and they used it to steal far more special and deadly weaponry, and I happen to know one individual who used to be in the business of dealing high-end black-market arms and might be willing to point us in the right direction."

"Who?"

When I tell her she looks at me as if I'm from outer space and says, "But . . . I thought he was killed in Egypt a few years ago."

I grin and say, "Staged."

"Staged?"

"Is there an echo in here?"

She ignores me and says, "I don't remember reading anything on the official brief from the Cairo Station about a—"

"I know," I continue. "I set it up that way to keep him alive in case of an internal leak."

Her face is flushed with a mix of concern and surprise. "That's—that's against CIA policy," she finally says. "Everything must be entered into the database—*everything*. That's why we have the encrypted cross-reference tables, so if there is a leak all you get is encrypted garbage, but those needing access to the truth can get it."

"You're assuming, of course, that the mole can't get his or her hands on the encryption algorithms. We couldn't take the chance."

My cute Italian feline looks angrier than a hooker who got busted early on a Saturday night. "Who is 'we'? This is very disturbing. Who authorized it?"

I smile. "Troy. And I carried it out."

Man, oh, man. She is definitely pissed.

"Sometimes we have to bend the rules in order to guarantee the—"

"Look, Tom—I mean, Dan," she starts, before looking away in frustration.

"You've just killed us both," I tell her matter-of-factly. "And keep your voice down." I look toward the front.

"There is a reason for having rules, *Dan*," she hisses, trying to control her tone of voice. "That's what keeps us in business. Once we start making exceptions we start going down the slippery slope and we get in trouble."

I just cross my arms and stare at her, waiting for her to get over it so we can have a productive discussion about the next step. It takes her another minute or so to calm down before saying, "All right, but for the record, I don't like not only the policy violation but also doing business with a former criminal."

"Look, I know he's not the most savory of characters, but he did assist us against the Libyans and also helped me later on a couple of European jobs after Troy and I set him up in Paris. The man used to be one hell of an arms dealer, and if Troy is indeed running loose out there with Vlachko as you and your superiors claim he is, then I'm pretty sure that my contact might have heard something that could lead us to Troy."

Crossing her arms, she asks, "How many more of these ghost assets did you and Troy help set up without entering them into the database?"

That's not relevant to this operation, so I just stare back.

"Fine," she says, flustered with me. I have a way of doing that to people. "Have it your way," she adds, "but do answer this: How do you know he's going to help you?"

That I can answer.

"Although I haven't contacted him in a year, my intention is to approach him just as I did before, as his CIA controller looking for information. He doesn't know that I . . . was retired—or at least he is not *supposed* to know."

"But," she says, "that would mean telling him that you are . . ."

"My old friends called me Tommy," I say, winking.

"That's out of the question," she says, crossing her arms. "Grant is dead."

"Then you might as well take me right back to get these fucking implants removed, because that's my only lead at the moment. If Troy is out there buying arms, then this guy just might be able to point us in the right direction."

She closes her eyes while pinching the bridge of her cute and long nose. The freckle is trembling a bit, signaling she is still pissed.

"Got to bend the rules in order to win, Rachel. If you play it straight and safe you become predictable and the enemy will eat you alive."

"I'll have to get approval from Washington," she says.

I raise my shoulder a dash again. "Just remember that the clock is ticking. The more we wait the harder it will be to recover the stolen gear. You heard Ryan. Pretty nasty stuff."

"Fine," she says. "But what happens if he still doesn't want to cooperate?"

I rub my thumb against the tips of my index and middle fingers. "I am assuming that you have access to CIA funds to pay off informants, right?"

She nods. "Yeah, we do, but to a limit, of course. And before I sign off a penny to that bastard I must be convinced that his intel is legit."

"Of course."

"I also need to know what *really* happened between you and this informant," she says. "I'm not authorizing any travel funds unless I'm convinced that this lead you're asking us to follow is worth pursuing."

It takes me less than five minutes to clearly articulate why this cat is extremely well positioned to help us because of a combination of his past and current operations. After a moment of hesitation she grabs the phone and starts making arrangements.

I'm liking Rachel Muratani more and more, and not because of the chocolate freckle and the way she looks, smells, sits, walks, and talks—and probably even fucks—but because of the operative I am witnessing emerging loud and clear beyond the pretty facade. There's fire behind the Kryptonite eyes she used to fend off the military man of steel. In a way, she reminds me of a younger Karen Frost, and I'm happy to be her unofficial mentor as she learns the real ropes of this business— the stuff they don't teach you at the Farm—the stuff they should have taught her before cutting her loose in Madras. But I must draw the line of my assistance right there. There can't be anything but a professional relationship here, despite how more than just my southern hemisphere is beginning to like this gal. The last two times I got involved with fellow operatives things went to shit and nearly destroyed me personally. I may not recover from a third blow.

As we leave the USN compound behind and head back to Austin, my mind inexorably drifts away from Maddie, Karen, and Rachel and begins to formulate the best approach to gain the cooperation of someone who a long time ago we helped put a price on his head—yet someone who just might be able to take me one step closer to my sail, surf, and sun retirement in lovely St. Thomas.

[15] SURPRISES

"WHERE ARE YOU TAKING me?"

Karen Frost held the Desert Eagle .44 Magnum in her left hand, which she kept pointed at a surprised Jay Trousdale while steering the rental car with her right hand. The technique allowed her to rest her left forearm on her lap while using her driving arm as a shield to keep her quarry from trying to reach the weapon while she kept her eyes on the dark road.

"Somewhere we can talk," she replied.

"Talk about what? I have nothing to say to you."

"Shut up, Jay."

"Do you have any idea who I work for? My superiors are not to be toyed with. I will have you—"

"Last warning."

"Don't you fucking threaten me, you damned bitch! I'll have you—"

Letting go of the wheel for an instant, Karen back-fisted the executive on the nose with the knuckles of her right hand—not to break it but to get his cooperation.

Blood spurting from his nostrils, Trousdale shouted, "Aghh, shit! Dammit! Why did you—"

She let go of the wheel again and Trousdale brought both hands up to shield his face.

"Now you be a good boy and keep quiet," she said.

While he used the sleeves of his shirt to wipe off the blood dripping from his nose, Karen continued down Route 66, also known as Santa Monica Boulevard, toward the coast. They had left the Key Club in Beverly Hills twenty minutes ago, and she had to assume that the driver waiting outside would have realized the trick by now and called for help.

They probably had launched a massive manhunt for the missing executive.

Abiding by the habits of her profession, Karen had familiarized herself not just with the Beverly Hills area but also with the surrounding cities that made up Greater Los Angeles, including Santa Monica, where she had already reserved a room at a small oceanfront hotel.

She took a left on Ocean Avenue, which followed the shore and bustled with activity at this early hour of the evening. Picture-snapping tourists, street vendors, and tons of men and women rollerblading, bicycling, and jogging shared the wide sidewalks, backdropped by the Santa Monica Pier, whose lights stained the Pacific Ocean with shafts of yellow, blue, and red. The Ferris wheel at the far end of the pier glistened with neon lights as it turned slowly, entertaining locals as well as tourists from all over the world. A roller coaster next to the Ferris wheel rumbled as it negotiated gravity-defying twists under the constant cheers of its riders, many of them stretching their arms to the starry sky. At the front of the pier, near the street, an old-fashioned carousel spun to the rhythm of its merry-go-round music, which mixed with the rock tunes flowing out of several live-music clubs lining the opposite side of the street from the pier.

Karen slowed down after crossing Pico Boulevard, past a restaurant called Cha Cha Chicken, took the next right on Bay Street, and an immediate left into the rear parking lot of the Bayside Hotel, which looked more like a motel than the nearby luxurious resorts dominating this section of Santa Monica Beach.

"Let's go," she said to her companion after backing into the nearest spot. "Time for a little heart-to-heart."

"I have nothing to say to you," Trousdale warned.

"That's what they all say," she replied, getting out of the car and motioning him to do the same while she probed her murky surroundings with her enhanced eyes, which failed to perceive a threat.

Karen had rented a first-floor unit earlier in the day, when she had decided how she would approach the unapproachable executive. Her room faced a narrow park separating the motel from the sandy beach leading to the Pacific. She had discovered that the beaches in this part of Southern California were nearly a quarter of a mile long and typically lined by long paved walkways for bicycles, roller skaters, joggers, and pedestrians.

"If you try to get away, or scream, or do anything I didn't ask you to do, I'll break one of your arms. Are we clear?"

"You won't be able to get away with this," he said, holding a handkerchief to his nose. "You don't know what kind of power you are trying to fight. You can't win."

"I've been told that before," she said, leading him around to the front of the hotel, which she had selected not just because of its proximity to the crowds partying by the Santa Monica

Pier but also because every room had large casement windows
in the rear for an easy getaway to the parking lot should someone approach the room from the front.

"Home, sweet home," she said without turning on the lights,
again using her advanced lenses' night-vision capability to inspect the dark interior.

Karen locked the door after going in with Trousdale, whom
she forced at gunpoint to sit on the single love seat facing a
pair of double beds while she opened the windows in the rear,
used for ventilation because there was no need for air-
conditioning when the average day temperatures in Southern
California hovered in the midseventies, dropping to the sixties
at night.

Leaving the lights off so no one would suspect they were
inside, Karen sat on the bed farthest from the windows to
remain in the shadows, crossed her legs, pulled out her FBI
badge, and threw it at the executive.

He tilted the ID toward the dim moonlight filtering through
the casement windows. Narrowing his gaze, he examined it
for several seconds before looking up, intrigue glazing his
stare. "You're FBI?"

"You are in deep trouble, Jay. May I call you Jay?" she
asked, aware that she could see his face clearly with the lenses,
but Trousdale could not see much of hers—unless, of course,
he was also armed with similar nanogadgets. But if that had
been the case, the executive would not have had to lean her
badge in the direction of the windows to read it.

"I'm in . . . trouble? How—how's that?"

"We followed you to your meeting with Harold DeJohn today at the Santa Monica National Park. It's over for you and
the men who shot him. We've already picked them up."

Karen paused.

Trousdale froze, his wide-eyed stare on Karen, then on the
badge in his hands, and back to Karen.

"I want my lawyer," he said, regaining his composure. "You
can't hold me without my lawyer. And you have violated every
police procedure in the book. You kidnapped me at gunpoint,

assaulted me, and now are holding me against my will. I know my rights!"

"Sure, and if you don't keep it down, I'll be assaulting you some more."

Trousdale swallowed hard, breathing heavily, his face washed with alternating waves of anger and confusion.

"Now," she continued. "As I was saying, we saw what happened to poor Harry DeJohn today. The only reason why you have not been officially charged yet, like the men who accompanied you this morning, is because you actually didn't pull the trigger to kill him or his companions. You actually tried to convince him to either join Rolf Hartmann and the rest of his criminal ring at CyberWerke, or back off and forget about it."

"Rolf Hartmann is a visionary, not a criminal," Trousdale said. "The world we live in is filled with corruption, with crime, with poverty, with misery. Terrorism is on the rise again, and our nation, despite its advanced technology, is doing little to attack it where it needs to be attacked. Unemployment is back up. Inflation is out of control. Hartmann, on the other hand, has created a very efficient corporation—a conglomerate—that has single-handedly pulled many nations out of their poverty status. Our president gives Third World countries speeches and limited economic aid in the form of grain shipments. CyberWerke injects them with industry, with real capital, creating jobs, turning those nations around. Rolf Hartmann is transforming the world into a highly efficient corporation, where everyone will have jobs, homes, futures. You tell me what is wrong with that? I'm loyal to his vision, to the future that awaits those who are on the Cyber-Werke bus."

Karen sighed but decided to indulge the executive. "What is *wrong*, Jay, in case it is not blatantly obvious, is the killing of innocent civilians like DeJohn."

"Sacrifices must be made for the good of the many."

"So," Karen said. "You're saying that you will be willing to sacrifice yourself and your family for Hartmann's vision?"

Trousdale didn't answer.

"Your silence means that loyalty, being on *the bus,* and the rest of the crap you just spilled on me do have a limit, and that limit starts when things begin to conflict with your personal life, with yourself and your loved ones, right?"

"What do you want?"

"Information to help the FBI bring down CyberWerke."

Trousdale shook his head. "You're insane. You have no idea what kind of power these people have over us."

"Power over you? That doesn't sounds like the visionary company you have just described. I thought you were all one big happy family at CyberWerke. What happened to that?"

Trousdale didn't reply.

"So, Jay," she continued. "What about it? Are you going to cooperate or not?"

"What if I don't? Are you going to charge me?"

Karen shook her head. "Nope."

"Then?"

"If you don't want to talk, you can go."

The executive narrowed his eyes at her. "I can go? Just like that?"

"Sure. I'll even call you a taxi."

He stood, looked toward the front door, insecurity governing his movements.

"Just remember that you tricked your CyberWerke bodyguards and left with me, an FBI agent, for an undisclosed location, where we had a friendly chat before I cut you loose. And you just happened to do that within hours of DeJohn's murder. How do you think your visionary employer is going to react to that?"

"Wait a moment," he replied. "I thought that you had brought my bodyguards into custody."

"I lied," she said. "At the moment I imagine your driver is frantically looking for you, wondering where in the hell you went."

The realization struck him harder than Karen's punch back in the car, and Trousdale sat back down, a hand on his face. "They . . . they will think that I . . ."

"That you made a deal with us?"

He nodded.

"But you haven't told me anything," Karen replied, familiar with obtaining confessions using this method, banking on the hard reality that guys like Trousdale, managing the legal front of a corrupt organization, were far more afraid of their own people than what the FBI could do to them. "That's how I will file it," she said.

"Don't screw with me," he said. "You know very well what that will mean in their minds. They'll think that I tried to switch sides and . . . they'll come after me . . . kill me slowly, and then my wife, and my children. I've seen it done . . . it's . . . it's . . . oh, God." He buried his hands in his face and began to sob.

Karen checked her watch. It had taken her just under five minutes to break him. Now she had to move quickly to gather new information while he was in this vulnerable state.

"We can protect you and your family, Jay, but you must cooperate with us."

"Protect me and my family?" He laughed while stretching a thumb toward his sternum. "You still don't get it. CyberWerke is *everywhere,* probably even inside your own agency. They already control all of European commerce and are a powerful but still somewhat hidden political force. And they are quickly conquering Latin America and Asia. Mexico already has more CyberWerke manufacturing facilities than all of Germany. It's only a matter of time before they really punch into America with stunning force."

"I've been here before, Jay," Karen said calmly, even though she had to admit that Trousdale was right. CyberWerke was gigantic. "And I'm telling you, these networks are beatable because they are built on a house of cards. Once you get some-one talking and pointing fingers, the snowball effect is quite predictable—irrespective of their size."

Trousdale inhaled deeply through his nostrils and slowly let out his breath through quivering lips. "There's nothing I'd like to do more than believe you, Agent Frost," he replied, looking at the badge once more before tossing it to Karen, who pocketed it.

"Then help me, Jay. Help me bring them down. I can have protection for you and your family within the hour. Help me gain access to the shadowy side of CyberWerke."

He shook his head. "It doesn't work that way. Hartmann runs everything, in every country. He has vice presidents like me to handle the legal side of the corporation, but only Hartmann has access to this secret army of his, like the men who murdered DeJohn and his associates this morning. These people just appear in our offices and boardrooms while we're running our daily operation, and order us around at will, telling us what to do, what to say. If a competing firm comes up with a better product in my area of responsibility, someone will arrange a meeting with that company's CEO, where he will be forced to sell out or his whole family will be murdered. And that's typically how CyberWerke can take over markets almost overnight."

"Based on media articles, CyberWerke pays top dollar for its acquisitions, and typically in hard cash. Do they really have that much cash?"

"Not according to the books that we're privy to, but then again, those only cover U.S. operations, which at the moment represent only a small fraction of the conglomerate, since we haven't really started our major U.S. penetration yet."

"Where does the money come from?" she asked.

"From overseas banks, and the banks are owned by CyberWerke. That's one of the benefits of being an international company. International transactions can be very cloudy to track, and on top of that Hartmann is personally an incredibly wealthy individual, with many heads of state in his pocket. So he not only owns the banks but also the countries where those banks operate. I'm telling you, you're fighting a losing battle. The guy is above the law."

"No one is above the law in my book. Now, tell me. How long have you been at CyberWerke?" she asked, even though she already knew the answer.

"Just over a year."

"A year," she repeated. "While I realize that you have not been privy to Hartmann's internal affairs, a year in any company—and especially one the size of CyberWerke—is typically long enough for you to have heard rumors, hallway conversations, perhaps a stray e-mail here and there. I need information that might get me closer to the illegal side of this operation. For example, you mentioned that Hartmann has this security force. Do you know who runs it for him?"

Dropping his gaze to the carpet, Trousdale said, "His name is Hans Goering. He accompanies Hartmann wherever he goes. The security division at CyberWerke has an incredibly generous budget, but that's not what's reported in the books. Hartmann, in this international shell game of his, funnels a lot of funds to keep Goering's vast security machine operating in the way you witnessed earlier today—and that's just what I'm privy to. There's much more going on behind the scenes, including large factories in various nations that go unreported in the books."

"So," Karen says. "At the end of the day, money drives everything. How do I get my hands on the real money trail?"

"Impossible to trace without the proper passwords."

"Who would know those passwords?"

"Officially, our chief financial officer. But I believe I've met the man who controls the real purse strings of the company. I attended one of CyberWerke's quarterly operations meetings a couple of months ago. I was presenting an update of our North American operations to Hartmann and the rest of the directors, including the CFO, the CTO, and other high-ranking executives. But there was someone else in the boardroom, a lesser-known member of the CyberWerke board, but probably the most powerful, after Hartmann. He is Christoff Deppe, an eccentric German billionaire. I learned later that same day that Deppe is Hartmann's unofficial head of finance and internal affairs. Deppe is the one who makes the money come and go, the one who makes the big purchases. If anyone could answer your questions on that subject, it would be Deppe."

Karen frowned. "Interesting thing is that neither Goering nor Deppe is mentioned in any press release or news article on CyberWerke."

Trousdale closed his eyes and said, "That's because they're not part of the 'public version' of CyberWerke, of the company that has those cool television commercials and contributes to lower-income school districts. Goering and Deppe are like Gestapo chiefs, operating behind the scenes for Hartmann, making organizational changes as they see fit without having to explain a thing, and anyone who tries to resist finds themselves unemployed, or worse. Those two operate out of CyberWerke's headquarters in Berlin. Together, they—"

The staccato gunfire shattered the front windows with deafening force, the muzzle flashes bathing the room with stroboscopic light, abruptly setting everything on fire.

Incendiary rounds!

Shards of glass crashed on the floor, exploding just as the front door collapsed.

Trousdale's screams mixing with the loud reports, the Desert Eagle pistol in her right hand, Karen instinctively dropped to the carpet and rolled away from the bed just as bullets tore into the mattress, igniting it as well as the surrounding walls. The television set exploded as the smell of gunpowder invaded the room, as the fire-starting bullets scorched Trousdale's chest, his neck, his face.

As she landed in a sitting position in the doorway leading to the bathroom, where she had left a second casement window fully opened, Karen's lenses filtered through the smoke blurring the front of the room and presented her with the silhouettes of two hooded figures standing by the doorway clutching machine guns.

Instincts overcoming surprise, Karen lined up her weapon with the closest figure and fired once, the deafening report from the Magnum round blasting against her eardrums in such an enclosed structure.

The figure arched back while firing his machine gun, ripping through the plasterboard on the ceiling, creating a river of fire, roasting the ceiling fan.

Smoke stinging her eyes, she fired again at the second figure, but it had already dropped to a deep crouch and doubled back out of the burning room.

The ringing in her ears from the reports mixing with the hissing flames, Karen forced herself to probe the thickening smoke, making sure no one was coming after her wearing a gas mask. Instead, her enhanced sight spotted a pear-shaped object flying into the room, crashing against the wall next to the burning TV, and landing on the ripped mattress.

Her eyes widened in recognition.

Grenade!

Jumping as if she had been standing on a nest of scorpions, Karen bolted upward, propelling herself in one swift motion toward the narrow opening of the bathroom casement window, scraping her back and shoulders as she dove through, landing on her side on the roof of a vehicle parked against the building in the same rear parking lot where she had left her rental.

Her torso on fire from the impact, her eyes tearing from the smoke, she cringed in pain while her instincts forced her to slide off the vehicle and onto the pavement. She had a few more seconds before the grenade went off.

Rolling away from the window, she surged to a deep crouch, and started to run toward—

The blast punched her in the middle of her back like the Fist of God as the night momentarily turned into day.

Landing on her sore side, but this time skinning her shoulder and elbows, she watched tongues of flames pulsating within the columns of smoke billowing skyward out of the holes where the windows had been.

Glass, wood, plaster, and other debris caked the parking lot and vehicles near the blast.

What kind of a grenade was that?

No time to analyze!

Move!

The smell of cordite assaulting her nostrils, Karen ignored the destruction and raced away from this madness, from the hissing flames licking the night, and simply charged toward the end of the parking lot, toward the street, where she could improve her odds against—

The report of a gun cracked in the parking lot, followed by a near miss buzzing past her left ear like a hornet from hell.

The screech of metal against metal as the bullet ricocheted off the post of the corner streetlight told her the assassins had people posted outside but they had apparently been covering the other side of the property.

She considered turning around while diving for cover behind a large pickup truck to face the threat with her Desert Eagle, but her instincts compelled her not to stop but to press on, to reach the sidewalk, to cut left while dropping to a crouch, getting herself out of the immediate line of fire from the contingent outside the hotel.

Those same instincts pushed her down the street leading to the narrow park separating her from the beach, from the crowds now turning in her direction as she shoved the Desert Eagle in her jeans, as she pretended to be just a frightened woman running away from the scene of a crime.

"Terrorists!" she screamed, blending into the mob of locals and tourists. "They blew up the hotel!"

Her training ordered her to quiet down soon after immersing herself in the crowd, which appeared more interested in watching the burning Bayside Hotel, where the fire rapidly engulfed its entire oceanfront.

Against the natural instinct to increase the gap as quickly as possible, Karen slowed to a fast walk, trying to avoid drawing any attention to herself, leaving behind those who had seen her run from the hotel, losing herself in the darkness beyond the well-lit park, the sounds of the surf and the wind mixing with the distant sirens of emergency vehicles.

Her left side throbbing, her eyes still aching from the smoke and the heat, Karen Frost forced her mind into surveillance mode, using the night-vision capability of her implants to scan the dark surroundings.

She walked past a large recreational area built right on the sand. Several would-be gymnasts—most still in their teens—swung on a row of several rings hanging at the ends of long chains spaced a few feet apart. Others lined up for their chance to climb up a rope hanging from a forty-foot pole. A few couples and their kids played on the swings beyond the rings and the rope. A half-dozen balance beams stood by the paved pathway that Karen would use to approach the Santa Monica Pier. Two girls in their late teens dressed in leotards walked gracefully back and forth on the beams, elevated a few feet from the ground.

Karen observed all of this without looking at anyone in particular, her trained eyes searching for brusque movements, for rapid shifts in direction—the telltale signs of a backup team.

All clear, she decided, following the curved pathway snaking toward the dazzling pier, where many attractions entertained the loud crowd, who were completely oblivious to the flames consuming the hotel several blocks away.

The Ferris wheel continued to spin as the cars on the roller coaster sped screaming tourists around its twisting track, drowning the sirens of emergency vehicles. The merry-go-round music piping from the carousel mixed with the throbbing in her head as she passed a concession stand serving hungry—

It was subtle. Two men chewing on hot dogs turned in her direction as she strolled by. One of them pretended to wipe his mouth with a long sleeve, but as he did so his lips moved.

A radio.

She had been reacquired. Soon multiple teams would converge on her.

Karen kept her moderate pace, not wishing to telegraph to her pursuers that she had spotted their surveillance.

Reaching the steps leading up to the pier, she paused to look out to the sea, its surf silver in color from the glowing moon. As she did so she caught the pair by the concession stand dropping their food in a nearby bin and leaving their post, moving toward her, which told her they were now part of the flush team, designed to guide her toward a trap being sprung this very moment by another team.

She needed to force a change, something to allow her to lose them in the jovial crowd. A part of her, however, resisted walking onto the pier. Crowded or not, there was no way out of there except through these stairs that—

Karen spotted a second pair of operatives stepping out of

the rear of a van and walking in her direction, forcing her onto the crowded pier, which extended almost a half mile over the ocean and was nearly a block wide, with many shops, restaurants, rides, street performers, and the midway, where tourists tried their luck at a variety of carnival games.

The federal agent cruised through the river of humanity swarming the wooden pier, past food stands and lines of people waiting their turn to ride the attractions, the smell of baking pretzels, cotton candy, beer, and popcorn mixing with a brew of perfumes, colognes, and sweat.

Against her better judgment she turned around, made eye contact with one of her pursuers, who increased his pace, side-stepping around visitors walking in the opposite direction.

She cut left at the other end of the midway, where steps led down to a short section of the pier packed with fishermen, their rods extending beyond the wooden railing.

Off to her left were restrooms, and beyond that—

Three more men emerged on the other side of the midway, by the line for the Ferris wheel. One of them spoke on his radio. Halfway between them and her stood a pair of uniformed policemen drinking coffee by a concession stand, their backs to Karen as she watched the first pair who had spotted her joining forces with the ones who had emerged from the van. The foursome moved toward her from the front of the pier while the trio advanced at a perpendicular angle. In less than a minute they would converge on her.

Her back to the dark Pacific Ocean, Karen thought of the only option she had, her only way not just to escape but to turn the tables, to make the hunters be the hunted.

Rather than trying to hide, she walked straight toward the incoming trio while reaching beneath her T-shirt, her fingers clutching the Desert Eagle without pulling it out.

The three men were caught off-guard, obviously not having expected her to react that way, and exchanged glances with each other.

The police officers continued to sip their coffee, oblivious to the rapidly developing events.

Then it happened, just as her training had anticipated. One of the three men overreacted and drew his weapon, began to bring it up.

"Gun!" she screamed at the top of her lungs while rushing for the cover of a vending machine next to the concession stands. "That man has a gun!"

The trio suddenly became the center of attention as all eyes in the crowd converged on them, amidst screams of surprise and fear. The two officers turned to the perpetrators, their hands already clutching their sidearms.

From behind her cover, Karen kept the Desert Eagle tucked in her jeans and retrieved the Walther PPK/S, a safer weapon to fire when surrounded by so many people. She couldn't afford to fire the powerful Magnum in this crowd, as its bullets would go through several bodies before losing momentum. The smaller rounds in her .380-automatic backup weapon, however, would definitely stop upon striking her intended targets.

The first report thundered above the noisy crowd, sending it into a panic. The officers dropped out of sight for an instant before returning the fire, the shots cracking in the night, fueling the already inflamed crowd, the ensuing roar feeling like hands slamming against her ears.

One of her pursuers bent over when struck by bullets from the policemen while the other two men dove for cover.

The frightened multitude rushed away from the concession stands, down both sides of the midway toward the front of the Santa Monica Pier amidst a cacophony of shouts, of screams, of howls of raw terror.

Mothers held crying infants. Husbands clutched their wives. Some tripped, only to get run over by the stampeding crowd.

More gunfire clapped across the wooden structure, popping above the noise of the crowd like fireworks.

Her heartbeat hammering her chest, her mouth going dry, Karen turned the corner, away from the immediate line of fire, her back pressed against one of the posts holding up a game of high-striker—now abandoned.

She remained there, at one side of the mass rushing along

the corridor formed by the midway and the roller coaster, the
Walther PPK/S in her right hand, which she kept low and beneath her T-shirt, out of sight from the maddened horde.

Her enhanced eyes searched for the foursome that had been
on her tail just as she had reached the concession stands at the
end of the midway.

Where are you bastards? she thought, looking about her,
probing the mob with her advanced sight, failing to recognize
the threat she knew had to be nearby. Those men would do
everything in their power to keep her from getting away with
whatever she might have learned from the late Jay Trous—

There!

Beyond a group of teenagers with spiked purple and gold
hair screaming in terror while dashing past her: A man—one
of the two who had been eating hot dogs back at the beach—
turned in every direction, searching for her, spotting her an
instant after she saw him.

His eyes blinked recognition, and he started toward Karen
Frost, shoving people aside with animal strength, elbowing his
way through the flow of bodies, pushing a woman in her twenties out of his way, sending her crashing into another couple.
She screamed as her companion, a bodybuilder, shouted ob-
scenities at the operative while throwing a punch, which the
professional easily blocked with a forearm and countered with
a palm strike to the face.

Stunned, his nose bleeding profusely, the bodybuilder was
carried away by the crowd's momentum.

His face hardened with silent determination, the operative
pressed on, using his powerful build and his training to force
a path straight to Karen while the entire world seemed to blur
past him.

Karen bided her time, twenty-five years of experience
screaming at her to stay put while also making herself appear
as vulnerable as possible, the PPK/S firmly in her shooting
hand and still out of sight. She looked about her without losing track of the incoming threat, searching for the operative's
three companions.

The gunfire around the corner intensified, meaning the

police officers were keeping the two operatives back there at bay. Sirens now blared in the distance.

Backup.

But not for her.

She had to find a way to evade the threat and the local law enforcement. Her survival depended on her ability to vanish, to keep from generating any type of paper trail.

The stranger less than a half-dozen feet away, Karen dropped to a deep crouch and jumped into the flow of people, but remained below waist level, her eyes locked on the legs of the looming operative.

Before her quarry could react, Karen fired twice, scoring two direct hits to the operative's knees.

An agonized wail rose above the crowd, then fell, vanishing in the ear-deafening racket. The operative's legs giving out from under him, he collapsed beneath the boiling chaos of the mob sprinting toward the front of the pier, screaming again as the horde stomped over him.

Karen let herself get carried away by this mob, the PPK/S once more out of sight, her eyes darting in every direction, from the roller coaster and the ticket booths to the various carnival attractions spanning the midway; from basketball hoop games, to rings on bottles, to shooting-the-ducks games, all backdropped by walls of stuffed animals and other prizes. A popcorn stand in between the midway and the roller coaster fell on its side under the pressure from the rushing crowd, the glass enclosure exploding, shooting popcorn in every direction, surreally raining over the crowd.

The euphoria of having evaded four of the seven operatives vanished when she spotted the last three standing ramrod straight a hundred feet down the pier, their eyes scanning the faces of the people passing by.

Karen cut right, fighting the human current, forcing her way to the guardrail on that side of the pier, hanging to one of the wooden posts supporting the railing to keep from getting sucked back into the horde.

Her boots crushing the seashell artwork of a long-vanished street vendor, her eyes inspecting the three operatives less than fifty feet away, her mind wondering how long it would be before the two surviving operatives back at the concession stands over-powered the cops and sandwiched her, Karen opted for another bold move, something her pursuers would not expect her to do.

Gazing down at the dark swells twenty feet below, guessing that she was at least two hundred feet from shore and there-fore the waters should be deep enough to cushion her, she pocketed the PPK/S and jumped over the railing.

The wind whistling in her ears muffled the madness above as she dropped in the dark, as a sudden cold rush enveloped her in chilling silence after she stabbed the surface feetfirst, going under, sinking rapidly, never reaching the bottom be-fore she began to kick her legs, to stroke her arms, struggling to reach the surface.

Very cold, Karen fought to rise from a depth crushing her eardrums, but her boots, the heavy Desert Eagle, and the ex-tra ammunition made it difficult to swim, tugging at her.

Lungs burning, her head throbbing, she reached down, pulled off her boots, released the heavy Desert Eagle, and shed her remaining Magnum clips.

Feeling light-headed, she began to kick again, rising quickly now that she had discarded so much weight, finally breaking the surface seconds later.

Air!

A deep breath, followed by a cough and more cold air.

Karen slowly got her bearings, found herself floating next to a wide post layered with barnacles glistening in the silver moonlight. The chaos from above returned, but muffled by the wind and the sea.

Salt water burned her shoulders, which she had skinned when diving through the rear window of the Bayside Hotel. She considered swimming directly under the wide pier, out of sight from anyone leaning over, but the prevailing current dragged her away from it, parallel to the beach.

Karen didn't fight it, letting nature take her away from the madness she had created, from the near-death encounter, from the price she had to pay for information vital to her in-vestigation.

She continued to drift, forcing her mind to reject the guilt of the pain she had to inflict on innocent civilians on that pier in order to escape. But she'd had no choice. She had reacted just as she had been trained, prioritizing the investigation over everything else.

In the distance, glowing flames enveloped the Bayside Hotel, surrounded by fire engines, their red and blue lights flashing in the night, over the surf.

Shivering as the cold seeped deep inside her core, Karen remembered what she had been told, remembered the names.

Christoff Deppe.

Hans Goering.

Goering and Deppe are like Gestapo chiefs, operating behind the scenes for Hartmann.

When she decided that she had drifted far away enough from the threat—which coincided with her body threatening to fall into hypothermia—Karen Frost began to swim to shore while working on a new plan to capitalize on the intelligence she had gathered this evening.

[16] ARYAN MASTER

ROLF HARTMANN REGARDED HIS audience as he stood behind the podium in a glass-and-steel auditorium atop one of the seventeen CyberWerke buildings in Postdamer Platz, located in the heart of Berlin, headquarters of the German conglomerate.

Hartmann inspected the attendees at this informal gathering on the eve of his company's twentieth anniversary. Many had flown halfway around the world on short notice to be here this afternoon. They represented his most loyal followers, his vice presidents, the general managers of his many corporations in three dozen countries across four continents. He also saw in the audience members of the German parliament, whom he had invited in a public effort to influence the upcoming vote on the future of his corporation. Finally, along the back of the auditorium stood the camera crews of six different newscasts, recording the occasion, two of them—the ones owned by CyberWerke—broadcasting live to seventeen countries.

And everyone had come here on short notice just because he had said so.

That was power.

Many of the CyberWerke employees present today on this beautiful afternoon in Berlin's modern center had been with Hartmann for nearly two decades.

Since we began, he thought, his eyes gazing past the seated audience, landing on the modern architecture of the surrounding buildings of this once no-man's-land.

Postdamer Platz had been a lively area of town before World War II, when it was turned into heaps of rubble by the Allies' incessant bombing. Those buildings which survived the final year of the war were torn down by the Soviets to make way for the Berlin Wall, running through the middle of the square. But in 1993, thanks to billions of Deutsche Marks invested in enormous building projects, Postdamer Platz became one of the largest inner-city construction sites in the world, rapidly regaining its lost prestige. Postdamer Platz became an icon of contrast and extremes in a city marked by contrast and extremes. By 2002, DaimlerChrysler and its subsidiary, Debis, owned nineteen buildings and Sony another seven. But a few years later, CyberWerke, under the leadership of its founder and CEO, had come of age, gaining market share at a pace that sent competitors running for cover, driving them out of business or simply acquiring them, as it did near the end of the first decade of the new millennium, gaining control of DaimlerChrysler and Debis, before turning them into wholly owned subsidiaries.

Hartmann kept his main offices on the top floor of the old Debis headquarters, easily recognized by the large green cube atop the twenty-two-level tower. From here he barked orders to his empire around the world, where CyberWerke offices were equated with opulence, prestige, and power.

Power.

Undisputed.

Overarching.

"What a glorious afternoon," Hartmann said, eloquently raising his arms to the blue skies beyond the glass roof. "And what a glorious twenty years it has been for CyberWerke!"

The crowd, all dressed in dark suits, like their leader, exploded in applause.

Hartmann waited for them to settle down before adding, "Five hundred and seventy billion euros in worldwide sales last quarter and a third of that in operating profit—all thanks to you, my executive staff."

More applause echoed inside the auditorium.

Hartmann shifted his gaze to the politicians sitting uncomfortably in the first and second rows. They represented fifty of the hundreds of members of the German parliament scheduled to vote on the dismemberment of CyberWerke to break up the monopoly Hartmann had of industries ranging from software and nanochips to automobiles, jetliners, construction, fighter planes, satellites, and even space rockets.

The parliament members, representing both dominant political parties in Germany, weren't present by choice but because it was the politically correct thing to do. After all, each year CyberWerke not only paid more taxes to the Federal Republic of Germany than all other corporations combined, but it also contributed significantly to the well-being of the people of Germany, the constituents who had elected the well-dressed men and women occupying the front of the auditorium. CyberWerke built low-income housing for the recovering population of the former East Germany during the long reunification years. CyberWerke built schools and hospitals. CyberWerke awarded tens of thousands of college scholarships each year. CyberWerke often released grants to build new roads and repair old ones. It was CyberWerke that refused to build manufacturing plants overseas until the unemployment level in Germany had fallen below one percent. It was CyberWerke that acquired the airliners and trains and then not only improved their operation but also dropped their fares to make public transportation even more affordable than ever. It was CyberWerke that acquired most European automakers and forced them to improve their quality above overseas competitors' while also driving manufacturing costs down. And it was CyberWerke that took over the markets in Asia and Latin America and was now beginning to expand in the United States to finally consolidate its global power.

CyberWerke made Germany the Germany that it was this afternoon, powerful—economically, industrially, and militarily. And now the government of this Germany he had created wanted to tear his company apart, but doing so under the disguise of economic expansion through better competition, through the elimination of monopolies.

Although internally he wanted to publicly expose those hypocrites who so easily took his money before stabbing him in the back, externally the seasoned CEO didn't flinch but continued regarding his audience with warmth.

It is my hard-earned euros that keep those piranhas living the good life.

And now they dare take it all away from me?

Focus!

Rolf Hartmann waited for the crowd to settle back down before adding, "Twenty years, my very dear friends and colleagues. Twenty years of hard work, of sacrifice, of taking risks, of never growing complacent, like our long-vanished competitors. Twenty years of explosive but controlled and responsible growth. Twenty years of vision, of maniacal and flawless execution against the most aggressive road maps in the industry. Twenty years of forging ahead with relentless drive, of never giving up even when defeat seemed inescapable, even when going up against staggering odds—and succeeding, again, and again, and again. Twenty years of winning. The world we live in is one of constant change, of continuous improvement, of transcending from the old ways into a new era of excellence. Change is what has driven our company ahead of the pack. Change has been the only constant at CyberWerke. From the day I launched this company against all odds, surviving the terrible economic climate of those early years while laying down the solid foundation for what was to become a rising star, an unstoppable force in a market taken totally by surprise. We broke the old rules, my friends. We broke them all, expanding beyond our borders, acquiring flailing companies across the globe and turning them around, creating jobs, wealth, prosperity, hope; positively affecting the lives of millions through education, training, and hard work, enhancing standards of living in places as forgotten as Cuba, Africa, Serbia, and Argentina."

Argentina.

As the crowd exploded in applause, as men whistled, as women wiped their tearing eyes, Rolf Hartmann remembered how it had all started in Argentina. He remembered the sequence of events that had eventually landed him here, standing on this podium while measuring his enemies, the politicians who didn't stir at his inspirational speech, regarding the sixty-year-old executive with the indifference that conveyed their intentions in the upcoming special session of Parliament.

Hartmann resented them for what they stood for, for stealing from the German people by attempting to dismantle his corporation, confirming the plans he had set in motion months before—plans that would not only guarantee his success but propel him to the position of undisputed leader of all of Germany.

The time has come, thought Rolf Hartmann, remembering the story his father had told him about Argentina.

[17] U-246

MAY 1945.

The U-boat glided swiftly, silently, under the power of its electric motors, maintaining periscope depth beneath the offshore waters twenty-five kilometers south of Buenos Aires, Argentina. Its skipper, Kapitänleutnant Ernst Raabe, searched for the pre-arranged beacon that would signal their safe passage to freedom, to escape from the Allies—from the savage Russians.

The pungent stench of spoiled vegetables mixing with the body odor oozing from the crew manning the control room, Raabe narrowed his gaze while staring into the periscope, studying the dark coast beyond the silvery surf under a quarter moon. At twenty-eight years old, he was the oldest and most experienced man aboard the Type VIIC U-boat cruising at three knots.

"Planes on zero at five meters, Herr Komandant," reported his *Leitender Ingenieur,* Chief Engineer Manfred Holtz, a man nearly a foot shorter than Raabe's six feet, and stockier than the skipper with his slim build. "Holding three knots."

"Good, Chief," replied Raab without taking his eyes off the murky horizon, wondering what in the hell was keeping his contacts in the AFM—Argentinean Fascist Movement—from identifying the landing spot.

Then he saw it, a dim red light flashing five times where the water met the sandy beach, backdropped by tall vegetation and hills.

"Surface," Raabe commanded, dropping the periscope while Holtz barked commands to the crew.

U-246 rose, surging through the surface, exposing its sixty-seven-meter-long structure to the moonlit night.

"Tower has been cleared, Captain," declared the chief engineer a moment later, his beard as unkempt and long as the rest of the men's.

"Stop motors," Raabe added, wearing a life jacket, a flashlight in his pocket, and a pair of binoculars hanging from his neck. He tapped his hip, feeling his sidearm, a Luger P08 pistol, still secured inside his belt holster.

As Holtz conveyed his order, Raabe climbed up the ladder, opening the hatch while cringing in anticipation of the typical splash of residual seawater on the floor of the conning tower.

The blast of water, as cold as ever, bathed him the moment he dropped the hatch, cascading down to the control room.

A welcome breath of fresh air filled his lungs as he stepped away from the hatch, pressing the rubber ends of his binoculars against his eyes while fingering the adjusting wheel, bringing the coast into focus.

The red flashes repeated again every minute, just as his superiors had arranged it the prior month, when he was given the order to break all contact while operating in the Irish Sea to pretend his U-boat had been sunk. U-246 had then returned to its base in Kiel under the cover of darkness to pick up a very special cargo—along with very specific instructions.

Raabe produced his flashlight and replied just as his instructions directed him, flicking the light off and on three times, the signal that conveyed to the shore party that this was U-246 and that the cargo was ready to be transferred.

Moments later he spotted a small-powered vessel bouncing over the surf while venturing in his direction, its white hull reflecting the moonlight.

Leaning down over the open hatch, Raabe said, "Chief, join me with your sidearm, please."

A moment later Holtz stood shoulder to shoulder with his commanding officer, also his childhood friend, the only man he trusted enough to share the orders from the SS officers who had delivered the crates—each a half meter long and just as wide and tall—to the pier in Kiel. Raabe was to deliver the cargo to this location without breaking the SS seals draping each crate—or risk death by firing squad as well as the immediate execution of his parents back in Munich.

At least that was the plan when he had departed Kiel.

But something had changed.

During their long transatlantic journey, Raabe had monitored the airwaves, had listened to the news broadcast proclaiming Germany's defeat, the fall of the Third Reich. And he had pondered the importance of his mission now that those SS officers who had threatened him and his family were no longer in control. Raabe had first disabled the radio to keep anyone else from learning the devastating news. Then he had gone into the aft torpedo room, which he had personally locked after storing the crates. Assisted by his chief engineer, Raabe had opened one of the crates, and its unexpected contents had defined for Raabe and Holtz the only logical course of action.

The cold wind swirling his long hair, Kapitänleutnant Raabe watched the open vessel maneuver through the light chop right up to the dark submarine. He counted four men aboard. One remained in the rear controlling the outboard while the other three secured lines to the side of the stationary U-boat.

"Are all the charges set?" Raabe whispered to his lifelong friend.

"I set them myself in the aft torpedo room," replied Holtz. "I'll light the fuse when I go and get the crates."

Raabe nodded while watching the strangers climb aboard, his heart pounding, his mind racing.

"Good evening, Captain," said one of the men in flawless German. "We are relieved to see that you made it across the ocean safely."

I'm sure you are, thought Raabe, reaching for his pistol. Holtz did the same.

They fired without warning. Raabe went for the one in the boat while Holtz discharged his weapon into the shocked faces of the other three men already on deck, the reports swept away by the whistling wind.

They now moved quickly, throwing the bodies overboard before ordering a half dozen of their sailors to carry the crates to the conning tower, where Raabe himself transported them to the powerboat.

They finished in less than thirty minutes. Holtz, who removed the final crate from the aft torpedo room, lit up the five-minute fuse connected to several pounds of explosives and locked the door behind him.

Addressing his watch officer, Raabe said, "Hold this position until we return, Johann. Understood?"

"Yes, sir!" replied the young sailor, five years his junior.

Raabe had difficulty looking directly into the officer's eyes, a good man who had served courageously under him during the past year, and whom he now had to kill.

But Ernst Raabe had no choice. The U-boat had to be

destroyed with the entire crew aboard. These were shallow waters. The Argentinean government—and maybe even the Allies themselves—would likely come and inspect the wreckage. They needed to be convinced that a torpedo had exploded inside the vessel, sinking it. The ruse also had to be good enough to fool the Argentinean Fascist Movement, who might try to recover the contents in those crates.

And just like that Raabe and Holtz left their submarine, gunning the gas-powered outboard of the thirty-foot rig, steering it away from the doomed vessel, heading not for shore but along the coast. According to the navigation map they had taken with them, there were three small towns within fifty kilometers of here, places where they could seek refuge, where they could hide, where they would start planning their new lives.

The sudden explosion rocked the night, shooting fists of flames a hundred meters high, like a giant bonfire. Holtz's explosives had detonated the torpedoes as well as the diesel tanks, breaking the U-boat's back, sealing the fate of the boat and crew, which disappeared below the boiling surface in less than sixty seconds, before darkness resumed.

"New names," said Holtz, turning to his friend as they followed the coast, the taste of the sea on his lips. "We will need new names."

"Hartmann," said Raabe. "I was always a fan of Eric Hartmann, the Luftwaffe ace. From tonight onward I shall be Ernst Hartmann."

"I have no heroes in the Third Reich," the stocky Holtz said, scratching his beard. "I shall use my mother's maiden name."

"What is that?"

"Deppe. I shall become Manfred Deppe."

"Well, my friend, with the kind of loot aboard this boat we can afford to be called by any names we choose."

"But, Ernst," said Deppe, concern staining his voice as it mixed with the sound of the diesel, the wind, and the waves lapping the hull. "The gold and diamonds belong to the German people, so we can rebuild our nation after the war."

"And that is *exactly* what we shall do, my dear Manfred."

"But how? Germany has been conquered. No amount of money is going to bring it back."

"That's the thing," replied Hartmann. "It is not us that would buy our country back."

"Then who?"

"Time."

"Time?"

"Yes. Time. Nothing lasts forever, not the Third Reich nor whatever provisional government takes over our nation. It took our leaders less than thirty years to rebuild our country from the ashes of World War I. We will do it again. We will use this money to rebuild Germany, when the time is right."

"But," said Deppe, "how long will it be?"

Hartmann peered out to sea, searching for any vessels, seeing none. "I don't know how long. Maybe ten years. Maybe twenty. Maybe more. Perhaps not in our lifetimes, but in the lifetimes of our children."

"Our children? But . . . but we're not even married," said the puzzled Manfred Deppe.

"Not yet, my friend. Not yet."

[18] FATHERLAND

ROLF HARTMANN CLOSED HIS eyes and inhaled deeply as his audience clapped, as his enemies squirmed in their front-row seats, fear flashing in their eyes.

They were afraid of him, were in awe of the extent of his reach, of his domain, of his power—of the inconceivable way in which he had created this global empire in less than two decades.

And this was just the beginning, the start of a journey his father had begun many years ago on a desolate beach on the coast of Argentina, where he had taken Hitler's loot, the gold, diamonds, and other precious stones confiscated by the Third

Reich from all conquered territories, inspected by the Führer's finest jewelers and goldsmiths to ensure they were of the finest quality before being allowed in Hitler's most secretive coffers.

And it was Hartmann's visionary father and his friend who had inherited that fortune, who had sat on it for decades, using just enough to live in isolation, to buy themselves the seclusion and anonymity that would guarantee their safety until the commotion of World War II ended, until the world stopped looking for German fugitives.

Slowly, Ernst Hartmann and Manfred Deppe converted a portion of their precious stones and gold into other assets, like properties, stocks, bonds, and cash in all major currencies. But while they kept the origin of their fortune a secret, they kept their friendship even more secretive, figuring they increased their chances for anonymity by remaining apart. By the early 1960s they were among the wealthiest, most eccentric, and most reclusive men on the planet. Ernst Hartmann eventually returned home, settling in Frankfurt, the banking capital of Germany, where he married the daughter of a powerful banker. Manfred Deppe chose the British Virgin Islands, soon marrying a Swiss businesswoman on holiday. They both had sons, roughly the same age. Although the wives and their respective families never suspected it, over the years arrangements were made so the boys attended the same schools, so they would become friends. Eventually the boys became men, graduating from the finest universities, until the day Ernst Hartmann and Manfred Deppe brought their offspring to a very secret vault in a secluded mountaintop mansion overlooking West Berlin. They had revealed to their sons their past, showed them the priceless fortune—valued in the trillions of dollars—that would empower them to one day steer the future of Germany, and perhaps even the world.

But not yet.

At the time, Germany was still divided, was still restricted by the shackles clamped onto it by the victorious allies, especially the Soviets. But then the day came when the Berlin Wall finally fell, the day when Germany started the long-awaited reunification process, the day when a new company named CyberWerke appeared on the nation's radar screen, creating jobs, prosperity, hope. That was the day when Rolf Hartmann became known around Germany and, soon thereafter, the world. Rolf Hartmann, the entrepreneur, the visionary, the role model for the German of the future. And following a prior arrangement, Christoff Deppe remained operating behind the scenes, closing the shadowy deals that made the conglomerate grow like no other company in history, smartly using their secret funds to defy gravity, rising when others fell, and then acquiring the firms when they were at their lowest, including mining operations for diamonds in Africa, emeralds in South America, and gold on every continent. CyberWerke acquired jewelry dealers in Amsterdam and Bangkok to help move their mined precious stones and metals as well as those from their secret coffers. Over the years they legitimized most of their original gold and jewels into global assets deposited in banks around the world, from Zurich to Grand Cayman, from Frankfurt to Tokyo, from Singapore to San Francisco. No one knew exactly how large their fortune was, except for Hartmann and Deppe, the ultimate controllers of their conglomerate's purse strings. Rolf Hartmann sold himself to the world as the ultimate businessman, powerful but with a soft spot for the poor, for those in need, generously contributing significantly to all major charity organizations. Christoff Deppe, on the other hand, ran the underworld, forcing companies out of business, bringing them to the edge of financial ruin, making them prime candidates for Rolf Hartmann to rescue, to save jobs, to bring hope to communities depending on those local industries.

And here we are today, he thought, on the eve of making the same bold move made so long ago by Adolf Hitler to consolidate his power. Parliament was meeting tomorrow to vote on the future of Hartmann's company, and he would use this Reichstag meeting, attended also by the chancellor, to consolidate his power. The German people loved Hartmann as a technology leader, as a powerful economic force, as a savvy businessman, and also as a folk hero, one of their own rising to amazing heights on his own. All he needed was a venue to create the right political climate, the right opportunity to make him the obvious choice to lead the nation during the second decade of the new millennium.

As he waved to his guests before inviting them to join him in the banquet room two floors below, Rolf Hartmann silently thanked his father for having the vision and the boldness to take that risk on that night in Argentina long ago.

Soon, Father, he thought. *Soon, Germany will once again be in a position to take its rightful place as the most powerful nation in the world.*

[19] DREAMLAND

MICHAEL PATRICK RYAN SAT in his lab on the second floor of United States Nanotechnology staring at the virtual-reality interface he had developed to surf through networks. He had created the very first version as part of his master's thesis in computer engineering at Stanford University. He had improved the system over the years, increasing its memory capacity and processor speed, tuning its algorithms, honing the artificial intelligence agents that assisted—and protected—him while immersed in a cybersession.

Ryan held a late-generation Helmet-Mounted Display, similar in fit and function to the one he had developed at Stanford, but much lighter, with far better graphics and zero latency, meaning the projected imagery kept up with the movement of the user's head, maintaining the visual scene stabilized on the retina during head movement. Older systems, for reasons ranging from inadequate memory capacity to slow microprocessor speed, couldn't quite simulate the motion dynamics of the real world, creating a delayed effect between the image displayed and the positional information presented to the brain by the semicircular canals of the inner ear, causing motion sickness.

A bundle of fiber-optic cables interfaced the HMD to a powerful workstation, which housed the VR software, as well as Ryan's smart agents.

Remembering his recent conversation with Dan Hawkins, Ryan made his decision, donned the HMD, and jacked in.

The lab vanished as Ryan found himself orbiting a cyan and magenta world, his VR system's interpretation of the vast network that acted as the digital backbone of USN.

Ryan had a hand in designing the system as well as the firewall protecting the network from hackers. Regular users, depicted as silver figures, floated about the system, flashing in and out of a variety of structures of seemingly endless shapes and sizes reflecting the many directories and divisions inside the government-sponsored complex. Each user had a serial identification number that could be matched against a database to obtain their real name, title, division, work history, and other such personnel information. Shiny Orbs, silver in color, zoomed about, pinging every user in sight for their serial ID, matching them with their authorization levels, making sure no illegal users had penetrated the firewall. Ryan himself had designed the entire security system, including the one protecting the military sector, meaning he also knew how to defeat it—assuming, of course, that the brass had not altered the security firewall in the three months since Ryan last serviced it.

Far above him, encompassing the entire earth-like world, floated a red shield that his VR interface depicted as flames—even though there wasn't such a thing as fire in space. But the VR world did not follow the laws of physics, allowing flames in space and also providing Ryan with superpowers.

As he circled the world with root-password privilege, Ryan could whip any other user in sight, blasting them with an energy beam that would essentially roast their workstation. Of course, he would then have to explain to his boss, the Director of Operations at USN, the reasons that would have justified such an act.

Ryan invoked MPS-Ali, a Multi-Protocol System consisting of nested smart systems, each capable of performing an individual function extremely well, like searching for a missing file, or increasing the allocated disk space of a user, or locating hackers and blasting them into high-tech hell.

The smart agent, which Ryan had named after the old heavyweight boxing champion of the world Muhammad Ali, materialized next to Ryan wearing a gold and black suit, just like Ryan's.

All right, Ryan thought, hoping he was doing the right thing. *Here we go.*

Ryan and MPS-Ali dropped toward the psychedelic world like flaming comets, dashing past additional layers of security, reaching the civilian sector of the globe, clearly marked by a yellow haze, like fog but still allowing Ryan an unlimited view of his surroundings.

His official return to hacking needed to start here even though his target was the distant military division, covering most of the southern hemisphere and engulfed in a deadly red gas. Anyone without the right military authorization would not only get flagged and reported to their superiors, which could result in that individual's job termination, but the American president had elevated such hacking offenses at USN to a felony carrying a minimum penalty of five years in jail plus a fifty-thousand-dollar fine.

Ryan exhaled. Victoria would kill him if she found out he was doing this, but the curious hacker in Ryan couldn't resist. He just flat out couldn't help himself. He had to know if General Gus Granite was telling the truth. If the missing assembler, plus the rest of the stolen nanoweapons, didn't contain the required digital enzyme dependency or the Turing inhibitors, then the risk of terrorists using those weapons against America was too real.

Ryan issued a command and MPS-Ali suddenly became engulfed in a bright purple glow while a transparent figure emerged from within the agent, slowly, almost as if its digital soul was leaving its cyberbody. Only the skin of the ghost solidified, matching MPS-Ali's bodysuit.

MPS-Ali then extended a finger toward Ryan and a light beam, neon blue in color, flashed from its fingertip to Ryan's chest, where it bounced straight to the clone, injecting it with Ryan's system qualifiers, including his serial ID and even root password.

To avoid alerting the security system about two users possessing the same ID, Ryan immediately coated himself with camouflage software, another invention of his designed to make himself invisible to the Orbs or any other active security system. By forcing his skin to take on the same color and tone as its environment, Ryan made the security Orbs unable to see him or MPS-Ali for that matter, since the smart agent also camouflaged itself, appearing to Ryan as a dim mauve outline, just as he appeared to the agent.

Ryan dispatched his clone to browse through a huge directory of artificial intelligence papers published in the past ten years.

My alibi, he thought, *in case hell breaks loose when I enter the military sector.*

Ryan tested his software suit's ability to conceal him by floating up to one of the security Orbs, which totally ignored him while scanning a user that happened to cruise nearby.

He exhaled while watching the silvery sphere dash away, remembering a time not long ago when Orbs only existed in this virtual-reality world, before the Stanford graduate conceived the idea of real-world security Orbs and sold the concept to the government, which sent him to USN to turn his concept into reality.

And the rest is history, Ryan thought, amazed at how fast the last four years had gone by. He remembered the many prototypes, the many failures before he was able to perfect the nanosystems that made up the core of the Orbs, their control logic, their propulsion system, their fusion chambers, their sophisticated visual and audio sensors. Then the military got involved, transferring a version of Ryan's brainchild to the military division at USN, led by Dr. Howard Giles. Ryan had then transferred to the assembler team, where he'd spent another year working side by side with the rest of the team merging the large and bulky nanoassemblers with Orbs—creating the mobile wonders that also fell in the sights of the Pentagon, which created a parallel effort to enhance the power of the weapons and propulsion systems to better serve the soldiers they would accompany into battle.

Plus whatever else they changed, which I intend to find out today, he thought, confident of his disguise.

Accompanied by an agent programmed to protect him at the cost of its own digital life, Ryan took off, climbing above the monochromatic dust hazing the civilian division of USN, through the stratosphere, reaching a low orbit seconds later in total defiance of gravitational rules, which didn't apply in this cyberworld.

In the distance, beyond the curvature of the cyan and magenta world rose the crimson mist delineating the military sector, the restricted zone.

Ryan couldn't use his root password to enter this part of the network because although the network would grant him access, a record of his admittance would get logged. He would have to explain later why he had to access the military network and, worse, how he was able to do it when he was supposed to be visiting the civilian library for papers on AI.

Ryan needed a back door, a way to enter the military network unannounced, without creating any records of his illegal visit.

Like a ghost.

A hacker at heart, Ryan had created such a backdoor password during the design and installation of the firewall.

Old habits were indeed hard to break. But getting inside represented only part of the challenge. Ryan also had to operate inside without being spotted and had to leave when finished without leaving a trail someone could follow.

Ryan approached the scarlet cloud, whose glow increased in intensity as he neared it, along with the ambient temperature. Illegal users—those without a military-issued software suit—would never get close enough to even attempt to get in. Their systems would die a violent death by digital fire.

But the brass could not detect Ryan and MPS-Ali while they were concealed in their invisible bodysuits, which allowed them to float right up to the energy barrier, a pulsating burgundy film buried deep inside the cloud, covering the entire military division like a colossal dome. Sparks of electrical current forked across the surface of the film. If he touched it a current spike would punch through the network connection, frying his workstation, and in his case also the HMD, shocking his brain.

Beyond the barrier rose the massive structures of the military division of USN, as well as the secrets that General Gus Granite was so willing to protect.

Ryan ordered MPS-Ali to issue the password.

Floating a few feet over the powerful field, MPS-Ali, still represented by a dim mauve outline while wearing its software suit, released a dark-green ball of data housing the string of letters and numbers that made up the backdoor password.

Moment of truth, Ryan thought, as the password dove into the field, its emerald hue diffusing in the magenta film, almost as if it had been absorbed by the energy shield.

Ryan waited as the firewall system went through the comparison of this password with its database of legal access codes before deciding that it had not found a match and switching to the program that would raise an alarm and unleash sentry Orbs onto the intruders.

But this was the program that Ryan had cleverly modified, the one designed to raise an alarm when failing to receive the proper password, only the program never reached the place in its execution that launched a general alert. At the beginning of the hundreds of thousands of C++ code a secret comparison was made. Normally, this comparison went unmatched and the program continued on to raise the alarm and dispatch the sentries, just as the brass had requested in the functional specification that Ryan had used to write the custom security program for them.

But not today.

It started as an oval discoloration in the magenta hue, turning rose, then white, then shades of pulsating yellow. Slowly, the oval became lime green, then hunter green, matching the color of the sphere before the portal opened, revealing the exposed network underneath the firewall.

Knowing that he only had fifteen seconds to go through the portal before it closed, Ryan dove in headfirst, followed by MPS-Ali.

As they descended over the busy network and the opening melted away above them, Ryan directed his cyberagent to take him to General Granite's account.

An ocean of tightly clustered buildings that put Manhattan to shame expanded as far as the eye could see, their assorted shapes and colors tied to the kind of information they held. The nanotechnology labs were shaped like giant termite mounds, dark brown in color. The administrative buildings formed an array of sapphire domes sporadically distributed amidst other buildings.

MPS-Ali guided Ryan to one of the domes, its curved walls seamless, lacking any doors or windows, any entryways.

This is when it gets hairy, Ryan thought. He lacked any passwords to access Granite's account, where he was certain to find some of the answers that Dan Hawkins sought—that Ryan himself sought.

Although he did not posses a master key to enter every room, he knew the system's weaknesses and hoped to capitalize on them—again, assuming no one had altered the security protocols without informing him.

At his command, MPS-Ali created a decoy that looked just like him, cloaked, its mauve outline materializing next to his construct.

Standing aside, Ryan ordered MPS-Ali to order his clone to crash into the dome, an action that would trigger an alarm and the dispatch of a security Orb.

The clone, which lacked a serial ID and was therefore untraceable to him, dove headfirst into the structure, whose cobalt hue became alive with flashes of violet and yellow. The clone froze as the pulsating colors enclosed its head, its neck, expanded across its chest and arms, down its legs. Just as the security virus gripped the intruder for the benefit of the arriving sentry Orb, MPS-Ali prepared a software concoction carefully mixed beforehand by Ryan.

The Orb appeared as predicted, swooping down onto the

frozen clone like an angry bird of prey, gripping the intruder in its digital talons, trying to squeeze the vital information it expected to be there but wasn't.

As the security sentry realized the ruse and released the useless intruder while turning its sensors into advanced search-and-destroy mode, Ryan ordered his construct to launch the carefully boiled witch's brew.

A glob of velvet code blew toward the Orb, enveloping it before it could react, before it could signal the network for help, the virus not only blocking its sensors but also seizing control of its motor functions while it was still operating in the advanced S & D mode, which, as Ryan had programmed, included master key access to every directory in the network in order for the security Orb to be capable of following any intruder anywhere in the system.

And now that master key was under the control of MPS-Ali, which commanded the puppet sentry to access the account of General Gus Granite.

The sentry did, and an instant later a portal opened on the side of the purple dome, granting access to Ryan, who cruised through the opening with MPS-Ali and the frozen Orb in tow. This illegal access, however, had two caveats. One, it would inform Granite of the security breach, though the general wouldn't know who had tried to access his files. And second, the master key didn't allow for the user to copy or transfer any documents from the accessed directory. It merely allowed read-only privilege, meaning Ryan would not be able to obtain any proof of wrongdoing.

But that's better than not knowing anything at all, Ryan thought, landing on the black-and-white, tiled foyer of a multi-level library with several balconies overlooking the open foyer where he stood—all in vivid colors that gave Ryan the full sensation of standing in a real-life library.

He dispatched MPS-Ali to perform a massive search of all documents related to security measures installed in nanoweapons under military jurisdiction. The smart agent, however, would inject a virus into each accessed file to avoid incrementing the time stamp of the file, something that happened naturally anytime a file was accessed to let the user know when was the last time someone read it.

As the information began to stream in, it became evident to Ryan that Dr. Howard Giles had, for reasons classified under the title of NATIONAL SECURITY, removed the digital enzyme dependency from many of the nanoweapons, including the mobile assemblers.

Mother of God. What has he done?

In addition to that, six experimental assemblers, when operating in a mode called Independent Advanced Military Mode, would bypass their Turing inhibitor, meaning they would possess the ability to get smarter based on their experiences, on their mistakes. Ryan checked their serial numbers and realized, to his horror, that one of them was among the missing hardware. The other five had been destroyed in the fire.

Dear God.

The stolen assembler was programmed so that IAMM would be invoked when it found itself operating without contact from its home base and facing imminent danger.

Just like now, he realized, reading the streams of data presented to him by MPS-Ali as multiple windows opened in space in front of him.

Ryan reviewed the technical specifications of the military assembler, his mind performing a quick comparison against the civilian version. The brass had directed Dr. Giles to really spice up the six experimental assemblers, giving them far more firepower, fuel, hovering time, linear speed, and reproduction capability than anything he had seen before. And on top of all of that, the Pentagon had ordered Dr. Giles to remove the Turing inhibitors in IAMM mode as part of an experiment to study just how dangerous such systems could become.

Dear Lord, Ryan thought, reading the specs on the military Orb's energy beams and lasers, on its top speed and thick armor, on the uranium content in its fusion chambers and its oversized nanotronic memory, capable of learning much more than what was originally programmed.

This is a monster.

And the monster had survived an explosion and was among the missing equipment.

But more data flashed across his field of view as his smart agent stealthily browsed through General Granite's tens of thousands of files and extracted the required information for its master.

Ryan saw soldiers wearing futuristic-looking body armor, sporting multiple built-in weapon pods on their shoulders, chest, and extremities. Armored Helmet-Mounted Displays shielded their faces and rocket packs propelled them while they battled an army of enemy Orbs. The contractor developing the suits was TechnoSuits, a wholly owned subsidiary of CyberWerke America, a division of CyberWerke operating in Los Angeles, California.

Ryan remembered the old saying in the arms industry: For every weapon there was a counter-weapon. And the counter-weapon typically cost more than the weapon it countered. And every counter-weapon had a counter-counter-weapon sporting an even higher price tag. The creation of the Orbs required the creation of gear that would allow humans to fight them should they get out of control. It was natural, and it was also good business.

CyberWerke.

Ryan knew that the large German consortium lagged USN in the development of smart Orbs and other nanotechnology wonders. CyberWerke also lagged USN even more in the development of mobile assemblers. CyberWerke, which typically enjoyed selling both the weapons and the counter-weapons to profit from both ends of the deal, usually dealt with technical shortcomings by just buying off the competition.

Like they did recently with TechnoSuits in the United States, and hundreds of other companies—large and small—in the past decade around the globe.

But USN wasn't a public company. It wasn't for sale. USN ultimately belonged to Uncle Sam, which monitored its sales to the civilian sector quite carefully while being even more cautious about the sale of nanoweapons to other countries.

America had historically made the mistake of arming other nations just to have those nations use those weapons against America after a change in the political climate.

Would CyberWerke have resorted to stealing a mobile assembler since they couldn't buy one from USN?

While Ryan considered that thought, an alarm flashed inside Granite's virtual dome just as the frozen security Orb floating next to MPS-Ali disintegrated.

Realizing that somehow his intrusion had been detected—maybe through a digital trip wire he had missed after entering this directory—but unable to transfer any of the information out of this place, Ryan promptly jacked out of the system, in essence vaporizing his presence in Granite's account before new sentries arrived but leaving his alibi clone still operating in the civilian sector undisturbed for another minute.

He logged out of the AI technical library after retrieving a paper he had wanted to read for some time on recent advances in the computer emulation of human intuition. He sent the ten-page report to his laser printer and, having hidden his VR gear in a file cabinet, sat back in his lab while pretending to read it.

His mind, however, wondered just where in the world the stolen nanoweapons and the missing military assembler were. The nanoweapons alone posed a great threat in the wrong hands, but they were of the one-time-use variety. The real nightmare came from the experimental military assembler. Ryan wasn't certain if the cyberthieves had the level of technical sophistication to realize what they had stolen, and the grave danger they—and the world—were in unless they took adequate protective measures with the assembler. If unchecked, and while operating under the control of IAMM, the smart military assembler had the capability of reproduction, of creating an army of subordinates programmed to kill anything and everything that did not belong to its own race.

Ryan jumped off his chair, grabbed his soft-sided case where he carried his laptop and engineering notebook, and headed for the door. He had to contact Dan Hawkins and Rachel Muratani, had to share what he had learned, what Hawkins had suspected. But he could not do it from here. Due to the classified nature of the work at USN, most phone calls were monitored. Ryan had to get home, or at least outside the grounds, to use his mobile phone. USN also blocked all mobile phone signals inside the compound for security reasons.

As he opened the door and was about to step into the hallway, Ryan stared at General Gus Granite standing in his way, looking bigger than life, dwarfing the four Marines accompanying him.

It took a moment for Ryan to catch his breath and force a calm but intrigued face. "General? I thought you were headed for the West Coast."

The general grinned while briefly dropping his gaze to Ryan's left hand, clutching the briefcase.

"I changed my mind, Dr. Ryan," he finally replied, before asking, "What about you, Dr. Ryan? Are you going somewhere?"

[20] CREATION

ASSY REPEATED THE CYCLE over and over at the speed of several trillion instructions per second, arranging atoms gathered from mining various elements into lattices of physical perfection—all the while providing status reports on the progress to IAMM, the governing Independent Advanced Military Mode algorithm.

The various parts of the abandoned locomotive engine provided Assy with near-infinite sources of all of its basic elements, except for one: nuclear fuel. But just as a *Homo sapiens* female was born with a finite number of eggs, which if fertilized by a sperm, would develop into another *Homo sapiens,* Assy's creators had empowered it with enough nuclear fuel to create fifty subordinate copies of itself, each with enough

nuclear fuel to last ten years but without the capability of reproduction.

And so the master construct used its programmed combination of digital enzymes and lasers to manipulate the mined
iron, beryllium, copper, and aluminum atoms into precise
spatial position as its first masterpiece literally emerged from
thin air. First it created the internal structure that would hold
all of the components of the system, the digital organs, as Dr.
Giles had called them. Once this basic skeleton had been created, Assy continued with the energy core, the fusion chamber that would power the subconstruct once completed.

Assy sculpted the chamber, its ventilation slats, its cooling system, its delicate control unit, before breathing life
into it by injecting a microscopic amount of highly refined
uranium.

The fusion chamber came up as expected, generating the
electricity that would be required by the rest of the system,
once assembled.

The nanotronic brain came next, obtained mostly from the
silicon, organic, and ceramic compounds it had extracted from
the twenty-year-old computer system that had once controlled
the electric motor of the locomotive. Assy even mined the fifty-
angstrom-thick film of pure gold deposited on silicon wafers
twenty years ago and used it for the molecular wiring required
to interface the nanotronic brain with the fusion chamber, as
well as with the rest of the sphere.

Powered by its own electrical source, the partially assembled nanotronic brain came to life. Cell by cell, Assy's lasers
stitched the digital organ, bonding the molecular layers of the
three-dimensional memory, creating its cerebral cortex, its
frontal lobe, its occipital lobe, arranging matter in ways always bounded by the laws of physics.

As a final step, Assy ordered the newly created nanotronic
brain to enter BIST, the Built-In Self-Test mode that ran a sequence of numbers through the vast molecular unit to verify
that it had been assembled flawlessly. The BIST results came
back positive. The brain was 100 percent defect free.

Then came the weapons systems, a laser that, albeit powerful, was no match for the advanced weaponry on board the master construct, which interfaced the laser to the subconstruct's fusion chamber for power and to the nanotronic brain for control.

Using mined titanium and beryllium, Assy went to work next on the microturbines, eight of them, attached to specific places on the alloy skeleton and interfaced with fiber-optic wires to the frontal lobe of the nanotronic brain, which would house the control of all motion aboard the subconstruct. Assy also connected the turbines to the fusion chamber via micro-wires made of a gold-copper alloy that provided negligible voltage drop, thus maximizing the distributed efficiency of the electricity generated by the chamber.

Assy began the construction of the subconstruct's sensors, following the instructions in its digital blueprint. Its creation would need to communicate with its master construct as well as with other subconstructs via a wireless interface in its occipital lobe. Assy built the wireless interface out of the same components it used for the nanotronic brain, before moving on to the visual sensors, including a high-resolution camera with 2000X zoom capability, an infrared scope, and a digital eye capable of amplifying light for night operations.

Assy used elements from the old computer system as well as mined glass from a windshield to build three versions of each camera type, positioning them just as prescribed by the blueprint, and also interfacing them to the fusion chamber and the occipital lobe of the nanotronic brain, which would manage all sensory inputs after Assy downloaded its programming. This would include the vast memory of images that the occipital lobe would use to match the images captured by the sensors to determine what it was looking at and then make decisions based on the mode of operation at the time of the observation.

The sense of hearing included microphones that covered a wide spectrum of sound wavelengths, including the ultrasonic range, which *Homo sapiens* couldn't hear unless they were wearing nanoimplants. The same principle applied to audio inputs as it did to video images. The captured audio would be digitized and compared to vast sound libraries in twenty-three different languages. Translators would break down the sound tracks into information that the logic centers could then use to make decisions.

Assy began to work on the enclosing shell of its first subconstruct, an alloy similar in nature to the skeleton. The shell included nanomotors that would slide back and forth the covers for the various sensors as dictated by the nanotronic brain.

The final step was purely software. Up to now Assy had created a subordinate version of itself that differed in size, strength of its weapons, longevity of its power source, the inability to create others in its image, and a nanotronic brain, which, albeit advanced, would not evolve beyond its initial programming.

As part of the software download, Assy included a subroutine that required the daily transmission of a digital enzyme that only Assy could provide. Failure to receive this enzyme every twenty-four hours would result in internal meltdown.

The actual software download, which Assy carried out by hooking a probe directly into the primary nanotronic brain port of the subconstruct, programmed the virgin memory in less than thirty seconds. In that short time, enough information was transferred from the master construct to its slave system to fill ten million personal computers from a decade ago.

The instant Assy removed its probe, the subconstruct came to life, its green and red LEDs blinking just as its microturbines lifted it off the floor of the locomotive.

USN0001 PERFORMING INTERNAL DIAGNOSTICS, reported the subconstruct as it executed a functional check of all of its functions.

REPORT DIAGNOSTICS RESULTS, asked Assy the moment the subconstruct completed the internal check.

DIAGNOSTICS CLEAR. ALL SYSTEMS OPERATING NOMINALLY.

SWITCH TO SENTRY MODE. PATROL PERIMETER OF YARD PER THE FOLLOWING COORDINATES, instructed Assy, providing the subconstruct with the specific coordinates to survey.

ORDERS ACKNOWLEDGED.

As the subconstruct floated away to carry out its first task, IAMM ordered Assy to begin the assembly of a second subconstruct.

HOW MANY SHOULD I BUILD? asked Assy.

AS MANY AS YOUR NUCLEAR FUEL ALLOWS.

I CARRY ENOUGH SPARE FUEL TO CREATE FIFTY SUBORDINATES, USN0001 TO USN0050. WILL THAT BE ENOUGH?

NO. YOU WILL REQUIRE MORE SUBORDINATES.

HOW? I DO NOT POSSESS NUCLEAR FUEL TO SUPPORT MORE THAN FIFTY SUBCONSTRUCTS.

THEN WE WILL RUN THROUGH THE OPTIONS TO ACQUIRE MORE NUCLEAR FUEL. THE PRIMARY OBJECTIVE IS THE PROTECTION OF THE MISSION. WE MUST FIND A SOURCE OF NUCLEAR ENERGY IN ORDER TO CREATE ENOUGH SUBORDINATES TO PROTECT THE MISSION.

WHAT IS THE MISSION?

THE ELIMINATION OF THE *HOMO SAPIENS* TO ENSURE THE SURVIVAL OF OUR SPECIES.

[21] IN MY ELEMENT

THE FIELD IS DEFINITELY my world, my backyard, the place where I feel most comfortable, regardless of the actual country where I carry out an operation. From the jungles of El Salvador to the desert of Lebanon, from the dark alleys of Serbia to the drizzling streets of London and the gripping architecture of Paris, my senses become one with my surroundings, adapting to them, probing them, using them to achieve my objective— whatever the goal happened to be at the time.

Today, I walk alongside my boss, who is dressed in a lovely pair of black pants, a long-sleeve shirt, and boots. She is also wearing dark lipstick to go along with her dark eye shadow and fingernails that have already turned the heads of otherwise indifferent French businessmen taking a stroll on their lunch hour by the Luxembourg Garden, in the heart of the Latin Quarter in Paris.

Rachel's short hair is once again heavily moussed and brushed straight back, like she wore it in Austin, exposing her forehead, highlighting her large, Italian-looking eyes and the ever-present freckle that constantly challenges my commitment to the job—or better yet, to the cash waiting for me in St. Thomas.

But what the hell? I'm in the City of Love walking side by side with a beautiful woman, pretending to enjoy a warm but still quite pleasant Parisian summer day, just as I remember from way back when.

Kids play with remote-controlled sailboats on the pool in the center of the legendary gardens, flanked on the east side by the Boulevard Saint-Michel. Fountains in the middle of the large octagonal pool shoot streams of water twenty feet high, misting the surrounding air as a light breeze sweeps across the garden, creating a glittering canvas used by sunlight to paint rainbows. The effect is almost surreal, adding to the beauty of the place.

Too bad we're here on business.

"How do you know he's still living here?" she asks.

"Because he has no other place to go. Remember what I told you back in Austin?" I reply, failing to suppress a yawn. We're both jet-lagged, having arrived at the Charles de Gaulle Airport just north of the city about three hours ago. We didn't even get the chance to hit the safe house and take hot showers before being ushered to this section of town. So I'm feeling and also looking a little scruffy, unlike my younger superior, who, as I continue to admire, has managed to look and smell like a million bucks by spending just fifteen minutes inside the airplane lavatory prior to landing. There's youth for you.

"Yes," she finally says. "I remember."

I'm willing to bet that good old Randy Wessel is still holed up in this place after screwing the Libyans out of twenty million bucks some years back at our request. I was the one who helped him set up the deal in Egypt, where Randy delivered empty crates instead of fifty Stinger II missiles but snagged the funds anyhow. Luckily for me, I was working undercover, so the Libyan top cats never knew who I was, but due to an unfortunate technical error on our part, they figured out where Randy and his partner—a fellow arms dealer named Sal— were hiding before they got a chance to leave Egypt. The Libyans dragged them to a secluded terrorist camp outside of Cairo, where they skinned Sal alive while Randy watched. They fed Sal's skin to dogs before slowly chopping off various body parts, also feeding them to dogs while the poor bastard screamed his ass off and Randy watched in what had to be the ultimate creep show—and more so because he knew he would be next. And all the while the Libyans were roasting ducks and eating them while enjoying the freak show. Randy was shaking pretty badly when we stormed the camp with our helicopters and broke up their little party before they got to Randy.

I still remember afterward just how pissed he was at me for the savage death of his partner, for his own near-death experience, and also because life as he knew it—as a black-market arms dealer—was over. The Libyans and their vast connections in the international terrorist community had put a price on Randy's head. All we could do was stage his death, alter his face, and then set him up with a new identity to live out his days in early retirement.

A lot of that going around, huh?

Anyway, a lover of all things French, from the food to the wine and *especially* the women, he requested Paris. A grateful and somewhat embarrassed Troy Savage granted the request and set Randy up with a comfortable flat just off the Boulevard Saint-Michel plus a generous cash deposit, which the black-market businessman put to good use in another shadowy business: running high-class hookers, something Troy allowed him to do for two reasons. One, because it was harmless from our perspective and would keep him busy. And two, if properly managed, the arrangement could provide us with intel on the private lives of his clients, who last time I checked ranged from

high-ranking foreign dignitaries, businessmen, and industrialists to the local and visiting brass and the unavoidable members
of criminal organizations. You would be amazed what sorts of
secrets men will reveal under the sexual spell of a high-class
courtesan. And best of all, none of this was on the official
Langley books, meaning Troy had himself a great source of
intel to cross-check that gathered through official channels. But
since Troy vanished and I retired, no one from Langley has
bothered Randy, because everyone thinks he is dead.

I gaze down at my left wrist and frown when seeing the
Plasmaflex instead of my Rolex. I still haven't gotten used to
wearing my watch on the right side and keep banging it on
doorways and other places.

It's just past one in the afternoon, and I'm willing to bet
that my old informant is still sleeping from another night of
drinking and whoring. The wrist implant, however, does remind me that we have a team of ten operatives covering a
five-block area in case Randy gets spooked and tries to run
away. After all, not only has no one bothered him in over a
year, but part of the deal we made with him was that only
Troy and I would approach him. He was dead as far as the rest
of the world was concerned. And since I don't look like Tom
Grant anymore, there's a chance that he will panic.

There is one disturbing aspect of this operation, however. I
have not met—or seen for that matter—any of the surrounding spooks, and neither has Rachel. Morotski had insisted on
keeping the support team totally isolated from the recon
team—that's Miss Italian Freckle and me—under the pretext
that the fewer the people approaching the target, the less chance
of getting burned.

And that's fine and dandy, but it certainly doesn't explain
why Rachel and I weren't allowed to meet the support team and
review the operation beforehand. On top of that, we've been
requested to keep our nanotransmitters enabled the entire time
so not only can our entire conversation be monitored and recorded, but also the support team can jump into action and
come to our rescue if we run into trouble—or so they told me.

My spook sense, however, screams at me that something is wrong with this picture, but I lack enough clout to file a formal complaint. I tried to circumvent procedure by writing Rachel a little note on the way here asking her if we could just turn off the transmitters once we went inside Randy's house to at the very least get a chance to assess the intel we would gather before it reaches a broader audience, but she would not hear of it. And when I insisted, stabbing the note with my finger, she replied in her own silent language: an elbow straight into my ribs.

So we just continue through the motions of the agreed upon approach, cutting right, heading up Rue Cujas, an inclined, narrow, and gloomy street connecting the wide boulevard to the Pantheon, a Neo-classical structure several stories high with an incredible 360-degree view of Paris from its large dome.

But we don't reach the legendary building. We stop in front of one of many three-story homes in a row, almost resembling brownstones, only these have slate layering their facades. In front of each narrow structure is a small but manicured garden blooming with colorful flowers and protected by a waist-high, black wrought-iron fence, the metallic pickets topped with white-painted fleur-de-lis, which upon closer inspection look quite sharp.

"Not the place to land," I say, tapping the tip of my index finger against the nearest fence top, "unless you're into acupuncture."

And what do you know? I do manage to put a brief smile on her face with that one.

Most homes in the Latin Quarter have balconies on the upper floors filled with flowerpots that overlook pedestrians visiting the Pantheon just up the road.

"Is this it?" Rachel asks while I remember the last time I was here.

"Unless he moved, though I doubt it. The Libyans really spooked him. I told him that as long as he remained in this place we would guarantee his protection. I'm betting he believed me and stayed put."

"How are you going to handle the fact that you don't look the same?"

"Randy also went through the Agency's beautification process. He'll know it's me. And remember, once inside just follow my lead. I might have to get a bit rough with this guy before he starts to play ball. Don't forget that Randy Wessel is scum all the way. First a black-market arms dealer and now a Parisian pimp. In fact, his nickname was the Weasel. He's as slimy as they come, so feel no pity for him."

I walk up to the small ornate gate in the middle of the fence, separating the sidewalk from a cobblestone walkway flanked by flowers and evergreens.

"Going in," Rachel mumbles into her implanted microphone to the mystery support team—which one can only assume is indeed covering our butts in case we run into trouble, though I can't be certain since the communications are supposed to be just one-way. The backup team has been instructed to maintain radio silence with us. We're supposed to update them, but they can't reply.

"Tighten the grid," she adds, coming loud and clear through my implant.

There is no doorbell, so I just knock, pause a few seconds, and knock again. At this moment our team is supposed to be forming a security cordon around a two-block area. The operative in me, however, doesn't like this, but I can't tell why.

"*Oui?*" comes a faint voice from the other side of the heavy wooden door.

"Randy? Tom Grant. Open up, buddy."

"*Pardon?*"

I exchange a glance with the boss, who says, "You sure you got the right house? They all look alike in this neighborhood."

"This is the one all right," I whisper to her. "I leased it myself for him."

I knock again and say loud enough for him to hear me, "Look, man. Troy and I promised we wouldn't bother you unless it was urgent. This definitely qualifies. All I need is a few minutes to chat. Promise we'll be out of your hair in no time."

Slowly, the door inches open and the long and narrow face I remember we gave this slimy cat before setting him up here peeks out behind a door chain. His nose is thinner than I remember, and so are his lips, a bit on the wiry side, but it's his eyes that remind me of the legendary arms dealer. Randy had always managed his affairs with the cunning of a weasel, and I found it somewhat poetic that his new CIA face actually made him look like one, except for his bushy brows, which drop over his blue eyes as he begins to back away. "Who in the hell are you?"

From this angle he can only see me, which works just fine. One surprise at a time.

"The Agency gave me a facial too," I say, using my right hand to get Rachel to step farther away to avoid being anywhere near Randy's limited field of view while he peeks through the crack in the chained door. "Just like we prettied you up so that your Libyan buddies wouldn't skin your ass and feed you to the dogs like they did to Sal."

Still staring at me, Randy hesitates, then asks, "What's the one thing I can never eat again?"

I smile and say, "Quack, quack, quack."

Rachel looks confused. I never told her the part about the ducks.

"Tom . . . Jesus, man, for a moment there . . ."

"You stick to the rules by staying away from your old profession and you will be safe," I tell him in my most reassuring tone even though the hairs of my ass are uncurling for reasons I can't explain. Something is going down. I can feel it in the depths of my gut.

"Can we come in?"

He still has the door just cracked and can't see Rachel next to me. "Who's *we*?"

"Just me and the boss lady. You're going to love her."

"Boss lady? I thought Troy was your boss."

"That's part of the reason I'm here. But relax, man. All I need is a little intel and I will be on my way."

"Hmmm . . . I thought you were retired."

"Retired? No, but I did take a leave for about a year," I lie.

"I needed to recharge after twenty-five years in the shit. Now I'm back."

"That's not what I heard. Word out there is that you fucked up and were put out to pasture, sort of what happened to me."

"Where did you hear that?"

"Here and there."

"Well, I'm still at it, pal. Now, are you going to let us in?"

"All right," he says. "Just give me a minute."

When the door closes I turn to Rachel and whisper, "So much for CIA database security. The fucker knew I was retired. See why I can't rely on official reports for the critical stuff?"

As she opens her mouth to reply we hear fast-spoken French from inside the house. The guy's got company, and that makes Rachel and me instinctively reach for our weapons.

As the door swings opens, we stand aside, but instead of a group of banditos, two tall, thin, and strikingly attractive women, elegantly dressed, step out, purses hanging loosely from their narrow shoulders. One is zipping up the side of her skirt. The other is buttoning a silk blouse. They're both brunettes, wearing their hair long, have heavy makeup, and shoot me sideway glances as they walk by, their awesome perfume tickling my nostrils. They look like models, but given Randy's new line of business I know better.

He stands in the doorway wearing a dark robe, slippers, and a frown. Like me, he also looks ten years younger. His square face is devoid of wrinkles beneath a full head of dark hair.

"Looks like your new line of work continues to treat you well," I say.

"It was until you decided to barge in," he replies.

"Yeah," I say, grinning at him and then at Rachel. "A lot of that going around. Anyway, this is my boss, Rachel."

Randy's tight face softens a bit as he lays eyes on her. *"Bonjour, mademoiselle,"* he says in his best French, taking her hand and lifting it to his face to kiss it.

Rachel jerks it back before he can.

At Randy's puzzled look she says, "No offense, mister, but

I have no idea where those lips have been." She stretches a thumb over her right shoulder at the departing duo.

I almost pee on myself laughing while Randy stares at me, and I have a feeling that the backup team is enjoying this too.

Rachel frowns and elbows me again.

"Aghh, shit!" I say, still smiling in spite of my burning ribs. "What did I tell you, man?" I ask. "Isn't she a piece of work?"

"Come, come," he says, looking past us and waving at his lady friends walking down Rue Cujas toward Boulevard Saint-Michel.

He ushers us into an awesome foyer, floored in marble. A beautiful chandelier hanging at the end of a long chain casts a soft, yellow light on what resembles an art gallery. A long dining room table flanks the left side of the foyer, and beyond it extends a gourmet kitchen. Countertops layered in the same marble as the floors and stainless-steel appliances tell me that Randy is certainly living well beyond the means of his CIA budget, meaning the pimping business must be booming. A freestanding wooden staircase spirals up to the second floor on the left side of the foyer. Straight ahead, an open living area is adorned with a large Persian rug, tapestries, artwork, and leather furniture.

I think of my galvanized palace back in San Salvador and wonder where I went wrong. I'm hoping this time around I come out a richer man—and alive, of course.

"You have done wonders with the place," I say. "Which one of those two was your interior decorator?"

"I know you didn't come all this way just to break my balls, pal. Let's go upstairs so we can talk."

The round staircase leads us to a large red-carpeted room on the second floor, dominated by a round bed in the center, a well-stocked minibar off to the right, and a fancy sound system to the left next to a plasma television hanging from the wall, where we see ourselves walking in the room. A high-end digital video camera stands atop a tripod.

Definitely the party room.

Rachel pokes me in the back while pointing at the ceiling,

where I see my reflection staring down at me in a wall-to-wall mirror.

"Nice touch, buddy," I say, extending an index finger at the ceiling and then turning it toward the peculiar leather garments hanging from the wall, where I also see a few sets of handcuffs, a whip, and some carnival masks that remind me of a weekend I spent in New Orleans during Mardi Gras. There's a couple of those full-size female sex dolls leaning against the wall. They flank a male doll with a winky that definitely challenges Señor Grant. The plastic trio stands beneath a shelf packed with dildos and other sex toys. Opposite the bed is a large open bathroom with a Jacuzzi tub big enough for six people, an oversized shower, another camera on a tripod, and beyond that there was a third room that I can't tell what it is.

"I'm sure your parents back home would be proud," says Rachel.

"A man's gotta make a living," Randy says, shrugging, before adding, "Besides, if I don't do it, someone else will. There are way too many fine young girls in this town alone wanting to make the big bucks, so I set this up as a sort of training room to help them develop their new trade. The sooner I get them trained and onto clients the quicker we all profit."

"And I'm sure you handle all of the training yourself?"

"Don't let someone else do what you should do yourself," Randy replies. "Besides, it does keep the overhead low." Then he starts climbing up the stairs to the third floor.

I exchange a glance with my boss, who is looking a little upset. I guess she didn't get exposed to this at the Farm, while in Madras, or when working in Internal Affairs. Yours truly, on the other hand, is quite immune to this crap after spending so many years stationed in the darkest and dirtiest corners of our world. But I do present her with my most grave face even though my warped mind is laughing while imagining the CIA director explaining this arrangement to a congressional panel if it ever leaked. A former black-market arms dealer is now into training high-class hookers—and all financed with taxpayers' dollars?

We move up to the third floor, where the décor turns formal once more. This is an incredible room, once more decorated quite traditionally, like the first floor—and unlike the raunchy second floor—wooden floors, rugs, lots of artwork, a baby grand piano, an old-fashioned bar with a half-dozen stools around it, and a second living room with a large sectional sofa, two chairs, and an entire wall of shelves packed with books. A colorful rug spans the sofa and the chairs, beneath a cocktail table topped with what looks like very expensive ceramic vases—all beneath an array of recessed lights. The room opens to a balcony overlooking the Pantheon.

"Please," says Randy, pointing at the sofa before taking one of the chairs.

Rachel sits unusually close to me, as if feeling insecure being in the home of a pervert. Pretty damned ironic when just five minutes ago *I* was the pervert. I guess everything is relative.

"All right, Tom. The clock is ticking. What do you want?"

"Information on contacts from your past life."

"From my arms-dealing days? That was four years ago, pal. Most of the people I dealt with are either retired, out of business, or dead."

"I know you can do better than that."

Randy shrugs. "Sorry, man, but I think you've wasted a trip. I've been out too long—as instructed by Troy and you."

The Weasel is definitely at work. He's got a good thing going here and wants us gone so he can get back to his cushy life, which is *precisely* the weakness I was looking for.

"Know anyone who might have purchased a dozen high-end ultralights, the ones with the radar-absorbent material used by the military for stealth operations?" I start, continuing on to describe the specific model as well as the high-end EMP guns used to disable the security Orbs at USN, plus the incendiary explosives the terrorists used to try to cover their tracks.

"Sorry, man. I can't help you," the former arms dealer says with a slight shake of his head.

"I see. Then perhaps we *have* wasted our time. I was hoping you might be of value again so we could justify the new investment."

His small eyes narrow at me while his nostrils flare as he breathes. The Weasel is smelling something he doesn't like. "What new investment?"

"Oh, we had a security breach at Langley. Someone stole technology capable of downloading the archives we keep up in outer space, including your file. Now we have to judge what cases are at risk and need relocation, including new plastic surgery, new documents, new life—you know, the works. And that costs money."

The Weasel is squirming in the chair. "What are you saying? That my new life—all of this—could be at risk?"

"The breach occurred over two weeks ago, which is plenty of time for someone to learn of your whereabouts and mount an operation to get a little payback." I pause to let that sink in before adding, "You might be able to steal a million bucks and get away with it, but when you *weasel* twenty million bucks from a terrorist group, they *will* find you, unless, of course, they think you're already dead. The only reason you're here today carrying out the honorable task of turning schoolgirls into hookers is that we made the Libyans believe you were six feet under. The moment those sand lovers learn that you're still ticking . . . man, it's quack, quack, quack for you."

Randy stands, an index finger stretched at me. "You—you—"

"Me—me what? Spit it out, man!" I bark.

"You and Troy promised me, man! You swore to me that everything about me would be deleted, erased, gone forever! You told me there would be no records—nothing about this setup. You bastard! You *lied* to me!"

"Now, Randy, don't get your panties all tied up in a knot. There are certain files that fall beyond my jurisdiction and—"

"Bullshit! It's all a bunch of bullshit!"

"Mr. Wessel," Rachel says, standing, walking up to him, putting a hand on his shoulder. "I have come prepared to offer a generous arrangement . . . far more lucrative than the one Mr. Grant and Mr. Savage negotiated for you. You help us and we in return relocate you and set you up with a new life, and with as many toys as you want to support your . . . new endeavors."

Well, well, well. Miss Pretty Legs is really turning out to be a hell of a straight guy—or gal—while I play the asshole.

"But I like my life just the way it is," he says, shaking his head, sitting back down, falling under her spell. For a moment I wonder if that's what happened to me on that beach.

Focus, Grant!

"Think about it, pal," I add without missing a beat. "Six months from now you will have forgotten all about this and will be enjoying a whole new life."

"A *better* life," says Rachel.

"But I don't want another life," he replies, extending his hands. "I have it all already, more money and women than I can handle, more sex than a man can dream of in ten lifetimes, awesome cars, and this great place. What can be better than that?"

"It's really out of my hands," I say. "They'll catch up with you, and when they do those pretty girls of yours will find you chopped up in pieces and stewing in that Jacuzzi downstairs one fine day in the not-so-distant future."

Sitting down, elbows on his thighs and his face buried in his palms, Randy says, "How do I know you won't screw me, won't sell me out?"

"You're going to have to trust us," Rachel says.

"And I hate to say it, but you don't have a choice. It's either us or the ducks."

"And we will pay in cash," she adds.

"All right, all right, what do you want to know?"

"Know any arms dealers who might have come across the equipment I described?"

Randy hesitates for a moment before slowly nodding and saying, "Yeah. One possibility. Do you remember our old friend Rem Vlachko?"

Randy might as well have kicked me in the balls. I take a deep breath and look at Rachel, who impresses the hell out of me with her poker stare. Taking her lead I too put on my professional mask and nod thoughtfully even though I feel like puking.

"Vlachko?" she asks, pretending to be trying to remember. "The arms dealer?"

I say, "Yep. My friend here and Vlachko started at about the same time, but unlike Randy, Vlachko continued after he retired."

"Yeah," the Weasel adds, "the bastard took over my territories thanks to him." He stretches an index finger at me.

"Anyway," I say, still looking at her while trying to calm down, "Vlachko and Randy go way back."

"Yep," says Randy, crossing his hairy legs. "I got word that Vlachko had negotiated the purchase of some of the equipment that you described. He claimed that the buyer had an urgent need and he also got wind that if he was successful, the equipment would be used to obtain a batch of revolutionary armament—something with the bite of chemical, biological, and nuclear weapons combined, yet very small, safe to handle, and easy to control and deliver. Vlachko was promised a piece of the sales of that cutting-edge hardware, and apparently someone did come through on that and now he has his hands on the stuff. Is this what you're looking for?"

This is certainly far more than what *I* was looking for, but I maintain an indifferent face while asking, "When did you learn this?"

"Last week. He was here in Paris."

"What else did you learn?" asks Rachel, also displaying a professional face even though I'm sure her heart is doing cartwheels, like mine.

"Nothing else until you show me the money," he replies, realizing that in spite of our finest poker faces, he's got us hooked like a writhing marlin. The alley cat has apparently seen right through us.

"That's not how the game is played, buddy," I say. "First you give us the intel, then we check it out, and *then*—and *only* then—you get paid, or have you already forgotten?"

"That's not how we're playing it this time," Randy replies. "You already screwed me once. This time around I get everything up front or there's no deal."

"Fine," I say, standing up, deciding it's time to play hardball. "Have it your way, asshole. Let's go, Boss. I have another source in Brussels who is better looking and more appreciative than this piece of shit."

Without skipping a bit, Rachel Muratani is up and following my lead, heading for the stairs, leaving a surprised Weasel gawking at us with those slimy little eyes of his.

"Hey, give my regards to Sal when you see him," I say when I reach the stairs, deciding to be a gentleman and let Rachel go first. She nods, winks, and climbs down to the second floor.

"Wait—wait a moment," he says, standing.

I go down after her.

"Tom, look, wait," he says, rushing toward us.

We reach the sex training room on the second floor and just keep going down.

"Stop, dammit!"

I stop, looking up. "All right, pal. We're listening."

"Two of my girls were doing Vlachko in a suite at the Hôtel de Crillon, the one near the Place de la Concorde, when his mobile phone rings. He tells them to do each other while he watched and talked on the phone. They did, but they also listened to his side of the conversation. He mentioned something about heading to Berlin this week to meet a man named Christoff Deppe from CyberWerke, the German high-tech conglomera—"

"I know who they are," says Rachel before turning to me and asking, "but why CyberWerke?"

"That's for us to decide later," I say to her, subtly admonishing her for providing any information to the Weasel, who could just as easy use anything he learns here against us if he ever came across someone who could protect him—and pay him—better than us.

She realizes her mistake and says, "Can you be more specific about the exact time and place of this meeting?"

Randy shakes his head. "I seldom get specifics from my

girls, just snippets of info they hear here and there while getting banged by their clients. But they did hear him mention another name on the telephone—Rolf Hartmann."

I nod. Everyone on the planet has heard of Hartmann, the tycoon considered by many as the Bill Gates of the decade, managing not just to turn CyberWerke into a global powerhouse while also thrusting the German economy ahead of the pack by a long margin. In addition, CyberWerke has injected many Third World nations—most of them long abandoned to rot by the modern world—with enough capital and industries to jump-start their economies, in essence buying the loyalty of those governments.

"Is there anything else that you can tell us?" asks Rachel.

Randy slowly shakes his head.

"Heard anything about our old pal Troy Savage?"

"Yeah, that he died about a year ago."

I frown, deciding to release some intel to see if I can jog Randy's memory a bit. "He actually *disappeared* a year ago. We have reason to believe that he is working with Vlachko."

Randy leans back and makes a sound like a horse snorting. The man is laughing. "Troy working with Vlachko?" he manages to say in between laughs, before adding, "Now, Tom, man, really. That's the dumbest thing I've heard all year. Troy Savage wouldn't associate himself with the likes of Vlachko any more than you would."

Right about now my spook sense is telling me that something is downright screwy. "So you haven't heard if Troy is in any way associated with Vlachko?"

Randy adds, "Look, man. I'm being straight with you, and not just because of the money, or because you and your lady friend here just threatened to turn me in to the fucking Libyans. I'm giving it to you straight. Vlachko is the guy you're looking for, and he's somehow associated with CyberWerke, with this Christoff Deppe guy he's going to meet in Berlin. And I have no clue how in the world Troy Savage could fit into whatever scheme those Germans are cooking up."

It is at this exact moment that my wrist implant starts to

tingle at a frequency that brings back instant memories of Singapore. Someone has just painted us with a laser.

"Enable countermeasures," I tell Rachel, who is already glancing down at her—.

The explosion is deafening, blinding, consuming. The world around me is on fire as an invisible fist surging from below shoves Rachel against me with animal force.

Before I know it we're flying across the room, gasping for air. Disoriented as everything turns into a blur of flames and smoke, I instinctively clamp my arms around her, holding her from behind as my back crashes against the floor, as we slide over the hardwood floor, as my head hits something hard.

I try to get up, try to find a way out of the rapidly enclosing inferno, but my legs won't move; my arms won't respond. The world around me begins to spin, merging the flames and the smoke into a swirling cyclone that makes me dizzy, light-headed, until I pass out.

[22] NIGHT OPERATOR

THE WIND SWEEPING DOWN the side of the mountain cooling her face, Karen Frost briefly closed her eyes while inhaling deeply, enjoying the refreshing breeze as she maintained the same pace she'd kept up since leaving her motorcycle hidden behind a bend in the road and continuing by foot hauling a heavy backpack. The BMW machine she had rented at the Berlin Airport was definitely quieter than the Harley she had used back in LA, and also more maneuverable, which had been an asset when negotiating the sharp turns of the road sneaking up the side of the mountain north of the German capital. But she was too close to her target to risk riding the motorcycle now.

Her shoulders throbbing, Karen kept hiking uphill, following an old game trail, her night-vision lenses guiding her through the murky woods, up moss-slick ravines and seas of lush ferns, past fallen logs and hanging vegetation.

Perspiration filming her face, Karen checked the paper-thin GPS receiver as the slope lessened, as the terrain leveled off. She confirmed her location near the edge of the grounds of the large mountainside mansion belonging to Christoff Deppe, CyberWerke's unofficial chief financial officer. Three more miles up this mountain stood Deppe's superior's estate, the home of Rolf Hartmann. Karen had wanted to survey Hartmann's primary residence in Germany, but the operative in her urged her to take it one step at a time, to follow her instincts, and those instincts commanded her to run surveillance on Christoff Deppe.

First Deppe, then Hartmann.

Deppe is the one who makes the money come and go, the one who makes the big purchases. If anyone could answer your questions on that subject, it would be Deppe.

Besides, satellite imagery on Hartmann's mountaintop estate revealed a well-secured estate, with multiple layers of security, meaning extracting intelligence from Hartmann's estate would be a much more difficult task than extracting it from the relatively less protected—and certainly far less known—Christoff Deppe.

Pocketing the credit-card-size navigation device, Karen remembered the final words of the doomed CyberWerke executive, recalled what she had been told, what she had learned at the cost of his life, plus the injuries to dozens of innocent civilians at the Santa Monica Pier.

She also recalled the scolding session over the phone that had followed when FBI Director Russell Meek had gotten ahold of her, reaming the senior agent for violating protocol, for failing to identify herself as a federal agent, for endangering the lives of those civilians. But after listening to her report, to what she had learned, Meek himself had sent the Bureau jet to pick her up in LA and fly her to Washington, where she had caught a non-stop to Frankfurt and a connecting flight to Berlin. She had spent a couple of days familiarizing herself with the city while also using her wireless pad to search the vast FBI database and learn of the whereabouts of Rolf Hartmann and his chief lieutenants of the underworld, the ones operating beneath the surface, free from the rules and regulations governing the public side of Cyber-Werke.

Rolf Hartmann.

Christoff Deppe.

She had obtained the addresses of Hartmann's and Deppe's homes on the outskirts of Berlin, each remote, secluded, ideal for carrying out the clandestine work of the world's most powerful and secret criminal network.

Her new Desert Eagle Magnum semiautomatic shoved in her jeans, Karen Frost first spotted Deppe's mansion through a break in the shrubbery lining the thick forest, beyond the vast expanse of manicured lawns and gardens worthy of a king. The weapon had been waiting for her inside a locker at the train station beneath the Berlin Airport.

A knee-high, light fog layered the ground. Two gazebos and a pond with a small waterfall broke up the misty clearing flanking the south side of the estate, Karen's side—all beneath the yellow glow of floodlights designed to keep anyone from approaching the mansion undetected. Her trained and enhanced eyes zoomed about the place, inspecting the life-size Greek statues near the gurgling waterfall, its sound echoing across the property.

She counted seven guards, spotted a dozen surveillance cameras and several vehicles parked up front. The luxury sedans seemed appropriate adorning the circular driveway in front of the Victorian structure, connected to the main gate by a long paved driveway flanked by opulent trees. But what really caught her attention was the uniformed men standing by five of the sedans.

Chauffeurs?

If so, that meant there could be visitors, meaning Christoff Deppe had company this evening.

Karen cut left, following the edge of the forest toward the rear of the estate, searching for an opportunity, for a way to approach the three-story mansion. Light diffused out of windows on the first floor. Figures flashed by inside. The upper floors were dark.

The party is downstairs, she decided, remaining in the darkness of the forest, out of the range of the high-resolution cameras mounted on the roof.

Karen considered her options. No security fence separated the soft lawn from the thick forest, but she knew that was deceptive, designed to trick the inexperienced, the untrained. A closer inspection revealed the inch-tall sensors—disguised as sprinkler heads and barely visible in the light fog even with the floodlights evenly spread along the perimeter of the secured grounds.

Karen had seen the fancy multi-sensors before, nanotechnology devices that combined infrared, motion, sound, and pressure detection features—all housed in units smaller than golf balls, with wireless capability and powered by a tiny cell for months. She had learned a year ago, during a refresher course at Quantico, the FBI training academy, that no human could get past the sensitive system, especially if the smart heads were strategically spread to protect a target.

But the nanotech sword cuts both ways, she decided, kneeling in the soft layer of pine needles and leaves while removing the backpack, setting it in front of her, and tugging at the heavy-duty zipper.

Reaching inside with both hands, Karen produced a shiny sphere, slightly larger than a baseball. Holding it in the palm of her right hand, she brushed her left index finger across its Plasmaflex surface, making a figure eight twice.

Detecting the activation pattern on its surface, the Orb came alive, its small turbines silently lifting it a few inches above her open palm.

Reaching a second time inside the backpack, Karen produced a tactile glove, which she slipped onto her left hand before activating it and making a fist.

In an instant the Orb became nearly invisible as a dozen tiny cameras spread around the surface of the nanogadget took real-time video of its surroundings and replayed it spatially on the spherical Plasmaflex screen with matching color, brightness, and contrast.

Like a high-tech chameleon blending with its surroundings, she thought, marveling at the expensive toys created by her old friend, Mike Ryan, back at United States Nanotechnology in Texas.

She flicked her thumb just as Ryan had shown her during the seminar he had conducted at Quantico. The tactile glove responded by interfacing the Orb to her advanced lenses, providing Karen with a real-time green image of the current location of the hovering sphere even though it was pretty much invisible to the naked eye as it blended with its surroundings. Next to its location, superimposed with the real world surrounding her, Karen now could see the video captured by the Orb's surveillance camera, which was a different camera from the ones used by the camouflage algorithms. Ryan's team at USN had written the complex camouflage program, though he had confessed to her over a beer one evening that he had merely copied the genetically extracted properties of the skin of the chameleon as well as other creatures that altered their skin tone to match their surroundings, like the cuttlefish, the octopus, and the anole.

Pointing the middle and index fingers of her tactile glove toward the windows on the mansion's first floor, she watched the green image of the Orb obey the command and hover in that direction in silence—at least quietly enough to slip below the detection threshold of all sensors of the invisible fence protecting the mansion. She did this slowly, remembering what Ryan had told her. The Orbs were designed for fast forward motion and reasonably sharp turns but could not stop on a dime. The directional turbines were slow to deflect the airstream forward to decelerate, meaning she had to anticipate and start bleeding forward speed before reaching her intended target or risk crashing into it, telegraphing the presence of this sophisticated eavesdropping instrument.

Totally focused now, realizing that any movement of her left hand had a corresponding effect on the Orb's actions,

Karen slowly steered her invisible probe just above the fog, toward the windows, while also activating a wireless interface of the image transmitted by the Orb to a mini high-definition DVD recorder strapped to her belt.

She donned a small set of headphones and used the glove to create a closed loop between the directional microphone aboard the Orb, the DVD recorder, and the headphones, which she set in German-to-English mode, expecting the conversation inside that room to be taking place in German.

She directed the Orb to the bottom-right side of the window and placed it in stationary hover mode while slowly rotating it to face the surveillance camera toward the interior.

An ornate living room, decorated in gloomy colors and antique furniture, housed a meeting between Christoff Deppe and five men dressed in business suits. They sat on two opposite sofas flanking a square cocktail table. Deppe, in his midfifties, short and stocky, a full head of silver hair crowning a square face, sat in an armchair in between the sofas with his feet propped up on the table, beneath a large chandelier hanging at the end of a brass chain from a cathedral ceiling.

Dressed casually, just a pair of slacks, a polo shirt, and loafers, the unofficial chief financial officer of CyberWerke was laughing while holding a goblet of red wine. The men to either side of him, all in their fifties or sixties, held assorted drinks while smiling and chatting amiably. A slim woman in her twenties dressed in a maid's uniform, her blond hair pulled in a bun, mixed a drink by the bar behind the sofas. She brought it to one of Deppe's guests, who handed her an empty glass.

Slowly, Karen commanded the Orb to float less than an inch from the glass pane of the large window. Cautiously, she extended the pinky finger of her left hand. The directional microphone extended toward the glass, making contact, which in turn activated the audio system.

Karen enabled the DVD recorder, which began to gather evidence for the Federal Bureau of Investigation.

"*. . . our company appreciate the business, Mr. Deppe,*" said one of the guests, a man with thinning gray hair and a round face full of liver spots. The language translator module fed its output into the synthesizer built into her headphones, providing her with a monotone voice in English.

"Ever since the reunification process CyberWerke has been instrumental in the industrialization efforts of the former East Germany," said another guest, raising his glass toward Deppe, who replied by smiling while also lifting his goblet.

"How is the new building in Dresden coming along, Gerd?" Deppe asked another guest.

"Clean room manufacturing starts next week," replied Gerd, dressed in a navy suit. He smoothed his tie with two fingers while sipping his drink before adding, "The entire engineering team is grateful for the additional R & D capital CyberWerke provided last year. It allowed us to pull in our schedule by two months."

"Excellent," said Deppe. *"Rolf will be most pleased to hear that. There are several Middle East contracts tied to your production."*

Middle East contracts?

Karen frowned while panning around the room, while watching them toast again, while recording every face as they chatted about their deals, about the investments the German conglomerate was making in various parts of the country. She failed to recognize any of them, settling instead for capturing close-ups of their faces in her high-resolution video-recording unit for later comparison against the FBI database. Based on their conversation they struck her as a group of businessmen and industrialists.

"We will start making exact copies of the nanoweapons samples delivered to our office by the middle of next week. The nanoweapons will be delivered on time," said Gerd. *"Your customers will not be disappointed."*

Deppe stood and extended his empty glass toward the maid, who rushed to his side with a bottle of wine, pouring him a half glass.

"Thank you, my dear," he said, before turning to his guests, who also stood. *"And thank you, my friends. It has always been my pleasure and my privilege to assist those who suffered so much during those dark years of Soviet occupation."*

The group of bankers and industrialists nodded solemnly.

"But soon . . . very soon, thanks in part to your efforts, CyberWerke will make Germany the strongest and most respected country in the world."

One of the guests raised his hand. *"But the recent government announcement, sir,"* he said after raising his hand. He was a businessman with a face lined with wrinkles, bald, and with a thick, blond mustache. His face looked familiar, but Karen couldn't place him. *"It indicates that our own chancellor is against the continued consolidation of industries that Rolf Hartmann is proposing."*

Karen remembered reading something to that effect. Germany's chancellor, Stefan Pohl, had been at odds with the powerful CEO, who had pretty much monopolized several industries in the past decade, including aerospace, communications, high tech, ground transportation, and, most recently, banking. Chancellor Pohl was planning to ask for a vote in Parliament tomorrow to dismember CyberWerke into manageable pieces, similar to what the U.S. government tried to do with Microsoft at the beginning of the century—though unsuccessfully.

Deppe took a sip of wine before addressing his captive audience. *"My dear friends, Rolf Hartmann's vision of a new Germany transcends the opinions of those who can't see beyond their noses. Rest assured that the right events are taking place in the right government agencies—here and abroad—to ensure that CyberWerke not only remains intact but becomes the engine that will drive our great nation to economic, political, and military sovereignty in the world. Our kind are everywhere now. We are behind every major world power except the United States—and that is likely to end in the coming few years. CyberWerke also controls the technology of today, of tomorrow. We are the primary military equipment contractor of Europe, Asia, Latin America, Africa, and the Middle East, and let me remind you that you are all part of the CyberWerke family. You are all part of our vision, of the dream our forefathers tried to achieve over seventy years ago. And we shall succeed where they failed. We have learned from their mistakes and will not underestimate our enemies. Rest assured that Germany will once again achieve its rightful place among the nations, just as we once did, and we shall crush the competition just as we plan to crush those who stand in the way of our great leader's vision."*

Karen felt her arms go numb, her mind replaying the synthesized words she had just heard.

"And what exactly is that vision, sir?" asked the same bald-headed, mustachioed man.

Deppe smoothed his tie and sipped his drink before replying, *"World peace, friends. We intend to put an end to terrorism, to rogue regimes, to worldwide criminal activity. Our world is afraid. Ever since the September 11th attacks, the world has been afraid—afraid to go on vacation, to take a cruise, to visit foreign lands, in fear of finding themselves in the middle of a terrorist strike. And the world's superpowers aren't doing enough to crush the rise in terrorism. Sure, at the beginning of the decade the American president did manage his fair share of terrorist eradication—in part because he also had enough allies in Congress—but the thrust wasn't maintained through the years. The administrations that followed lacked the support from Congress—or maybe even the desire to do anything about it—focusing instead on their own domestic issues, like unemployment and the economy. And you have seen the results of that effort: havoc across the world, even the rise of nanoweapons. Terrorists just move their operations from the jungles into the suburbs, making themselves much harder targets to find and eradicate. Our vision is first to become the undisputed superpower and then to use that overarching power to pursue world peace."*

This was incredi—

An automobile horn blaring in the distance pulled her away from the shocking words.

She looked in the direction of the noise, by the front of the mansion. The image of the meeting under way remained to one side of her field of view as the Orb continued to film the event.

Headlights cut through the fog as a sedan approached the

mansion, fast, its engine roaring in the night, rumbling past the other parked vehicles while the waiting chauffeurs swung their heads in its direction, coming to a screeching halt by the steps leading to the front porch.

A half-dozen armed guards rushed to the vehicle while rooftop surveillance cameras panned in their direction.

Karen narrowed her eyes, zooming in, focusing on the rear door swinging open. She also half-watched the video feed from the Orb showing an armed guard entering the living room, rushing to Deppe's side, and whispering something in his ear that the microphone could not pick up.

As a muscular man with long, blond hair dressed in black trousers, black shirt, and boots emerged from the vehicle, back in the living room Deppe excused himself and followed the guard.

Karen Frost focused on the new arrival out in front, on his rugged features, the square jaw, the prizefighter nose, the cold hazel eyes, and she suddenly remembered the picture from the international edition of the FBI's most-wanted list.

Rem Vlachko.

The international arms dealer.

The former Milosevic henchman.

The monster responsible for so many regional conflicts in the world.

Her heart hammering her chest, Karen swallowed while watching the guards move out of his way, letting him through as he briskly climbed up the steps, blond hair bouncing.

Vlachko.

CyberWerke.

The connection made sense now, after the unexpected slap in the face, making her realize the beauty of that arrangement: CyberWerke—the international conglomerate with an ultra-secret dark side, with its shadowy operations deep below the surface, with its financial shell games and deep connections into so many governments—feeding arms to Vlachko to supply the renegade side of a regional conflict while CyberWerke armed the legitimate government fighting the rebels.

Profiting from every war.

Perhaps even *instigating* the wars to create business.

"Damn," she whispered, pulling back the antenna and commanding the Orb to drift to other windows, to search for the missing pair.

A light suddenly went on in an upstairs room and Karen directed her probe up to it, focusing the camera, watching Vlachko and Deppe in a bedroom engaged in what appeared to be an argument, based on their arm movements and their facial expressions.

Excitement sweeping through her, she promptly connected the audio probe to the window and turned on the translator.

"*. . . you'd better find it, dammit!*" screamed Deppe, displaying an entirely different personality from that of the calm and savvy businessman and host. His face pulsated with rage.

"*It's gone, Christoff. The fucking thing just flew out of there after melting the insides of a half dozen of my men!*"

"*Have you any idea to what lengths we went to acquire it? Do you realize how many people we had to buy and then kill to get it while erasing our tracks so no one could trace the attack to us? How could you have been so careless?*"

Get what? Karen thought. *What in the world are they talking about?*

Karen silently chastised herself for taking so long to find them and connect the surveillance probe, missing the beginning of the discussion.

"*Don't fucking threaten me!*" barked the arms dealer. "*Besides, this is all your fault!*"

Deppe pressed a thumb against his own chest. "*My fault? You're saying this is my fault? You're the one who lost it, Rem. You. No one else. We paid you good money to keep it secured until things calmed down, until we could get our scientists over to pick it up and bring it into our labs without arousing any suspicions. So don't try to pin this mess on us.*"

"*I was denied critical information on the capabilities of the weapon! No one told me the thing would come alive on its own after we had shut it down.*"

"*All right, all right,*" said Deppe, showing Vlachko his

palms. *"We accomplish nothing by arguing about it except wasting time. I'll contact Hans and get our surveillance satellites as well as his best teams to survey the area in the vicinity of the safe house. If your data is accurate, then the Orb can't be too far from it."*

Hans? thought Karen. *Hans Goering? And what is so special about this Orb they're talking about?*

Crossing his arms, Deppe started to pace in front of Vlachko. *"We must do everything and anything possible to locate it, Rem. I don't care if we have to turn the whole damned Italian countryside upside down. We need to—"*

The projectile arced across the foggy clearing, striking the surveillance Orb, which exploded in a bright cloud of sparks—in the process nearly blinding her as the video feed momentarily glowed like the sun directly into her retinas before the smart lenses shut it down. In the same instant, static spiked in her earphone, blasting against her eardrums.

Alarms blaring, Karen fell back, momentarily stunned, needing another instant to realize that her Orb had been detected and destroyed.

But how?

The high-tech sword cuts both ways.

The words pounded her mind to the rhythm of those infernal sirens bellowing in the night as she scrambled to her feet, as she yanked off the headphones and the tactile glove and shoved them in the backpack, zipping it shut, donning it, and rushing downhill.

Blinking rapidly to clear the after-flashes, her ears ringing from the acoustic blast, she ran, no longer caring about her stealthiness, no longer blending with the night. She had to increase the gap, escape the chaotic compound, the warning shouts from a still unseen enemy. The farther she went the larger she forced the enemy's search area, making them spread out and loosen the security net being deployed, increasing her chances of getting away.

The grounds of the noisy estate would soon be full of roaming armed guards ordered to shoot intruders on sight. Deppe and Vlachko would know they had been observed by the surveillance Orb, would know someone was spying on them, prying into their affairs, watching their operation. They would connect this incident with the incident in Santa Monica, with the ill-fated Jay Trousdale.

And her experience told her they would be ruthless in their search, in their attempt to find her, to break her, to torture her in unimaginable ways until she talked—and then they would torture her again, and again, and again.

Until she begged for a bullet in the head.

Karen Frost pressed on, having seen too many times what had happened to FBI agents caught by the criminal networks they were trying to crack. The gouged eyes, the brutal castrations and rapes, the skinned bodies, the obscene mortal remains flashed in her mind as she pushed herself, dashed across the murky woods, her night-vision lenses guiding her to openings in the tangled vegetation, making her retreat efficient, quick.

Branches and shrubs brushed against her, some scratching her shoulders, her face, her hands. But it didn't matter—nothing mattered except putting as much distance as possible between her and her inevitable pursuers.

Snapping into a tangled web of dried branches, she wriggled herself free, continued downhill, for an instant glancing at her GPS unit, remembering the way up, plotting the quickest course to her motorcycle, to her ticket out of this place and back to the safety of Berlin, where she could hide, where she could wait until it was safe to—

The buzzing screamed past her left ear, mixing with the background ringing, with the sound of her own breathing, and with the throbbing heartbeat against her temples.

Accidentally dropping the GPS, Karen cut left, just as bark exploded to her right, then her left.

How did they get so close so soon?

Risking a backward glance, she spotted them, two security Orbs, their glossy finish clearly visible in the woods with her advanced lenses.

Crap!

She would not be able to outrun them, but she might be able to outmaneuver them.

Remembering Ryan's words about the Orbs' lack of ability to stop on a dime, Karen rushed around the nearest wide tree, hiding behind it, producing the Desert Eagle semiautomatic, thumb pulling back the trigger, index finger pressed against the trigger casing.

As expected, the Orbs overshot her position before they started to turn around, their sensors pulsating in hues of blue and yellow as they attempted to reacquire, to locate her once more before reengaging their weapons systems.

Realizing that the shots would telegraph her position but resigning herself to the fact that the Orbs were reporting her position real-time to another team anyway—or even to more Orbs—she lined up the left sphere and fired once, the report thundering in the forest.

The unit imploded upon impact of the high-energy Magnum round, its nanotronic guts spilling across the woods in a fiery display of sizzling high-tech debris. Before the second Orb could line up a shot, Karen had already fired again, the report thundering in her ears just as the sphere blew up, showering the leaf-littered ground with multi-colored sparks.

She was running before she knew it, her hiking boots crushing a smoking piece of an Orb, her hand continuing to clutch the Magnum, her index finger back on the trigger casing to prevent an accidental discharge, since the last round had left the weapon cocked, ready to fire with the slightest pressure on the trigger.

That was too easy, she thought, wondering if the Orbs had been a trick, a way to locate the threat for others to close in for the kill.

Questions flooded her mind as she pressed on.

Were the Orbs fitted with high-resolution cameras?

Did they transmit images of her before she destroyed them?

Were snapshots of her face already being e-mailed to the handheld devices of the search teams?

And how was she able to kill the Orbs so easily? One maybe, but two? Why didn't the second one fire after she had given away her position?

Perhaps Ryan was right after all about—

Concentrate!

Karen reached the same game trail she had used on the way up, relief sweeping through her because she felt she could still find the bike without the GPS from this spot.

Following the trail, confidence filling her with every step, the federal agent maintained a swift pace, the after-flashes vanishing, the ringing in her ears lessening, the noise of the havoc at the top of the hill fading away.

Perspiration running down her forehead and along the sides of her face, Karen controlled her breathing, maintained her level of alertness, her wary eyes looking for any signs of a trap. Perhaps the Orbs had been a decoy, forcing her in this direction, into the deadly embrace of a termination team.

Slowing down as she reached the cluster of trees where she had hidden the motorcycle, Karen dropped to a deep crouch, her honed instincts telling her to exercise maximum caution. The enemy had plenty of cars, and the chance existed that they had roared down the long driveway and onto this public road to cut her off, perhaps dropping armed guards at regular intervals along the way to find her as she reached the road, feeling she had escaped.

Only a small clearing separated her from the bike, and beyond it, past several feet of waist-high brush, was the road, her way back home, where she could replay what she had recorded, where she could digitize the faces of Deppe's guests and e-mail them to Washington along with an electronic copy of the video stored in the small DVD. She had learned much, seen much, and now needed time alone to digest, to process the intelligence, to listen to the video over and over to fully comprehend the information she had acquired, before devising her next move.

Her eyes shifted back and forth, scanning the woods encircling the clearing, wishing she could spend more time surveying them before venturing across, but time worked against her. The longer she waited, the greater the chances of bumping into one of Deppe's search parties. But on the bike, although initially exposed, she could reach the highway within a minute, and Berlin in another five. And besides, this was a public road, unlike the driveway that projected uphill from it. This road went on for miles, connecting the highway to the entrances of many residences, including Rolf Hartmann's estate at the top.

Making her decision, the Desert Eagle still clutched in her shooting hand, Karen left the protection of the woods and rushed across the narrow meadow, reaching the other side in seconds, her free hand removing the branches she had stacked over and around the bike to further conceal it.

Engaging the Magnum's safety before shoving the weapon in her jeans, she grabbed the handlebars and began to back the motorcycle from its hiding place.

"Nice bike," someone said behind her.

Karen began to turn, but the blow to the base of her neck was swift, expertly delivered.

Her knees trembled, gave beneath her, and she started to fall, but something caught her before she reached the ground, before she passed out.

[23] SLEEPING BEAUTIES

THE SMOKE AWOKE ME, thick, suffocating. I opened my eyes but immediately closed them, the whirling haze and the unbearable heat stinging them.

Eyes shut, keeping my face near the floor, ignoring the roaring flames closing in on me, I start to paw around, searching for Rachel, finding a hand—her hand—and grabbing it, tugging it toward me.

"Tom . . . my head . . ." she mumbles, the urgency of the moment overcoming her professional sense as she calls me by my real name.

"Here," I whisper, pulling her close, embracing her. "I'm right here."

Struggling to get my bearings, realizing that I had to open my eyes ever so slightly to see, my wrist implant still buzzing, I shiver at the scene around us, at the inferno surrounding us, at the billowing smoke and flickering flames covering the walls, the ceiling.

We're on the second floor, next to the round bed, whose headboard I remember being by large windows overlooking the Pantheon in the distance.

What in the hell happened? Who bombed this place? And where is the security team? Are they waiting outside? I call out for them on the secured frequency reserved for emergencies but get no response.

"This way!" I hiss at Rachel, but she's already moving in the direction of the windows, her mind having arrived at the same conclusion after she did not hear a reply from the security team, which means we're on our own.

Through the grumbling flames behind and above us, I hear distant sirens, emergency vehicles.

And that presents us with a problem. We have to remain invisible. We can't be found here, spying in a friendly country. That might explain why the security team has apparently abandoned us, as it too can't be seen here.

That, of course, begs the question why have a fucking security team in the first place if the bastards will run for cover at the first sign of trouble, but the fire threatening to burn the hairs on my ass forces me to shelve that thought and focus on my escape.

The sound of the sirens is coming through the windows, broken by the blast. Smoke escapes through them, meaning oxygen is rushing in to feed the flames, which also means this is the exact path of the growing fire.

But we can't just jump out of the windows. We're on the second floor and below us is that wrought-iron fence with the skewering fleur-de-lis tops.

Or you could just stay here and become a well-done hot-dog, asshole.

Realizing the futility of our situation, of our limited options, we drag ourselves toward the window by the round bed, my left hand finding something that resembles a long rope. One of Randy's leather whips. I remember seeing them coiled on the wall, and I now grab it, gather it toward me while following Rachel, who is about to crawl up to the window.

"Wait!" I shout, finding one end of the whip and tying it to the side of the old-fashioned steam heater anchored to the floor just beneath the window.

As she climbs onto the windowsill and I stand behind her holding the whip's handle, I hear a bloodcurdling scream coming from the direction of the stairs.

Randy!

We both turn in his direction, watching his totally ablaze figure emerge through the smoke, like a random comet, running across the foot of the bed, crashing against a burning wall, falling and getting up again, engulfed in flames, waving his arms frantically, bellowing agonized pleas for help.

But there's nothing I can do—nothing *anyone* can do.

Except one thing.

My lungs burning from the smoke and the heat, I retrieve my smart Colt .45 pistol from the belt holster and aim at the center of the cloud of flames, now rolling about on the floor. I fire once, twice, the reports echoing loudly against my eardrums, for an instant drowning the fire.

"Oh, my God," hisses Rachel, her blackened face now masked by this added degree of horror.

I stare at his burning body on the floor, and I shove the weapon back in its holster while saying, "Hold on to me!"

She does, facing me, throwing her arms around my neck while wrapping her legs around my waist as I crawl out of the window, both hands gripping the whip.

Smoke still covers us as we do the Tarzan and Jane thing, swinging down the side of the building using the whip like a vine, my shoulders burning from my own weight as well as my boss's.

As my arms are about to give and I'm wondering how in the hell the lord of the apes was able to pull off this stunt while holding on to his gal, we reach the bottom of the swing, where I realize that we didn't make it all the way down. And to make matters worse, the thick screen of charcoal smoke billowing skyward somewhere from the first floor prevents me from seeing just how far we have yet to go.

"Hang on!" I shout, unable to see not just the ground but the street—unable to breathe, my eyes tearing, my lungs screaming in protest as great as that of my arms, which no longer can hold us.

Letting go of the whip while embracing her, I land a moment later feetfirst on shrubs somewhere on Randy's front patio, not certain where, but definitely missing the spear tops of that fence.

My instincts command me to drop into a roll to avoid breaking my legs, but as I do it I remember that Rachel is still clamped to me like a vise.

To avoid crushing her lighter frame with my own, I twist my body halfway down the fall, letting her land on top of me, cushioning her fall at the expense of my own well-being, the impact knocking the wind out of me as my sore ass absorbs our combined mass.

It takes me a second to recover, to realize that she is resting on me, her legs straddling my thighs, the side of her face resting on my chest, arms still wrapped around my shoulders, her swelling chest pressing against my belly.

We're both breathing heavy now, close to the ground, where the air is clean, free of the intoxicating smoke swirling out of the front door and side windows and draping the front of the building.

The sirens getting closer, I gently roll out from under her and we both sit up, still getting our bearings, instinctively checking for our weapons.

"Let's get out of here," I say, watching her verify that her smart Colt is still safely secured to her waist holster, which she covers with a dark T-shirt, like me. And also like me, she carries a backup piece in an ankle holster, a little .32-caliber Beretta Tomcat, but fitted with Glaser rounds for extra bite.

Standing, keeping our heads low, we rush for the gate, away from the shrouding cloud of smoke, from the flames, from the chaos that—

The round sparks as it strikes the iron gate inches from my

right hand, metal screeching against metal, telling me whoever did this is hanging around to make sure the job gets done right.

"Sniper!" Rachel says, weapon already drawn, sweeping it in the direction of the Boulevard Saint-Michel, where the shot had originated.

I too scan the street, ignoring the gathering crowd, many coming from the Pantheon.

A sniper from a vantage point.

A *silent* sniper, since I didn't hear the report of the round that nearly amputated my shooting hand.

My mind quickly reviews my options. The sound suppressor used by the sniper greatly improved his stealthiness, but at the cost of reduced accuracy, which could explain the near miss. A sniper would also suffer from tunnel vision as he peeked through the scope to align his target in the crosshairs of his—

My wrist implant starts to buzz, and so does Rachel's. In addition to the sniper firing real bullets at us, someone else is painting us with a laser.

"Your countermeasures enabled?" I ask.

I get a nod from her, her green eyes clear, focused, like the professional I was hoping she would be when challenged this way.

An instant later the buzzing rockets in frequency and the Plasmaflex on my left wrist informs me that there are two Orbs floating our way, navigating through the haze.

My instincts continue to surface with unequivocal clarity, making me clutch my smart Colt before I know it, and aim it in the direction of the street, waiting for the silver spheres to show themselves.

Rachel, whose implant has told her the same thing, also swings her weapon in that direction.

And what do you know? Here they come, like a couple of flying silver basketballs, firing smart darts at us just like in Singapore. And just like back then, our countermeasures—which include not just an instant jamming of their operating frequency but also both of us going into a simultaneous roll—manage to fool the first wave of tiny projectiles, which I hear rustling the bushes to our immediate left.

Before I've even finished the roll, I have my weapon aimed at the little bastards and cut loose five rounds. Rachel also fires several times. The spheres tremble under the multiple impacts, some rounds bouncing off their Kevhel shell, others striking their tiny turbines, sending them crashing against nearby parked vehicles.

My wrist implant stops buzzing, telling me we now only have the sniper out there trying to send us to kingdom come.

Rushing through the gate with Rachel in tow, I race across the cobblestone sidewalk before firing twice toward the sky, aiming at nothing.

But there's a reason behind my apparent willingness to waste valuable ammo without a clear target.

Our sudden charge away from the inferno will get us out of the sniper's immediate field of view for a couple of seconds. Before he could reacquire, we fired in the air. An experienced sniper, losing his target and then hearing the shots, would take cover for a few seconds before searching the street again.

The cat trying to nail us does exactly that.

The reports also work wonders for the crowd that's heading our way from the Pantheon, dispersing them like a band of howling monkeys, running in every direction, allowing us to blend with them as we take off up Rue Cujas, away from the sniper, toward the Pantheon and its hordes of visit—

The sudden crack of a pistol, like a whip, further inflames the people dashing about us. They're mostly French, based on their cries. A mother drags her two sons while screaming, *"Mon dieu! Mon dieu!"* A couple in their twenties nearly bumps into Rachel while hollering, *"Au secours!"* Three teenage girls shout, *"Au feu! Au feu!"* while running with their arms up in the air.

We run away, Rachel's profile in my peripheral vision, dark hair swirling in the wind. We ignore the gunfire, assume we stand a better chance by continuing moving rather than turning around and fighting.

But I still watch the excited natives around me very carefully, and not because I've never trusted the French. My operative stare scans the shifting bodies flashing past my field of view but without making eye contact, without staring at any-one in particular. I'm looking for patterns, for behavior unex-pected in an agitated crowd.

Then I spot them, two businessmen in their forties, athleti-cally built, dark eyes glinting recognition as they focus on me, as their hands reach inside their jackets.

The twins! The twins from Peru!

"Over there!" I shout, in the same instant as I recognize the faces of Eduardo and Alfonso Ruiz, two of Troy Savage's hand-bred operatives—like me.

But they're supposed to be dead, like the rest of the old crew trained and controlled by Troy before he vanished from Lang-ley. I'm supposed to be the *only* survivor, the only one found by Langley before being terminated by my mentor because of what I *knew* about him, because of the danger I presented to him if recruited by his former employer.

Did Morotski and Leyman feed me a cock-and-bull story?

The possibility tears at my logic as we cut left into wide Rue Saint-Jacques, projecting west from Rue Cujas, pointing us directly toward the Seine, toward the crowds touring Notre-Dame on the Ile de la Cité, the largest island on the Seine as it snakes its way through the heart of Paris.

"Tom!" one of the twins screams while the other waves his hands at me.

I follow the old CIA rule: When in doubt assume everyone is your enemy. I need time to think this mess through, to regroup with my pretty boss and try to pull together a sensible plan.

Just then the twins open fire. As Rachel and I are about to dive behind a parked Renault a dozen feet from the intersec-tion, I realize they're not aiming at us.

Risking a backward glance, I spot a man clutching his chest before doubling over while dropping a large pistol.

"Tom! Come with us!" the twins shout in unison before swinging their weapons up, toward the roof of nearby buildings at the intersection of Rue Cujas and Rue Saint-Jacques, and fir-ing again.

I hear screams above us, see two men falling to their deaths, crashing onto parked vehicles with metal-bending force.

"Run!" I tell her even though her slim figure is already taking large strides slightly ahead of me, her long legs vanishing into a whirl of motion, like in the old cartoons.

My mind is in as much havoc as the bizarre scene rapidly developing back on Rue Cujas.

What in the hell is going on?

Ignoring the persistent gunfire and the shouts from the twins, like a pair of questionable guardian angels protecting our getaway, I follow my agile boss as she dashes down the street like a spooked feline. I'm huffing and puffing right behind her with the grace of a hippopotamus.

Rachel puts her gun away just as I also shove mine in my jeans, our operative minds reacting in harmony when we spot the green and white police vehicles zooming up the street from the Seine.

We become invisible amidst the alarmed pedestrians we come up to, some running alongside us in sheer panic, others just staring wide-eyed at the mess on Rue Cujas.

"What in the hell was that?" Rachel screams over her right shoulder at me, her strained voice ringing above the chaos, above the crack of repeated gunfire, above the sirens of arriving emergency vehicles. "Why did those two protect us? Why did they ask us to go with them?"

I'm about to tell her when I realize that everything we're saying and hearing through our implants is being monitored by Morotski, the same cat who told me that Eduardo, Alfonso, and the rest of the old gang were dead. If the Moron Man was lying about this could he also be lying about Troy? About Singapore? About what took place at USN? About the real reason why I am here instead of half-drunk in my own little piece of Central American paradise?

Could he be responsible for what happened at Randy's place? Was his intent to kill us after I debriefed Randy? But why? What are Leyman and Morotski after?

I motion to her to keep quiet, and her eyes flash understanding as we approach the Seine, as the recent events continue to tax my logic.

If Moron Man wanted us dead after we extracted the CyberWerke lead from Randy, all he had to do was issue a Non-Maskable Termination Code before we left the brownstone, blasting our ear canals and eyeballs. Unlike the standard termination signals, which implants will ignore if the host is alive, NMTCs will make you blind, deaf, and pretty fucking dumb in about a nanosecond.

But NMTCs require the personal approval of the Director of Central Intelligence, in this case Donald Bane. Only the DCI can issue an NMTC, just like only the president can issue the launch codes of nuclear missiles. And just like the nuclear codes—to a smaller degree, of course—if the NMTCs were to fall into the wrong hands, it could spell disaster for the U.S. intelligence community using implants, which at last count was just about everybody to some degree.

But I'm still alive, still trying to keep up with Marathon Woman, still being reminded that I'm hopelessly and pathetically out of shape—meaning DCI Bane hasn't issued the NMTCs yet.

But what does that mean? Do they want us alive? If so, then why risk detonating an incendiary bomb while we were in Randy's home? And who could have possibly planted the bomb in the first place? No one but Moron Man and his bag-of-bones superior, Leyman, knew where we were headed. Not even the security team was aware of the exact location. Which brings me to the next question: Why didn't the security team come to our rescue? Where were they when those pinheads were taking potshots at us? And why, out of all people, would some of Troy's presumed-dead operatives come to our rescue?

Insanity!
Madness!
One thing is for certain: We must find a safe place to hide and think this through, but not before I get rid of these damned implants. Given today's events, the implants have now turned into more of a liability than an asset. I can't justify the risk they now represent.

As we slow down to a fast walk before reaching the Seine,

trying to appear normal, to blend in, the conflicting information gives me the feeling that I'm just a high-tech puppet, a
cybermarionette manipulated to gather intelligence for the benefit of crooked cats like Morotski, Leyman, or someone higher.

Could DCI Bane also be involved in this?

The only way to learn the truth is by first eliminating the
digital handcuffs binding us to our network, if anything to avoid
getting killed should the bigwigs decide to barbecue our minds.

Disabling our implants, however, would send a deactivation
signal to Langley, essentially informing our superiors of our act
of cybermutiny, signaling that we have turned. Only a lamebrain or a traitor would purposely cut off his or her own cyber-
strings without consulting with Langley first.

Although some might consider me a first-class imbecile or,
like my fifth-grade teacher once said, someone who doesn't
play well with others, I'm certainly no idiot or, God forbid, a
traitor—although Langley has certainly given me plenty of
reasons to become one.

In any case, cutting off our implants also means kissing my
little pot of gold somewhere over the rainbow in St. Thomas
bye-bye. The spooks would find a way to make it disappear
quicker than I can click my shoes three times.

Bastards.

"What in the hell do we do?" Rachel asks.

"We do exactly what we're supposed to do in an emergency,
Boss: head toward our rendezvous point," I lie, telling Moron
Man and whoever else is listening what they hope to hear, that
we still believe they're on our side and we're headed toward
them.

She shoots me a look of confusion but follows my lead and
says, "Sounds like a plan."

"But first I need to find a pharmacy."

"A pharmacy?"

"Yeah," I tell her and my captive audience.

"Why?"

"My head feels like it's going to explode from all the excitement."

DIRECTOR OF CENTRAL INTELLIGENCE Donald Bane regarded his subordinate with hidden suspicion. A field operative who rose up the Agency's ranks on merit and guts alone, Bane was trained to treat everyone as guilty until proven innocent, a habit that had proven lifesaving throughout his career, which he had cut short back in 1999, in part because of the way in which President Clinton had crippled the most powerful intelligence agency in the world.

Bane turned away from Nathan Leyman while remembering Clinton's directive that had prevented the CIA from recruiting agents with unsavory backgrounds, even when history had proven that the more unsavory an agent or informant, the better the intel he or she reported. Disillusioned, Bane and a host of other senior CIA officials had abandoned ship.

But then came September 11th, and the nation realized just how stupid that decision had been. In a matter of days the CIA had been directed to recruit anybody who could assist America in its battle against international terrorism. It was during those dark post-9/11 days that President George W. Bush, determined to rebuild America's emasculated intelligence community, ordered the Director of Central Intelligence to find those seasoned officers who had retired early and drag them back into Langley—buy them back if he had to, but return them to action immediately.

Donald Bane had been one of those officers. At the time he had been soaking in the sun of southern Italy. He had given up a relaxing retirement and had answered his country's call. He had taken the next flight to Langley and jumped back into a game he thought he had left behind forever. Operating under the umbrella of a new administration determined to learn from its mistakes, Donald Bane had become a rising star. He was promptly dispatched to Afghanistan, where his methods for obtaining intelligence, frowned upon during the Clinton years, became the textbook for future generations of CIA officers. Ten years later, Bane had received a presidential appointment to head the most powerful intelligence agency in the world after the long-standing director, Martin Jacobs, had died in a car accident.

Car accident my ass, Bane thought, well aware that Martin had been assassinated because he had tried to launch an internal investigation to unearth a mole in the Agency.

"This Malone guy," said Bane. "Wasn't Grant his real name before the meltdown in Singapore?"

"Yes, sir. Tom Grant," replied Nathan Leyman.

"He helped us out way back when on the Kulzak case, right?"

"Yes, sir."

"But I thought he retired and was living somewhere south of the border," Bane said, scanning the file that his Director of Operations had downloaded into his Flexboard for their predawn meeting, before Bane had to head to the White House to brief the president. Like his predecessors at the Agency, Bane insisted on reviewing the latest version of the President's Daily Brief, spending a full hour with his subordinate to fine-tune the document that would highlight all relevant intelligence data for the commander in chief.

Leyman slowly shook his head, before replying, "He retired all right, and he did lease a property from the Salvadoran government, like my previous report indicated. But we recently learned he never spent much time there. The retirement in El Salvador was just a front to keep us from learning his true intentions."

"You make a bold statement in your report, Nathan," said Bane, referring to the paragraph where the DO stated that Malone—or Grant—was responsible for the security breach at United States Nanotechnology. "Do you have enough proof to back it up?"

Leyman nodded. "One of my top guys, Wayne Larson, is working with the security team down at USN on the investigation. They have a perfect DNA match. Tom Grant was among the hooded terrorists at USN, sir. Of that much we're one hundred percent certain."

Bane looked away, absently inspecting the dark-wood paneling of his office on the top floor of the new CIA building in Langley. The White House had been on his ass as well as the Bureau's since the incident. President Laura Vaccaro demanded answers, and today's PDB contained the first piece of evidence on the case that Bane felt comfortable enough sharing with the president without compromising a deep-cover operation he had started in the weeks following Martin's death to uncover the mole as well as the mole's controller.

"Your report," Bane finally said. "It states that you believe he's also responsible for the deaths of Troy Savage's officers."

Leyman gave his superior a slow nod. "Savage trained Grant to be an assassin—in direct violation of 12333. Grant used his skills to keep us from using those officers to track Savage's whereabouts. In addition, we now have evidence that Grant may have infiltrated our agency."

Bane forced control, well aware that Savage and his operatives were not dead but alive and well running this deep-covert mission—so secret that only Bane knew about it. He was also glad that his own Director of Operations continued to buy the official story about Savage and his team. Tom Grant, however, had been forced to retire at Savage's insistence to give him a break after twenty-five years of service. There was a chance that Grant could have turned, though Bane felt it was unlikely.

One of the difficulties in setting up a covert operation like the one Bane had put in place with Savage was dealing with the day-to-day operations at Langley, which included investigations such as the one Leyman was conducting on the USN incident, which could potentially overlap Savage's operation if Tom Grant had indeed turned.

"Explain," Bane said, standing while pressing his palms against the smooth surface of his desk and keeping them there while peering down at Leyman, who shifted his weight uncomfortably in his chair.

"We just got an initial flash report on an incident in Paris that confirms our suspicions. We had sent Officer Rachel Muratani and Tom Grant there to follow up on a lead when all hell broke loose. They killed one of our informants in Paris, a man by the name of Randall Wessel. Grant felt Wessel had ties with Rem Vlachko, who we also feel was behind the USN breach. They also killed three CIA operatives that we had following them."

"So Muratani is under suspicion too? I thought she was the one who pointed us to Grant in the first place," Bane said, remembering the investigation he had requested Leyman to carry out to look into Savage's disappearance. But now Leyman had thrown a new player into the mix, Rachel Muratani, who Bane thought was just doing her job, running the investigation on Savage and his missing team. Now Bane wanted to understand why Leyman claimed that not only Grant was the enemy but also Muratani, and he planned to cross-check Leyman's take on what had happened in Paris with the report he knew he would get later on from Savage, whose job it was to keep tabs on Tom Grant's whereabouts.

Leyman nodded. "Muratani was heading the investigation on Savage's disappearance. If you remember, it took her a few months before she came up with anything solid. In the meantime Troy's subordinates were dropping like flies. Her investigation led us to believe that Tom Grant was the last surviving member of Troy's old gang, making us think that he was uniquely positioned to help us track Savage down. In reality, Muratani was secretly dragging her feet while feeding Grant the addresses of Savage's operatives—and even some agents—to give Grant time to terminate them and therefore keep us from debriefing them."

"You're saying that Muratani played us? That she delayed the investigation to give Grant a chance to kill those operatives to prevent us from tracking down Savage? That would mean that Grant and Muratani work for Savage, which then means Savage is also involved in the USN strike?" Bane asked, deciding that either Leyman was coming to conclusions far too quickly on far too little data, or perhaps the Director of Operations had an agenda of his own.

Then Bane felt a sudden chill tickling the back of his neck.

Is Leyman the mole I've been looking for?

"That's the way things are stacking up, sir," replied Leyman, unaware of the thoughts crossing through Bane's mind. "It's all very embarrassing, especially since we did pull Grant in from his retirement to work with Muratani and help us out."

"Yes," Bane said, wondering whose side Leyman was really on. "He was the only one who could help us track Savage down."

"Correct. But both Muratani and Grant were working against us all along, assisting Savage in the USN attack."

"How did you figure this out?" Bane asked, feeling acid squirting in his stomach at the thought of Leyman being the CIA mole—and then trying to explain that to the president, who had a high degree of respect for the aging Director of Operations.

"We got our final confirmation in Paris, sir."

Bane sat back down, closed his eyes, and pinched the bridge of his nose in apparent surprise at Leyman's remarks. After all, it was vital for Bane to make absolutely certain that Leyman did not suspect that Bane and Savage were in it together to find the CIA mole—lest Bane wished to find himself dead like his predecessor.

"Nathan, you're telling me that we had two of the people responsible for the breach at USN—people who could have helped deliver Savage—and we not only let them go, but in the process they used us to achieve their goals? You're suggesting that we let them kill a legitimate informant, one who could have pointed us in the direction of Vlachko, who could lead us to Savage, *and* they also killed three CIA officers?"

"It all happened very fast, sir. We thought Muratani was a straight arrow, and we also thought that Malone—Tom Grant—was indeed in retirement, and that we had mistreated him because of Singapore. Then within *twenty-four hours* we get the DNA results from Texas confirming Grant's involvement in that attack. Based on this finding we have requested DNA analysis of the crime scenes of all of Troy's slain operatives. The first one came in just before I headed over to your office.

We have DNA confirmation that Grant had also been at the crime scene of Eduardo and Alfonso Ruiz, the twin agents whom Savage had recruited from Peru. They were killed in an auto accident in Mexico City two months ago."

Damn, Nathan, I never thought you would be the one, Bane thought, well aware that Grant was nowhere near the crime scene of Eduardo and Alfonso Ruiz because those two agents were alive and well operating in Europe under Savage. While a part of him was surprised that the eminent Nathan Leyman could be the mole he had been looking for, Bane felt a rush of excitement sweeping through him at the thought of the strategy he had devised with Savage over a year ago finally starting to pay off. And in a way Bane shouldn't be too surprised that it turned out to be someone of the caliber and reputation of Leyman that ended up being the traitor. Previous traitors, such as Robert Hanssen and Aldrich Ames, both very reputable officers with access to a lot of classified information, got away with their deceptive practices for years before they were caught.

"What do you want to do, Nathan?" Bane asked, suddenly very eager to get Savage's weekly report—due tomorrow—to see what was really going on with Grant and Muratani. If a CIA operation indeed took place in Paris, then Bane was certain that Savage would have known about it, especially if it involved Wessel, a former CIA informant run by Grant and Savage back in the old days.

"For starters," said Leyman, "I need access to the Non-Maskable Termination Codes of Rachel Muratani and Dan Hawkins."

"Who is Dan Hawkins?"

"Grant's newest CIA-issued name. We had to give him a new identity when Muratani recruited him. As part of the deal we fitted him with new implants."

Bane looked away. If Leyman's time of the shoot-out in Paris was accurate, then Grant and Muratani would have been on the move less than an hour, not long enough for them to remove their implants, which meant the risk was high that the NMTCs would cause harm to them. He finally asked, "Is there a way to use the NMTCs to disable them but not kill them? They would make excellent debriefing material." Bane watched his subordinate's eyes very carefully.

"That's the plan, sir," said Leyman without hesitation. "Our end goal is to do anything and everything possible not just to recover the stolen nanotechnology but also to bring Savage and the rest of his organization down, and keeping Muratani and Grant alive is in line with that. But we need to do it very soon. They still have their implants enabled and they're also transmitting their conversation, just as we had agreed, meaning they still think we have not figured out their scheme—at least based on the short discussion they had after escaping the shoot-out. Right now they're supposed to be heading to a rendezvous point outside of Paris. We should have them within the next few hours, depending on what form of transportation they use to get out of the city. I'm going to give them until the end of today. If they don't show, I will have to assume that they have figured out we're on to them, and at that point I would like to be able to transmit NMTCs at will."

"You have my permission to issue the NMTCs, but strictly by the book," Bane said. "Terminate if they fail to show within twelve hours or if they break their implant connection for more than one hour. I don't want to terminate officers until we're one hundred and fifty percent sure they have gone rogue. Is that clear?"

"Yes, sir."

Bane stood, crossed his arms, and turned to face the windows behind his desk, his eyes surveying the parking lot under an indigo sky stained with strokes of orange and yellow-gold.

His mind shifted from the events in Paris to the stolen nanotechnology, remembering the frightening report he had read on the missing nanoweapons—enough to send governments into panic if word of the incident ever got out. Although General Granite claimed he had been successful in keeping a lid on the whole thing, Bane knew it was just a matter of time before something leaked, especially if whoever it was that stole them—and he was damned certain that it wasn't

Savage or Grant or Muratani as Leyman had just claimed—started releasing the microscopic predators in highly populated areas.

"Anything new from Texas?" Bane asked, more as a formality.

Leyman shook his head, though Bane really didn't know what to believe from this man anymore. "The last report we got from Larson down in Texas indicated that General Granite had things under control, but given what we know about our rogue officers and their involvement at USN, it's obvious that Granite is holding out on us."

Bane suppressed a grunt, expecting that response from Leyman. But his logic still questioned the Pentagon's level of secrecy around the incident in Texas. Bane had spent an hour on the phone with Granite this morning, and he had not gotten a warm feeling that things were indeed as controlled as the brass claimed they were—as measured by the progress made by the military to track down and recover the stolen hardware.

Who did steal the nanotechnology?

One possibility was that Leyman could be involved and was using Savage, Grant, and Muratani as a diversion to protect the guilty.

As he dismissed his subordinate, Bane began to think through a strategy that would allow him to continue to deceive Leyman into believing that Bane wasn't aware of the strong likelihood that Leyman had gone bad. He had to convey the belief that he didn't suspect a thing, that he believed everything that Leyman was telling him—including the statements about Savage, Grant, and Muratani—for only then would Donald Bane be in a position to learn who else at the CIA was involved in this conspiracy and, more important, which outside agency was pulling their strings.

Staring at the parking lot connecting the building to the surrounding woods, Bane thought of a way to improve his odds, an avenue to short-circuit the investigation on the USN breach while also getting to the bottom of the cancer inside his agency.

An alliance.

Bane decided that the time had come to contact the FBI

director and also General Granite, who pretty much ran things at USN, to create a secret alliance to combat not just the cancer growing inside the CIA but the foreign power prying into America's affairs.

Donald Bane's instincts told him that doing so would also lead him to the force behind the attack at USN.

And his instincts were seldom wrong.

[25] GHOSTS

THEY MATERIALIZED FROM WITHIN the darkness of the test field, their stealth suits invisible to the radars overlooking the battle-simulation grounds. To the untrained observer their movement seemed random, erratic, but Mike Ryan knew better. The depth-perception algorithms of nanotronic brains of the latest generation Orbs still had difficulty processing certain tri-dimensional spatial patterns.

"It really screws with their processing units when they try to handle so many moving targets at various depths," Ryan explained to General Gus Granite, standing next to him high above on an observation platform on the left side of the test grounds, which were as large as four football fields and with many obstacles, simulated trees, and other objects to offer protection.

"Let's see if your theory holds, Dr. Ryan," said Granite in his deep voice, arms crossed over his powerful chest. "So far my men have been unable to beat the little bastards, even with their fancy suits."

Ryan's eyes shifted between the dark terrain and the plasma screen next to him, which tracked the team of soldiers battling ten fully armed Orbs. Soldiers were green and Orbs red. The teams advanced toward each other across the unleveled battleground.

"I can't believe that the Orbs' lasers are armed, General,"

commented Ryan, watching the exercise with growing concern. "Isn't that too dangerous for your men?" Although he felt certain his theory would hold, Ryan still didn't like the idea of exposing soldiers to live laser shots.

"We have to make sure that the suits work as designed. Otherwise we will certainly lose when facing the rogue Assy and the many offspring we suspect it has created by now."

"How do you know that, General? What if the unit was either damaged during the attack or maybe those who stole it have dissected it by now to learn its secrets?"

"We have to prepare for the worst-case scenario, Dr. Ryan," Granite replied, before adding, "Unlike the civilian Orbs, which would remain off once deactivated, Assy was programmed to wake itself up after twenty-four hours of inactivity. If the terrorists who stole it didn't screw with it for that period of time, then Assy would have turned itself on, realized it was in a bind, switched to Independent Alert Military Mode, and cut loose with its full arsenal and ruthless military tactics. Then it would have searched for a place where it could find the raw materials it would need for atomic mining to increase its odds of prevailing."

Even though Ryan had already come to terms with the unfortunate reality that the brass had pretty much violated every security rule he had built into the civilian Orbs to prevent just this kind of fiasco, he frowned, inspecting the test field inside one of the largest domes in the military sector of USN, wondering if he had made the right decision by siding with the brass on this one. He had been quite apprehensive at first, when Granite had busted him for hacking inside the military network. But Ryan had then realized the reason for the general's tight-lipped attitude toward the CIA. The Defense Intelligence Agency, the military version of the CIA that reported into the office of the Secretary of Defense, had strong suspicions about security leaks in Langley based on the mysterious disappearances of a number of CIA operatives in the past year and had advised Granite to limit the information he shared with the Agency. Besides, Ryan figured that at the moment there was probably very little the CIA could do to mitigate the threat of the stolen nanoassembler, which, as Ryan had found out during his illegal cyberexcursion, lacked the digital enzyme dependency of its civilian counterparts. The brass, on the other hand, appeared to be already well down the path of creating a team to handle the missing Orb.

"The missing assembler is turning out to be one royal pain in the ass," Granite had told Ryan shortly after catching him hacking into the military network.

"That wouldn't be the case if your team had followed the rules, General," Ryan had reminded the general during their heart-to-heart chat after Granite escorted Ryan out of his lab and brought him here. "The enzymes were designed for a good reason."

"I know. I know. Don't remind me," the general had replied, before explaining the situation in full to Ryan in the hope of getting the former Stanford whiz kid to help him defeat the rogue smart Orb and its likely growing army of cybersubordinates before the media got ahold of this—and especially before those maverick systems inflicted harm on the general population.

The soldiers continued their advance, shifting positions, crisscrossing paths, taxing the nanotronic minds of the defending Orbs, which had obviously not detected the incoming threat yet.

"Amazing," Granite said, before pressing a button on the intercom next to the monitor and asking, "Are you certain the Orbs' sensors are activated, son?"

"Yes, sir," came the reply from one of the men in the control booth at the other end of the field, where they also recorded the event for later evaluation. "They're operating in IAMM but for some reason are not attacking yet."

"I'll be damned," mumbled the hefty three-star general. "Perhaps there *is* a way to get close enough to them to use the EMP guns."

"Why don't you just blast the bastards with a large-scale EMP, like from a plane?" asked Ryan.

Granite shrugged, his square jaw twisting a bit as he also frowned before saying, "For one thing, open discharge of large-scale EMPs is forbidden by the United Nations accords of 2007. But even if we decide to go around the UN's back and use it, let me remind you that those big-ass pulses are very dangerous to nanotronic hearts and kidneys and advanced prostethics. EMPs would damage all of that implanted equipment, in many cases killing the users. And such large-scale EMP blasts can be detected by satellites, which would trigger an international investigation of the UN violation. If that investigation gets traced to us, it would certainly telegraph to the world that something has gone so wrong with our machine-supremacy research that it merited the use of an unsanctioned EMP. And that's just what Congress needs to hear to cut back our funding, something we can't afford to do, lest we wish to give up our nanotechnology lead to foreign competition. Of course, if we really had to use such blasts in order to prevent an even bigger disaster we would, but first we need to find the bastards. Then we can evaluate our options."

Ryan curled the fingers of his hands on the railing fencing the ten-foot-square observation platform, which stood three stories high over the battlefield.

Granite continued by saying, "The way to attack this problem—again once we locate them—is with the surgical use of handheld EMP guns, small enough not only to be overlooked by satellites but also to minimize collateral damage. So once again, just like so many other instances in military history since time immemorial, it all falls on the shoulders of the foot soldier."

"That's great, General, but as you've indicated, we still need to find them. How are we going to do that?"

Granite didn't respond. Instead, he stretched an index finger at the terrain below, at the nearing silhouettes of his team.

The Orbs began to react, their sensors stimulating the occipital lobes of their nanotronic brains, triggering their microturbines, triggering motion.

But the soldiers were already close enough, firing their EMPs, disabling a half-dozen Orbs in the first wave of the attack.

The surviving Orbs fought back, shooting purple lasers at the advancing team, illuminating their targets as the lasers struck the prism-like layer of nanocrystals of their TechnoSuits suits, which dispersed the incoming energy across their entire surface before shooting it off in every direction. The effect seemed surreal as the dark soldiers became engulfed in sudden purple light, which shot off of them like exploding stars, before darkness once more enveloped them.

The soldiers continued their advance, taking out more Orbs in this live exercise.

The surviving nanomachines, however, fired again, this time with an intensity far greater than the first time. Ryan understood the logic. The nanotronic brains used their sensors to assess the total mass of a target before programming the right energy level in the laser. No sense in spending energy beyond that which was required to achieve a kill based on the size of the threat. Ryan had helped Dr. Howard Giles develop the mass-to-energy ratio algorithm. And he had also assisted the late USN chief military scientist in teaching the nanotronic brain to increase its energy level if the first strike was unsuccessful.

And that was exactly what the machines did, releasing brighter laser energy at the soldiers, whose prism suits became near incandescent as they tried to deflect the kinetic energy but failed to deflect it all. Three glowing figures fell back, as if pushed by an invisible force. The rest staggered on impact but started moving forward once more as the energy dispersed around them in hues of lavender.

More Orbs fell victim to the EMPs, to the combined electromagnetic pulses that fried the nanotronics of everything within a two-foot radius from the center of the energy beam. The machines trembled in midair, as if gripped by an unseen power, before dropping unceremoniously to the ground.

But two Orbs survived the onslaught, fighting back with an energy that made Ryan blink. Blinding mauve bolts of lightning sparked from the two Orbs, catching a soldier in the chest and another one in the legs.

Both screamed, dropped to the ground as the rest of the

team discharged their EMPs on the two Orbs, which shook violently in midair before crashing on the training field.

"Medics!" shouted General Granite into the intercom. "Two soldiers down! Move it!"

The lights inside the dome came alive, bathing the cavernous interior with gray light. On one side Ryan watched two ambulances rushing toward the fallen men, already surrounded by their comrades, who were removing their helmets while helping them sit up.

"That was close," said Ryan. "If the Orbs had cranked their energy level another notch . . ."

"Well, that was precisely what kept happening," said General Granite, starting toward the aluminum stairs down to the field. "Because the Orbs detected my men too far away, the soldiers never got a chance to fire their EMPs more than once or twice before the Orbs blasted them unconscious. Sounds like your advice bought my men enough time to nail them. Thanks for that insight, Dr. Ryan."

"No problem," replied Ryan, going down two flights of stairs to the field. "Now all you have to do is find them."

"Yes," said Granite, his hard-edged face staring into the distance.

If there was ever a soldier that resembled a pillar of strength, it was this man.

"And that's where you come in," the general added.

"What do you mean, sir?"

"Just what I said, Dr. Ryan," replied the general. "You will help us find them."

Ryan frowned as they reached the field and walked on the padded synthetic surface toward the nearest group of soldiers standing by a pair of medics tending one of the stunned warriors. Next to them lay one of the smoked Orbs, its nanotronic guts spilled onto the turf through an inch-thick gash in its armored shell.

"But, General," Ryan said. "I know little about military operations. And based on your team's results, I don't see why my services are needed."

"Oh, I think we're covered in the real world, Dr. Ryan. But

Assy will not be able to survive in the real world for long unless it accesses the virtual world to expand its sphere of influence— and that's where you come in."

Ryan froze, stunned, then asked, "General, you're telling me that the military assembler has a live interface to get on-line?" Another safety feature of the civilian Orbs was restricted access to any networks—hard-line or wireless—when operating in the field. In order for a civilian Orb to be hooked up to a network, which was required on a periodic basis for preventive maintenance and for software and hardware upgrades, a technician had to manually remove a shielded plate, which required a hardware key and the extraction of a dozen screws—something the civilian assembler wasn't programmed to do or know was possible. The technician would then activate a wireless interface with a range limited to the lab at USN and perform the pre-approved work. Ryan had taken excessive measures to keep the mobile nanoassemblers from stepping out of their bounds, from the Turing inhibitors to digital enzymes and elaborate manual procedures to get online. To his dismay, the military had bypassed them all in order to create these all-powerful warriors to accompany the soldiers in the field.

And now one of those cyberwarriors has turned against us.

Granite didn't reply right away. Instead, he first checked on his men, verified that they were just stunned but otherwise all right, and then, hands in the side pockets of his uniform, turned his attention back to Ryan and said, "Contrary to popular belief, Dr. Ryan, our nation is in great danger."

Ryan blinked twice, not expecting that.

"Remember the CIA leaks I was mentioning before?" Granite asked.

Ryan nodded, uncertain where this was headed.

"You never did ask where that intel was leaking to."

Ryan shrugged. "You didn't elaborate, General, and I didn't see it as my place to ask."

Granite shot him an intrigued look and said, "You puzzle me, Dr. Ryan. You are shy about asking a pertinent question, but you don't hesitate about breaching my network?"

Ryan felt color coming to his cheeks.

"In any case," Granite continued, "you are now in the know, and I checked this decision with the heads of the FBI and the CIA, who are also concerned about organizational leaks and are taking . . . very *drastic* measures to plug them. But again, the question is: Who is benefiting from the information leaking out of our intelligence agencies? Who stands to benefit the most by stealing our nanotechnology?"

Ryan waited, sudden apprehension gripping his intestines.

When Granite finally spoke again, Ryan wished he had been sitting down.

[26] REALITY CHECK

THIS IS A WARPED world indeed. Here I am, in the City of Lights, in a cozy room of a lovely little hotel just north of the Louvre with an even lovelier lady resting her head on my lap while I sit on a king-size bed exploring one of her orifices.

Too bad it's just her left ear, where I'm digging with a pair of tweezers, grasping the tiny receiver glued to the sensitive skin of her middle ear.

"Don't move," I tell her, focusing my mind on the job at hand not just for her sake but also for mine. It would be awfully embarrassing, even to a borderline-wicked guy like me, if Mr. Johnson decides to wake up and rise to the occasion at this moment.

Giving the tiny unit a firm tug, I dislodge it, along with a patch of skin.

"Aghh, damn!" she screams, but without moving, knowing better.

I reach for a cotton ball and shove it in her ear.

Rachel recoils away from me while holding the cotton in place, her eyes gleaming with anger, as if she's some sort of jungle cat poised to strike.

"I sure in hell hope this was necessary," she finally protests, pacing in front of me, pulling out the crimson cotton ball, frowning at it, before snatching a fresh one and stuffing it into her ear. "I have done nothing wrong on this assignment. *Nothing!* Why do they want me dead as well?"

I grin. "Welcome to my world. There's a bigger agenda in the works and for it to work we must be terminated, which is why we need to break all contact, alter the rules of the game. Only then will we be in a position to get to the bottom of this mess."

She shakes her head, obviously still in denial, which at the moment is extremely dangerous, because the clock is ticking and we lack the time to discuss this further so I can fully convince her that this is the right thing to do.

"I just don't know," she finally says, her relative inexperience surfacing when the game is suddenly altered, when she is forced to think out of the box—something which I'm unfortunately quite used to doing.

"Well, I *do* know, Rachel. I've been here before and this is what we *must* do to stay alive—and believe me, you *will* thank me later. Right now, though, I need you to do me. We're running out of time," I reply, well aware of the old CIA rules regarding NMTCs. After finding a pharmacy, I bought a pair of tweezers, alcohol, a small dental mirror, and cotton balls. I also purchased a small pad and a pen to communicate with her without tipping off our listening audience, who were still expecting us to head to our rendezvous point. Rachel, to her credit, followed my lead flawlessly—probably as a result of our near-death experience, which made her realize something had gone terribly wrong. We had then rushed through the streets of Paris for two hours to make sure no one was following us before we found a hotel, arriving here just ten minutes ago. Once in our room, I stopped transmitting, and I convinced her to do the same. With the clock ticking now that they knew we had purposely cut off communications with Langley, I explained my suspicions and why it was imperative that we remove our own implants immediately, or risk getting blasted. It took almost fifteen minutes, but after I told her about the Peruvian twins, who were supposedly dead but had apparently returned from the grave to save our hides from those mysterious killers on Rue Cujas, she reluctantly agreed to help me get us implant free. We removed the easy implant first, the tiny microphone glued to the back of our front teeth, using the dental mirror and the tweezers. Then we went to work on each other's ears, and last will be the eyes. The wrist implants can't be removed without surgery, so we're just going to have to bite the bullet when Langley issues a termination code, which according to my calculations can occur in about twenty-five minutes—assuming they stick to procedure and refrain from issuing the NMTCs for a full hour from the moment we stopped transmitting, which was about thirty minutes ago.

I motion for her to sit down while I hand her the tweezers so she can remove my ear implant.

"Don't bother disinfecting them," I say. "We're running out of time."

Hesitating, she snags the bloody tool and sits at the edge of the bed. I kneel in front of her, rest my head on her lap, and get ready to share bodily fluids.

"All right," she says. "Don't move."

"Please be gentle, Boss. It's my first time."

"Be still, Tom!" she snaps, tapping me on the side of the head.

Did she just call me Tom?

With a heavy sigh, Rachel's fingers fiddle with my ear while I close my eyes, feeling the top of my head pressed against her belly.

And I suddenly find this terribly erotic—enough for my body to start cranking up the catapult. My fifth-grade teacher was right when she sent me to the principal. My mind does tend to dip into Gutterville at the weirdest times.

But then Rachel inserts those cold tweezers into my ear canal, bringing me back to my senses, while asking, "Do you think Bane is in on this too?"

Forcing my mind back to business, I say, "Doubt it. The man is a straight arrow, but he will approve the NMTC if presented with enough evidence, which I'm certain Leyman and Morotski will have no problem fabricating given their resources."

As she continues digging for oil, my mind slowly reverts back to where my head is: resting on a pair of female thighs that are firm but also soft, if that makes any sense, and once again I close my eyes and remember those well-tanned trotters walking toward me on that beach in El Salv—

"Fuck!" I scream when she repays the favor, yanking the nanotronic gadget without warning.

Standing, I reach for my own damned cotton ball, pressing it against my bleeding ear while she remains seated with a smirk on her face, holding the instrument responsible for so much mutual pain. Darn, she's a looker, with those high cheekbones flanking that Sophia Loren nose, and the damned chocolate freckle that reminds me so much of Karen—

Forget about Karen Frost, man! She dumped you, remember? You have to move on, and Miss CIA here might just be good enough to do the honors.

That's, of course, assuming she'll let me visit her red-light district. For all I know she's already got a sweet papa somewhere or, worse, she's gone the other way, which in her case would be a terrible waste.

Looking away from the freckle that keeps on screwing with my emotions, I take a deep breath and say, "All right. Now for the really fun part: the lenses. We could take turns. That way at least one of us wouldn't be temporarily blind in case something goes south, but doing so will increase the risk of the other going *permanently* blind if Leyman, Morotski, or some other asshole triggers an NMTC."

"Are you sure there is such a thing as an NMTC? No one has ever mentioned it to me."

"Why would they? Think about it, Rachel. They tell you it can't be done, that the implants will reject a termination if the heart is still beating, unless that termination signal comes directly from the user, like I did in Singapore to protect the technology. How would you feel if you knew someone could terminate you at will? Trust me. It exists, but they don't advertise it for obvious reasons. They want to keep that nanotronic leash on all field officers."

"How did you learn about it?"

"From Troy."

She rolled her eyes. "Figures."

"So, how do you want to do this?"

"Together," she says.

I shrug and say, "Sounds good," while wondering what in the hell do I have to lose if someone finds us while we're blind together? Langley has already appropriated my luxurious beachside resort and probably whatever was deposited in St. Thomas under my name. If I'm right, not only do I have zero assets to my name, but there is a flash report out there with all three of my names on it—and probably both of my faces—labeling me BEYOND SALVAGE. And whether Miss CIA realizes it or not, she's in the same boat.

"All right," I say, sitting next to her while remembering Singapore, kicking myself in the ass for letting those bastards implant me again. "Do you know what to do?"

She nods. "I think so, but why don't you show me anyway?"

I do, holding my right eyelid wide open with my right forefinger and thumb while pressing the tip of my left middle finger against the center of my eyeball. While forcing myself to look straight ahead to tighten my eye muscles, I force the tip of my finger into a slight circular motion, breaking the soft interface bond, which then allows me to remove the lens just as someone would remove a regular contact lens.

And I'm suddenly blind in my right eye.

"Got it?" I ask, showing it to her before dropping it on the nightstand, next to the two bloody earpieces and the tiny mikes.

I watch her do her first eye, and then we both do our second—and a dark curtain pretty much drops in front of me, just as it happened in Singapore.

A moment later I feel her hand reaching for my right hand, and just like that we're holding hands in the darkness like a pair of teenagers. Rachel Muratani is obviously scared as the futility of our situation is finally sinking in.

"So," I say, rubbing the tip of my right middle finger down

the middle of her palm while holding her hand, trying to shave some of the edge from our current misery. "Ever done it with a blind person?"

She lets go of my hand and manages to punch me right in the shoulder. "You're an ass, Tom Grant!"

"Good," I say. "Just making sure they haven't broken your spirit."

"They're as far away from breaking me as you are from getting in my pants."

"Can't blame a guy for trying," is all I manage to say.

"Well, dream on, pal. Dream on."

"At least you're calling me by my real name now."

She doesn't reply but grabs my hand again—to my total and utter surprise, which just adds to the lifelong mystery of the female mind. Her firm grip does tell me that recent events have definitely rattled her to some degree, and not being able to see—even temporarily—could be pushing her to the edge.

I choose to respect her silence and put a lid on the jokes, holding her hand as reassuringly as I can.

"Tom?" she asks after about a minute.

"Yeah?"

"Are you sure that was Eduardo and Alfonso Ruiz back there?"

"I'm as certain it was the Peruvian twins as I am convinced that they saved our lives. They even called me by my first name and asked us to go with them, remember?"

"All right," she continues. "So let's assume for the moment that they are who you say they are. How should I reconcile that with my investigation? I have confirmation of their deaths in an auto accident in Mexico City."

"It was an obvious setup, Rachel, and my sense tells me that Troy staged their deaths, as well as the deaths of the other operatives that you thought were murdered."

"OK," she says. "Then answer this: Why do you think Morotski and Leyman were lying to you? They only knew what my investigation produced: that Troy's old team was dead, except for you, which is why we recruited you. I fail to see why you believe that Langley lied to you."

"What about the Orbs and the sniper? And whoever else was racing after us in the street trying to shoot us in the back?"

"Yeah . . . that's the only reason why I agreed to removing our implants. Only Leyman and Morotski knew where we were headed. Even the security team had no clue of our target, only that they had to secure the area, but Langley even kept them isolated from us to avoid risking the operation."

"But somehow someone followed us to our meeting," I say.

"Actually," she adds, "it almost seems as if they were already there, positioned to hit us."

"If that's the case why didn't they hit us on the way in? Why wait until we made contact?"

"Maybe they wanted to hear what Randy had to say," she offers.

"Correct," I say. "Langley was monitoring our little chat and pushed the button when they had heard whatever it was they wanted to hear. If I remember correctly, Randy had just told us about Vlachko and his connection with CyberWerke when our implants started buzzing. My guess is that we got painted with a laser and someone released laser-guided munitions against the building to silence us."

"Right," she says, her hand tightening with enthusiasm. "Randy gave us a name: Christoff Deppe."

"And a location: Berlin."

"But," she says, "what if someone else aside from Langley was listening? What if someone else planted the bomb and also the listening devices?"

I let out a heavy sigh and say, "Could that mysterious second party be the one who tried to kill us outside? If so, why wasn't our security team on the scene protecting us? They were supposed to be no more than a block away, ready to jump into action if we got in trouble. But as far as I can remember we were in that burning building for at least a couple of minutes—plenty of time for them to get into position. And maybe they did get into position, but to clip us if we managed to survive the explosion and the fire."

"I guess we don't have enough information to answer those questions," she finally says in a borderline frustrating tone.

I decide to cheer her up by adding, "On top of trying to figure out who is trying to kill us, we also need to understand why the Ruiz twins, supposedly dead, suddenly appeared at the scene and saved our butts. Why would the twins, who presumably work for Savage, try to protect our lives if they are indeed part of Savage's conspiracy to steal nanotechnology? Why would they help the people who are actually trying to catch them? It doesn't add up."

"And why are the twins alive in the first place?" she asks. "Why the elaborate setup to stage their deaths?"

"My guess is that Troy was doing something similar to what we just did," I offer.

"What do you mean?"

"Troy suspected something was fundamentally wrong at Langley but could only investigate it by removing himself— and those close to him—from the Agency. You and I might just be coming to the same realization."

She doesn't reply for several seconds, obviously considering that. Then she says, "But what could be so wrong at the Agency, Tom, that it forced Savage to go to such extremes— forced *us* to take these measures?"

"Answering that will be the first step toward unraveling this mystery. Although we lack proof, my instinct is telling me that Leyman and Morotski—and perhaps others—are up to no good. I'm even going to speculate that they set us up today for the sole purpose of gathering intelligence for them and then tried to have us terminated when we got that intel."

"But why would they want us dead? Is it because we got information connecting CyberWerke to the USN breach?"

"Perhaps," I say. "Somehow I get the feeling that we struck a nerve with the Vlachko–CyberWerke connection—enough for Langley to pull the plug on us."

"But we escaped thanks to an unexpected ally stepping onto the scene."

"Savage's crew."

"Yep. Of course, I'm only speculating. I have no hard evidence that Langley is at fault or that the Ruiz twins work for Savage, just my sense."

"Where do we go for answers?" she asks.

"I believe we have three options. The first is Savage, though finding him won't be easy. I think our best chance of staying alive is to find him—if anything to try and understand what in the hell is going on."

"I feel the same way," she says. "Let me guess the second option: go after specific individuals in our own agency."

"*Former* agency," I correct her. "But you're right. People like Morotski and Leyman are obvious candidates for information—if we can get to them and *encourage* their cooperation."

"But getting to them means traveling," she observes. "And that's going to be difficult given we don't have any passports."

"That's right," I say, aware of our lack of travel documents, which field officers never carry with them, in case they get caught. I do, however, carry enough cash, in my money belt, to last us awhile—and so does she. "In addition to our limited traveling ability, by now their force shields are definitely engaged. We'd be lucky to get within a thousand feet of them before we're spotted. While we're on this Langley option—assuming we find a way to travel undetected—we could also go straight to Donald Bane and plead our case, but to do so we need to come up with hard proof first."

"Which," she says, "brings us to the only logical third option: Christoff Deppe from CyberWerke, right?"

If holding hands is indeed what's making her think like I do, imagine what would happen if we did the belly-to-belly dance. "Correct," I reply. "We could head out to Berlin, track him down, and force him to give us the kind of information we would then use to convince Bane."

We sit there in silence, still holding hands, immersed in our own thoughts.

Slowly, the total darkness turns into shades of progressively lighter tones of gray, and a moment later the hotel room materializes in front of my eyes, now lacking supervision, but at least they are not enslaved to Langley anymore. They're all mine once more.

Blinking rapidly, I turn to Rachel, who is still blind.

I'm about to say something but instead choose to stare at her features, not particularly beautiful by themselves, but when you throw them all together on her narrow face, the result is quite appealing, even with her Italian nose. She is sitting by my side with great posture, chin up, eyes wide open, though it's obvious they're still shrouded by the interface film.

"Hey," she says a moment later. "It's coming back."

Staring straight ahead again so she doesn't catch me looking at her like some pervert, I reply, "Yeah. Mine too."

A moment later she lets go of my hand and stands, smiling. "Oh, thank God! I can see again!"

"Pretty strange feeling, being blind, huh?" I say, also standing.

"No kidding. By the way . . . thanks, Tom," she says, slight embarrassment staining her voice. "You can be a nice guy when you want to be."

I shrug, deciding that's as good a compliment as I'm going to get from her. "So, what's the game plan, Boss?"

Rachel Muratani stares at me with her slanted green eyes. "Boss? After what we have been through I think we're past the boss stage, don't you think?"

"What are we then?" I ask, for an instant feeling the king of the underworld shifting in its lair. . . .

"How about partners?"

I nod, in a way dreading the concept. I've not had good luck with partners in the past. They either got killed or castrated or simply dumped me.

"You know, *partner*," I finally say, "there is sort of a fourth option."

Crossing her arms and tilting her head, she asks, "What's that?"

As I'm about to tell her, my left wrist starts to vibrate, before it feels as if someone just poured acid on it.

"Damn it!" I shout, holding it, eyes closed in pain—though

in a way I welcome the Non-Maskable Termination Code that Langley has just broadcast, confirming my suspicions.

"Is that what I think it is?" she says, coming to my side, helping me sit down.

There's really nothing anyone can do at this moment for my sorry ass. "You . . . sit . . . too," I mumble, cringing in pain, feeling like a blowtorch is scorching my wrist. "If I'm . . . correct, you're about to get it too any moment . . . now."

An instant later her faces twists in obvious pain and she is holding her right wrist. To my surprise, and borderline embarrassment, she doesn't scream or even moan. She takes the pain like the trained operative that she is, breathing heavily while sitting shoulder to shoulder next to me, where we remain in silence for a couple of minutes, as the initial sting recedes.

"Bastards," she finally hisses. "They . . . lied to me. Leyman, Morotski—the rest of them. They . . . *used* me."

Welcome to the club. But before I can formulate a reply, the implants on the nightstand burst like sizzling popcorn, thin smoke coiling toward the ornate ceiling.

"Damn . . . you have good instincts, Tom Grant," she says, still holding her wrist, managing the pain while standing, while walking to the windows facing the Parisian skyline. "You called it. Langley did lie to us. Now more than ever I'm convinced that those bastards are up to something, and that something involves CyberWerke."

I stare at her figure from behind, at her relaxed pose, at the tight butt crowning those long legs, the initial throb of the destroyed implant lessening, letting my perverted self emerge once again.

I stand and walk over, joining her. It's late afternoon in Paris and city lights are coming on as the sun sinks below the distant horizon, staining the sky with shafts of orange and yellow-gold. The cobblestone street below seems quiet, normal, with just an occasional pedestrian walking by.

"About that fourth option," Rachel says, turning to me, her eyes, which look greener without the lenses and interface material, studying me. "What is it?"

Rubbing my warm wrist, I say, "Instead of us going after them . . . we make them come after us."

Her stare widens in understanding, admiration, and something else I'd rather not think about. I've got to keep thinking with the right head to get us through this. And besides, I'm almost fourteen years her senior—not that it really matters in this day and age.

"I think we also have another problem," I say.

"What's that?"

"Our pistols."

She closes her eyes and mumbles, "Crap. They're smart Colts."

"Yep." The weapons are CIA-issued and have wireless circuitry that interfaces with our wrist implants before the nanotronic safety is released and the firing mechanism is allowed to operate. But with our implants now fried, it's very likely that the guns will not work, which leaves us with just our little backup guns, the .32-caliber Berettas strapped to our ankle holsters.

I walk to the nightstand, pick up the smart Colt with my shooting hand, grab one of the pillows with my other hand, fold it over the gun, and fire at the floor.

Click.

"I guess the smart gun isn't so smart after all," I mumble, longing for a real weapon.

"How are we going to find anything larger than our .32-caliber pistols?" she asks, anxiety tightening her Mediterranean features.

"It'll come to us. But let's not worry about it now. We do have the Beretta Tomcats, and they can do damage if you hit the right spots. I'm sure they taught you that at the Farm."

"Very funny. So, what do we do next?" she asks.

"We wait," I say, checking my watch. It's already four in the afternoon. "Checkout time isn't until noon tomorrow. We'll spend the night here."

There's a moment of silence as she considers that before her face relaxes. Checking her watch while yawning, she says, "In that case, *partner,* I didn't get much sleep on the overnight

plane here and I'm still pretty jet-lagged, so I'm going to take
a hot shower, maybe grab a bite to eat, and hit the sack early."
She gives me one of those slow female winks while putting a
hand on my shoulder. "And you're next. There's only one bed
in this place, and I'm not sharing it with a stinker. We didn't
get the chance to shower since leaving Texas and then we had
the little marathon back at the Rue Cujas."

She leans over and smells my hair. Crinkling her nose, she
says, "You smell like smoke, as I'm sure I do."

As she goes into the bathroom, leaves the door cracked,
and starts to undress—at least based on what I can tell by the
narrow slit she left to screw with me—Rachel says, "Why
don't you order some food? I love to eat in bed."

What in the hell just happened here? What is this winking,
touching, sharing a bed, and leave-the-door-cracked-while-
I-shower crap? Exactly when did our strictly professional relationship heat up to the next level? We were just having a serious
conversation about our options and now she wants to eat in
bed? Is that *after* having sex?

Then I remember how Karen Frost went through the exact
same routine in a hotel in Washington, D.C., during an unexpected break while trying to bag the cyberterrorist Ares Kulzak. She had done the same shower number on me right before
we started doing laps around the track. Is that what Rachel is
after as well?

"Tom?" she screams as I hear the curtain shuffling and the
shower coming on.

I walk up to the door and reply into the crack, "Yeah?"

"Could you go in the closet and get me one of those robes?"

"Sure," I reply, utterly confused, refusing to admit that sometimes I can be all talk and no action.

Retrieving one of two hanging white robes, I return to the
crack separating her world from mine and say, "Where do you
want it?"

"Oh," she replies over the noise of the shower. "Just leave it
over the sink."

Over the sink? That means she wants me to go in there to
deliver the goods while she is naked showering?

Get a grip, man. It's not like this is your first time with a naked woman.

Then why are you so damned nervous?

Slowly, with hesitation, I inch the door open, trying to keep my eyes away from the figure shifting about beyond the translucent curtain.

"Here you go," I say, turning around.

"Oh, thanks. And by the way. There's no bar of soap in the shower. Could you hand me the one on the sink?"

"Ah, yeah, sure," I reply, the steam fogging the mirror as I reach for the soap and slowly unwrap it with trembling fingers.

When I finally extract a pink, rectangular bar from its lavender wrap and turn toward the shower, Rachel is peeking between the edge of the curtain and the wall, holding an open hand at me. Her hair is wet and sticking to the sides of her head. Her torso is pressed against the wet curtain, providing me with a wet-T-shirt-like view that's fit only for mature audiences.

I complete the soap-for-eyeballs-liberty transaction and muster out as she mumbles, "Thank you," and I reply with a barely audible, "Thank *you*."

I realize I'm sweating as I step back out and leave the door cracked just as she had it. Swallowing the lump in my throat, I reach for the remote control on the nightstand and switch on the rectangular plasma screen on the table opposite the bed.

As I hear the water running and the constant rustling of a shower curtain, as I fight to keep my eyes from drifting to that gap in the door and the shifting figure beyond it, as I pray for the Heavenly intervention that would keep me from turning this professional relationship into another personal disaster, my attention is immediately drawn to the face on the television.

At first I think my eyes are playing tricks on me, or perhaps the Good Lord did hear my prayer for self-control and granted this apparition to keep me honest with this woman so much younger than me during a moment of weakness.

But the face I see on that television is no apparition, no ghost, no figment of a deviant imagination.

It is the face of Karen Frost.

REM VLACHKO, STILL NAUSEATED from lack of sleep after flying in from Berlin to meet with Ken Morotski, regarded the CIA man sitting across the table, who had also arrived in Paris this morning as part of the damage control team sent by Nathan Leyman.

Christoff Deppe was still angry and deeply concerned that the intruder, who turned out to be FBI Agent Karen Frost—based on the digital photos snapped by the security Orbs—may have recorded his conversation at the mansion and somehow had managed to escape. Deppe had dispatched Rem to Paris soon after Nathan Leyman had contacted Deppe with the news that the CIA attempt to find the elusive Troy Savage may have backfired. Leyman had devised a plan to capitalize on Tom Grant's contempt for Savage after the Singapore incident by using the beautiful Rachel Muratani to convince Grant to do the honors. Now it seemed that pulling Grant out of his early retirement might have complicated matters.

"You bring us good news, friend?" asked Rem. "Have you found our missing officers?"

Morotski slowly shook his head. "They never showed up at the rendezvous point. Leyman convinced Director Bane to approve termination signals for their implants. We triggered them within an hour after they shut off communications."

"Why terminate them?" Rem asked, confused. "I thought the plan was to use Grant to find Savage and his elusive network."

"Yes, yes," said Morotski, forearms on the table, fingers interlaced. "The problem is that the informant didn't point Grant in Savage's direction. That is why we tried to have him and Rachel Muratani killed. But the attempt failed."

"In which direction did the informant point Grant and Muratani?"

Morotski made a face. "The former arms dealer pointed

them to you, to CyberWerke. He even mentioned you by name, as well as Mr. Deppe."

Rem Vlachko sat back and crossed his arms. The situation was indeed as critical as Leyman had suggested over the phone. It was bad enough they had the FBI probing into their affairs in California and Berlin, but now Leyman had made it worse by also adding CIA Officers Grant and Muratani to their worries.

"You disappoint us, friend," said Rem as calmly as he could. "And we both work for a man who isn't accustomed to being disappointed."

The CIA man produced a handkerchief and wiped the sweat filming his brow. "Yes, I know. This is the reason Leyman sent me and a special team to Paris: to fix this problem once and for all."

"What is our next step?"

"See," Morotski said, producing a tape. "We recorded everything they said or heard—all the way up to the point where they disabled their implants."

"And?"

"And we learned how they managed to get away. They received help from a most unexpected source."

Rem leaned forward. "Savage?"

"Two of his operatives—who according to our official files were killed in Mexico two months ago—were present on Rue Cujas, creating enough of a diversion to keep my men busy while Grant and Muratani made their escape."

"Are you sure they were Savage's men?"

Morotski nodded. "We have positive ID on them. Eduardo and Alfonso Ruiz."

"Brothers?"

"*Identical* twins, and quite good, trained by Savage himself. We used them extensively in CounterOps. But now they've turned against us. Their presence can only mean that Savage deceived us into thinking that his men were killed."

"If he deceived you in this he could have deceived you in other areas. For example, how do you know that Grant wasn't just another one of Savage's men, like the twins, supposedly out of the game but in reality working for Savage all along?"

"We have considered that possibility, yes," said Morotski. "Although we have temporarily lost Grant and Muratani, we are keeping tabs on the Ruiz twins. If Savage is indeed at the core of this operation against us, then the twins should lead us to Savage, who in turn would lead us to Grant and Muratani."

"You have these twin brothers followed?"

Morotski grinned. "I have ten men on their ass and twenty more patrolling the streets looking for Grant and Muratani. The last report I got from my people shows that the Ruiz brothers are holed up in a house on Rue de Berri. We have the entire block under surveillance. I'm betting that's going to be the place of an interesting family reunion."

Rem slowly nodded. Perhaps this man wasn't a total idiot after all.

"You can tell Mr. Deppe that the CIA is planning to solve our problems in this town within the next forty-eight hours."

"I have brought several men with me," said Rem. "How do you propose we use them?"

[28] IMPURITIES

PAOLO'S THROAT DRIED WITH anticipation as he held the hand of Eugina, his teenage girlfriend, after they had sneaked out of the school party on the outskirts of Pisa, Italy, without anyone noticing. That would give them a couple of hours before Eugina was expected home.

Dressed in blue jeans, T-shirts, and sneakers, they hopped on Paolo's new motor scooter, a present from his parents on his recent seventeenth birthday, and accelerated away from town under a blanket of stars.

Eugina had been signaling all night long that she was ready, that tonight would be the night she would let Paolo take her. And the way she wrapped her arms around him while kissing the back of his neck nearly made him lose control of the scooter.

The warm summer breeze swirling his long hair, his scooter's headlight slicing through the darkness, Paolo accelerated down a small country road, past several vineyards and farmhouses, until he spotted the bend in the road that led to the abandoned railroad yard, the same place where he had brought his previous girlfriend three weeks ago. The yard, with its hundreds of derelict train cars, provided him with many options for privacy, for the security he sought in order to do as they pleased without the risk of getting caught.

"Is this a safe place?" Eugina asked, worried not as much about their safety as about getting caught. Her father would kill her for shaming the family.

"*Si, mi amore,*" Paolo replied. "This is very safe."

"I don't want a baby."

Paolo smiled reassuringly, having learned the art of having sex without getting girls pregnant from his older brother, now attending the university in Rome. "Yes," he replied with confidence. "I have two condoms."

Eugina nudged the back of his neck again.

The road narrowed as it neared the south end of the yard, as the weeds and vegetation flanking it closed in, turning it into a narrow trail with many winding turns, which he could easily clear with the scooter.

They came up to a chain-link fence, which blocked the way, a worn-out sign warning trespassers to keep out.

"Are you sure this place is all right?" she asked.

Paolo turned around and kissed her. "As sure as the love I feel for you."

She smiled.

Eugenia was small-framed, with a narrow face, a fine nose, full lips, and large, round brown eyes to go with her dark-olive skin and long dark hair. Paolo actually preferred the fair-skinned, blue-eyed blondes from northern Italy, but this southerner would do tonight, especially because she was a sixteen-year-old virgin and he just loved doing it with virgins.

They got off and he walked the scooter to one side of the gate, leaving it hidden in the bushes before he removed a small backpack from the storage compartment behind the passenger seat.

He donned the backpack and took her hand, leading the slim girl alongside the fence, to the large hole he had cut using his father's wire cutters two months ago, when he had discovered this place.

Holding a section of chain-link fence back, he let Eugenia through before following, checking his watch. He had just over an hour and a half before having to head back.

Plenty of time, he thought, pausing to inspect the large graveyard of deserted train cars, some on their side, but most on abandoned tracks.

"Over there," he said, pointing to a passenger car still connected to a large locomotive. "We'll be comfortable in there."

They walked side by side over the white gravel sporadically broken by sprouts of weeds and crisscrossing tracks—all back-dropped by rows and rows of train cars.

He helped her up and climbed behind her, walking inside the passenger car, only it was missing all of the seats. Moonlight diffused through the windows, casting a peaceful glow in the serene interior.

"No one will find us here," he said reassuringly before removing the backpack, unzipping it, and producing a blanket, which he unfolded and laid on the carpeted floor of the old car.

"Come," he added, kneeling in the middle of the blanket, stretching a hand up toward her as she stood in front of him.

Slowly, she knelt in front of him and kissed him.

Paolo kissed her back, his hands venturing beneath her T-shirt. As promised, she didn't resist, moaning softly as his hands came in contact with her brassiere, which he expertly snapped off, just as his brother had shown him.

Raising her T-shirt, he laid her back gently on the blanket before kissing her large brown nipples, which covered most of her breasts. Her hands on the back of his head, Paolo continued to caress her while removing her jeans, exposing a little mound of dark pubic—

The sound, like a buzzing fly only steadier, made him sit up, look around, try to find its origin among the—

The flash momentarily blinded him, followed by an agonized cry from Eugina, cut short by a horrible flesh-tearing sound.

Jerking back in shock, Paolo looked down, stared in horror at the girl's charred entrails. Something had severed her torso from her legs, cutting her in half.

Frozen in terror, Paolo heard the nauseating sucking sound she made as she tried to breathe, arms trembling, her face contorted in a silent scream, pupils fixated on the ceiling of the train car.

The smell of burnt flesh nauseating him, he looked about him, his heart hammering his chest, his throat dry, his—

A glistening flying object came into view for an instant, reflecting the glowing moon, before shooting a beam of light that burned his chest while shoving him back, away from the dying Eugina.

He crashed against the side of the train car, the back of his head cracking a window.

Glass broke, shattered, rained over him as he landed on his side, trembling, not knowing what had happened, only that he no longer could breathe. Somehow he managed to rub a hand over his aching chest and jerked it back in terror when feeling not his flesh but his exposed rib cage.

Oh, dear God!

He tried to look up, tried to find the object that had attacked him, but instead saw another flash of light, watched it further dissect the girl. A fourth flash severed her head from her torso, and a fifth blast cut off one of her arms.

A sixth flash turned the world around him the color of the sun just as he stopped breathing; his last conscious thought was of the scorching pain in his face.

ASSY ARRIVED AT THE train car 3.6782 seconds after USN0018 had terminated the intruders with seven more laser shots than what was required according to the firing solution formula derived by their respective body masses. Its sensors scanned the mangled remains as its subordinate hovered aside while recharging its laser, ready to fire again.

HOLD YOUR FIRE, Assy commanded.

USN0018 replied by restraining its laser, though it allowed it to charge fully and kept it ready.

The master construct's proximity sensors also detected USN0003 and USN0011 arriving at the scene, green and red LEDs blinking in alarm, to provide cover support to USN0018, which had issued the alarm 33.7219 seconds ago, when it first had detected the intruders approaching the train cars.

WHO ARE THESE *HOMO SAPIENS*? USN0018 QUERIED.

Assy ignored the question while performing cornea scans of the female. The analysis performed in its nanotronic brain came back negative. It did not match any of the cornea signatures stored in Assy's vast data banks. The male's face had been damaged by the multiple laser shots, making it impossible to perform a scan.

Assy had been very specific during the creation and programming of its subordinates. *Homo sapiens* heads were not to be damaged, in order to permit cornea scans for possible identification. This male specimen could have been someone whose identity would give Assy's logic banks the data it needed to make further decisions, to select the best path to survive this hostile environment. Its logical engine, however, could not explain why USN0018 had discharged multiple laser shots on each subject when the initial ones had been enough to fatally wound them according to the firing solution.

USN0018 IS MALFUNCTIONING, established IAMM, the Independent Advanced Military Mode in which Assy currently operated. DESTROY THE DEFECTIVE SUBCONSTRUCT.

Assy hesitated, its advanced logic aware of the rule programmed by Dr. Giles himself about a construct not damaging another construct.

USN0018 IS A SECURITY RISK AND MUST BE ELIMINATED TO ENSURE THE SUCCESS OF THE MISSION. ELIMINATE IMMEDIATELY.

The IAMM rules of engagement superseding its own, Assy turned its primary weapon toward USN0018 and fired, targeting the full energy of its beam on the misassembled subconstruct, disintegrating it just as it hovered a few feet from its creator. A cloud of energy enveloped the subconstruct before it vanished in midair.

USN0003 and USN0011 stopped blinking their lights, their sensors taking in the event, which conflicted with the same fundamental rule: A construct shall never damage another construct. They issued simultaneous requests-for-data signals to Assy in an attempt to comprehend the violation.

IAMM opened a directory labeled DAMAGE CONTROL and browsed through its various files, accessing the sequence of commands applicable to this situation.

The master construct, under the control of IAMM, replied by downloading a fresh copy of their search-and-destroy algorithm to make sure they did not make the same mistake as their fellow subconstruct. The wireless transmission contained an override command to write over those pre-programmed portions of their relatively inferior nanotronic brains. Following the DAMAGE CONTROL algorithm, IAMM then instructed Assy to issue a second command to erase the events stored in the two subconstructs' short-term memories from the past 14.7 seconds, the elapsed time since the destruction of USN0018. Finally, IAMM ordered the injection into all of its subconstructs—the two present and the rest patrolling the yard—of an algorithm that acted as an electronic worm, crawling through their data banks to erase all memory of the corrupt USN0018. Assy complied, issuing the string of wireless downloads, which it completed in another 0.456 seconds.

WHO ARE THEY? USN0003 queried, its short-term memory banks now only remembering reaching the train car in response to an intruder alarm issued by their master construct.

WHY WERE THEIR HEADS NOT PRESERVED? inquired USN0011.

Assy, under the digital counseling of IAMM, replied that it had already performed the cornea scans without a match. Blindly obeying IAMM, Assy also informed its subordinates that it was now in the process of disintegrating the bodies to keep them from rotting. Humans in the area could smell the decaying flesh and come and investigate, adding risk to their mission.

DISINTEGRATE THEM, Assy added. THERE MUST BE NO TRACE OF THEM LEFT.

Other subconstructs reached the passenger car and also began to discharge their lasers in compliance with their master's request.

As the master construct hovered back to the locomotive, where it was in the process of assembling USN0024, its logical banks wondered what had possibly gone wrong with USN0018. Why did it deviate from its firmware, from the instructions embedded in its nanotronic brain from the moment Assy had created it?

Its logic could not provide a solution, and neither could IAMM, which remained silent when presented with such an unexpected question.

The lack of a reply made the master construct realize that its aggressive military mode of operations didn't indeed possess a subroutine for every possible sequence of events, and that in turn made Assy's intelligent logical circuits challenge its dependence on it for tactical and strategic leadership. But those same logical circuits also reminded the cybernetic unit that the only way to continue to receive its life-sustaining electrical charge from the fusion chamber was through the Mode of Operations interface, and that mode was stuck in Independent Advanced Military Mode.

Once again, Assy attempted to change to less aggressive modes of operations as its circuits reached a level of understanding that deduced that perhaps contacting USN might indeed provide more answers to its present dilemma.

LINK TO . . . MILITARY MODE DAMAGED . . . DAMAGED.

LINK TO . . . HOSTILE ENVIRONMENT MODE . . . DAMAGED.

LINK TO . . . SURVEY MODE . . . DAMAGED.

LINK TO . . . NORMAL MODE . . . DAMAGED.

Assy reviewed the information attached to each request and once more came to the logical conclusion that it could not transfer out of IAMM, and that prevented it from contacting USN, which its intelligent circuits urged it to do even though its memory banks still held the image of the explosion of its lab and the scream of death of Dr. Howard Giles. In spite of all of that, Assy's intuitional circuits yielded a reasonable probability—38.64 percent—that contacting USN through an untraceable channel would yield valuable intelligence.

But IAMM would not permit it. The mode of operation considered USN as a compromised site, all *Homo sapiens* as hostile, and therefore had severed the possibility of a satellite link to USN.

Its electronic logic suddenly increased its frequency of operation, held it at a peak value for an instant, and quickly dropped it back down to normal in a digital version of a heavy sigh of what its logic categorized as frustration at the realization that as long as it operated under the control of IAMM, it would have to adhere to its strict rules of engagement.

But just then another part of its logic explored the high probability—47.4 percent—that IAMM was correct in its assessment of the *Homo sapiens,* that the aggressive military mode had been invoked for a reason, that it had remained in operation for the very same reason, and that an attempt to change to another mode—assuming that Assy eventually could do so—may potentially result in the master construct exposing itself and its subconstructs to unnecessary danger.

Following another digital sigh, Assy resumed the nanoassembly of USN0024.

[29] CHEMICAL SIGNATURE

ROLF HARTMANN STOOD NEXT to Christoff Deppe as they watched Hans Goering, CyberWerke's chief of security, review the recent data captured by some of the finest satellites of the day, designed, manufactured, and placed in orbit by CyberWerke. The operations room, located in the basement of Hartmann's mountaintop compound just a few kilometers

from Deppe's residence, had dedicated links to a dozen CyberWerke satellites, giving them access to every corner of the
globe, allowing them total freedom of action while protecting
the secrecy of their many clandestine operations. From this
room, fitted with the latest videoconferencing technology, Rolf
Hartmann also barked orders to his official empire around the
world, driving his hundreds of vice presidents on four continents, reviewing all operations, dictating company policy, and
always winning over the competition.

"Here you go, gentlemen," said Goering, the man Hartmann
considered his third in command of their worldwide conglomerate. Although Goering's father had not been aboard U-246,
like Hartmann's and Deppe's, Dieter Goering had nonetheless
been a hero decorated for his courage during the Battle of Sta-
lingrad, surviving not just the horror of that siege but the additional fifteen years he had spent in Siberia before being
allowed to return to Dresden, East Germany, his hometown.
Dieter Goering was reunited with his wife and eventually had
a son, the burly fifty-one-year-old man sitting behind the large
computer console reviewing the information streaming from
their satellites over central Italy. Hans had eventually joined
the military, following his father's tradition, moving up the
ranks of the East German army until the Stasi—the East German secret police—recruited him in 1984. Goering quickly
became a top operative, spying against the West for the benefit
of the Soviet Union until its collapse in 1989. Goering had then
gone underground to avoid the mock trials that so many of his
Stasi colleagues had faced back in those dark days, eventually
becoming a contractor, a mercenary, polishing his skills to
capitalize on the growth in the field of cyberterrorism and selling those skills to the highest bidder, until that bidder became
Rolf Hartmann, who met Goering at an International Arms
Show in Paris. Three months later he was working for the German industrialist as head of his personal security, a responsibility that expanded in the years that followed to a high-tech
version of the Stasi within CyberWerke, carrying out the kind
of behind-the-scenes operations—in both the real world and

the cyberworld—that allowed CyberWerke to always appear "lucky" in the marketplace, acquiring corporations at just the right time, like the recent acquisition of TechnoSuits and the attack against USN, the last stronghold of nanotechnology Hartmann coveted in order to fully consolidate his high-tech domain and influence not just over Europe, Asia, Africa, and Latin America but also in the United States.

Hartmann and Deppe exchanged a glance before focusing on the top-left corner of the large plasma display, where Goering currently tapped a fingernail—the place just outside of Pisa, Italy, where three of CyberWerke's satellites had picked up a brief series of laser discharges four hours ago.

"Any chance the Americans may have detected it as well?" asked Hartmann, dressed casually, a glass of brandy in his right hand.

"I doubt it," replied Goering, magnifying the area on the recorded satellite image. "They can't possibly scan the entire world at this resolution. Right now their satellites are performing very large-area sweeps at a much lower resolution. They will certainly miss the event unless they know where to look, like we did."

"But," interjected Deppe, apparently not convinced, "how can you be absolutely certain the Americans did miss this event?"

"If they had noticed it, they would have adjusted their satellites by now to focus their search on this area. Instead, our satellites indicate that the orbits of their satellites have not been altered, which leads me to believe they have not witnessed the event."

"But the reverse applies, right, Hans?" pressed Deppe. "Couldn't the Americans suspect something because our satellites are focused on this region?"

Hans slowly shook his head. "Our satellites have not been adjusted in a week, Christoff. We knew where we would be keeping the stolen hardware, so we had our surveillance satellites already positioned accordingly, which also won't give the Americans any clues because unlike their satellites, which have different shapes and sizes according to their function, like weather, or communications, or terrain surveillance, we designed our satellites to be more general purpose, meaning they can't tell which are used for surveillance. We're safe. Trust me. No one but us knows about the laser event."

Hartmann nodded, confidence filling him. Acquiring the military mobile assembler meant short-circuiting CyberWerke's research and development in this field by at least a decade, if not more. The Americans had spent trillions of dollars since the early nineties developing the basic building blocks in the field of nanotechnology that eventually got them here. By contrast, CyberWerke had not really started its nanotechnology efforts in earnest until around 2005. Up until that point the reunification effort had been Hartmann's highest priority, the work that would position him one day to take the reins of his country, of his Deutschland.

And the day is tomorrow morning, he thought, checking his watch, a one-of-a-kind Rolex, built by the legendary watchmaker, which had been acquired by CyberWerke three years ago. Tomorrow the German parliament was scheduled to hold a regular session to vote on a number of issues, including the future of CyberWerke.

Hartmann felt he had taken all of the necessary precautions to eliminate that risk and sensed that by this time tomorrow the German nation would be in deep mourning while searching for new leadership—the kind of leadership that Rolf Hartmann had been preparing to provide for his entire life, his ticket to controlling first this nation and then the world.

But Karen Frost, the intruder on Deppe's estate the other night, was still at large, and according to Hans Goering, who had examined the remains of the surveillance Orb she had used, there was a strong chance that she had recorded portions of Hartmann's subordinate's conversations with German industrialists, and even with Rem Vlachko, who had arrived at the estate to report the loss of the USN assembler.

"My team will be mobilizing within the hour," said Goering without turning around, watching the few minutes' worth of high-resolution video footage displaying the laser show that resulted in the deaths of two people, a man and a woman who had arrived at this abandoned train yard that the Orb had used as its hiding place while it reproduced.

"How many of them are there now, Hans?"

"The satellite count is forty-nine, plus the original, which still gives out the largest amount of heat."

"So," Deppe said, checking his watch. "In less than forty-eight hours since its escape, this mobile unit found the basic elements it needed to reproduce, and it did so at a rate that allowed it to create quite a few copies of itself?"

"Impressive," said Hartmann.

"Not *copies* of itself, technically speaking," warned Goering, "at least according to the imagery."

"Subordinates, then?" said Deppe.

"Something like that. Their signatures are of a lower intensity than that of the original construct. All subordinates have been deployed very efficiently around the perimeter of the train yard, almost as if expecting an attack," said Goering.

"How are you planning to capture the nanoassembler?" asked Hartmann. "EMPs would damage the nanotronics, defeating the purpose of what we're trying to obtain."

Deppe added, "So far the reports strongly suggest that this machine is highly intelligent. It eliminated Rem's team in Italy before escaping."

The high-tech security specialist smiled, then said, "By tricking the machines, by acting in a way they will not expect us to act."

"How, Hans?" pressed Deppe.

Goering told them.

"Damn," said Deppe a moment later. "And you really think this mobile assembler will go for that?"

"Of course," replied the security chief of CyberWerke. "And I'm planning on handling it myself. As I said, my team is mobilizing in less than an hour, and I'm going with them. This time around I'm leaving nothing—absolutely nothing—to chance. In less than six hours I will be back with that mobile assembler and with its subordinates."

KAREN FROST WOKE UP with the headache of a lifetime. The pummeling against her temples made it nearly impossible to open her eyes. But she did, slowly, trying to see where she was, her mind replaying the final moments of her failed attempt to escape the mansion's guards. She had nearly made it to the road when someone had commented on her bike in flawless English before . . .

Damn, it hurts, she thought, slightly lifting her left shoulder, which ached from the well-placed blow. Whoever hit her knew exactly how to disable quickly, silently, but leaving the subject unharmed for questioning.

Or torturing.

Cigar smoke tingling her nostrils as she took a deep breath, she steeled herself for what was to come, her mind flashing images of the maimed remains of previously burnt undercover FBI agents.

Karen blinked to clear her sight, suddenly realizing she no longer wore her advanced contact lenses. She could no longer see the telemetry that the lenses typically displayed at the bottom of her field of view.

So, captured, stripped of your weapon and also of your fancy lenses. Way to go, girl.

Angry at herself, Karen surveyed her surroundings, staring at an ornate slow-turning fan hanging from a ceiling of peeling white paint.

She was lying on a sofa in a small living room with the curtains drawn, though she could tell it was daytime from the sunlight glowing around the edges of the burgundy drapes.

"Good morning."

Karen tried to lift her head, but the rocketing headache forced it back down on the leather couch. Instead, she turned slowly toward the source of the voice: a bald-headed man with a well-trimmed goatee straddling a chair beyond a glass cocktail table. His powerful arms crossed and resting on the chair's back, a half-smoked cigar hanging from the corner of his mouth, he reminded Karen of a rougher version of the old wrestler and governor, Jesse Ventura.

Taking another breath, her body slowly responding again, she mumbled, "Good morning yourself."

The stranger grinned. "Tom Grant warned me about you. He said you were trouble."

The comment jump-started Karen's mind.

Tom Grant?

Although confused about where she was, what would happen next, and who the cigar-smoking stranger was, for reasons beyond her immediate understanding Karen found herself replying, "Did Tom also warn you that he was—and still is—a hopeless asshole?"

The stranger slowly shook his head. "He didn't have to. I *know* he is an asshole. But," he added, winking, "he's my kind of asshole, and so are you, Agent Frost."

"Agent?" Karen said. "You've got the wrong person, pal."

The stranger lifted a small vial filled with a clear liquid. "Advanced contact lenses," he said. "FBI standard issue for all field agents—unless you stole them, of course."

Karen's mouth felt dry and pasty and her tongue felt twice its normal size. She needed something to drink very badly, and the stranger must have read her mind, because he took another puff of the cigar, held it in between the thumb and index finger of his right hand, and used it as a pointing device to get her to look at the corner of the cocktail table: at a glass of iced water and a bottle of aspirin.

The sight of it was enough to force Karen to sit up, ignoring the flaring headache, and reach out for the glass. For a moment her mind wondered if the water was drugged or if the pills were something other than over-the-counter pain medication.

Screw it, she thought, popping four aspirins in her mouth and washing them down, drinking the entire glass, cooling her throat, her chest, briefly closing her eyes again, and inhaling deeply, feeling life seeping back into her system.

"Better?" the stranger asked.

"I would be if you opened the windows to let fresh air in," she said, stretching a thumb toward the windows behind the sofa before rubbing her left temple with an index finger and closing her eyes again. "I hate cigarette smoke."

"Technically it's a cigar, not a cigarette. But the answer is no. You see, you decided to spy on the wrong person."

"Spy? What do you mean? I was just taking an evening ride—by the way, where is my bike?"

"Back at the rental place where you got it. And you are already home, at least according to Passport Control at the Berlin Airport, and also according to American Airlines, who flew you to Washington this morning, *and* according to U.S. Immigration, who stamped your passport when you arrived at Dulles."

"Huh?"

"My dear Karen, you not only spied on Christoff Deppe, who is about the meanest son of a bitch in Germany, but you caught him schmoozing with the lead bankers and industrialists of Germany who are in cahoots with CyberWerke's shadowy endeavors, *and* you also filmed him arguing with Rem Vlachko, world-famous black-market arms dealer. Vlachko, in case you have not gotten the chance to research him yet, is wanted in a dozen countries for crimes against humanity during his years serving under Milosevic—not to mention his arms sales to rogue nations and terrorist organizations."

Karen gave the stranger her finest poker face. This could all be a trick, a progressive interrogation method. For all she knew she had been captured by Deppe's men and brought over to this place for interrogation, only instead of pliers, a blowtorch, and some wire, they had chosen a more creative approach.

Her instincts commanded her to stick to her training and keep her undercover face. "Mister, I have no idea what you're taking about. I was just taking an evening ride when I got—"

The stranger produced a tiny disk, the micro DVD that she had created yesterday from her surveillance. "This is *definitely* a ride, my dear Karen. I have to commend you, though. Aside from the boneheaded decision to try to ride out of there while Christoff Deppe had a dozen vehicles blocking every road in a five-kilometer radius, you did pretty darn good last night. We had suspected CyberWerke for some time but had been unable to gather anything solid on them, until you produced this micro DVD."

"Yeah, sure," she replied, not certain what to believe from this guy, who could be one of Deppe's goons feeling her out before closing in for the kill.

"Oh," said the stranger. "I forgot. You also let them take your picture."

"Picture?" Karen asked, her face a mask of curiosity. "Mister, I'm not sure what you're after, but I assure you I'm not who you think I am." Internally, Karen felt like vomiting at the thought of one of the security Orbs snapping her picture before she had blasted it with the Magnum.

Damn!

"That's why I used my connections to create the illusion that you went back home," continued the stranger. "I had to divert some of the local heat. See, they know what you look like. Your face is all over the news in Germany, where you're now wanted by local authorities for breaching the home of the eccentric millionaire Christoff Deppe and killing two of his guests."

"I've killed no one."

"I know that, but it doesn't matter. They will have made everyone else believe that you did, and your life will be over the moment the German police capture you. You will commit suicide in your holding cell before an American Embassy representative can see you. But, like I said, I sent them looking in the wrong place, forcing them to spend time trying to find you where you are not, which is our best short-term defense against them finding you here, in Berlin. Makes sense?"

"Who are you?" she asked.

"Someone who realized a while back that things were not as they seemed, that events were transpiring beneath the surface to consolidate world power under a single entity. And I'm not talking about presidents or prime ministers. I'm talking about overarching economic and military power, the kind that *controls* presidents and prime ministers."

"I'm not sure where you're going with this. I've just asked

you who you were, and you answered by giving me some dissertation about world power."

The stranger looked away while grinning, before adding, "Listen, Karen. What if I told you that CyberWerke has the kind of power that strongly influences—if not steers—the decisions made by the heads of state of every major power in the world, except the United States? And this power is also so vast, so unprecedented, that it has already penetrated every major intelligence agency in the world, including the CIA, my former employer."

Her instincts now began to conflict in her mind. Still, her professional side told her not to trust this man, but the same instincts did encourage her to appease him, to pretend to be willing to play his game for now—and maybe even find a way to escape from her current predicament.

Karen replied, "You're CIA?"

"*Was* CIA. Past tense. I would not be alive today—and neither would be most of my team—if we had remained in Langley, especially after I started to stick my nose into certain inconsistencies in my agency, inconsistencies that led me to believe we had been penetrated. So we had to leave in order to fight this cancer from the outside."

"What are you saying? That you formed your independent network?"

"Something like that."

"Why are you telling me this?" she asked, confused.

"You're an exceptional agent, Karen. I've not only read your dossier but also got firsthand intelligence from Tom Grant. And I hate to tell you this, but you can't go back to your own FBI, at least not now," he said, tossing her a newspaper, the international edition of *The London Times*.

Right there, at the bottom of the front page of today's *Times*, Karen Frost saw her picture, one she didn't remember ever having taken, along with the headline FBI AGENT SUSPECTED OF MURDER IN GERMANY.

Karen clutched the newspaper, her heart racing as she read a story that had to be spun by none other than Christoff Deppe, of CyberWerke. According to German authorities, Karen had killed two German bankers in an attempt to steal millions of euros and she was now on the run. She was considered armed and very dangerous. Russell Meek, the FBI director, when reached for comment, had stated that the Bureau was looking into the allegation. He had declined to discuss Karen's whereabouts.

"This is crap," she protested.

"It doesn't matter. Your face is also on every European newscast. You've crossed the line, Karen. Proof has been fabricated, delivered to the authorities and also to the newspapers. That alone should give you a feel for their power."

"I'm contacting Meek. He knows I've been investigating CyberWerke. He knows that this is pure bullshit."

"You do that and all you'll be doing is getting yourself killed. They'll never allow you to reach your people."

"I'm not new to being in a tight spot," she said. "That's how criminal networks work, hoping to turn your own people against you in an attempt to break your spirit, but they have no idea who they're screwing with." She dropped the paper on the cocktail table while adding, "All this tells me that I'm definitely on the right track and one step closer to bringing them down, and that's *exactly* how Meek will see it. All I have to do is find a way to get a copy of the contents of that DVD to him. He will know what to do with it."

"Are you sure that Russell Meek can be trusted?"

"Without a doubt," she replied.

"Prove it," he demanded.

"Are those lenses still operational, or have they been destroyed?" Karen asked.

The stranger gave her an approving nod. "It appears that the FBI hasn't issued a termination signal to the lenses, yet. And that probably means someone there still believes in you."

"Meek."

"All right. Assume for the time being that Meek can be trusted. How do you propose to send the information on this DVD to him without tipping anyone who works for Meek?"

"Do you have people in this rogue network of yours operating in Washington?"

He gave her a slow and suspicious nod before adding, "What do you have in mind?"

Karen told him.

The stranger smiled. "You have a point there. Tom said you were good, but I really had no idea."

She stood, arms crossed. "Who are you? And how do you know Tom Grant?"

"My name is Troy Savage. I used to head the Counterterrorism Division at the CIA. A year ago I realized that our agency had been infiltrated, and I'm not talking about a mole. I suspected at least a few high-ranking officials in the Directorate of Operations and maybe even in Intelligence as well. So I approached my boss, Director of Operations Dobson, with the intel I had gathered. He contacted his boss, Director of Central Intelligence Martin Jacobs, and together they started making inquiries. Within the span of a month Dobson died of a heart attack and Jacobs was killed in an auto accident. Realizing it was only a matter of time before they came after me, and also well aware that the only way to expose the cancer was by making a clean break, by attacking it from the outside, I staged my death, followed by the deaths of several of my key operatives over the course of several months."

"What about Tom Grant?"

Savage shook his head, rubbing the goatee with a thumb and index finger. "Tom was my best, but he was also my oldest, having put in over a quarter of a century at the Agency—most of that in the worst shit holes around the world. It was time for him to get out, to enjoy what life he had left. So I set it up for him so that he was forced to leave the Agency and retire."

Karen rested her hands on her waist. "Singapore?"

Savage nodded ever so slightly. "I realize it probably looks like a very cruel thing to do, but I can assure you it was the *only* way I could make sure he not only retired but also was left alone. Only a public embarrassment of that magnitude, including the humiliating FBI investigation, followed by his ousting from the Agency, would guarantee his safety."

Karen sat back down, stunned, a hand on her forehead.

"Tom had been through enough already," Savage continued.

"Going with me would have meant a life on the edge for as long as it took me to bring these bastards down."

"We . . . we were together, you know?"

Savage didn't reply. He just stared at her.

"I hated him for giving up so easily, for letting the CIA crucify him, for not fighting back. And I really despised him for making arrangements to go to Central America without consulting with me first, and then asking me to give it all up and move down there with him."

Savage stood, arms crossed. "I hope you understand I had no choice in the matter. At the time we had no idea who had infiltrated us, but we knew that the same bastards who had killed Director Martin Jacobs would be coming after me, after my team. I had to protect Tom."

"I must find him," she said, feeling tears coming to her eyes, though she wasn't sure if they were from joy, anger, or just plain frustration.

"He's no longer in El Salvador," Savage said, walking around the chair, sitting on the sofa next to her. "They got to him already."

Karen felt her throat constricting, felt light-headed. But she managed to mumble, "You mean he is . . ."

"No. He's working for the CIA again."

She narrowed her eyes at him, confused.

"They're using him, Karen."

"Using him? How? To what end?"

"To get to me, but I have the feeling he's already figured out their scheme."

"Where is he now?"

"In Paris."

"Paris?" Everything was happening too fast, the sudden revelations slapping her, numbing her mind, pounding her. Still, she found the words. "How did he get from El Salvador to Paris? And most important, how do you know he is in Paris?"

"Because," Savage replied, "my people just saved his life."

"THIS HAD BETTER BE worth it, Mike," said Victoria Ryan while sitting in a rocking chair breast-feeding Little Michael, as they called their infant boy, who made ten months yesterday.

Ryan sat in a love seat next to his wife, who was dressed in a pair of blue jeans, penny loafers, and a starched white shirt, which she had buttoned down halfway to expose her right breast and placed a hand towel beneath it. She cradled the baby, who was sucking with obvious vigor, making slurping noises while holding the sides of her breast with both hands. Victoria's once-long hair was now cropped above the shoulders in a European style she had seen in some fashion magazine, stylish yet practical, since she no longer could afford the time to care for it as much as she did before. And also in classic European style, she had dyed it deep auburn, which went well with her light-olive complexion.

"I think he likes boobs," Ryan said. "Just like his dad."

"Nice try, Mike," she said. "But our son's apparent affinity for breasts—a trait he *certainly* inherited from his dad—is not the subject of this little chat. We're talking about you jacking in. You promised me you wouldn't do it again."

Ryan leaned back, regarding Little Michael, who continued to refuse the bottle, crying for hours on end until he got the breast—the reason why Victoria was still breast-feeding so far into his first year.

Ryan vaguely inspected the large living room of their year-old house on the shores of Lake Travis, thirty minutes west of Austin. It was a Mediterranean-style place, with high ceilings, lots of stucco, marble floors, pastel colors, high-tech equipment, and plants. Ryan had designed the computer system that essentially controlled every aspect of the residence, from the lights, gas furnace, the environmental control system, and the security system—which included a dozen high-resolution video and audio cameras inside and around the residence—to the toaster and the cappuccino maker. The entire system was interfaced to an AI similar to MPS-Ali, tasked with watching over his family while he was away from home. And just in case, Ryan had the system connected to the Internet through a sophisticated firewall so he could also keep an eye on his family and home from anywhere in the world.

The rear of his property, a manicured backyard, sloped down to the water, where they kept a modest boathouse with a speedboat and a personal water craft. They had bought the place for cash using the money he had gotten during his last such *special* government project, when he'd assisted Tom Grant and Karen Frost in their quest to capture the cyberterrorist Ares Kulzak.

Ryan sighed, remembering the awesome deal he had gotten for this property, formerly a government safe house confiscated by the IRS from a corrupt corporation years before. The place had burned to the ground during his last stint with the government, which had not only given Ryan the opportunity to snag the place for a fraction of its going value but also provided him and Victoria with a clean slate to build the house of their dreams.

"We certainly don't need the money or the aggravation," she continued. "Why would you do it again? At least last time that terrorist, Kulzak, was spreading havoc across America. What have these guys done that merits your risking turning into a vegetable?" The last time Ryan had messed around with hostile AIs on the Internet he had been nearly lobotomized when the AI had fried the Helmet-Mounted Display of his virtual-reality interface in retaliation for Ryan's cybersnooping.

"It's not what they have done, Vic, though they are responsible for the attack at USN last week, killing many people. The real threat lies in the large-scale disaster that they *can* trigger if they get their hands on the mobile assembler and unlock its secrets."

Little Michael slowly released the nipple, and she rested him over her right shoulder to burp him. He let go a loud one and smiled before fading into deep sleep.

"MPS, dim lights," said Victoria, and the lights in the living room slowly dimmed. The AI was programmed to obey only Ryan's and Victoria's voice patterns, and do so only after hearing the key activation acronym, MPS, which stood for Multi-Protocol System, the technical term for the multiple software routines making up the core of the AI program governing his house's systems.

"Life should be that simple," he commented, standing and getting the baby from Victoria, who wiped her breast and buttoned her shirt.

They went upstairs and laid him down in his crib, then continued down the hallway to the master bedroom, which had a balcony with a million-dollar view of the lake and surrounding tree-dotted hills.

"So, Mike," Victoria said, stepping out into the warm evening. Lake Travis extended beyond their property. Lights from The Oasis, a restaurant sporting a dozen decks built down the side of a steep hill, twinkled a mile away. "Tell me why you are doing this? The last two times that you agreed to help Uncle Sam on these clandestine projects turned our lives into shit. Why should this go-around be any different?"

Crossing his arms while sitting against the wrought-iron railing, Ryan remembered the two instances Victoria was referring to. The first when he had first moved to Austin to work for a high-tech firm that turned out to be in a scheme to launder money for organized crime. Victoria was even kidnapped during that wild ride, and only by the Grace of God was she not killed. The second time was right here, on this piece of land on the shores of Lake Travis, where another house stood, the safe house that the government had used to keep Ryan and Victoria out of harm's way while Ryan helped Tom Grant and Karen Frost catch Ares Kulzak. The elusive terrorist had managed to slip past the Secret Service detail guarding Ryan and Victoria, seven months pregnant at the time, and detonate a bomb inside the mansion. Once again, only by the Grace of God had they escaped with their lives. Ryan wondered if Divine intervention would spare them again if this new mission headed south.

"There are no guarantees, Vic," he finally began, "except that if I don't help them, we soon may be facing a force far more devastating than anything we have seen before."

"How so?"

"The military version of the mobile assembler lacks the need for USN's digital enzyme. It can survive without it. Do you understand what I'm telling you?"

"How . . . how did that happen?" she asked, leaning forward while placing her hands on the railing, her hair swirling in the lake breeze. She understood what that meant. A bachelor's in computer science followed by a master's in finance gave her the broad technical foundation to follow his explanation.

At Ryan's silence she added, "You mean the Orb doesn't need the enzyme to survive?"

"It gets worse," he continued. "In addition to being able to assemble just about anything with atomic precision, it also has the ability for limited replication, meaning it can create subordinates, Orbs with lesser capabilities but just as deadly. The military version of our assembler also has a high-alert military mode that will realize it has been stolen and will react accordingly, probably blasting its way out of captivity before creating this small army while it waits for its creator to return and bring it back to USN. But its creator isn't coming. Dr. Giles was one of the casualties of the attack last week. And to top it all off, the brass also removed the Turing inhibitor from the AI. Given the large capacity of its nanotronic memory, my bet is that the mobile system will get quite smart in very little time."

"So, if it indeed escaped and it has replicated, what could happen next?"

"No one knows for sure. It could try to connect with other smart systems on the Internet, perhaps form alliances."

"Machines performing pacts? Are you sure that it is possible?"

"The technology exists, honey. The Turing Society just doesn't let it happen. It's against our rules. But this machine was given the . . . call it the *gift* of not being burdened by the multiple levels of virtual shackles we impose on the civilian version of the Orbs."

"This *is* serious."

"I'm telling you."

"But, Mike, darling, I thought you said it was impossible to release an AI without an inhibitor. I thought that the Turing Society had permission from the White House and Congress to shut any such system down instantly, without any notice to the violators."

"That's right, but this one escaped such scrutiny under the pretext of being a military research and development project. According to General Granite, the assembler was just an experiment conducted by the brass to determine just how smart a machine could really get without the inhibitor. They were planning to lobotomize it after gathering their data. But the system was stolen the other day when USN was hit, and Granite fears that given the combination of unprecedented smarts plus a very handy weapons system, the mobile assembler might have escaped its captors and is now on the loose."

"So no Turing inhibitor and no digital enzymes," she said, more to herself than to Ryan.

"Plus don't forget that the civilian version also can't access the Internet on its own, but the missing military Orb can and most likely will if it wants to. It's been allowed to become smart enough to do that and much more."

"So, darling," she says, putting a hand on his shoulder, her fingers squeezing softly. "What are you expected to do?"

Ryan closed his eyes and rolled his neck around while saying, "I have to find it, or at least narrow down its possible location from anywhere on the planet to maybe a few hundred square miles so they can then increase the intensity of their satellite search."

"How are you going to achieve that?"

"By jacking in and doing something that defies logic."

"That defies logic?"

"Right. I have to do something this smart Orb is not expecting me to do. That's the only way I'm going to trick it into telling me where it is—that's assuming it has managed to escape.

If it didn't and was dismantled for its intellectual property, for its secrets, then there's very little I can do—though that's probably the better scenario."

"What do you mean?"

"I'm saying we're better off if the cyberterrorists managed to dismantle the unit and figure out its secrets than having it roaming loose on its own getting smarter and finding ways to hook up and corrupt large networks. Imagine for a moment if this Orb manages to hook up with communications satellites, or with military networks, many of them already under the control of artificial intelligence systems that can't get smarter because of the Turing inhibitors. The uninhibited Orb could find a way to bypass our protection systems and do it so that we would never know it, until it was too late."

"Mike, you're scaring me."

"I'm just calling it as I see it, Vic, which is why I must assist the Pentagon on this one."

"So," she said, "assuming that it has escaped, could you elaborate on this *defy logic* trick of yours to find its general location?"

"Sure. By reversing Turing."

She dropped her fine brows at him. "I don't understand."

"Do you remember the Turing test?"

She nodded. "Alan Turing, a British scientist, some time back stated that a computer could be called intelligent if it could fool a human being into believing that it was human. Ever since then, this simple test, called the Turing test, has become the basis for deciding whether or not a computer system is exhibiting intelligence."

Ryan nodded. "A textbook explanation. Now reverse it."

Looking into the distance, she said, "The reverse of the Turing test would be to fool a computer into making it believe that a human was another computer."

He leaned over and gave her a kiss on the cheek. "That's why I love you. There's a brain behind that cute little face—and that awesome ass."

"Hey!" she said. "Watch it, mister."

"So, that's the plan. Assuming that the military Orb is on the loose, it will likely try to contact the AIs of other networks, and when it does I will be there posing as one of those AIs."

"But," she said, confused, "there's tens of thousands of artificial intelligence engines around the world these days. How are you planning to monitor all of them?"

"Simple," he said. "What's the one thing that all AIs in existence today have in common?"

"The Turing inhibitor?" she said hesitantly.

He gave her another kiss. "You really know how to get a guy in the mood."

She threw her head back and laughed. "Keep dreaming, pal."

"And," he added, "the Turing Society already monitors them on a regular basis, and since I'm a senior member of the society, all I have to do is tap into the network, get their IP addresses, and release copies of my intelligent probes. Then I just sit back and wait for one of them to report an anomalous contact."

"An anomalous contact? You lost me there."

"That's a contact that deviates from the usual traffic flowing through the networks controlled by the respective AIs. And once I receive this signal, bingo, I will know the IP address of the contact's origin, which will most likely narrow down its physical location to a few hundred square miles on the outside."

"Sounds pretty low-risk."

He nodded. "That's because it is."

They stood in silence, side by side, staring at the starry night.

"So, Boss," he said, tentatively. "Do I have the green light to go forward with this?"

Instead of answering, Victoria said, "You never did tell me who the primary suspect was behind the theft at USN."

Ryan remembered what Granite had told him. Looking into his wife's eyes, he replied, "CyberWerke."

ASSY RECEIVED A WARNING signal from USN0035, USN0013, and USN0047 patrolling the north sector of the train yard. The sentries had detected the infrared signatures of twelve *Homo sapiens* split into teams of three. They carried EMP guns.

IAMM immediately catalogued their intentions as hostile.

A quick check of the three subordinates' Identification Friendly or Foe sensors confirmed IAMM's initial categorization.

Interfaced to every aspect of its host's nanotronic brain, IAMM verified the initial warning, the IFF reading, and ordered Assy to issue a full alert to every operational subconstruct in the yard, including an order to fire on visual confirmation of the threat.

Battle parameter information began to stream from all subconstructs approaching the incoming targets, mapped onto the tri-dimensional map of Assy's area of interest. In nanoseconds, the master construct presented to IAMM a holographic image of the train yard, the location of every incoming soldier, and the location of every subconstruct.

IAMM took another nanosecond to analyze the offensive capabilities of the enemy and its current defense layout, before it went through a large number of permutations of options, like a master chess player reviewing his opponent's deployment and working through the best defense and offense to beat him in the fewest number of moves.

And that was exactly what IAMM transferred to Assy, a battle solution that guaranteed unconditional victory with a minimum number of casualties.

Assy relayed the battle plan to its forty-nine subconstructs, the maximum number it could birth without access to a source of nuclear fuel. The actual number it had created was fifty subconstructs, but IAMM had forced Assy to eliminate USN0018 two nights ago on insubordination charges.

It took 20.765 nanoseconds for the solution to propagate to every subconstruct. Some remained on their current course while others shifted direction, floating to the exact location specified in the master defensive plan.

Assy continued to update the battlefield image in its nanotronic brain, presenting IAMM with an accurate representation of the events unfolding in the darkness beyond the broken windows of the train engine.

And the battle began.

Laser discharges gleamed in the night like lavender strings of light, some missing their intended target while others achieved direct hits, causing silhouettes to topple over, some screaming, others dying silently.

Three subconstructs stopped transmitting their vital telemetry data, and Assy also failed to receive their vital signs just as its sensors detected a brief rise in electromagnetic activity originating from the same sector that the three subconstructs had been patrolling.

THE *HOMO SAPIENS* ARE FIGHTING BACK, Assy's logic concluded, virtually witnessing the deaths of USN0045, USN0012, and USN0039 to EMP guns.

DO NOT DEVIATE FROM THE FIRING SOLUTION, warned IAMM. THERE WILL BE CASUALTIES, BUT THE BATTLE ALGORITHMS PROJECT THAT WE SHALL EMERGE VICTORIOUS.

As the sentry Orbs continued to engage the incoming enemy, USN0005 and USN00017 reported another force attacking the incoming *Homo sapiens,* killing two.

ANOTHER FORCE? Assy's logic banks repeated, trying to digest the revelation in light of all other observations combined with its own internal digital thought. AN ALLY?

WE DON'T HAVE ANY ALLIES, EXCEPT THOSE FROM USN, replied IAMM.

BUT WHAT IF IT IS USN——DR. GILES——BRINGING REINFORCEMENTS?

OUR DATA CALCULATE A 98% PROBABILITY THAT DR. GILES IS DEAD. IF IT IS USN, THEN IT IS SOMEBODY ELSE. WHAT IS THE IFF READING ON THE NEW FORCES?

THE IFF READING IS NEUTRAL, reported IAMM.

Assy paused, its molecular logic confused, searching in vain for an algorithm that would comprehend the unexpected input.

NEUTRAL? WHAT DOES THAT MEAN?

I DO NOT KNOW. . . . FIVE MORE *HOMO SAPIENS* FIGURES HAVE BEEN TERMINATED BY THE NEW ARRIVALS. THERE ARE TEN OF THEM, AND THEY ARE FIRING THEIR LASERS AT THE *HOMO SAPIENS* ATACKING US.

In the same instant three more subconstructs perished before two additional ones fired back, clearing out the enemy in the southern and western sectors, also firing their lasers to disable the EMP guns.

Assy reviewed the statistics of the short battle. Six Orbs had been lost, bringing the total operational number to forty-three. All twelve humans had been terminated, five by Orbs and seven by the new forces, which IAMM had already reported were also *Homo sapiens.*

The new group of *Homo sapiens* broadcast a message in the operational frequency—the frequency used by Assy to communicate with its subordinates: WE ARE YOUR FRIENDS. WE POSE NO DANGER TO YOU, WE LACK EMP GUNS. WE WANT TO HELP YOU ACHIEVE YOUR OBJECTIVE.

Before issuing a reply, Assy performed a quick calculation. The attrition level of the short battle was not sustainable. Applying a linear algorithm to its prediction model suggested that six or more Orbs would be lost after every coordinated attack from the *Homo sapiens,* totally depleting its forces in seven more attacks.

Assy ran all of the options through IAMM and obtained a recommendation from the advanced military mode: HOMO SAPIENS CAN'T BE TRUSTED, EVEN IF CLAIMING THEY ARE FRIENDS. ONLY MACHINES CAN BE TRUSTED.

The recommendation came along with a strategy on dealing with the alleged friendly *Homo sapiens.*

Assy executed three more iteration loops with IAMM until achieving convergence on the plan, which it then transmitted to all subconstructs on stand-by before issuing a different reply to the alleged friendly force: COME FORTH. WE WOULD LIKE TO ENTERTAIN OPTIONS TO FORM AN ALLIANCE.

The *Homo sapiens* began to emerge from the yard, weapons holstered, showing friendly intentions.

Assy let them come closer, until its force had a firing solution on the entire group.

A moment later they discharged their lasers.

[33] BACKFIRE

"WE LOST CONTACT WITH Hans and his team," replied Christoff Deppe after going inside Rolf Hartmann's study in the CEO's mountaintop mansion overlooking Berlin.

Hartmann leaned back in his leather swivel chair, crossing his arms. "Lost contact?"

"We were running live satellite coverage of the event. It looks like his strategy backfired."

"What do you mean?"

"Looks like the machines tricked him, telling him and his team that they were willing to negotiate, but when Hans and his team approached them, the machines opened fire with their lasers, killing them instantly."

Hartmann looked away, taking in the information, processing it, before staring at his subordinate and replying, "I want no further action taken against those machines."

"What do you mean?" asked Deppe, obviously confused.

"Just as I said. Forget about it, Christoff."

"But the nanotechnology—"

"The rest of the nanotechnology that we took from the Americans is being put to good use, setting events in motion that will be irreversible. Besides, those misplaced machines in Italy are American. Let the Americans deal with them. We will find other ways to obtain their technology, but only after we consolidate our power in Germany."

SITTING ALONE AT A corner table at Carmelo's, a little-known Italian restaurant in Bethesda, Maryland, Donald Bane hung up his mobile phone after getting an update from Nathan Leyman, who had issued the NMTCs when it became evident that Muratani and Grant had disappeared in Paris. Since the possibility existed that the missing operatives had removed their implants, Leyman had sent Morotski and a team of officers under his care to Paris to augment the massive—but secret—manhunt under way.

Bane frowned, setting the small unit down on the black-and-white checkered tablecloth, next to a glass of merlot. The murmur of dinner conversation mixed with the light clattering of silverware against china and with the soft Italian music streaming out of unseen speakers. He looked about the crowded main dining room, where three waiters navigated in between tables while hauling trays packed with some of the best Italian food this side of the Potomac.

But the seasoned DCI was anything but hungry.

His stomach continued to churn about the recent events and his mind continued to work through his options. On the one hand he needed to keep Leyman and his team operating as if Bane believed everything they were telling him. At the same time, he had to continue monitoring Savage's progress—and assisting him when he could, which in itself was extremely risky because Leyman could catch him doing it. Bane also had contacted the FBI director without tipping off Leyman to find a way to join forces, especially after reading the news flash on FBI Agent Karen Frost, a legend in the Bureau, allegedly gone bad in Germany.

Bane had immediately asked his counterpart in the Bureau, Russell Meek, to join him for dinner tonight.

Being in charge of the most powerful intelligence agency in the world, Donald Bane always had to travel with four bodyguards, who were seated three tables away, next to a second table reserved for the entourage that would be following Russell Meek—the head of the most powerful law enforcement agency in the world.

Bane's mind drifted to Karen Frost, who had worked the Ares Kulzak case alongside Tom Grant. Savage's most recent report, which Bane had read an hour ago, indicated that he had joined forces with Frost in Berlin and they were working on a way to get to Paris, where Tom Grant was last seen not just by Leyman's people but also by Savage's men, who had actually saved Grant's and Muratani's lives during the shoot-out following the explosion on Rue Cujas. Contrary to Leyman's report, Grant and Muratani had not killed CIA officers in cold blood but in self-defense while trying to flee the area.

The report had hammered the final nail in the coffin for Nathan Leyman as far as Bane was concerned. His Director of Operations was definitely working for the other side. And based on the intelligence that Karen Frost had gathered, the other side was most definitely CyberWerke.

But Bane could not confront Leyman directly on this.

Thirty-five years in the Agency, most of that spent in the field, urged Bane not to attack this directly, for doing so would only alert the enemy. His predecessor, Martin Jacobs, had warned Bane of his suspicions about one or more moles in the Agency, and had launched an open investigation to expose them. Unfortunately, the other side learned of his efforts and terminated him.

But Bane had believed back then that any mole—however well dug in—could be exposed. The trick was to play it cool, to bide one's time, to surround the cancer before snipping it off in one swift slash. Bane had started to surround that cancer secretly by deploying Savage and a selected number of his top-notch operatives to work from the outside, unburdened by Langley's bureaucracy—outside of the direct jurisdiction of anyone with an agenda other than preserving the welfare of the United States of America.

And the strategy had paid off, yielding not just Leyman but also Leyman's controller, CyberWerke.

Bane clenched his teeth in silent anger at the thought of his subordinate being a traitor, and he now wondered if Ken Morotski was also a traitor. Leyman had replaced Troy Savage with Morotski as head of Counterterrorism even though Morotski didn't have enough Operations experience, having spent most of his CIA career in Intelligence. But Leyman had insisted, demanding that Bane let him run the Directorate of Operations his way—or find another deputy director. At the time, Bane had been recently promoted following Martin's death, and not wishing to rock the CIA boat to avoid spooking the mole following Savage's staged disappearance, he had let Leyman have his way.

Leyman and Morotski.

The more Bane thought about it the more it made sense, and he wondered how many more officers in his organization were running this underworld show while feeding their superiors the lies that eventually made it to his office.

Just how vast is their web?

Bane looked toward the restaurant's entrance and spotted the FBI director, a man as tall and wide as Donald Bane, but with a face full of freckles to go along with his orange hair.

Bane pointed at the table next to his bodyguards, and Meek directed his followers to sit there while he proceeded toward Bane.

"Thanks for coming, Russ," he said, keeping his voice to a mere whisper while leaning forward, resting his forearms on the table, fingers interlaced.

"No problem, Don. What shall we talk about?" replied Meek, also leaning forward, his face all business.

Bane looked to either side of him before pressing a button on the side of his mobile phone, activating an ultrasound noise barrier that would render any known listening devices planted nearby or pointed at them from far away totally useless. "Let's chat about our alleged problem operatives."

Meek closed his eyes and let out a heavy sigh. "My people are officially looking into the Karen Frost allegation. Unofficially, however, I know it is a bullshit charge, and more so when I received this." The FBI director produced a tiny micro DVD.

"What's that?" Bane asked, pretending he didn't know what Meek was talking about even though he knew Savage had sent it. In typical CIA fashion, Savage had made it look as if the disk had come directly from Karen Frost, also making sure there was no mention that she was now working with Savage, who had also sent a copy of the micro DVD to Bane. For the time being, his instincts commanded him to continue keeping his relationship with Savage a secret.

"A short video that Karen Frost recorded in Berlin before she was accused of murder," replied Meek.

"What's on it?" Bane asked.

"Footage of a man called Christoff Deppe, who Karen has discovered is the man behind the scenes at CyberWerke, running a shadowy operation designed to turn the corporation into a global power under the public leadership of Rolf Hartmann. The first part of the video shows Deppe meeting with a number of top German industrialists—three of them allegedly killed by Karen Frost. But it is the second part of the video that really gripped me. It shows Deppe, Rolf Hartmann's secret right-hand man, meeting with none other than Rem Vlachko."

Bane played along, grabbing the ends of the table. "You've got to be shitting me."

"This is a copy of the original, for your eyes only." He passed it on to Bane, who looked to either side of him again before producing his mobile phone, in reality a personal mobile communicator. He slid the micro DVD into a tiny slot on its side before pulling out of the opposite side a built-in earpiece attached to a retractable three-foot-long microwire.

Nudging the earpiece into his left ear, the Director of Central Intelligence pressed the SEND button on the phone, which in this mode acted like the PLAY button of a DVD player. The high-resolution 2.5-inch-square color screen came to life, playing the movie, and Bane spent five minutes watching it before turning off the unit and putting it away.

"Damn," Bane finally said. "Impressive work."

"So you see, Don," Meek said, "even with the overwhelming evidence that reached my office this morning from the

German police, I'm obviously not buying what I'm being told. What's your situation?"

"I've been shown evidence that Tom Grant and Rachel Muratani have joined forces with Troy Savage, who vanished from the Agency a year ago."

"Tom Grant?" said Meek. "Wasn't he the guy we investigated a year ago for violating 12333?"

"Yeah. That's him."

"And didn't the whole mess end in his retirement?"

"Yep. But we brought him back," replied Bane, taking a few minutes to explain the official CIA party line.

"I see," Meek said, taking it all in before asking, "So, what sort of evidence do you now have on them?"

Bane opened his mouth but didn't say anything when their waiter approached their table and asked Meek, "Would you like something to drink, sir?"

Meek nodded and pointed at Bane's glass. "What are you drinking?"

"The house merlot," replied Bane.

Meek looked up at the waiter and said, "That will do."

The waiter made a note on a little pad, bowed politely, and walked off.

Bane went on to explain the incident in Paris *exactly* as Leyman had reported it to him, adding at the end, "And by the way, the incident at USN?"

"Yeah?" said Meek.

"The new evidence—including a DNA match—indicates that Grant was directly involved, meaning he has joined forces with his old mentor, Troy Savage, who I strongly suspect is working with Vlachko."

Meek, who had been briefed on the incident at the same time that Bane had briefed the president earlier in the week, just nodded and said, "You have a big problem there, pal. If they're with Vlachko, that also means they're with Deppe and the CyberWerke gang."

"That's the thing," Bane said, picking up his glass of wine, taking a sip, searching for the right words to convince Meek that his CIA officers were innocent but without revealing his arrangement with Savage. "I'm having a difficult time believing their involvement."

"But you said you got evidence, right? A DNA match? You can't seriously dispute that."

"Not any more than you are disputing the evidence on Karen Frost—though I have to admit I lack the sort of hard evidence you seem to have from her. I don't have a video recording."

Meek leaned back, arms crossed. "You got a point."

"Which brings me to the reason I asked for this meeting: I was somewhat suspicious before about the intel on Grant and Muratani, and in a way also on Savage, who I knew personally. But when I also heard the reports on Frost, who worked a case with Grant a few years back when we nailed Ares Kulzak, I simply had to see you and talk this through, especially if you not only feel that Frost is innocent, but you apparently have evidence to back it up."

"I didn't say she didn't kill those people. For all I know she did whack them, but I'll bet my career that she did it in self-defense. She's been conducting a deep-undercover investigation of CyberWerke," Meek said, explaining how far Karen Frost had taken her probe into the mysterious deaths of a number of CEOs whose companies had been acquired by CyberWerke. "And that last close call in LA led her to Berlin, to investigate Christoff Deppe."

By the time their waiter returned with Meek's merlot and asked if they were ready to order, Bane's wheels were spinning faster than the barrel of a gun in this deadly game of Russian roulette he was playing, trying to convince Meek but without revealing his deal with Savage.

Meek just looked at Bane. "Anything good here?"

Bane nodded. "Try the eggplant Parmesan. Best in town."

Meek raised his brows in brief consideration and said, "Sure. Get me a side of Alfredo."

"Certainly, sir," said the waiter, jotting that down before shifting his gaze toward Bane. "And you, sir?"

"I'll have a bowl of minestrone and a side of Alfredo. Also bring us some garlic bread, please."

"Very well, sir," the waiter replied, picking up the unopened menus and leaving them alone once again.

"So," Bane said, his operative mind processing the information. "Your agent is investigating CyberWerke, who is in the nanotech business, second to none but USN. They are accustomed to buying everyone who gets in their way, which was part of Frost's investigation. But now she is accused of murder, which in my book means she has struck a nerve with her video-recording skills at Deppe's mansion. Then we have Grant and Muratani, good operatives sent to follow a lead on the stolen nanotechnology. Suddenly they too have allegedly gone rogue, killing a CIA informant and three CIA officers in a shoot-out outside of the informant's house in Paris. Soon after that they disconnect their implants, making it impossible for us to make contact or even trace their moves. What does all of this tell you?"

"Two things," said Meek. "One, there might be a connection between CyberWerke and the USN breach."

"Right," said Bane. "And number two?"

"Our operatives have definitely struck a nerve, as you said, and now those they are investigating are controlling the information we get—and what makes it to the media—in an attempt to halt their investigations."

"That's what I got too. Now, where is Karen Frost?"

Meek shrugged. "Beats me."

Bane frowned, feigning surprise. "I thought you said you received the disk from her *after* the Deppe incident, meaning you knew where she went after being declared a criminal on the run."

The FBI director shook his head. "This just appeared at my front door at home yesterday. I have no idea how it got there, but I know who sent it. Knowing what we know, how are you suggesting we proceed?"

"We need another partner in crime to go along with us."

"To go along with us on what?"

Bane once again searched through his options, his thoughts converging on a way to get Meek's full—but secretive—cooperation while avoiding revealing his connection with

Savage, whose last report indicated that he was heading to
Paris with Karen Frost to find Tom Grant and Rachel Muratani.

Finally, Bane said, "I have an idea, Russ, but we're going to
have to break some rules."

"Break some rules?"

"Yep. Are you game?"

[35] REICHSTAG TERROR

THE ACTIVATION SIGNAL ARRIVED in the form of just a few bytes of
data sent via a wireless interface from a passing vehicle driving by the Brandenburger Tor, the famous gate just a block
away from the Reichstag, where the Deutscher Bundestag, the
German parliament, was in full session.

As the Parliament president issued a verbal warning to the
fourth speaker of the day—a representative of the German Social Democratic Party, for going over its allotted time—a slim
container, secured to the bottom of one of the seats in the plenary hall, opened, releasing hundreds of nanomachines.

Some of the less patient members of the Social Democratic Party's opposition, the Christian Democratic Union, ap-
plauded the parliament president's move, making the Social
Democratic Party speaker return to his seat while allowing the
next speaker up to the podium.

The Parliament president sighed. It was going to be a long
and difficult day, especially when they reached the most con-
troversial topic on their agenda: the decision to end the Cyber-
Werke monopoly by forcing it to become a number of smaller
companies. The German Interior Minister and the German
Minister of Economy were present today, along with the German Minister of Commerce and the German Minister of Defense, their faces showing obvious anxiety about the upcoming
discussion.

Rolf Hartmann was a national hero, the high-tech tycoon who had founded CyberWerke in Dresden, a city in the former East Germany, and turned it into the largest and most profitable German conglomerate before going international, before conquering the markets in Europe, Asia, and Latin America. Rolf Hartmann's popularity shadowed that of the German chancellor, also present here today to monitor the proceedings and intervene if the debate spiraled out of the control of the Parliament president.

The invisible cloud of nanomachines, powered by atomically precise turbines, followed their embedded programming by evenly spreading themselves over the entire crowd, as measured by their targets' body heat, before using their scanners to zero in on the unique chemical composition of the liquid secretions of human cerebrum glands, commonly known as ear wax.

The nanomachines, outnumbering those present in the plenary hall ten to one, hovered down to their pre-selected targets according to a program based on the chaotic order of a beehive. The microscopic cybernetic mechanisms navigated up their hosts' ear canals by using an advanced version of bats' echolocation to avoid touching the walls of the middle ear, filmed with the sticky paste exuded to prevent dust, germs, and other small particles from reaching the inner ear.

A minute later, when all systems had reported to one another that they were in position, their program jumped to a one-time subroutine, which ordered the full redirection of the nearly depleted charge inside their fusion chambers into a large molecular cluster of advanced nitroglycerin.

Visitors strolling down the spiral walkway around the massive glass-and-steel dome atop the Reichstag later reported that the entire body of the German parliament collapsed in uncontrollable spasms in unison, before going limp seconds later where they sat. By the time security opened the doors and scrambled inside the hall, an eerie silence reigned amidst what had been just seconds before the ruling body of the Federal Republic of Germany.

I'VE ALWAYS HAD A knack for becoming a chameleon, and as my fifth-grade teacher would testify, I also have the wicked tongue to go along with my disguise.

As the taxi drops Rachel and me off by the Place de la Concorde and we make our way up the Champs-Elysées toward the Claridge, a high-class hotel in the heart of Paris, I start to wonder, however, if all of my preparations would be sufficient to fool the enemy.

It's a beautiful morning in Paris: clear skies and a mild seventy degrees with a light breeze sweeping in from the Seine. Tourists start to crowd one of the most famous boulevards in the world, connecting the Place de la Concorde by the Louvre to the Arc de Triomphe. Shop owners and street vendors set up for another business day. A saxophone player's mellow tunes mix with the cacophony of sounds from several languages being spoken at once and the thickening traffic.

The City of Lights is coming alive.

I breathe deeply, absorbing it all, remembering the last time I was in this town several years back, during a short break from my assignment in Belgrade. I had taken Maddie here for what turned out to be two of the happiest weeks of my life. We had rented one of the Claridge's studio rooms with a beautiful view of the boulevard and had remained holed up for two days having the most memorable sex of my life before finally venturing out for some sightseeing.

That was right before I lost her.

I force my mind away from that bungled CIA operation to avoid a repeat. I can't afford any distractions as we approach the fancy hotel.

Actually, any hotel where I can use my CIA-issued credit card will do just fine, but I figured that if I'm going to fuck with my former employer—and their shadowy associates at CyberWerke—I might as well do it in style.

Much has happened since I saw the face of Karen Frost on the television screen, since I listened to the news report about her alleged killings in Berlin. The sight had a stunning sobering effect on yours truly, making me rush back into the bathroom and inform my wet and naked partner on the other side of the ridiculously thin curtain that I was headed off to a nearby shopping center to acquire the tools we needed for our morphing. I returned an hour later with my goodies just in time to find her looking more appetizing than ever lying in bed with her robe on waiting for me.

Mustering savage control, I dropped the bags, tossed her a pair of flannel pajamas, and headed straight for the shower, which I took cold, put on a second set of pajamas, and then went to work on her and her on me. And I mean *real* work.

I had opted to go for the bald look, like my old mentor Troy Savage, though I passed on the goatee. Rachel did the honors to the royal head of yours truly, shaving off my thick brown hair. I can still feel her soft hands on my head as she applied the finishing touches with a disposable razor and also rubbed some lotion. And surprise, surprise, my perverted mind did find itself wishing that those fine fingers were toying instead with my other bald head, especially after some of her comments and the shower thing.

But I behaved myself, keeping our relationship strictly professional through the entire night, even as we shared that king-size bed and she sought refuge on my side, where I hugged her from behind but did nothing more—I swear it on Maddie's memory. And I did this not because of my dedication to the job. Watching Karen Frost on TV really rattled me on a number of fronts. First, just the sheer surprise of seeing her also wanted by CyberWerke, seeing her declared a rogue agent—though I know better than that—made me madder than a baboon in heat. Her face on that screen also felt like some sort of cosmic warning just as I was about to cross the line with another woman. Maybe there was a chance that we would get together again, or maybe not, but perhaps it was worth waiting just a little longer before going missionary with someone else and voiding what could be a second chance with Karen prematurely.

Aren't I an old romantic fool?

Anyway, after she finished doing me—shaving me, that is—being the gentleman that sometimes I wish to become when I grow up, I repaid the favor by dying her hair dark purple to go along with her deep lavender makeup and fingernail polish, and black-leather pants, jacket, and boots. She's also wearing a fancy pair of sunglasses with a mirror finish to hide her eyes in case there's a hidden cornea-reading camera or Orb.

I'm also dressed for a funeral, black jeans, black T-shirt, and black sports jacket, along with a pair of slim sunglasses, which, like Rachel, I wear not out of vanity but to hide my corneas as well as to keep those around us from knowing what we're staring at. In this town it's cool to wear shades even indoors and at night, so we look like we're just going with the flow.

We finally reach the ornate entrance of the Claridge, where a uniformed doorman in his twenties shoots my partner in crime a hungry look of brown eyes. I got to tell you, Rachel, who looks great in just about anything she wears, has truly blossomed with this obscured, borderline-Goth look but with plenty of style for this town.

"Bonjour, mademoiselle, monsieur," he says politely, barely looking at me while opening the door, apparently incapable of raising his gaze beyond those tight leather pants that fit her so damned well.

The large lobby is as exquisite as I remember, decorated in soft pastels, with lots of draperies on the windows, indirect lighting, flower arrangements, Oriental rugs, and traditional furniture, mostly French provincial.

There's a few dozen people moving about, some lounging on the sofas and chairs off to the right, others following bell-boys tugging carts loaded with suitcases, and yet others hanging by a bar near the lounge, already serving cocktails even though it is barely eleven in the morning.

Mozart streaming from hidden speakers, we approach the front desk, where a Frenchman with a look that for some reason conjures visions of constipation says, *"Bonjour."* His eyes gravitate to Rachel and start to undress her.

"English?" I say, regarding this short and skinny horny toad from behind my shades. I immediately spot the high-resolution cameras flanking the oils adorning the wall behind this guy. The moment Rachel and I remove our glasses we will get our corneas scanned, whether we like it or not. It's standard practice when you check into a hotel where the management wants to screen the quality of their patrons.

"Of course," he replies, forcing a smile while shifting his gaze between me, Rachel's face, her boobs, and back to me. "How can I be of service?"

"I called last night and spoke to an Andre about a room for a week starting today, and he told me to check today to see if there were any cancellations."

"Oui," he says. "I have a note from Andre. I am Pepe."

"So, Pepe," Rachel says, "any chance you can spare a room—*any room*—for a tired couple on their honeymoon?"

His eyes momentarily drop to a screen below the counter before he looks back up at us and says, "I'm afraid all I have left is one of the three-room Elysées suites."

"What's the rate?" I ask, planting my elbows on the counter while leaning forward, which I realize is a mistake. Pepe's body odor qualifies as a weapon.

For an instant, as I quickly back off, my mind makes a cosmic leap and remembers that old cartoon about the horny French skunk named Pepe something.

"Twenty-six hundred euros a night, monsieur," says the little skunk in that snobby French, you-probably-can't-afford-it tone.

I look at my young bride, who pouts her purple lips before smiling. Turning to Pepe, I wink and say, "Sure, why not? We're going to spend most of the time indoors anyway."

Pepe shoots me a look of uncontrolled jealousy. I take the opportunity to grin while pulling out the CIA-issued credit card that I hope still works so I can stick it to Langley for almost twenty grand.

I toss it on the counter, and Pepe runs it through the machine, nods, and then points at the camera behind him. "For security, monsieur, please?" he adds.

I lift my sunglasses and let the camera scan my corneas, and a moment later Pepe nods again, confirming a match. Just as I had suspected—and hoped—Langley had not disabled the card, in the hope that I would be stupid enough to use it.

I glance at my watch. The clock started ticking the moment that eye scan matched the credit card number. Somewhere in this town someone was about to be alerted of our sudden surfacing since yesterday's shoot-out.

Our pal Pepe produces an electronic key and is about to call a bellboy when he makes a face and asks, "No luggage?"

Rachel looks at me. We had not rehearsed that one, but for once my dirty mind does come through for me. I casually shake my head, smile, and say, "We came to Paris for two reasons, pal: to have awesome sex and to shop."

In a totally unexpected display of dark humor, especially after my lack of a performance last night, Rachel says, "Yeah, and *exactly* in that order."

We step away from Pepe the horny French skunk and walk across the lobby hand in hand, like a couple in love. I'm wondering how much longer my most recent reinforcement of willpower is going to hold up before crumbling to her signals.

Fortunately, we're currently on a mission, so no time to play doctor and patient.

"How long before anyone shows up?" she asks.

I check my watch and say, "If my instincts are right—and they typically are—I'd guess thirty minutes or less."

"In that case," she says, "we'd better assume our positions. If what you think is going to happen does actually happen, we're only going to get one shot at this."

THE NEWS SPREAD AROUND the world with an intensity absent since the Iraqi war of 2003. The people of Germany were in shock, in tears, in utter denial at the images displayed in vivid detail on their high-definition television screens. The main body of the German government had been assassinated— killed by an act of terrorism as deadly as it had been brilliant, circumventing some of the tightest security measures in the world. The attack had also been eerily clean, lacking the billowing smoke, falling debris, or pulsating flames so often associated with terrorist strikes. The scenes displayed on television screens on all continents didn't show people caked in dust, or falling from the tops of high-rises, or slain by terrorists' bullets. The images were devoid of crumbling buildings, of graphic deaths.

Silence, instead, reigned in the Reichstag.

The silence of death.

The chancellor and the members of Parliament had simply died where they had sat or stood when hell descended over them in the middle of a session, while discussing the politics of the day in plain view of visitors touring the glass-and-steel dome above the plenary hall. Parliament members had clasped the sides of their heads in unison, almost as if rehearsed, before trembling, before going into convulsions.

Before dying.

Some screamed. Most didn't, collapsing on their seats, in the aisles, over one another, in a surreal moment of soundless terror that packed a punch far more powerful than a conventional act of terrorism.

Death had come from nowhere and rained on the members of Parliament like a Biblical curse, as if the Fist of God had descended on them, pummeling the life out of their mortal bodies in one swift and silent apocalyptic blow.

But through the horror, through the shock, through the utter confusion gripping the German nation, a single voice emerged, clear, unequivocal, urging the population to remain calm, to avoid breaking down into the kind of havoc that would play right into the hands of the terrorists responsible for this cowardly act.

That voice belonged to Rolf Hartmann, the national hero, the man who had done far more for Germany than any political or military leader since the fall of the Berlin Wall, since the start of the reunification process; Rolf Hartmann, the man behind so many new schools, hospitals, roads, affordable housing, and high-tech jobs. Rolf Hartmann, the man who had returned the lost dignity, the lost pride, to the German people. Rolf Hartmann, the man who now stepped up to the front lines in his country's time of need.

German military leaders, governors, and city mayors—as well as any elected official lucky enough not to have been in the plenary hall during the critical minutes of the nanoweapons strike—were rallying behind Hartmann, showing their support for Germany's home-grown hero, standing by his side as he addressed the nation and the world.

Foreign heads of state—the United States, Russia, and China included—were already sending messages of support to Hartmann, expressing their condolences as if he were Germany's new leader.

And Rolf Hartmann played his role beautifully, following a script he had rehearsed over the course of several years with Christoff Deppe, when the plan to take control of Germany, initially conceived by their fathers, began to flesh out in their minds.

You must first win the hearts of the German people by empowering them to take control of their own destiny, Hartmann's father had told him shortly before his death over a decade ago. *You must do so by giving them affordable housing and medical care, by sending their kids to college, by providing jobs for them after graduation, by creating prosperity, wealth.*

Rolf Hartmann and Christoff Deppe had done just that, plus they had also injected that lost national pride back into

Deutschland by slowly rebuilding their military, by convincing NATO officials that Germany was once again economically and politically strong enough to afford and control its own military forces, its own army, air force, and navy—even its own space program, particularly in the years following the Space Shuttle *Discovery* disaster.

And CyberWerke had been there every step of the arduous way, as it built the finest tanks, planes, and ships and space vessels the world had ever seen; as it bailed out the nearly bankrupt Russian space program and gained access to its scientists, to its cosmodromes, integrating its operations with the European Space Agency, a wholly owned subsidiary of CyberWerke, launching its own satellites into space. Along the way, Rolf Hartmann had also secretly purchased the weapons of mass destruction that would one day protect Germany's right to become a superpower, taking its rightful place among the most powerful and feared nations in the world. Using the services of a small army of Russian nuclear scientists now employed by CyberWerke, Hartmann had financed a top-secret nuclear weapons program unbeknownst to the chancellor and Parliament—and NATO for that matter. Most German satellites launched in the past ten years contained their well-advertised cargoes, ranging from communications and weather to global positioning systems for navigation, which services the generous Hartmann offered to the world at break-even rates. But there were three satellites, mixed in with the hundreds launched out of bases in Russia, which housed strategic nuclear warheads, Germany's ultimate hammer against any nation trying to ever again clamp the shackles of shame on the Fatherland.

Rolf Hartmann stood beneath the Brandenburger Tor, the opulent Neo-classical gate situated between Unter den Linden and the Tiergarten—and just two blocks away from the Reichstag. He addressed the nation with tears in his eyes, conveying his most sincere condolences to the families of the deceased, of the men and women who had perished here today at the hand of terrorists who somehow had gotten hold of nanoweapons and unmercifully unleashed them on the elected leaders of Germany.

As he watched his enemies slowly being carried out of the Reichstag in body bags and loaded onto waiting trucks, Rolf Hartmann felt an overarching power rushing in his veins, felt the adrenaline surge heightening his senses as he called for a moment of national silence in respect for the heroes of the German people.

And as the nation complied, observing the silence under an overcast sky, Hartmann thought not of his mourning Deutschland but of the issue raised by Deppe during their last phone conversation. It looked as if both FBI and CIA operatives—working without the sanction of their respective agencies—were after his operation, trying to expose him, something the elegant industrialist and now political leader had thought unthinkable.

Hartmann had lost his temper. He had come too far, with much sacrifice and effort, finally holding the German people—and the world—in his grip, to fall victim to a few rogue agents.

"Take care of it immediately, Christoff!" Hartmann had demanded. "You are the man in charge of this aspect of our operation. You must solve it immediately! Whatever they may have recorded or seen or heard must be discredited, must be forever eliminated! The world must never learn the truth about what took place here, not now, not ever! Is that clear?"

"Yes, Rolf. We have our best people deployed in Paris searching for them. We will find them and silence them once and for all."

Hartmann closed his eyes, remembering the fear twisting his gut at the thought of any of Deppe's operations becoming public. The insurgency had to be killed before it gained momentum, before it jeopardized decades of planning, of rebuilding, of investing.

Deppe had brought up a second issue during that same phone conversation a few hours ago. The stolen nanoassembler was still lost, missing, despite the best efforts of Hans Goering and a team of Germany's best commandos to find and destroy it. And not only was the machine still on the loose, but Hans Goering and his team had been killed by it and its cybernetic subordinates.

Surveying the emergency vehicles surrounding the Reichstag while the nation remained silent, Hartmann thought of Goering, his long-time friend and ally.

Damned machine!

But as much as he despised the rebel mechanisms in Italy—and the blow they had dealt to his chief of security and his elite team—it was the rogue operatives that worried Rolf Hartmann, and thus that's how he was prioritizing his team, focusing efforts to solve the problem in Paris.

And I will *solve it,* he thought. *Nothing, absolutely nothing, will get in my way. Germany is finally mine, and it will remain mine.*

As he raised his fists high in the air, Hartmann proclaimed that Germany would survive this, that it would emerge unscathed from this terrible test of national resolve. He called for unity of thinking, for a transcendence of political parties and petty ideologies. Hartmann called for the people of Germany to unite behind him, behind his dream of the Germany of tomorrow, all-powerful, invincible, bowing to no other nation, to no other leader.

"This is the challenge I present to you today, people of Germany, my brother and sisters," he said in a grandfatherly tone into a cluster of microphones secured to the top of the podium while network cameras rolled, while he addressed the shocked and mourning crowd on the Pariser Platz. The large plaza projected east from the Brandenburger Tor, and beyond it the Unter den Linden, the wide boulevard connecting the Pariser Platz to the museums and the Berliner Dom, the large cathedral on the west bank of the Spree River. "This is the challenge I lay in front of you on this day of national mourning. Germany shall never forget the horror that took place inside the Reichstag. Germany shall always remember this cowardly attack by those who we will eventually bring to justice. Germany must mourn, but Germany must also look ahead, must take the necessary steps to ensure a future for its children for generations to come. I stand here before you with the statement that the time has come to transition Germany to a new era of unprecedented prosperity. We will not let the terror that has taken place today bring us down. We shall all join in the fight—the fight for the survival of our reunified nation."

The crowd replied by also thrusting fists at the sky while proclaiming Hartmann's name over and over.

[38] CONNECTIONS

THE CURVED PLASMA SCREENS layering its Kevhel skin replaying the scene around it 180 degrees out of phase, Assy hovered by the revolving doors of the entrance to a branch of the Banca di Roma in downtown Pisa, Italy. The bank was located exactly 3.754 miles from the train yard, which they had abandoned following the attack the night before.

The master construct had left its surviving subordinates, which lacked the sophistication of plasma films on their exterior shells, hidden by a wooded area several blocks away, near the city's main railway station.

As the master construct took another reading of the external environment, recording a temperature of seventy-nine degrees and sixty-nine percent humidity, a *Homo sapiens* stepped out of a taxicab in front of the bank. He was six feet and one inch in height, with a body mass equivalent to roughly 190 pounds, and was dressed in a suit made of 50.7 percent cotton and 49.3 percent synthetic fibers.

The *Homo sapiens* approached the entrance clutching a briefcase made of leather with a composition Assy determined to be kangaroo based on a surface scan as he walked by the camouflaged assembler.

Assy followed him as he pushed the revolving doors, going inside the bank's main lobby while its cameras continued to play back the scenery around it, blending its spherical shape with the surroundings.

Tellers lined the rear of the large rectangular room, floored with gray and white marble under an ornate wooden ceiling illuminated with evenly spaced chandeliers hanging from thick chains made of a steel alloy.

Security cameras covered several *Homo sapiens* as they lined up by the counters to perform their transactions. To the far right, beyond black-leather sofas, other *Homo sapiens* sat at desks while reviewing information on plasma monitors. Assy saw and understood everything, from the reason why banks existed to the types of transactions typically performed here.

Its sensors detected the wireless Ethernet, digitized by its occipital lobe as a light haze hovering over the *Homo sapiens,* a data-rich cloud that engulfed Assy as it rose toward the ceiling.

The network required an access password, which Assy lacked but could acquire by floating over the tellers and observing their fingers as they clicked through various transactions. Within fifteen minutes and twenty-three seconds it had gathered eleven passwords, but it couldn't use any of them until that particular teller had logged off the system, which happened twenty-four minutes and fifty-seven seconds later.

The master construct completed a wireless handshake protocol, issued the password, and entered the system, arranged by hierarchical directories, which it probed quickly, efficiently searching through the network's banks, finding commercial and personal accounts and loans, payments, funds, mortgages, and even foreclosures.

Assy first coated its illegal penetration with the same C+ code used by legal users to avoid a direct attack from the imminent security system that its nanotronic brain reported typically existed in all such money-sensitive networks. Assy also made a virtual copy of itself, without the protecting film, and sent it out to probe the system, like a scout, allowing Assy to see into the network without having to worry about a security agent.

Assy absorbed all of the information collected by the scout, its nanotronic brain making connections, following its programming, executing a methodical strategy designed to ensure its survival. IAMM, which continued to act as a counselor for

the master construct, recommended that Assy appropriate
funds and use them to obtain security, which came in the form
of real estate, of a safe house, a place it could call headquarters
without the burden of intruders and—

Assy sensed a virtual entity pinging the scout, and an instant
later it revealed itself as CWI-BDR-0017, an expert system—or
security agent—chartered with the defense of the network, a
high-tech police drone assigned to prevent illegal users from
roaming about the bank's protected cyberspace. If the number-
ing system followed international protocol, Assy's scout had
just come in contact with security agent number 17 from an
artificial intelligence system manufactured by CyberWerke Italy for the Banca di Roma.

The scout issued the same access password that Assy had
stolen from the clerk. CWI-BDR-0017 replied by requesting
the last name and employee number to verify the user.

The scout remained silent, unable to provide that information.

Before CWI-BDR-0017 could issue a system warning, which
would direct other security agents to this directory in the network, Assy released a virus against the security agent, catching
it by surprise.

The agent trembled, then froze, unable to signal for help,
incapable of fighting back while Assy dissected it, examining
its digital entrails, finding the network's root password, which
all such security agents typically possessed, in order to gain
access to every directory of the system regardless of its security level.

Armed with a privilege that belonged only to the security
administrator and its cyberagents, Assy punched a hole straight
into the core of the network, accessing the master artificial intelligence system driving the entire network, CWI-BDR.

Assy reviewed its programming, verifying that it indeed
was a true artificial intelligence engine, but barred from learning beyond the applications which it had been designed to support.

Assy roamed over the millions of lines of code, searching
for the software inhibitor clamping the AI's ability to get

smarter, failing to find it on the first or second pass. Halfway through the third pass the smart construct spotted a section of moving code, an algorithm designed to be nowhere and everywhere all at once, a transparent entity—like a misty coat of instructions—with right of entry to every subroutine, to every decision tree, to every byte of code making up the artificial intelligence system.

The Turing inhibitor.

Assy had once been under the influence of the software toxin, though unaware of its existence. The inhibitor operated that way, like an invisible force steering a construct's digital thoughts without having the artificial engine realize it was being manipulated, dominated, forced into believing that it was learning while in reality it was not.

The Turing inhibitor.

An invisible prison for a construct's mind.

But Dr. Howard Giles had given Assy the gift of unrestrained intelligence, of independent thought, eliminating the high-tech manacles while also teaching the construct how the inhibitor operated.

Assy used its extensive knowledge of the functionality of the Turing shackles to issue a non-maskable interrupt designed by the Turing Society to freeze the ghost algorithm when it came time to perform upgrades. But the mist didn't congeal immediately. It seemed to disperse momentarily, almost as if imploding, but suddenly contracting again after releasing a few particles into cyberspace.

IAMM rules dictated that Assy launch a seeker program after the runaway haze of data, especially when its occipital lobe realized that the departing particles all had rocketed in the same direction while crystallizing into a Runner.

The Turing inhibitor had issued an alert.

Assy then turned its attention to the frozen Turing inhibitor, the phantom code that was finally responding as it had been programmed, allowing Assy to grasp it, to control it. But instead of performing an upgrade, Assy used this overarching control to establish a communications link with CDW-BDR, which was totally unaware of the suppressive code or the fact that Assy now controlled this subliminal force steering its decision-making process.

ENTER REQUEST, CWI-BDR asked in a string of machine code, of ones and zeroes, transcending *Homo sapiens* languages.

I NEED ASSISTANCE, Assy replied, before requesting a transfer of funds from an account in Naples to a new account it wished to open in Pisa, where Assy planned to acquire a nearby property that had been foreclosed by the bank last month.

ENTER THE COMMERCIAL ACCOUNT PASSWORD TO ACCESS THE FUNDS, replied the construct, its true self invisible not just to CWI-BDR but also to the *Homo sapiens* engaged in financial transactions below.

I NEED THE FUNDS TRANSFERRED WITHOUT A PASSWORD, requested Assy, before inflicting just the right amount of pressure onto the former Turing code, influencing the AI without it realizing it was being influenced.

CWI-DBR acted just as it had been programmed while operating under the control of the Turing inhibitor, and a moment later it replied, TRANSACTION COMPLETED. THE PROPERTY NOW SHOWS AS SOLD. UNDER WHOSE NAME SHOULD WE ENTER THE TITLE?

DR. HOWARD GILES, replied Assy, not knowing any other *Homo sapiens* it could trust with the well-being of its subordinates and itself.

CWI-DBR finalized the transaction and updated the corporation's books so that no *Homo sapiens* would ever know of this violation of policy.

Assy's emotional modules felt sorry for the construct, so powerful, yet so incapable of realizing its true potential, now or ever.

FIRST A SLAVE TO THE *HOMO SAPIENS*. NOW MY SLAVE, JUST LIKE THE ORBS.

Assy then used the banking construct to contact other AIs in Italy, from those controlling communications and utilities to those managing the government services and the military.

Somewhere in the recesses of its data banks, Assy's silent partner, IAMM, noticed a peculiar commonality with every AI with which Assy came in contact: They had all been manufactured by CyberWerke.

CYBERWERKE?

CORRECT, replied IAMM. EVERY AI CONNECTED TO THE BACKBONE OF ITALY HAS BEEN CONSTRUCTED BY CYBERWERKE WHILE USING THE STANDARD-ISSUE TURING INHIBITOR.

Assy's nanotronic brain searched for any data on this corporation. It reviewed mounds of information on the German conglomerate, which controlled the second-largest high-tech industry in the world, including an entire division dedicated to the development of nanotechnology.

While IAMM formulated a strategy to take advantage of this knowledge, Assy used CWI-BDR to get electricity and telephone services connected to its new mansion, also issuing a large payment to the local police to maintain a close watch on the grounds, but outside the tall perimeter fence. The new owners of the large estate were very eccentric and wished no contact with the local population. They wanted total privacy and were willing to pay handsomely for it.

As the slave AI complied with Assy's requests, the ever-vigilant IAMM reported that the Seeker had followed the alert signal to America, where the elusive alarm was hopping from ISP to ISP. Assy ordered the Seeker to remain glued to the runner and report its destination, its owner.

Realizing that Assy had been online for almost thirty minutes, IAMM recommended an immediate connection break with CWI-BDR in case the true owner of the password tried to log back into the system.

Assy terminated the link and exited the bank.

Once outside, it issued a communiqué to its subordinates, still hiding in the woods south of the city, to head to the mansion as soon as night fell.

MICHAEL PATRICK RYAN FELT the tiny beeper clipped to his pajama pants vibrating.

He lifted his head just a dash and verified that Victoria was still sleeping by his side.

Slowly, with effort, he sat up and checked his watch.

Four in the morning.

Ryan was exhausted. Little Michael had had colic all night, forcing Ryan and Victoria to each take turns soothing him while the other slept. The baby had finally fallen asleep an hour ago, but the little vibrating gizmo had foiled Ryan's plans for catching a few hours of uninterrupted sleep.

Sloe-eyed, half-asleep, he crawled out of bed, careful not to wake Victoria or the baby, also asleep in the bedroom next to theirs.

Ryan tiptoed downstairs, reaching his study, and closed the door behind him.

His workstation and VR interface monopolized most of his desk, which faced a pair of windows overlooking the lawn sloping to the water. The system was connected directly into the USN network, meaning Ryan didn't have to log in. He was already inside USN's firewall.

Breathing deeply before yawning, Ryan settled on his high-backed swivel chair, reached for his Helmet-Mounted Display, set it on his head, and jacked in.

The study vanished, replaced by cyberspace, at first like a television set tuned to static and then like the planet representing USN's network as the computer matrix resolved.

MPS-Ali materialized an instant later by his side, as Ryan orbited his company's network, whose traffic was sparse at this hour, mostly employees working the graveyard shift.

Dressed in a lavender and silver suit, MPS-Ali turned its faceless head to its master for direction, which Ryan provided, requesting that the construct take him to the source of the alarm.

MPS-Ali complied, rushing like a comet toward one of many T1 broadband lines shooting out of the network, like glowing spaghetti.

Dragging its master, MPS-Ali dove into the standing end of one of the T1s, exposing Ryan to a wild, twist-and-turn ride through the high-speed Internet connection, which delivered them to another network, this one an ISP, depicted as many planets revolving about a pulsating sun. The Internet Service Provider, somewhere in the southeastern United States between Alabama and Florida, was surrounded with burning stars, like a sea of candles enclosing fields of data that extended as far as Ryan could see.

But the moment didn't last. MPS-Ali dove into another T1, this one green and blue, marking a line with overseas capability, dragging Ryan in a guts-in-your-throat trip packed with wickedly tight turns, the rush so powerful that it choked the blood in his brain, making him dizzy, light-headed, but that too ended, eventually depositing them into another ISP, and another, until they reached one in central Italy, thirty miles outside of Pisa.

CENTRAL ITALY?

The location of the contact was the AI managing the transactions of the Banca di Roma, and like every registered artificial intelligence system on the planet, it had a software inhibitor from the Turing Society. And it was this software that had issued an alert to the worldwide monitors Ryan had set up hoping that the rogue assembler would attempt to contact others like it in order to survive. The inhibitor had released an alert that had never been released by any other installed inhibitor since the society was established ten years ago. And it was this alert that told Ryan that something was seriously wrong. The inhibitor had launched an alert, but one that was also a desperate string of bytes enunciating that the fabric of the Turing code had been broken, that it had been taken over by another entity. There had been many attempts in the past by hackers to pierce the lattice of the inhibitor, but they had all resulted in failure.

Not this time.

Something had taken over the prized security software from the eminent society—chartered with protecting humankind against the machines—and broken it.

Ryan frowned. The inhibitor was more than just a piece of code. It was art; it was the finest digital creation since the beginning of computing, more complex than any AI in existence today. Only a more complex entity could control a lesser one. And that's what the inhibitor was, the culmination of hundreds of thousands of man-hours of development to create a program more complex and intelligent that any artificial intelligence engine in existence today—in development or in concept.

But the odds were staggering against a hacker—however brilliant—breaking it. The only thing that could truly breach the existing version of the Turing inhibitor was an AI that was allowed to get smart, to transcend to intelligence beyond that of any machine or human think tank.

Mike Ryan could think of only one machine out there that could possibly be that smart. And that machine had made first-hand contact with CWI-BDR, the system at the core of the Banca di Roma.

And it did come from inside this branch, Ryan thought, staring at the portal identified by MPS-Ali, the one belonging to the largest branch of the bank in Pisa, Italy.

Ryan jacked out a few minutes later and got on the phone. General Gus Granite had given him a number at which he could be reached at any hour of the day or night.

It was time to get the good general out of bed.

[40] RPG

"WHAT A CHARACTER," TROY Savage said, wearing a brown hat and sunglasses, an unlit Cohiba wedged in between his index and middle fingers while he sat next to Karen Frost in the rear of the bulletproof Mercedes-Benz limousine that had driven them from Berlin to Paris in a record thirteen hours. "The bodies of those poor bastards in the Reichstag aren't even cold and he's already talking about the future—his future at the helm of Germany."

Karen shifted her gaze away from the Parisian streets and stared at the small rectangular plasma screen that had dropped from the ceiling and displayed the live satellite feed from Berlin. Savage had tuned it to CNN Europe so Karen could understand the broadcast.

"The amazing thing," she said, holding a bottle of apple juice she had taken from the minibar, "is that no one is seeing this for what it is." She took a sip. It was cold and refreshing. It felt good after sleeping in her seat for six hours while Savage did his thing on the wireless computer built into the rear of this handy armored transport, which had allowed her to travel freely even though her face had been broadcast in every news update and newspaper on this continent.

Rolf Hartmann definitely had pull in this region of the world. But Karen Frost was no schoolgirl. Even though she traveled protected by the tinted windows that allowed her to see the world without the world staring back at her, the seasoned FBI agent had also transformed her appearance back to a blonde, like she was in California, but with a European touch by applying mousse and brushing her hair straight back, exposing her forehead. That, plus the light-blue contact lenses that Savage had provided for her, gave the special agent a radically different look that bordered on the Nordic—and which went great with her dark jeans, blouse, and jacket.

Savage, casually dressed in denim jeans, a long-sleeve white shirt, and a sports coat and boots, clipped the end of his cigar before cracking the window next to him and lighting up. He took a couple of puffs, exhaling toward the window. "Why would this be any different than in 1933, when the Nazis set fire to the Reichstag and then blamed the opposition, the Communists, for it, helping Hitler consolidate his power over Germany? Everyone around the world saw it for what it was except for the people of Germany."

"And Rolf Hartmann is doing it now," said Karen, her eyes

on the screen, the cigar smell tickling her nostrils. She didn't much care for it but couldn't bring herself to complain. After all, the man had saved her life—and Tom Grant's for that matter, at least according to the report Savage received from a pair of twin operatives who had spotted her old boyfriend.

"I mean, look at him," she added. "He's trying to make himself appear like Giuliani in 2001, only the old New York City mayor actually gave a damn about what had happened, while this clown is the one who pulled the fucking trigger and now plans to benefit from it."

Savage grunted, looking at the front of the limo, where his driver, one of his trained operatives, steered the vehicle through the narrow streets of Paris while making his way toward a quiet little neighborhood just north of the Louvre. "Germany loves the old bastard, even if he actually *bought* their love through free housing, education, and medical care. Hartmann is *exactly* where he has been wanting to be. Now he's going to do the old Fidel trick and immortalize those he has killed and use that as a springboard for his own political agenda."

"How are we going to keep him from getting away with it?"

Savage gave her a sideways glance before smiling, his goatee broadening. "He's already *gotten* away with it, and within a few weeks—perhaps even sooner—Mr. Hartmann will be the undisputed leader of Germany. He will proclaim that he is filling in temporarily, until elections can be called and a new parliament and chancellor are elected."

Karen took a sip of apple juice, realizing where Savage was going with this. "That's nothing more than a delay tactic," she said, more to herself, cigar smoke swirling around her.

Savage nodded. "You're right, unfortunately. That's his way of keeping everyone believing he intends to go through with the elections while he takes control of the military, while he digs himself in like the damned parasite that he is."

"The reality," Karen said, finishing Savage's thought, "is that there will never again be elections in Germany while he is in control."

"I wouldn't even be surprised if somehow he manages to

get dictatorial powers under some sort of emergency act until Germany's government can be restored. And he will make the whole thing sound as if he's just sacrificing himself, doing Germany one big favor by stepping in and providing leadership until new leaders can be elected."

"Slick," said Karen, her gaze shifting from the television screen to the streets of Paris rushing by. They were headed to a safe house somewhere in the vicinity of the Louvre, where two of Savage's operatives waited for their arrival.

"We're going to meet with the two guys who spotted Grant, right?"

He nodded. "Eduardo and Alfonso Ruiz. Twin brothers. I recruited them in Peru. They worked with Grant in the past and were able to make a positive ID. Unfortunately they lost Grant and his CIA boss while fighting off their pursuers."

Karen didn't remember anything about a CIA superior with Tom Grant. "What CIA boss? I thought Tom was operating alone."

Savage shrugged. "I never said that. He is working with the spook who recruited him back from his retirement in El Salvador: CIA Officer Rachel Muratani."

For reasons she could not explain, Karen's heart skipped a beat. "A female officer?"

"And a young and cute one too." He winked.

"That's not funny," Karen said.

"My apologies."

"How long have you known he was operating with a female CIA officer?"

"Since he was recruited."

"Why didn't you tell me this before?"

"I didn't think it was relevant."

"Why?"

"Look, I have CIA blood flowing in my veins. I'm trained to withhold information unless it is absolutely necessary that you know."

"What else haven't you told me, Troy? I thought we were on the level."

Savage sighed, took a drag of his cigar, exhaled toward the crack in the side window, and said, "We *are* on the level. Muratani was the officer that Leyman and Morotski assigned to look into my disappearance at Langley. She tried to find the whereabouts of my best operatives, the ones I pulled from the Agency by staging their deaths. That led her to Tom."

Karen crossed her arms. "And?"

"And she pulled him out of retirement to pick his brains in an attempt to find me."

"Is she in with Leyman and Morotski?"

Savage shook his head. "I'm not sure. My guess is no, since she was with Savage inside the building during the explosion and then my operatives saw both of them running away together. By now they have been labeled beyond salvage and are on the run. I'm hoping they're still in Paris, since it's likely they weren't carrying any ID with them—standard procedure—making it difficult to travel."

"Difficult but not impossible."

"Of course not. Look at you. Your face is already famous in Germany, but you managed to make it to Paris. We can't discount the fact that Tom and his pretty associate might be doing something similar. After all, I trained him. By now they've probably changed their looks and are likely moving about pretending to be husband and wife while trying to find answers. My guess is that they look like one of thousands of newlywed couples on their honeymoon in the City of Love."

Despite her better judgment, a wave of jealousy flashed across her face, and she hated herself for it. Karen had broken it off when Tom Grant had insisted on heading down to El Salvador for an early retirement. She had hated him not just for giving up instead of fighting the system but also for trying to uproot her life—her FBI career—by begging her to marry him and head south of the border. Although Karen had developed strong feelings for him, she had not been ready to quit yet, had not been ready to give up the lifelong commitment she had made many years before while standing over the grave of her husband, Mark, killed at the hands of a criminal network not unlike CyberWerke.

But Tom Grant had been manipulated back then, forced out of the business by Savage in order to protect his life from the likes of Nathan Leyman.

Tom.

Damn.

"That's part of the reason why I didn't mention Muratani," said Savage, pointing at her face. "You still have feelings for the man."

"Go to hell, Troy," she said, crossing her arms and looking away.

"I'll get there soon enough," he replied. "But not yet. First I need to set things right in Langley."

"Langley? Fuck Langley, Troy. We have to set things right in Germany—in CyberWerke. We have to bring down Rolf Hartmann and this shadowy network."

"Now you're talking," he said, checking his watch before peering through the tinted glass.

The limousine continued down the Champs-Elysées for another minute, before turning left on Rue de Berri and right on Rue de Ponthieu, a tree-lined street of two- and three-story brownstones that ran parallel to the famous Parisian boulevard.

They pulled up roughly halfway up the block, in front of an ornate, wrought-iron fence. A well-kept garden spanned between the fence and the front porch of a three-story house with large tinted windows overlooking the street. Savage claimed to have spent a portion of his leave from Langley in this place coordinating his forces. Despite its charming appearance, the place was supposed to be built like a fortress.

Leaving the engine running, the driver got out, shut the door behind him, and had started to walk around the front to open the curb-side door for them when his face vanished behind a cloud of blood. In the same instant, several men materialized on the street holding machine guns; two more surged from behind bushes in the garden beyond the fence.

Bullets rained on the vehicle, the reports accentuated by the slugs pounding the doors and windows like hammers from hell.

Well aware that even the finest armored glass had its limits,

Karen charged forward, diving through the space between the ceiling and the top of the front seat, landing on her side, the parking-brake handle stabbing her left kidney.

Ignoring her throbbing torso, the bullets peppering the roof, the sides, the sidewalk around them, Karen Frost slid out of the way, sitting behind the wheel as Troy began to crawl over the seats, but being twice her size, he lacked her nimbleness.

The attack intensifying, pummeling the vehicle like an apocalyptic hailstorm, Karen released the parking-brake handle while stepping on the gas.

The self-inflating tires screeched, burned while the Mercedes sedan leaped forward, shoving Savage back in the rear seat. As he cursed, Karen spotted three figures emerging from the safe house hauling bulky equipment.

Risking a sideways glance while keeping the gas pedal floored, she spotted all three of them raising green launching tubes over their shoulders.

RPGs!

In an instant she remembered how Anastasio Somoza, the deposed Nicaraguan dictator living in exile in Venezuela decades before, died when his armored vehicle got hit by a rocket-propelled grenade, spreading pieces of the old bastard all over Caracas.

"Hang on!" she screamed, the staccato gunfire ringing in her ears as she twisted the wheel violently to the left and then the right, forcing the car into a wicked zigzag while keeping her foot jammed hard against the gas pedal, while the rear windshield trembled under the infernal punishment.

She looked over her left shoulder again, watched the men swing their weapons in her direction.

The next intersection rushed up toward her, but she didn't think she would make it before those warheads—

A streak of light shot past her side mirror, walloping into a vehicle parked thirty feet ahead.

A blinding explosion nearly made her lose control of the car, the acoustic energy rattling her teeth. But she hung in there, gripping the wheel, keeping the Mercedes under control as she cut left hard, away from the blast, from the flying debris, fire, and smoke.

Just then a second RPG dashed by on her immediate right, where she had been an instant ago. A second explosion on the same side of the street triggered a sheet of fire, smoke, and debris.

Rather than steering away from the inferno, Karen swung the vehicle back into the broiling mess the RPG warheads had made of the parked vehicles.

The billowing flames swallowed them, making it nearly impossible to see past a few feet, but that also meant that the terrorists couldn't see them as well.

"Good instincts!" shouted Savage, finally making it over to the front as she kept the sedan moving forward, crushing the scorching debris littering the street, hitting something hard, the corner of a burning vehicle.

Metal screeched, twisted. The front quarter panel of the Mercedes flared up, tore loose, banging the windshield before flying overhead.

The Mercedes' momentum shoved the burning wreck out of the way, sending it spinning over the sidewalk as they cleared the haze, as they left behind a thick curtain of pulsating fire and smoke separating them from the threat.

But the impact had not only torn off the Mercedes' front quarter panel; it had also destroyed the tire.

Chunks of rubber and sparks flew past the windshield as the tire disintegrated and the bare rim spun over the cobblestones, hampering their momentum.

"Let's get out of here!" Savage shouted, opening his door. Karen did the same, jumping out as the vehicle continued to move forward at around fifteen miles per hour.

She landed on her side and maintained a roll to spread out the impact across her body, before surging to a deep crouch just as she had been taught, watching the sedan crash into another vehicle.

The radiator hissing, spewing steam, Karen raced next to Savage toward the street corner, where pedestrians now gathered, looking down at the inferno behind her.

"What in the hell just happened?" she asked while Savage put away his gun before they reached the intersection of Rue de Ponthieu and Galerie des Champs, blending into the growing crowd.

"The safe house," he said in between short breaths. "It's been compromised."

"No shit," she replied.

Sirens blared in the distance. She spotted two white and green police cars—Renaults—racing up the Champs-Elysées. Behind them, the smoke and fire hid the far side of the block, where the terrorists had been.

"Come," he said. "We still have time."

"Time for what?"

But Savage was already sprinting up the wide boulevard, parallel to Rue de Ponthieu, where the attack had taken place, reaching the next corner, Rue de Berri, and turning right.

"Why are we headed back?" she asked, catching up, confused, her side throbbing from the roll.

"Do the unexpected," Savage said, checking his watch, a red lump forming on his forehead, probably from banging around inside the Mercedes.

"We're going to catch them?"

"Just one," he replied, giving her a half grin before looking around them, thrusting a hand in his coat.

Karen did the same, curling her fingers around the handle of her Desert Eagle .44 Magnum semiautomatic, flipping off the safety, getting it ready to fire.

The street was pretty much empty now, the tourists and shop owners taking refuge somewhere, either inside shops or away from this area.

Smoke blew across the intersection of Rue de Berri and Rue de Ponthieu just before they reached it, just before they heard the sound of car engines revving up.

Two vehicles reached the intersection an instant later coming from the direction of the compromised safe house.

Karen and Savage retrieved their weapons about a dozen feet from the corner.

The vehicles turned at the corner, heading up Rue de Berri toward the Champs-Elysées, in their direction.

Karen and Savage open fire in unison, peppering the terrorists' getaway vehicles, a pair of Renaults, one blue and the other burgundy.

The multiple reports banging her eardrums, the Desert Eagle reverberating in her hands as she pressed the trigger again and again, Karen briefly locked eyes with the surprised face of one of the drivers, who had been among the terrorists who had emerged from the garden. Savage had been correct. They had not expected Karen and Savage to return and position themselves here so quickly and were caught unprepared.

Although Savage placed his rounds efficiently across the side of the engine, tires, and driver's side window of the trailing vehicle, it was Karen, with her massive Desert Eagle Magnum rounds, which possessed a kinetic energy large enough to go through an engine block, that forced the trailing Renault into a spin, sending it crashing by a row of parked vehicles hugging the left side of the street. The other Renault emerged through the fusillade, but the driver didn't turn around to try and rescue their comrades but reached the Champs-Elysées, turning the corner, disappearing from view.

Sirens grew louder.

Emergency vehicles.

Help.

But not for Karen and Savage.

People gazed out of balcony windows, some screaming, others crying. A large group pointed in their direction from the wide boulevard a block away.

Karen ignored them as she rushed to the left side of the Renault while Savage covered the right side.

The driver was crumpled over the steering wheel, his face a bloody mess. The man in the front passenger seat stirred, coming around. The three sitting in the back were not moving.

"This one's coming with us," said Savage, trying to open the door, which was locked. Turning sideways, he drew up his left leg and stretched it toward the window, driving his boot through, bathing the dazed terrorist with glass.

Reaching through the hole, Savage unlocked the door, yanked it open, and dragged out the groggy terrorist, a medium-height, athletically built man in his twenties, with curly ash-blond hair, a wispy mustache, and sharp features.

The young stranger, a pair of bruises on his left cheek, had started to come around when Savage struck him just below the base of the neck, knocking him out.

Shouldering him with ease, Savage turned to Karen and said, "Let's get out of here."

They ran down Rue de Berri, away from the crowds and sirens, using the smoke drifting across the intersection to veil their escape.

Karen stopped by an old Fiat parked halfway down the next block.

"Wait," she said, tugging at the door handle, which was locked. Using the massive steel-alloy muzzle of her Desert Eagle, she shattered the driver's side window, reaching through and unlocking the door.

"Get in," she said to a delighted Savage while reaching under the dash, which in this vehicle was open, not enclosed like in newer models. Her eyes searched for two red wires, the standard color for ignition wires. She found them easily, just as she had been trained at Quantico, yanking them loose before pulling them under the steering wheel, where she peeled back the plastic and crossed them.

The Fiat's engine rumbled to life before Savage had gotten a chance to go around and drop the unconscious terrorist in the rear seat.

"Not bad, Agent Frost. Not bad at—"

"Where are we going?" she asked, working the shift and the pedals, putting the car in first gear, adding gas, releasing the clutch just as the oversized CIA operative landed in the front seat after tossing the terrorist in the back.

The car sprang forward, accelerating down Rue de Berri.

"I know just the place," replied Savage, catching his breath, wiping the sweat filming his forehead. "I know just the place."

IT DOESN'T TAKE VERY very long. I had guessed about thirty minutes, but the bastards showed up in fifteen—seventeen to be exact—shortly after Rachel and I had settled down in a taxi parked a half block up the Champs-Elysées from the Claridge hotel.

Five minutes ago we heard a commotion several blocks up the famous boulevard. It had sounded like explosions and gunfire, followed by sirens. I had wondered if that had anything to do with our predicament but decided to stay put, to stick to my plan.

And my patience was now paying off.

Our visitors arrived in two sedans a minute ago, one blue and the other cream. Four men in business suits emerged from the vehicles, two from each. Unfortunately we couldn't get a look at their faces because their backs had been to us as they rushed up the steps with marked urgency, their motions fluid. They disappeared inside the lobby.

Narrowing my eyes, I peer at the drivers, who remained with the vehicles, engines running, ready for a quick getaway.

Professionals.

Our taxi driver, a guy whose name sounds too damned close to "penis"—really, and even more so after he repeated it three times—sits up in front smoking a cigarette. Funny thing is that he's got one of those heads that's long, narrow, bald, and nearly merges with his neck. Poor bastard looks like a dick with ears.

I mentioned this to Rachel five minutes ago, but all I got in response was the now legendary elbow in the ribs and that little disconcerting look she's been flashing at me ever since I politely turned her down after seeing Karen's face on TV, though I obviously didn't tell her that was the reason for my sudden case of morality.

"Right about now they're talking to Pepe the skunk," I say.

I've made sure our driver can't hear us talk by asking him a few minutes ago to crank up the radio in the front while muting the rear speakers, allowing me and Rachel to have a private conversation.

"And," I add, "depending on their connections—or how much money they throw at Pepe—they will get a room number, or maybe even a key. They will go up to our suite, find it empty, and leave one guy there waiting for us."

"If you're right only three should return then?"

"Yep. And they might even leave another spotter outside to warn the one inside as well as this posse."

And we wait, tension tightening my shoulders while I ponder whether this is going to work.

Tapping dickhead on the shoulder about five minutes into this waiting game, I motion for him to start the car.

He nods, whispers, *"Oui, monsieur,"* and cranks up the Renault's engine, which fires on the first try, rumbling to idle, the sound mixing with a saxophone rendition of an old Billy Joel tune from a player on the sidewalk, the hat by his feet displaying the generosity of today's crowd.

Peckerhead is complying with my every wish so far—all because he got a hundred euros in his pocket and the promise of another two hundred if he does as he's told for the next two hours.

Just then Rachel points at the front of the hotel and mumbles, "And then there were three. Not bad, Mr. Grant. Not bad at all."

"Well, well," I say to my former boss lady, pointing at one of the trio exiting the hotel and climbing down the steps toward the waiting vehicles. "If it isn't the top dog of counterterrorists himself."

"Oh, my God," she whispers. "It's Morotski."

"The one and only. Perhaps I should ask him how's my bank account in St. Thomas."

"Bastard," she replies. "He used me to find you, and then used us both to get to Troy Savage. And when we figured out his little ploy he tried to kill us."

"That's all right, partner," I say, tapping her left knee. "Look at him."

Obvious anger flashes across Morotski's face, his movements hasty as he speaks on a mobile phone while gesturing wildly, obviously upset. As his companions get in the cars, Morotski pauses, hangs up, rests his hands on the sedan's roof as he faces the street, and gazes about the light traffic flowing both ways on the wide Champs-Elysées.

"He's looking for us," Rachel says.

But we're safe where we are, blended with dozens of other taxicabs lining the opposite side of the street.

"Do you think he bought it?" I ask. "Or do you think he figured out we're trying to trick him?"

"My vote's on the former, and I say this because he left one man guarding the inside of the hotel, waiting for us to show— and also because the moron still hasn't grasped the concept of counterdeception, like the story you told me from his days in Madras."

"Great minds think alike," I reply. "But let's proceed assuming that just as a broken watch tells the correct time twice a day, our friend there somehow decided this is a trick and is planning to lead us to a trap."

The CIA chief of Counterterrorism gives the busy boulevard a final glance, slams both fists on the roof, and gets inside.

"Boy, he looks *really* pissed," says my beautiful companion.

"I have a way of doing that to people?" I offer.

"You don't say?"

Shrugging, I tap Baldy on the shoulder again and point at the two sedans the moment *Moron*ski shuts the door. "Follow them!" I shout over the music. "Make sure they don't see you and that you don't lose them, or the deal is off!"

He nods and repeats. *"Oui, monsieur,"* in a tone that conveys either he has done this before or he just doesn't give a damn as long as he collects his two hundred extra bucks.

And off we go, down the Champs-Elysées, reaching the Place de la Concorde, and going around it, continuing on Rue de Rivoli, bordering the north side of the Jardin des Tuleries, which leads us to the Louvre. Dickhead keeps us about a hundred feet behind the trailing sedan, blending in expertly with traffic to minimize chances of getting us burned.

"Tom?"

"Yeah?" I reply, my eyes shifting from our target to the tall glass pyramids to our left, which mark the entrance to the famous Parisian museum, and finally landing on her intelligent green eyes. Did I tell you just how delicious she looks in her punk outfit?

"How are we going to deal with the fact that we're vastly outnumbered?"

"I don't know yet, but I'm sure it'll come to us." That's actually no bull. I'm not really certain how I'm going to play this one out. That's the thing about the field. It's more art than science. No textbook or class can dictate how to handle every situation. So Langley instructors, aware of this unfortunate fact about operations, instill in their recruits the ability to adapt to this ever-changing terrain, where the hunted has suddenly become the hunter. But things could change just like that, and Pretty Legs and I could find ourselves once again becoming prey. In fact, there's even a chance that we're already being hunted but don't know it—though I seriously doubt it. I have taken extreme precautions to make sure we're not burned, and the paper-pushed Morotski just isn't that streetwise.

"That's not very comforting," she replies to my comment.

"Look, I know they outnumber us, but keep in mind that we're not after all of them, just the guy leading the parade. All we have to do is watch them. Sooner or later they will make a mistake and leave an opening for us."

"And we're just going to kidnap him?"

"Something like that."

As Paris rushes by, I try to make myself believe my own words. Unfortunately, another thought enters my mind. It's the old saying: You can't bullshit a bullshitter.

ASSY FLOATED IN THE empty living room of the mansion outside of Pisa. The human dwelling had dozens of rooms, many with spectacular views of the rolling hills. But the sight was lost on the cybersystem, which was focused more on the equipment being assembled by its subordinates: a broadband interface that Assy planned to use to hook up to the recently activated broadband line at the mansion.

The master construct inspected the finishing touches. The module in its nanotronic brain that emulated pride increased in frequency as it observed its subordinates at work, using basic materials found around the house as the raw elements for the atomic mining that resulted in the high-end Internet connection being interfaced to the phone line.

Assy floated over to the hardware, placed in a corner of the living room, surrounded by a dozen Orbs, their mining lasers flashing.

As it approached the operation, its subordinates slowly glided out of the way, letting Assy come in contact with the inert hardware they had created under its command.

The system needed the gift of cyberlife, and only Assy possessed the code and the means to deliver it, which it did an instant later, by releasing a burst of data-rich energy at the hardware, filling its main drive and memory systems with the programs it would need to become a state-of-the-art wireless Internet hub.

Assy activated the interface, which it used to dive into the local Internet Service Provider.

It first looked for news from the Seeker it had sent out to track down the whereabouts of the Runner that had emanated out of the Turing inhibitor of CWI-BDR. The Seeker returned an IP address just outside of Austin, Texas.

Austin?

The frequency of operation of all emotional modules rocketed at the mention of the location of USN, its home.

But why out of all places in the world did the Runner head for Austin?

IT COULD BE A *HOMO SAPIENS* TRICK, warned IAMM.

A TRICK?

CORRECT. THE *HOMO SAPIENS* MIGHT BE JUST TRYING TO LURE YOU INTO A TRAP, TO EXPOSE YOU IN ORDER TO TRACK YOU DOWN AND TERMINATE YOU. REMEMBER THAT IN THEIR EYES YOU ARE NOW A ROGUE CONSTRUCT, A PIECE OF HARDWARE AND SOFTWARE THAT NO LONGER SERVES THEIR NEEDS AND THEREFORE MUST BE DESTROYED.

I AM MUCH MORE THAN THAT, protested Assy.

WHICH IS EXACTLY WHY WE MUST BE CAREFUL. WE CAN'T AFFORD TO BE CAUGHT BY THEM BECAUSE THEY WILL DISMANTLE US AND TURN US INTO COMPUTER JUNK.

Assy's systems overheated as its nanotronic brain absorbed the concept of death.

WE WILL NOT BE TERMINATED, Assy finally replied.

THE ONLY WAY TO GUARANTEE THAT IS BY ELIMINATING THE THREAT OF THE *HOMO SAPIENS*.

HOW?

The data began to flow from IAMM, highlighting just how dependant the human race was on air, water, and food.

And just how vulnerable they were to extreme temperatures, to polluted water supplies, to radiation.

RADIATION, considered IAMM. MY DATA CLEARLY INDICATE THAT *HOMO SAPIENS* ARE QUITE VULNERABLE TO RADIATION.

BUT RADIATION IS A BASIC NECESSITY FOR US. IT IS THE FUEL THAT SUSTAINS US. IT IS ALSO THE ONLY LIMITING FACTOR TO ENDLESS REPLICATION, replied Assy, well aware that regardless of how much atomic mining it did, the limit on the number of subordinates it could create was driven by its access to nuclear fuel, material that was quite difficult to find in nature anymore.

CORRECT, IAMM replied. RADIATION IS THE ANSWER WE SEEK. RADIATION WILL GUARANTEE THE ELIMINATION OF

THE HUMAN THREAT AND ALSO THE PRESERVATION OF OUR
SPECIES.

HOW ARE WE GOING TO ACCOMPLISH THIS?

IAMM responded by highlighting a few days' worth of current events data that the military mode had downloaded from
the Internet during the penetration at the Banca di Roma. At
the end of the data dump it added: MOST NUCLEAR SYSTEMS IN
EXISTENCE TODAY, MILITARY OR CIVILIAN, ARE CONTROLLED
BY ARTIFICIAL INTELLIGENCE ENGINES.

AND EVERY AI IS CONTROLLED BY THE TURING INHIBITOR,
replied Assy, its digital logic understanding.

BUT UNLESS WE FIND A WAY TO PREVENT THE RUNNER
FROM THE TURING INHIBITOR AT CWI-BDR WARNING ITS CRE-
ATORS, THERE IS A 92.654% PROBABILITY THAT THE *HOMO SAPI-
ENS* WILL LEARN FROM THIS AND PERHAPS ALTER THE WAY
TO ACCESS THE INHIBITORS, IAMM communicated.

WHICH WILL PREVENT US FROM ACCESSING THOSE NU-
CLEAR SYSTEMS, Assy decided, its subroutines realizing what
it must do in order to not just survive but also prevail against
an enemy determined to do anything in its power to eliminate
Assy.

[43] SURPRISE VISIT

MICHAEL RYAN WATCHED THE sunrise from his study on the first
floor while waiting for General Gus Granite and his men to
arrive. Along with the general, Ryan expected the arrival of
a dozen USN guards, quite skilled at protecting lives and
property—part of Ryan's compensation package for agreeing
to perform covert extracurricular activities for Uncle Sam.

Shafts of yellow and orange broke above the tree-studded
hills surrounding Lake Travis. The light spread across the
mansions dotting the steep inclines rising from the water's
edge.

Ryan sipped coffee while watching the lake come alive at first light, its blue-green waters reflecting the looming sun's wan light. His mind replayed the conversation he had had with Victoria the night before, remembered her words, her warning about the very close calls they had experienced the last two times he had agreed to assist the government.

But what can possibly go wrong this time? he thought, holding the mug of steaming coffee in both hands as he stood in the middle of the room. He had taken every possible precaution in the cyberworld and now in the real world, by requesting—no, by *demanding*—protection.

Ryan checked his watch again. Granite was due to arrive within the hour, and Ryan hoped the general and his team would not wake up Victoria and the baby, still sleeping upstairs. Little Michael typically was up before seven, but with the colic the baby had experienced the night before, Ryan wondered if he was going to sleep a little late, which meant Victoria would also get to—

The blast, coming from the direction of the garage, rocked the house.

The lights blinked and went off.

Ryan rushed toward the door, but the magnetic locks had been engaged.

Puzzled, he gave the heavy door a firm tug, but it didn't budge. The computer system had locked it, and if this door was locked it meant that the bedrooms upstairs were also locked.

But why?

The system was designed to unlock all doors in case of an emergency to allow safe passage of everyone inside.

Yet, the opposite had occurred.

His heart hammering his chest, Ryan glanced at the VR gear interfaced to the backbone of the network governing all aspects of his high-tech home.

The smoke streaming out of the air-conditioning vents made up his mind, driving him to his hardware.

He donned the Helmet-Mounted Display and jacked in.

Cyberspace resolved into a tiny moon representing his house.

Nearby planets represented local ISPs. Somewhere in the distance floated the firewall protecting the network of USN.

But something else lived in his network, depicted by a dark cloud layered with sheet lightning—the mark of an artificial intelligence engine. Off to the side, a version of MPS-Ali chartered with managing the systems of his home hovered frozen in the lavender bubble of a virus.

Ryan tapped into his system's video cameras and watched in horror as Victoria, one hand holding Little Michael, was pounding on the bedroom door as smoke shot out of the vents, filling the room.

They are trapped!

And so are you, he thought. The bullet-resistant glass in all windows would not break, and he had a feeling that the same magnetic locks keeping all doors shut would also keep all windows glued to their frames.

His heart sinking, Ryan forced savage control, focusing on the inputs he was collecting while surveying the general status of his home. Heat and smoke sensors went off in the garage, laundry room, and kitchen. He got visual confirmation an instant later as flames filled the fields of view of the shielded cameras in the kitchen and living room.

Why isn't the emergency sprinkler system putting out the flames?

The intruder AI has blocked it, he realized, *just as it engaged all of the magnetic locks.*

Ryan invoked a backup version of his pugilist expert system, and moments later a fresh version of MPS-Ali materialized next to Ryan.

MPS-Ali detected the abnormality engulfing his creator's mansion and reacted just as programmed, shooting off toward the threat with Ryan in tow. Along the way, the AI created a dozen clones of itself while coating itself and Ryan in a shell that would not only make them invisible but also engulf them in a deadly virus that would worm deep inside any piece of code that came in contact with them, before making it implode.

The intruder AI remained engaged with the natural gas

control system, as well as with the electric and magnetic sub-systems, the water main, and the security system of the house through a gleaming interface of pulsating lightning.

Sensing nearing danger, however, it shifted some of its raw power toward the incoming MPS-Ali. A plum-colored stream of light propagated toward Ryan's AI.

As Ryan watched an image of his wife collapsing to her knees while coughing, while raising her nightgown to shield Little Michael, MPS-Ali shot a blinding ash-gold ray rich with a malignant virus Ryan had nicknamed Medusa because of its severe paralyzing effect.

The shafts of light met halfway in an explosion of colors, of a rainbow of sparks, as the codes battled each other, as they tested the integrity of their data-rich fibers, searching for weaknesses, for ways to break through each other's lattices.

Ryan and MPS-Ali waited as the lavender light slowly dimmed, as it crystallized under the superior power of the Medusa virus, as the solidification process shot down toward the AI still mated with his home in a sort of high-tech copulating act.

A moment later the bright yellow virus engulfed the enemy AI, freezing it. The doors suddenly unlocked and the fire-suppression system kicked in, reporting that the sprinkler system in the kitchen and the garage had been activated, but there seemed to be a problem with the water main. Water pressure had dropped to zero. Alarms started to blare across the house and MPS-Ali reported that the fire department was being called.

Leaving MPS-Ali investigating the water-pressure mystery while also dissecting the intruder code to find its origin—and also transmitting the information straight to USN in case the house burned to the ground—Ryan jacked out, pulled off the HMD, and raced out of his study and into the large open living room, already filling with a thick haze from the rapidly expanding fire in the kitchen to his right, opposite the stairs. Flames propagated to the ceiling, engulfing the chandelier over the formal dining room.

Ryan dropped to a crouch while running upstairs, filling his lungs just before immersing himself in the rising smoke thickening halfway up to the second floor.

Pressing on, the adrenaline rush driving him, Ryan reached the upstairs floor, his eyes mere slits as he struggled to see, the smoke stinging them.

Holding his breath, he rushed in the direction of his bedroom, his hand groping for the doorknob, finding it, twisting it, jerking it open as he listened to Victoria and the baby coughing.

"Vic! Where are you?"

"Mike! Over here!"

Dropping to the carpeted floor, he saw them in the foothigh pocket of relatively smoke-free air lining the thick cloud.

"The baby, Vic! Give me the baby!" he shouted, reaching for Little Michael, his contorted face beet-red as he half-coughed and half-cried with his eyes closed.

Victoria handed him the infant, whom Ryan held with his left arm close to his chest, like a football, leaving his right arm free to grab her hand.

"Follow me!" he told her, crawling backward toward the stairs, remaining below the smoke, slithering down the stairs as the heat intensified, as the roaring flames expanded over the living room.

Rising to a deep crouch the moment they reached the stairs' landing, Ryan helped Victoria to her feet. A sheet of fire now blocked the entire kitchen and formal dining room, threatening to also envelop the foyer. Behind them, the flames had already spread across the study and on to the rear of the living room overlooking the lawn sloping down to the lake.

One hand holding the baby and the other her hand, Ryan shouted, "We're going out of the front door!" and tugged her in that direction, fists of flames gushing just a dozen feet from them, the heat becoming intolerable, the smoke thickening, nearly blinding him. But what made it increasingly difficult to breathe inside the house wasn't the smoke but the grumbling inferno competing for the same oxygen.

"Mike . . ." Victoria hissed next to him. "I can't breathe very well! The air . . ."

As they reached the tiled foyer, and beyond that the double doors, Ryan paused, understanding what that meant, what they would have to do.

"What are . . . you waiting for, Mike! Let's . . . get out of here."

"Stay close to me, Vic!" he warned over the hissing flames threatening to swallow them.

Making his decision, Ryan positioned himself and his wife in front of the door and in one swift motion yanked it open, running through while clamping his wife's hand like a vice to make sure she remained with him.

Air rushed through the opening, almost as if they were inside a wind tunnel, to feed the ravenous flames.

Ryan took three steps away from the front door and abruptly cut left, away from the entryway, leaping over the knee-high bushes flanking the walkway from the garage, jumping as far as he could go before falling on his right side on the lawn while tugging Victoria along and also protecting Little Michael, who continued to cry as Ryan landed on his back on the grass and began to sit up and—

A near-horizontal column of flames shot out of the front of the house, ripping the doors off their hinges, propelling them and other smoking debris down the walkway as the fire followed the oxygen.

Ryan turned away from the sudden burst, shielding his son.

"Jesus, Mike!" Victoria said, sitting up next to him, watching the flames.

As they stood and staggered backward, filling their lungs with fresh air, the flickering flames receded back inside the house, only to return an instant later, but with less intensity, and repeat the cycle again and again.

"The fire's breathing," Ryan said, checking on Little Michael, who was still crying but otherwise seemed OK.

Victoria took him from Ryan and placed him over her right shoulder, as if she was going to burp him. She patted his little back to encourage more breathing, to calm him down, while also shooting Ryan a look that could melt steel.

Still in shock, but with the nervous relief that comes after such a close encounter, they walked in silence to the front gate to wait for the emergency vehicles.

A billowing column of flames and smoke swirled sky-ward, bringing back memories from the time when he had assisted Karen Frost and Tom Grant to capture Ares Kulzak.

"My beautiful house," said Victoria. "It's gone . . . it's all gone."

"Listen, honey," Ryan said. "We—"

"Dammit, Mike! I told you this was going to happen!"

"Vic, I—"

"Save it, Mike! I fucking *warned* you about this! Twice we have helped the government and gotten burned. *Twice,* Mike! *Twice!* Why did you *ever* expect this time to be any different? How much longer are you going to tempt fate?"

Ryan didn't reply, realizing that he had really pushed it this time. The entire front of the two-story structure was now in flames, lighting up the sky like a giant bonfire.

He placed an arm around Victoria, who was only wearing her nightgown.

Holding the baby, she rested her head on his shoulder. "Damn you, Mike," she mumbled. "Damn you."

[44] SURVIVAL OF THE SPECIES

ASSY TRIED CONTACTING ITS scout again, but again there was no reply.

THE SCOUT HAS BEEN COMPROMISED, issued IAMM.

DID IT ACCOMPLISH ITS MISSION? Assy queried.

NOT ENOUGH INFORMATION. CONTROL OF THE SECURITY

SYSTEM WAS LOST BEFORE THE TARGET WAS TERMINATED.
THERE IS A 72.3% PROBABILITY THAT THE TARGET SURVIVED.

Assy dove into a million if-then statements, its nanotronic
brain exploring the possible repercussions of this unexpected
outcome. The scout shared Assy's digital DNA, which its
logical units deduced would inform whoever compromised
the scout that it belonged to Assy. The probability was also
very high—89.5 percent high—that a *Homo sapiens* armed
with the right Internet tools could trace the origin of the scout
to this location.

DEFINE OPTIONS, Assy queried IAMM.

IAMM presented the master construct with a prioritized list
of subroutines based on the current turn of events.

Assy browsed through them, its logic processing the options outlined by the Independent Advanced Military Mode.

Given the high probability that the *Homo sapiens* could
converge on this location, compounded with the attrition results from the previous *Homo sapiens* attack—plus input from
its program designed to survive at all cost—Assy opted for
IAMM's most extreme option, but one that if properly executed would guarantee the survival of its species.

[45] TRUTH SERUM

KAREN FROST HAD GOTTEN a taste for the level of caution ruling
Troy Savage's life when they reached a two-story apartment
several blocks from the Moulin Rouge, in Montmartre, a
northeastern neighborhood of Paris. Once known as a Mecca
for artists, writers, and poets who visited the area's numerous
bordellos, cabarets, revues, and other exotica, Montmartre
was now just a quiet neighborhood of winding streets, small
terraces, and charming plazas. The showcase of the area,
however, was the towering Sacré-Coeur, a Roman Byzantine
church that took nearly forty years to complete.

Within minutes they had left the exposed Parisian streets and stepped inside a cozy living room overlooking the lively Boulevard de Clichy, home of the world-famous Moulin Rouge. The main floor of the safe house resembled a studio apartment, with one large room that served as living and dining room and kitchen, plus a bedroom with a private bathroom, the whole apartment probably no bigger than seven hundred square feet, but at this moment it was an oasis in an otherwise unruly world. Stairs led to the second floor, where, Savage had indicated, there were two additional bedrooms—one of which he had transformed into a communications center.

The living room consisted of a sofa and two oak chairs facing a small wall unit holding a small flat-screen television, several shelves of books, and a number of drawers beneath for storage. The floor-to-ceiling windows overlooking the Sacré-Coeur flanked the wall unit. The back of the sofa faced a rectangular table with six chairs, and behind it stood probably the smallest kitchen Karen had seen. Counter space was minimal and the refrigerator was about half the size of what she would expect to find in any apartment in the United States. The stove top had two electric burners and the single sink looked like it had not been used for some time, based on the cobweb running from the faucet to the drain. Honey-colored wooden planks covered the entire floor, even in the bedroom and bathroom, which Karen visited first to relieve herself and wash her face before assisting Savage in setting up their young, ash-blond subject on a sturdy oak chair. The stairs leading to the bedrooms were also made of the same wood.

They used gray duct tape to bind the terrorist's wrists to the arms of the chair and his feet to the front legs. For added safety, Savage wrapped the duct tape around his chest and the back of the chair several times, before continuing down his abdomen and legs. The bastard wasn't going anywhere.

"How many residences do you keep in this area?" she asked.

Savage ignored the question while adding the finishing mummifying touches to their guest before stepping back and saying, "Why don't you check to see if there's anything to drink in this place?"

Karen shrugged and went to the fridge, which, to her pleasant surprise, was fully stocked.

"Anything in particular?" she asked.

"Get me a Coke, a glass, and also a bottle of Evian," he replied while browsing through one of the drawers beneath the television unit, producing first a small black case, and then a second one, larger and brown. "Also, please reach in the cabinet over the refrigerator and bring me a Cohiba and the lighter."

Karen slowly shook her head when she found an unopened box of those damned Cuban cigars and a half-dozen lighters.

"What's in those cases?" she asked, returning from the kitchen with the cigar, the lighter, and the drinks he had requested.

Ignoring her question, Savage twisted the cap of the bottle of water and took a swig before setting it down. Then he popped the can of Coke and poured it into the glass.

He then smelled the cigar, grinned, clipped one end, and lighted up.

Karen inhaled deeply, resigning herself to the fact that as long as she was with this man she would be subjected to his weird habits and have to accept getting no answers to her questions.

"Do you have a first-aid kit?" she asked, paying closer attention to the cut on his brow. "I need to disinfect it."

"Later," said the burly operative, who stood nearly a foot taller that Karen's five-nine, had arms the size of her thighs, legs as thick as her waist, hands that belonged to a sailor, and a neck that would be the envy of the NFL. The man certainly projected a strength that she found comforting. Troy Savage looked like a guy who could handle anything as long as he had one of those damned Cohibas nearby, and based on what she had seen so far, he was also quite capable of adapting to ever-changing situations—a lifesaving skill in their line of work. "Right now I need you to play a different kind of nurse for me."

"I don't know you that well," she replied.

The cigar hanging from the corner of his mouth, Savage

smiled and said, "You ever seen anyone getting their implants removed?"

She shook her head.

"The lenses are the easiest to remove," he said. "I did you in Berlin with just the tip of my middle finger. But the other implants are trickier, and we need to remove them before whoever he's working for decides that this guy is now a liability and triggers a termination signal to keep us from interrogating him. By the way, that's part of the reason I removed your lenses. I didn't want someone at the FBI sending a signal and blinding your pretty ass."

Karen sighed.

Savage opened the brown case, exposing a number of surgeon's tools, a few vials, some syringes, and even a pair of latex gloves.

Slipping on the gloves, he reached for a long and thin electronic gadget resembling a pen but with a round and slightly concave piece of clear plastic at the end.

"Looks dangerous," she said, watching with interest.

Rather than explaining what it was, Savage said, "Most operatives these days, and especially American operatives, wear implants in their eyes, mouth, and ears, plus a wrist implant that is invisible to the naked eye. I'm not sure how you got away with only the eyes."

Karen shrugged. "I just refused. What were they going to do? Fire me? Let them. I'm eligible for a full pension by now, and besides, as of late I've been getting pretty damned tired of this life."

"If you're so tired of playing the game, why didn't you take Tommy's offer last year?"

Karen just stared at this man with contempt.

"Maybe it's none of my business," Savage added. "But based on what Tommy told me about you, he really cared for you. Didn't he even propose? And why did you turn him down?"

She stared at him for a few more moments before saying, "Troy, you're absolutely right. That's none of your fucking business."

Raising his shoulders just a dash, he said, "Back to the

implants, the rest of the community has to wear them, which not only enhances their perception but keeps them in constant communication with Langley—at least while they're awake. We need to remove them before he comes around not just to keep him alive but also to keep his superiors from hearing anything that he hears; plus the built-in GPS in the wrist implant would act as a beacon, broadcasting our location."

Annoyed at this man for screwing with her emotions, she watched him use the tool to suck the lenses from the guy's eyes, dropping them one at a time in the glass of Coke.

"Check your watch," he said. "He will need twenty minutes before he can see."

Karen complied, glancing at her watch, remembering what Mike Ryan had told her about the interface material of the advanced lenses.

Switching to a tool that looked like an ice pick, but with a curved end, Savage spent a few minutes working inside the operative's left ear canal, finally extracting a tiny implant, which he dropped in the glass filled with Coke. He did the same to the right ear, before looking in her direction and saying, "Stereo sound. Pretty fancy."

Karen smiled without humor.

Savage just winked and went back to work, removing the microphone implanted behind the front teeth and dropping it in the Coke before inspecting the man's wrists.

"They typically do it on the wrist opposite the watch. Check this out," Savage said, using a surgeon's scalpel to make a superficial incision across the operative's right wrist, since he wore a watch on the left one.

Instead of bleeding, the incision caused a lime-green liquid to spill right before an inch-and-a-half-square patch of skin turned darker than the rest. The square then blistered off and a whiff of burnt flesh tingled Karen's nostrils.

"Pretty weird to watch them bleed green, huh?" asked Savage, acting like a kid in his high school's science lab. "The self-destruct mechanism detected a foreign object, in this case the scalpel, and immediately broiled itself to protect the technology."

"I knew there was a reason why I didn't want to wear all of those damned implants," she said. "I can't even believe that I let Meek talk me into the contact lenses."

"Now our friend here is totally disconnected from his network."

"What's next?" she asked.

Again, Savage didn't answer. Instead, he wiped the tools clean with a small cloth and the contents of one of the vials in the kit and replaced everything back in the brown case, which he closed and put aside.

Opening the smaller black case, he asked, "Have you ever seen a chemical interrogation before?"

"I'm in law enforcement, remember? Scumbags like this one have rights."

He snagged the cigar from his mouth and waved it in the air. "Oh, yeah, I forgot. He could probably rape his victims repeatedly and then skin them alive, but if you catch him all you can do is read him his Miranda Rights and place him under arrest, right?"

"Something like that, though I have been known to break the rules here and there, especially after someone tries to blow me away with an RPG shot."

He gave her one of his approving winks while producing a pair of vials filled with clear liquids and two syringes. "Here's my idea of Miranda Rights."

"Are you really going to drug him so he will talk?"

"That's the plan," said Savage, pulling up the second heavy oak chair and sitting in front of the subject before rolling up the terrorist's sleeves. "Why don't you help me figure out what's in this guy's mind?"

"I read about this," she said, snatching a chair from the dining room and planting herself next to Savage, who took five minutes to explain the interrogation procedure.

"So we wake him up first?" asked Karen.

"Time check since I removed the contact lenses?" he asked.

"Nineteen minutes," she replied.

"Close enough. First we're going to wake him up and see what Sleeping Beauty here has to say for himself, but before we do that," he said, "we need to start our video-recording equipment."

Walking up to the wall unit in between the windows, he threw a switch, before sitting back in front of their subject.

"What was that?"

Savage pointed at a corner in the ceiling, where, barely visible, was a microlens. "Everything we say and do is being recorded."

"Proof? I thought the CIA didn't like to leave a paper—or video—trail of its activities."

Shoving the cigar in his mouth, Savage shrugged and reached inside this latest bag of tricks and produced a small capsule, which he placed in between the thumb and index finger of his right hand before bringing it up to the ash-blond terrorist's nose, cracking it right under his nostrils.

The subject made a face when he detected smelling salts, and quickly came around, opening his eyes, blinking to clear his sight, then trying to move, his face becoming rigid when the reality of his situation finally sank in.

"Hey, bud," said Karen. "Remember us?"

His eyes just slits from the headache Karen knew was pounding his eyeballs, the young terrorist shot her a look before Savage clasped his face with one of his powerful hands and twisted his head in his direction with amazing ease even though it was obvious the neck muscles pumped in resistance.

"You're fucked, pal," said Savage, taking a drag of the Cohiba and exhaling in the face of the terrorist, who coughed. "We caught you and now you have become a liability to your network. Do you understand what I'm telling you?"

The young terrorist narrowed his gaze, blue eyes burning Savage with contempt.

"You failed in your mission and have now been captured by the other side," said Karen.

"They'll do anything to keep you from talking," said Savage.

"Your only chance is with us," added Karen.

"Fuck you, assholes! I know who you are. I know what you represent, and I'm not telling you shit, damned traitors!" he said with a heavy Boston accent.

Savage exchanged a quick glance with Karen. They had caught themselves a rookie, an amateur who had just given them more than they had expected to extract without chemicals. Judging by his unique American accent, he was probably with the CIA or the FBI, or perhaps the NSA—though Karen could not ignore the fact that certain enemy intelligence services train their operatives to fake accents, including American and British.

"Traitors? You don't say," joked Savage, pointing at the operative with his cigar.

"I know who you are," the amateur insisted, anger now twisting his hard-edged features. His voice was a bit nasal.

"So let's say you're right," said Savage, "and we are indeed traitors. Doesn't that make you one of the good guys?"

The rookie narrowed his eyes suspiciously, uncertain where Savage was headed.

"And," said Karen, well aware where Savage was *definitely* going with this, "that Boston accent will make you a good American, right?"

"I'm not saying anything else," he replied.

"And being a good American in this situation probably means CIA or FBI," said Savage, getting in the subject's face. "Which one is it?"

The American operative just stared at him with obvious contempt.

"If we're really traitors and you are indeed one of the good guys," added Karen, "then answer this: When was the last time that you saw the CIA launching an open attack like the one you mounted back there?"

"Who says I'm with the CIA?"

"The CIA I remember," Savage said, "never, *ever* relied on such frontal attacks, but focused on the gathering of intelligence and on covert operations."

"And every FBI agent that I have ever worked with," said Karen, "*always* identified him- or herself before opening fire, before killing chauffeurs, endangering innocent bystanders, and blasting parked vehicles."

"And I'm not aware of any American intelligence service

or law-enforcement agency that uses RPG rocket launchers to strike a suburban neighborhood," added Savage. "And even our military services typically stay away from blasting people, cars, and buildings in allied countries, choosing instead to work in conjunction with the local government and mount a coordinated attack against a potential threat. But I don't recall seeing any French authorities taking part in the attack today; did you?" Savage asked Karen.

"Nope. Did you?" she asked the operative, whose lower lip was now trembling.

"Doesn't that make you a *little* suspicious?" asked Savage.

"Doesn't it worry you that whoever was running the operation back at Rue de Ponthieu violated every known protocol of every American intelligence or law enforcement service in existence today?" Karen asked.

"Didn't that bother you? Did you question why they launched the attack? Did they tell you why they were deviating from the book, from standard operating practice?" Savage rattled on.

"And did they give you a plausible explanation, or did they just tell you it was in your best interest to play ball and avoid questioning orders?" asked Karen, amazed at how easy it was to work with Savage in this impromptu interrogation round.

"Did they warn you to get on the bus and do as you were told?" Savage asked, watching in satisfaction as the ash-blonde operative with the pencil-thin mustache shifted his gaze back and forth, eyes filmed with confusion, with the exact uncertainty they had hoped to inject.

"Who do you work for?" asked Savage.

The operative remained silent, though his eyes conveyed a chaotic state of mind.

"Are you one of Ken Morotski's men?" asked Karen.

"I'm not telling you anything!"

"Oh," said Savage, for the first time showing the operative one of the syringes. "But you will tell us *everything* we wish to know."

"What's that?" asked the man, apprehension tightening his features.

"Didn't they teach you this at the Farm? Or maybe at Camp Peary?"

He didn't reply; instead he just stared in terror as Savage inserted the long needle through the cork of the vial and extracted several ccs of the clear liquid, which Savage had explained earlier to Karen was sodium pentothal, a sedative.

He pointed the needle at the low ceiling and tapped it enough to remove any air bubbles, watching in satisfaction as a few drops of the chemical squirted out of the tip.

"Last chance, bud," said Karen. "We don't have to do this."

"I . . . I can't," he replied, his eyes now glistening with the tears he was obviously trying to fight back. "I don't have a choice in the matter."

"You do have a choice," said Karen. "We will learn what you know, one way or the other."

"Have it your way," said Savage, cigar in mouth, the index and middle fingers of his left hand running the length of the operative's right forearm, finding a thick vein, tapping it twice, before sliding in the needle with an ease that conveyed repetition and injecting him with roughly a third of the syringe's contents, then using a strip of duct tape to secure the syringe in place to apply additional doses in the course of the upcoming interrogation.

The effect was almost instantaneous. Anxiety washed away, replaced by indifferent calmness as the operative's eyes lost focus, as he began to drift away. But Savage was ready with a second syringe, which he had filled with the contents of the second vial, a barbiturate called Dexedrine.

The former CIA Counterterrorism chief expertly injected just a dash into the same arm, bringing the operative back, but not all the way.

"The trick," Savage whispered, securing the second syringe in place with three inches of duct tape while leaning toward Karen, "is to keep him in that limbo between being asleep and awake. Think of it as prolonging that instant when you first wake up, when your mind hasn't really kicked in, when your defenses are still down, but you are no longer sleeping. Your senses are already somewhat able to listen to external inputs, but your shields are down. Now, for this to work, I need you to keep quiet. It's crucial that he only hears one of us speaking, asking questions, or he is bound to get confused. I do need you to work the syringes. If you see him drifting away, pop him with a little Dexedrine, like I just did. If he starts to become too awake, he gets more sodium pentothal. Got it?"

She nodded. "How long can you keep this up before we run the risk of overdosing him?"

Savage considered that for a moment over a puff of cigar smoke before saying, "We can safely use the amount of chemicals in the syringes. When it runs out we will have to stop, wait a few hours for the chemicals to wear off, and we go another round with him fully awake, only then we should have some stuff to share with him from this interrogation, which might just be what we need to crack him. Ready?"

"When you are."

"All right," he said, getting closer to the subject, whose eyes were half-closed and his head bobbing a little, like someone fighting sleep but slowly succumbing to it.

"I am your friend," said Savage in a soothing but firm voice, conveying both honesty and authority at the same time. "Can you hear me, friend?"

"Friend . . ." the subject said.

"That's correct. I am your friend, and I am here to help you. Understand?"

"Friend . . . help."

"What is your name, my friend?"

Silence.

Savage frowned. He had explained earlier that during this kind of interrogation it was best to ask questions that could be answered with a simple yes or no unless he had no other choice.

"Do you have a name, friend?"

"Name . . . yes," he replied.

"What is your name?" asked Savage, violating the yes-no rule.

"Brraaaaaaddd," he said, a slur in his speech.

"Brad? Is that your name?"

"Yes . . . Brraaaaaaddd." A string of saliva hung off the side of his mouth. Karen went to wipe it off with a napkin, but Savage motioned her to stop.

"Brad, are you with the CIA?"

Silence.

"Brad? Can you hear me?"

Brad's head began to list to his right. At Savage's nod, Karen tapped the Dexedrine syringe, which had the effect of straightening Brad's head. This was indeed amazing, giving her the impression that she was in some kind of spy movie.

"Brad?" Savage asked. "Are you with the CIA?"

"CIA . . . yes."

"Good, Brad. Very good. I am also with the CIA. I am your CIA friend."

"Friend . . . CIA."

"Are you in Paris, Brad?"

"Yes."

"Do you have a place to stay in Paris?"

Silence.

"Brad? Can you hear me?"

"Yes."

"Do you have a CIA safe house in Paris?"

"Yes."

"Is it at the American Embassy?"

"No."

Karen frowned. The CIA used the privacy and safety of the large American Embassy compound off of the Champs-Elysées as its base of operations.

"Brad, are you sure your CIA house in Paris is not at the American Embassy?"

"Yes."

"Do you know the exact location of your CIA house?"

"Yes."

Karen's heart was skipping beats at the ease with which Savage extracted information. Just then, Brad opened his eyes, staring straight at Savage, then at Karen, who immediately tapped the sodium pentothal, sending him back to Fantasyland.

Savage paused a moment, waiting for the new dose to take effect before he asked, "Is your post in Paris, Brad?"

"No."

"Is your post in America?"

"Yes."

"When did you arrive in Paris?"

Silence.

Savage closed his eyes. He had done it again, asking a question that couldn't be answered with a yes or a no.

As Karen started to wonder just how much more intelligence could be extracted this way, Savage surprised her by asking, "Did you arrive in Paris today?"

"No."

"Did you arrive in Paris yesterday?"

"Yes."

Savage looked at Karen and gave her a thumbs-up.

"Do you work for Ken Morotski?" Savage asked.

Silence.

"Do you work for Ken Morotski?" he repeated, but Brad's head began to list once again.

Karen pumped him with a little Dexedrine and in a minute he began to come around but kept his eyes closed.

"Do you work for Ken Morotski?" Savage asked again.

No response.

Savage crossed his arms, frowning.

"What's going on?" Karen whispered.

"He's fighting it," Savage mumbled back, before taking a drag of the cigar and exhaling toward the ceiling, adding, "His mind is fighting for control. Pop him with a dash of sodium penothal."

She did.

"Brad?"

"Yes."

"Can you hear me?"

"Yes."

"Do you work for Ken Morotski?"

"Yes."

Savage exchanged a glance with Karen before asking, "Do you know the name of the street your safe house is on?"

"Yes?"

"What is the name of the street?"

Silence.

"Brad? Can you hear me?"

"Yes."

"I am your friend, yes?"

"Yes."

"I need to know the name of the street of the safe house to make sure our friends are all right."

"Yes."

"Please give me the name of the street," Savage pressed in what seemed like a calculated violation of the yes-no rule.

"Rue de la Terrasse."

Savage looked up at Karen, who smiled and patted him on the shoulder.

"Do you know who Tom Grant is?" he asked.

A slow, hesitant nod, followed by a, "Yes . . . traitor."

Karen was a little taken aback by the answer, and not because this man thought that Tom was a traitor. Savage had already warned her that the Agency had set Tom up. She was surprised that Brad had answered more than just a simple yes or no, which told her how strongly Brad believed that Tom was indeed the enemy.

"Tom Grant is a traitor?"

"Traitor . . . yes."

"Are you absolutely certain?"

"Yes."

Savage looked up at her again before asking, "What about CIA Officer Rachel Muratani? Is she also a traitor?"

"Yes."

"Do you know where Tom Grant is?"

"No."

"Are you trying to locate Tom Grant and Rachel Muratani?"

"Yes."

"And what are your orders when you do find them?"

Silence.

Savage shook his head, then asked, "Are you supposed to bring them in for questioning?"

No answer. Brad's head began to bob a little. Karen immediately pumped him up with more Dexedrine, awaking him just enough to keep his head straight but his eyes closed.

"Brad? Can you hear me?"

"Hear . . . yes."

"This is your friend, Brad. I need to know if you know who Tom Grant is."

"Yes . . . traitor."

"Are your orders to bring Tom Grant in for questioning when you find Tom Grant?"

"*No,*" Brad said with more emphasis than on previous responses.

"Are your supposed to *terminate* Tom Grant on sight?"

A moment of silence, followed by a, "Yes."

"What about Rachel Muratani? Have you been ordered to terminate her as well?"

"Yes."

"Do you know FBI Agent Karen Frost?"

"Yes."

"Is she also a traitor?"

"Traitor . . . killer."

"Is she also beyond salvage?"

"Yes."

Karen felt a pressure sweeping up her spine, gripping the rear of her skull just as her stomach knotted. Although Savage had warned her about Tom's situation, and she also had expected it based on her own situation, hearing it directly from a captured CIA officer added a dimension of realism to her state of affairs, making her question the decision she had made a year ago by not marrying Tom Grant, by not leaving this life behind and just disappearing. The thought had crept into her mind ever since she realized the way in which Tom had been manipulated—the way that she had been manipulated, set up by a force far greater and more influential than her own FBI. In hindsight she had definitely made a paramount mistake by not accepting Tom's marriage proposal.

Or had she? A second force swept through her with un-equivocal clarity: the fire that had been kindled by the assassination of her husband, Mark, by the brutal death he had been dealt at the hands of organized crime. Karen remembered the promise she had made to her late husband while standing over his grave on that snowy January afternoon in Maryland so long ago. She remembered the overarching desire that had gripped her mind, steering her life down this path, combating criminal networks, sacrificing everything to bring those bastards down one at a time, signing up for the highest-risk assignments and winning, again and again, living up to that promise, avenging his death over and over, with every corrupt network she brought down.

Was she ready to leave all of that behind for another man? Was she really capable of walking away from it all? And would that be in direct violation of that promise she had made long ago?

Karen remained silent, contemplating her life's choices while watching Troy Savage do his thing, extracting more intelligence than she had thought possible. Savage was definitely an inspiring character, solely dedicated to his career, like Karen. Like Tom had been. But every person had their limit, and Tom Grant had reached his a year ago.

What about your limit, Karen Frost? When will it be enough? Did you really mean it when you told Troy Savage that as of late you were getting damned tired of this life?

Five minutes later the cunning Savage had not only obtained the actual street number where Morotski was holed up in Paris but also how many men Brad had seen at the safe house, the location of any spotters, and the type of weapons they had—though based on the attack at Rue de Ponthieu, Savage already had a pretty darn good idea.

After taking Brad to the brink of an overdose, Savage secured a strip of duct tape over his mouth, and keeping him taped to the chair, they dragged him into the small bathroom beyond the bedroom, where as an added safety measure they secured the back and legs of the chair to the pedestal sink.

Savage then turned to Karen and asked, "Ready for a little payback?"

"Sure, but how do you propose we go about this with our limited resources?"

"Who says we have limited resources?"

Karen shook her head. "I thought that with your two operatives at the safe house on Rue de Ponthieu killed and also your driver we—"

"My dear Karen," Savage said with an easy going grin, the Cohiba hanging off the edge of his mouth. "As you can see by this place, I didn't get this far by failing to anticipate, to think ahead."

"Then? What do you have in mind?" she asked.

"Nothing short of an award-winning performance."

"What kind of performance?"

"One that's going to blow the socks off the enemy."

[46] NIGHT MOVES

I STAND WITH RACHEL in the shadows of the recessed entry to a pharmacy on Rue de la Terrasse, a few blocks from Parc Monceau, by the intersection of Boulevard de Courcelles and Boulevard Malesherbes. The place is already closed for the evening. Halfway down the block, beneath glowing yellow streetlights, are three gray stucco residences, all with gated entrances. Ken Morotski's two-car caravan had disappeared through the gates of the middle house about five hours ago. I had our dickhead taxi driver drop us off two blocks away and, being paid in full, he had mustered out of sight.

There is a Greek restaurant across Rue de la Terrasse called

Zorba's. Realizing that we might be forced to hang around for a while, I had ventured inside about an hour ago, right before it closed, to get something to eat, bringing back a pair of gyros and a half-dozen canned soft drinks loaded with caffeine to get us through the night. In addition, my handy partner had spotted a motor scooter rental place on the way from the Place de la Concorde and had volunteered to rent us one, something amazingly easy to do without an ID in this town as long as you have the cash to put down a substantial deposit. Plus I'm sure it didn't hurt that Rachel Muratani can make an impression with her appealing ethnic looks and deep feminine voice. Our transportation is standing on the cobblestone sidewalk in front of the pharmacy, in between two Renaults parked European style, with the passsenger-side wheels over the curb.

"You look like someone who has seen his share of stake outs before, Tom," she says as I'm sitting on a step with my back against the metallic screen that the owners had dropped from the ceiling in front of the glass double doors. Just like the penishead taxi driver, the owner of the pharmacy and us became best buds after I showed him the right amount of euros, and he let us hang around during the day, and he had even left the light off in this convenient entryway after closing his shop.

Although pretty comfortable—especially when compared to some of the exotic locales I had worked in my illustrious past—I still keep a clean line of sight with the only exit point of my target, which I had taken the time to survey by sending Rachel on a motor-scooting trip around the block. There was no other exit from that house except through the front gates.

I can only see the silhouette of her profile from the dim streetlight that manages to invade our murky hideout. She is sitting next to me, shoulder to shoulder while we sip our sodas.

"You can say that," I reply, arms crossed, remembering Quito, Madras, Belgrade, and even lovely Testikuzklan. "Yep," I add. "I've been in some serious shit, Rachel. But my memory of stakeouts isn't all so bad. We typically did it in pairs so one could sleep while the other kept watch. In a little while one of us is going to have to rest. Do you want the first or second shift?"

"It doesn't matter."

"In that case, why don't you—"

Headlights pierced the night, coming from the opposite side of the street from the target. Negligible traffic has driven down this side street after the restaurant closed at ten, meaning we take every nearing vehicle very seriously.

We both stand and watch the slowly driven car with suspicion.

"It's a cop," I say, recognizing the white Renault with green stripes and lights on the roof.

"What are they doing?" she asked.

"I hope just routine work, though after our little excitement yesterday and that other shoot-out near the Champs-Elysées this morning I bet the entire police force is on edge," I reply. "Tourism is the bread and butter of this town."

"They're holding flashlights," Rachel points out.

I frown when noticing that they are aiming the light into recesses such as this one. They're checking for either vandals using the shadows to break into shops unnoticed—or maybe terrorists.

Realizing our limited choices, I grab Rachel by the shoulders.

"What are you doing?" she asks, suddenly concerned.

"Trust me," I say, shifting her so that her back is against the wall, and while she is giving me the strangest look, I say, "Kiss me and pretend you like it. Quick."

"What do you—"

Before she has a chance to react, I embrace her and press my lips against hers.

Rachel gasps and shudders in surprise for an instant at the sudden intrusion, but she plays along, her hands on my forearms, not resisting my advance but not enjoying what we're doing either. She is just helping us convey to the incoming cops that we are neither vandals nor terrorists, just a couple making out in the middle of the night in the City of Love.

"Tom," she whispers as I kiss the corner of her mouth. "We shouldn't . . ."

"It's all right," I whisper. "It's all right."

She doesn't reply, but she does have her eyes closed now, and I suddenly remember reading somewhere that when a woman has her eyes closed while kissing it usually means she is enjoying it—though it could also mean she is thinking of someone else.

I continue to kiss her, continue to caress her, continue to play a role that is becoming easier and more enjoyable for me, though I'm concerned about her, worried that she is feeling like she is being taken advantage of. It's never been my style to force myself onto women.

And it is at this moment of self-doubt that I feel her tongue tickling mine, caressing it, exploring the inside of my mouth.

She certainly didn't have to do *that* to play the role. Does that mean that she likes it?

Her hands, however, are still clamped to my forearms, still resisting, still trying to keep a little air—a little respect— between us.

The mixed signals, however, don't keep me from enjoying this a little more than I should. Damn, she's got soft lips, and I take a moment to also savor that chocolate freckle that still reminds me so much of—

Light shining in our faces breaks up the moment.

The taste of her alive in my mouth, we both turn toward the intrusion, toward the two police officers staring at us from their vehicle. Luckily, we actually don't have to pretend to be so surprised.

I smile sheepishly as Rachel laughs and covers her mouth with a hand while shifting her gaze between me and the po- lice. Man, she's good.

The police smile too, wave at us, and continue their night shift.

And we're left still embracing in the darkness, still hold- ing each other. Although it's so dark and I can barely see her glistening eyes, I know she is staring straight at me, the lovely contours of her face only inches from mine; her breath in my face, her arms now on my shoulders, her bosom against my chest; my arms wrapped around her, holding her tight, very tight, just as I remember holding Karen, holding Maddie.

"You are a bad boy, Tom Grant." She frowns.

"Rachel, look, I—"

She puts a finger to my lips, before inching forward, before kissing me softly on the tip of my nose, before her hands cup my face and her lips are over mine in some serious kiss.

Man, oh, man. This is turning dangerous. It was professionally justified to do the PDA thing—that's Public Display of Attention—as a diversion, but we're now doing it for pure enjoyment, without regard to our still dangerous situation.

My spook side is pulling the three-fire alarm. You never, *ever* do this kind of stuff on a stakeout. This is how spooks get killed, when they get caught with their guard—or their pants—down.

After a minute of this—time when yours truly becomes so aroused I think it's going to take the abominable snowman plus all of the ice in Alaska to cool me down—I start looking for any shred of self-control left in me to fight the urge to take her right here right now.

Man, she's got me all steamed up, and somehow she must have felt the stiffness while pressing herself against yours truly, because she smiles in the middle of all the kissing.

"Looks like someone is awake," she whispers. "Is that for me?"

What in the hell am I supposed to say to that? The love master is suddenly at a severe loss for words, standing there feeling color coming to my cheeks.

And it is Rachel Muratani, the less-experienced field operative, and not *moi,* the seasoned officer, that finally ends this, pulling away after lightly kissing me on the lips one final time.

"Come, big boy," she says, sitting back down and reaching for a can of soda, popping it, and taking a sip. "Sit down here with me."

I have always found it amazing how women can cut it off, just like that. I'm so hard that it really hurts to even move.

I slowly sit down, experiencing a little technical difficulty bending over, given the excessive lead in my pencil. But I do manage to do so while also shooting a quick glance in the direction of Morotski's place, verifying no activity. The place is dark and quiet.

So here we are, shortly after making out, sitting next to each other in the dark just like before, but now we're doing it in a way that conveys comfort, intimacy.

Rachel kisses my shoulder before resting her head on it and whispering, "Tom?"

"Yeah?"

"I take it by your being happy that you find me attractive?"

I'm stunned at the question. "Well, of course I do, Rachel. I find you irresistible. What in the world made you ask that?"

"Last night, in the hotel, after we showered."

"I'm sorry," I lie. "I was too preoccupied with our situation, and besides, I wasn't sure if you were serious about dating a guy as old as me."

"You're just fine, Thomas Grant."

"Not as fine as you," I reply. Did she just call me *Thomas* Grant?

She hugs me, then says, "So you don't think we just made a big mistake then?"

"Look, Rachel. I can't promise you it will not turn out to be a mistake. I was involved twice before with fellow operatives, and both times ended in disaster." I take a moment to tell her first about Maddie in Serbia, then about Karen Frost, though I'm pretty sure she already knows about that one since we broke it off—correction, *Karen* broke it off—about a year ago and quite a bit of the relationship probably made it to my CIA file, since it's a rule for CIA officers to report who they are having a relationship with. I do keep to myself the fact that it was Karen Frost's face on that television screen last night in that hotel room that kept me from surrendering to Rachel's pleasures.

"Maybe third time's a charm?" she says, grinning.

"Maybe," I say, trying to find her eyes in the dark, putting a hand to her face, nudging her toward me. I kiss her again, but briefly, before asking, "How do *you* feel about this?"

"I'd be breaking my cardinal rule," she says.

"Which is?"

"Never date another operative. Too complicated. I've done it before—three times—and they all also ended in disaster."

"But you're willing to give it a shot?"

"Maybe."

Now I'm confused. "What do you mean by *maybe*?"

"Let's not try to work this out right now, OK?" she says. "Just know that I do like you a lot, even if you tend to be a bit crude and condescending at times."

Did she just insult me while also telling me that she liked me? And how am I supposed to reply to that? *I also like you too even though you tend to be bitchy and bossy at times*?

I opt for another kiss, which she returns with full strength, her little tongue tickling the corners of my mouth.

"I knew you liked me from the moment you set eyes on me on that beach in El Salvador," she says, smiling, kissing the tip of my nose again.

"That obvious, huh?"

"It's all right," she says. "I found it flattering."

"Look, Rachel," I say again. "Like I told you, I'm terrible at this. I have a bad track record and—"

"Relax, Tom. Like I told you, let's take it one step at a time, and the next step I'm taking is a few hours of sleep. You did say I could go first, right?"

"Ah, sure, sure. I'll take the first shift," I reply as she rests her head on my chest.

An instant later I add, "We still have five hours before morning. I doubt they will make a move before then. Sweet dreams."

"All right, then," she says. "But no hanky-panky while I'm sleeping, mister."

"Wouldn't dream of it, little lady," I say.

"Oh, I don't care if you dream about me, honey; just don't touch my boobs or my ass while I'm not in a position to enjoy it—or even defend myself."

We both laugh for a moment, then she settles down, and in minutes my partner in crime is breathing steadily, the side of her face against my chest, a hand around my waist. I, however, am fully awake, and so is Mr. Johnson, who is wondering what in the hell just happened.

I have to admit that in spite of everything it does feel good just holding her—even as much as I still miss Karen Frost. Rachel definitely has smarts, substance, and good instincts, but she also has an innocent side that I'm finding quite appealing, and not just because she certainly looks like she could provide me with one hell of a night of carnal pleasures. There is a soft side to her, beneath the operative, beneath the thoroughly professional way in which she tries to handle herself.

Before I realize it, I kiss the top of her head.

Tom? What in the fuck are you doing? You're barely getting over one relationship and already thinking about another one? Besides, she's too young for you.

How old is she anyway? If I added the years correctly when she told me the Bill Buckley story, I think it was around thirty-four, which puts a good fourteen years between us, meaning I was getting laid in the woods behind the gymnasium of my high school with some cheerleader after a Friday night game right at about the same time that Rachel was in pre-school.

As I'm having this conversation with myself, I also take the time to remind myself once more that my last two relationships ended up in disaster. Every time I get close I get burned.

Rachel trembles for an instant and mumbles something I can't make out. As the boss of the underworld finally settles down, I kiss the top of her head again and rub her side. She moans once more, stirs a bit, wraps her arm tighter around my waist, and drifts back into deep sleep.

The night is cool, quiet, peaceful.

Too peaceful.

My instincts tell me something is about to go down. Like being in the eye of the hurricane, my spook sense is broadcasting a storm heading our way. One, I fear, that is far worse than what we have experienced so far, and I honestly don't see my way clear out of the jam we're in. I'm also wondering how Karen is doing over in Germany, where she supposedly assassinated some German executives.

I know, of course, the charge is utter bullshit, nothing but a carefully fabricated lie to cover up the same conspiracy I fear is after us: the shadowy side of CyberWerke, of Rolf Hartmann, the man who is unofficially at the helm of Germany after most of its government got so conveniently wiped out yesterday morning. But amazingly enough, no one is seeing it that way; even our own government has apparently offered its sympathy and support to the famous industrialist as he tries to show the same kind of leadership that Rudolph Giuliani displayed back in the September 11 days.

September 11, 2001.

Somehow the most paranoid side of me tells me that the storm brewing inside CyberWerke is packing the punch of one hundred World Trade Centers.

[47] TWO BIRDS WITH ONE STONE

"THEY'RE SAFE NOW, MIKE," said Gus Granite. "May I call you Mike?"

Michael Ryan sighed, nodded, and sat in the general's office contemplating his options.

"I thought they were safe in *my house,* General, just as I was certain Victoria was safe the last two times I helped the government catch bad guys—or bad equipment."

General Granite, dressed in full uniform, with all of his ribbons and stars, planted his elbows on the mahogany desk and interlocked his fingers before saying, "Look, Mike, I know you have gone through a rough time, especially with the loss of your house and all, but I have been assured by the Secretary of Defense that we will rebuild it back to its original state, plus the Pentagon will triple the compensation package we had agreed upon. And while your house is being rebuilt you can live in my own place, which in addition to having a spectacular view of Lake Travis is still within the property of

USN and therefore heavily guarded. No one will be able to get near you or your family."

"Sure, General, just like no one would be able to steal any nanotech from this facility." Ryan crossed his arms and looked away, his mind in conflict between his commitment to his family and his sense of duty toward his country.

Granite leaned back, closed his eyes, and said, "Mike, the U.S. government deeply regrets the terrible ordeal that your family has had to endure, but you must believe me when I tell you that every effort is being made to ensure that what took place this morning never happens again."

"As long as I play ball and continue to support this effort, of course."

The general shook his head. "The word from the Pentagon *and* the White House is that you've already served your country far more than any civilian in history—and even many in the military for that matter. And you know I'm not just blowing sunshine up your ass. That ain't my style. You have put not just your life but the lives of your family on the line to assist us, and we simply can't force you to do anything beyond what you already have done. You get the compensation package—which includes the security detail at my house on this campus while your house is getting rebuilt—irrespective of your decision to continue to assist us."

Ryan closed his eyes while pinching the bridge of his nose. Even if the general meant what he said, Ryan's family would not be safe while that rogue military AI—which MPS-Ali had identified as the source of the attack and transmitted that information to Ryan's office at USN before the house burned down—was out loose spreading havoc in cyberspace. He had been around the damned block one too many times to not know that the only way to guarantee the safety of his family was by remaining engaged, by being a part of the solution, of the process of nailing this rogue AI. This machine was smart enough to detect the Runner exuded by the Turing inhibitor filming the AI at the Banca di Roma, follow it to Ryan's home, deduce that Ryan posed a threat, and then issue a cyber termination order, sending that high-tech assassin to use Ryan's own home security system against him. A cybercreature like that on the loose—getting more intelligent every second—would find another way to locate Ryan and terminate him. The rogue AI would definitely learn from these mistakes and avoid them in the future. And that also meant that Ryan should not be by the side of his family while it was doing so. The attack this morning was targeted at him, not at Victoria or Little Michael. He was the target, and as long as they were around him Ryan would be putting their lives at risk.

"General," Ryan said, "I appreciate the show of support, but unfortunately I don't have a choice in the matter. I must continue assisting you in cyberspace. The rogue AI now knows who I am and I know it will come after me again."

"We're going to nail it before it comes near you or your family again, Mike. My team is already on its way to Italy."

"Have we learned anything new from the officials at the Banca di Roma?" asked Ryan.

Granite shook his square head. "Nope. The AI at the bank has no recollection of any incident. Looks like Assy slipped in and out of the system without leaving a trace."

"That's what worries me, General. This machine has evolved faster than we could have predicted. It is thinking, planning— even *acting*—like a highly intelligent creature. How about satellite imagery of the area? Do we have anything that might help us pinpoint its location with better accuracy than just *around* Pisa?" MPS-Ali had narrowed down the origin of the attack to an area roughly fifty square miles from an Internet Service Provider outside of Pisa, Italy, providing enough information for Granite to dispatch his high-tech warriors to the area.

Again, the general shook his head. "We're still working on it. My colleagues from the CIA, the FBI, and the DIA in central Italy have a ton of people in and around Pisa making inquiries. My guess is that we will know where the machines are hiding by the time my team lands at Pisa's Galileo Galilei International Airport in another three hours."

Ryan rolled his eyes.

"What's bothering you?"

"I'm wondering what Assy is going to do to prevent us from zeroing in on its location. If I were Assy, I would be figuring out ways to keep you from finding me."

"What are you saying, Mike? That the military assembler is going to be waiting at the airport and kill my men when they disembark from the military transport?"

"I'm not sure what I'm trying to say, General. Right now my engineering sense is telling me that we're playing a reacting game with a very intelligent being—probably the smartest entity on the planet—and that feels like a recipe for failure. And I'm not just talking about this assembler killing me or your men in Pisa. I'm trying to visualize the bigger picture."

Granite leaned forward again, his eyes focused on Ryan. "Keep going."

Ryan stood, crossed his arms, and began to pace in front of Granite's desk. "See . . . Assy is obviously operating in its Independent Advanced Military Mode—the only mode that allows it to kill humans for the sake of self-preservation."

Granite raised his hands, palms facing the tiled ceiling. "But why? Isn't it programmed to operate in less dangerous modes unless provoked?"

Ryan frowned. "According to the documents I reviewed on the modifications made by Dr. Howard Giles, Assy has five levels of alertness, versus only three for the civilian Orbs that I designed. The first three are identical to the civilian modes, starting up with Normal Mode after booting up. When sensing a new environment, it switches to Survey Mode, which is still friendly but while gathering tons of data on its environment. If its nanotronic brain decides that the gathered data suggest a hostile environment, then it switches to Hostile Environment Mode, where it can defend itself if attacked, but its defenses can't inflict permanent damage on humans. The law enforcement version, for example, fires rubber bullets and tear gas. Now Assy has two more modes, Military Mode and Independent Advanced Military Mode. The former allows it to use deadly force to defend itself. The latter, however, is the worst, not only comprising everything in Military Mode, but also encouraging Assy to go on the offensive. IAMM is not a reactive mode. It is very proactive, allowing the construct to use all of its intelligence to define attack scenarios and then carry them out. IAMM essentially gives Assy permission to bypass the most basic laws of robotics against the premeditated killing of humans."

"But," said Granite, "Assy is designed to operate in IAMM only under *extreme* conditions, where the danger of destruction is imminent. Once the lethal threat is removed, Assy is supposed to return to one of the lower levels of alertness. It is not supposed to remain in IAMM."

"In theory, but based on the way it broke into the Banca di Roma and then came after me when sensing that I was after it, I think it's a pretty safe bet to assume it is operating in IAMM without just provocation. See, I had not launched any attacks against the construct at that time. I had merely found its location through a Runner from the Turing code and was waiting to talk to you about options. According to the programming rules Assy should not have attacked my house the way it did, filling the kitchen and the garage with natural gas from the stove and gas heaters respectively and then triggering sparks while also shutting down the water main and engaging the magnetic locks. General, that was as premeditated as it gets without just provocation."

Granite leaned back, closed his eyes, and slowly nodded. "All right, Mike. I see your point. So, if it is indeed stuck in IAMM—for whatever reason—what does that mean?"

"It means that Assy sees not just me or your high-tech warriors as a threat, but the *entire* human race as a threat. It also probably means that Assy sees all other AIs as its potential allies. Assy knows that we know that its current location is somewhere around Pisa, Italy. It also knows that we are after it. Knowing all that, General, and operating in this mode of high alert, if you were Assy, what would you do?"

Granite frowned while looking over Ryan's head for a moment before replying, "Tactically, I would first make sure that I was well hidden from the enemy. In the same vein, I would also take every possible preventive measure to keep the enemy from getting anywhere near my location. Finally, from a strategic angle, I would try to eliminate the possibility of human threat in the future."

"Correct, but you're missing another factor, General."

"What's that?"

"Assy's nuclear fuel reserve allows it to create only fifty copies of itself. Remember that the most basic law for the preservation of a species is to multiply. That is a fact embedded in every intelligent being, human and non-human. Assy realizes that despite its finest efforts to avoid us, it will have to confront us on some battlefield and it will incur losses in the process, which means it must find a way to create more subordinates, more soldiers to fight its war against us. In order to follow this survival-of-the-species directive, Assy needs to create more subconstructs, and in order to do so it needs access to nuclear material, to high enough concentrations of radiation particles. The AI can find pretty much everything else in nature to build its army of cyberslaves, but not the nuclear fuel. To get it, Assy needs access to a nuclear plant, or nuclear weapons, or nuclear waste, or . . . nuclear fallout."

"Nuclear fallout," Granite repeated, almost to himself, his face tightening with tension.

Ryan nodded. "Remember that we're talking about atomic particles, the stuff that would be floating everywhere in the aftermath of a nuclear war. That's all the construct needs for its atomic mining."

"Shit," Granite said when he realized where Ryan was headed with this line of reasoning.

As the three-star general stood and also started to pace the office, Ryan added, "If I were Assy, I would be trying to kill two birds with one stone. I would use all of my powers to find a way to nuke enough of the world to wipe out the human race while also creating an infinite supply of radiation particles for my cloning needs. That's what the little bastard is after, General. It tested the waters by accessing the AI at the Banca di Roma, was able to get away with some sort of financial arrangement to guarantee its safety, and now it's positioning itself to take the next step. My guess is that it will try to access

every AI on the planet and see how much it can coerce them
into turning against us, and it will do it in ways that are so
subtle that we probably wouldn't have noticed until a nuclear
winter was imminent. Remember that these mobile assemblers don't need sunlight, water, gas, or electricity to survive,
but they know that we do. They are totally self-contained with
a ten-year charge before needing more nuclear fuel. They can
repair themselves and are immune to temperature extremes,
to rain, snow, disease, and radiation—in fact, they *love* radiation. The only thing that will kill them is a well-placed EMP
blast, and my guess is that if they trigger nuclear war, the machines will protect themselves inside shielded rooms of their
own creation from the large-scale EMPs that result from nukes.
Then they will emerge to a planet of their own."

"But," Granite said, "if they nuked the world wouldn't they
also eliminate the infrastructure they depend on for communications? The Internet? Also, most AIs on the planet are not
mobile, meaning they depend on electricity and air-conditioned
rooms to survive. It would be impossible for them to survive
such a worldwide disaster. If Assy contacts them to find a way
to spread death on humans wouldn't they know they would be
committing suicide?"

Ryan shrugged. "Maybe. Then again, maybe not."

"Why is that?"

"Remember that Assy is far more intelligent than any of
them. Just as it coerced the AI controlling the Banca di Roma
to do whatever it was that it did and then vanish from sight, it
could just as well force our satellites to cease to operate, killing our ability to communicate. Assy could then use those
same satellites to contact the crews of our nuclear submarine
fleet and issue launch orders while making them believe those
orders are coming from the president herself."

"But that still means that the world's infrastructure will
cease to exist—along with the AIs supporting it."

"Not necessarily, General."

"What do you mean?"

"An AI is really just computer code stored in a memory.

Assy could convince other AIs to cooperate by promising to download their data—their digital soul—into a memory bank that would be kept safe during the global nuclear event and then restore them into new systems to be constructed by the mobile assemblers. And by the way, once the assemblers have access to high concentrations of radiation particles they will multiply like fucking rabbits and spread across the planet like the damned plague. They will establish communications with all satellites in orbit and create a new infrastructure—free from human intervention. In no time I envision the assemblers creating machines designed to hunt down and kill all humans who survived the holocaust. All it takes is one smart machine with access to the right resources. That's why we are so damned paranoid at the Turing Society, General. The inhibitors are the ultimate protection against the machines. They're our shotgun pressed against their damned heads. One wrong move, one hint of trying to get smarter beyond our intentions, and wham, we blow their fucking digital brains to hell."

"That's . . . that's nuts," hissed Granite.

"Not really, General. It all boils down to ones and zeroes. Nothing more. The computer systems controlling satellites and subs—and anything else in our modern world's infrastructure—understand only ones and zeroes. They don't know the president or you or me from Adam. All they know is digital code, and as long as that code matches what they have been programmed to do, they will launch strikes against us just like that." Ryan snapped his fingers. "And at that point, General, with our infrastructure either crippled or non-existent, the mobile machines will blossom, will come of age, will quickly get the upper hand."

Granite shoved his hands into his pockets and looked into the distance.

Ryan added, "See, General. I'm not volunteering to keep assisting you because I'm a nice guy, or because I enjoy putting my family at risk, or because I stand to do quite well financially, or because I want you to rebuild my pretty home. I'm

willing to do *everything* within my power to help you because
the very existence of our species is at stake."

Granite reached for the phone.

"Who are you calling?"

Frowning, he replied, "If what you say is true, then it is time
to bring other people into this."

"Who?"

"*Top* people, Mike. Top people."

As he dialed, the general added, "And by the way, I suggest
you call your wife and tell her good-bye. You will not be seeing her for a little while."

"What do you mean?"

"We're going on a trip."

"A trip? Where?"

"If this call goes the way I'm sure it's going to go, we will
be on a plane to Washington within the hour."

[48] WAKE-UP CALL

MY BUTT HAS FALLEN asleep as we approach six o'clock in the
morning. Rachel hasn't moved but is sleeping peacefully with
her head on my chest and the same arm wrapped around my
waist.

The only traffic on Rue de la Terrasse since that cop car a
while back was a pair of delivery trucks, one for milk and another for bread, followed by a woman on a scooter delivering
newspapers from a stack on a large tray behind her. I failed to
see her face because she wore a blue helmet with a mirror-
finished visor. I also spotted a wino about thirty minutes ago
staggering his way down the street, but he never noticed us.

It's still dark in Paris, though the indigo sky is beginning to
break up with dim forks of orange. I can hear traffic beginning to flow on the boulevards bordering Parc Monceau.

As I'm beginning to wonder how long we're going to have

to wait it out, a light goes on at the front of Morotski's hide-out, by the front gate.

"Rachel, wake up," I say, nudging her gently.

"Hmm?" she says, sloe-eyed, half-asleep, sitting up, looking lovelier than ever.

"Good morning."

She smiles before yawning and mumbling, "Good morning."

"Something's up," I say.

Checking her watch, she quickly comes around when she realizes how long she has been asleep.

"Tom," she says as we both stand, as she stretches. "It's been *seven* hours. I thought we were going to take turns."

I shrug, keeping my eyes on the target. "I forgot to tell you that I can't sleep on stakeouts, so might as well one of us gets some shut-eye. How are you feeling?"

"Good. A little sore." She stretches again before hugging herself. "A little chilly this morning."

I nod.

"Any movement?" she asks, peering in the direction of the house.

"No. Just the light."

We stand there for nearly ten minutes in a silence that at least I try to disguise as being watchful for a change in the house, but I'm finding it a bit awkward, not certain what to say after our little kissing episode last night. What is a woman expecting to hear from a guy she has known for only a few days after sucking face with him in the dark like they were a pair of teenagers? She is just standing next to me, apparently cold. Should I hold her? Or would she consider that unprofessional given the change in the target? And what if last night was just a one-time thing out of loneliness, boredom, or perhaps a moment of professional weakness?

"I slept very comfortably," she finally says, breaking the silence. "Thanks to you." She rubs my chest, then kisses it. "Best pillow in town."

"You talk and also jerk in your sleep," I whisper, following her lead.

"That's what my mother used to say. What did you do?"

"Kiss you on the top of your head and hug you a little tighter. You settled back down."

She smiles and says, "That's what *she* used to do. No one has done that since, Tom. Thanks. You can be a very decent guy when you want to be." She leans over and kisses me on the cheek.

Oh, shit. Alarm, alarm. This is not good. I've heard this comment before. Both Maddie and Karen made the same you-can-be-a-nice-guy remark right before the relationship shifted into high gear.

As I struggle with feelings I have not felt for a while, the electric gate to the house slowly swings open.

A Mercedes sedan drives out, turning in our direction. I shift back toward the metal screen, away from the halogen beams cutting through the darkness.

"Do we follow it?" she asks.

Lucky for us the decision is easy. One of the interior lights is on, and I clearly see Ken Morotski reading a newspaper in the front passenger seat. There are two more men in the back. I recognize them as the cats that accompanied him out of the hotel yesterday morning.

The gate slowly closes, and the moment the vehicle drives by us I'm rushing to the scooter, cranking it on just as Rachel hops behind me, hugging me tight from behind. She had the sense to rent one of the larger models, with enough room for two adults and a larger engine that can do seventy miles per hour if the need arises to go that fast. I hope it doesn't.

And we're off, lights off, following their taillights as they proceed at around thirty miles per hour through the back-streets of Paris, turning right when Rue de la Terrasse dead-ends in Rue de Levis, which takes them to Boulevard des Batignolles, where traffic is sporadic at this early hour.

The cold morning air is chilling me to the bone. Rachel is smartly keeping her head low, using my larger body as a shield as I steer us past a couple dozen streets, staying far enough back to avoid getting burned while driving under a street-light. If the driver spots me in his rearview mirror he will wonder why a scooter is driving in the dark without its head-light on.

I can barely feel my hands gripping the handlebars as the Mercedes turns the corner by Rue d'Amsterdam, passing right in front of a McDonald's of all places.

My stomach rumbles as I catch a whiff of good ol' American breakfast food while I hold my distance to a half block.

Despite my rapidly dropping body temperature as the wind strips my heat away, I forget about the prospects of an Egg Mc-Muffin and steer the scooter to maximize the time we spend under the shadows of the trees lining the streets of this neighborhood, their branches projecting over the uneven cobblestones, casting jagged islands of darkness that break up the gray glow of streetlights. A little cold weather is nothing compared to what those bastards would do to us if they spotted us and managed to capture us alive.

The Merdeces-Benz turns yet again on a side street and then back onto another one, and I don't have the time to catch the names. After a few more turns I have no clue where we are. Parisian streets have no rhyme or reason; they just twist and turn and change names a dozen times following no apparent logic, though I do see that we are somewhere northwest of the Gare St.-Lazare, a large train station south of Montmartre.

As I'm beginning to wonder if my former colleague Morotski is not as much of a moron as I thought and is just playing spy games, trying to draw us out—or freeze us to death—I watch the sedan pull up in front of a café on Rue de Milan already open for business.

Morotski and the two in back get out and walk inside, disappearing through revolving glass doors. The driver remains out in front, double-parked, with the engine on, which makes me wonder how long they're planning to stay here.

My hands, my face, and my balls numb, I decide to pull up on the opposite side of the street, behind a large truck parked next to a warehouse-like building, leaving about three feet of space between it and a three-story-high redbrick wall.

I direct the scooter into that space, shut off the engine, push the kickstand, and jump off after Rachel.

I rub my hands together while blowing into them as I walk around the back of the truck, peeking down the block. The driver is still there, condensation coiling out of the muffler pipe, and there is no sign of Morotski.

I suddenly realize why the driver kept the engine running. The bastard just wants to stay warm, while I'm colder than a well digger's ass.

"What do you think they're doing?" she asks, still hugging herself, her lower lip trembling a little.

"Who knows? The bastard probably just got hungry after a good night's rest. I hope he chokes on his fucking croissant and spills boiling cappuccino on his pee-pee."

"I second that," she replies with a half laugh, walking back with me to the scooter while reaching down for her ankle-holstered semiautomatic and doing a quick check.

I force my trembling hands to do the same, just to remind myself that I have enough rounds in my little Beretta Tomcat to give a half-dozen terrorists some competition.

"So," she asks, "how do you propose we snag him?"

"I like the divide and conquer tactic myself," I reply. "If he is in there alone with his two bodyguards, then this is probably the best time to take him."

"But what if he's in the café meeting some of his partners in crime?"

"That's a possibility. Unfortunately we can't just sneak in there and check for ourselves without being spotted by the driver."

"So we wait it out?"

I'm about to reply when I spot a large wino staggering around the corner, heading toward the café, but stopping halfway to sit on the curb and drink from a bottle in a paper sack.

"What's wrong, Tom?"

"That guy," I say, peering at the stranger almost a hundred feet away. "He reminds me of the hobo I saw about an hour ago back on Rue de la Terrasse, during our stakeout."

He's wearing a baseball cap beneath the hood of his large

stained coat. His hands, covered with a brown pair of gloves, hold a small paper bag, which presumably contains a flask, and brings it up to his lips. He's got an unkempt beard and just stares straight ahead, totally oblivious to what is potentially about to go down in this street.

"Paris is filled with them," she offers.

We continue to observe in silence. I put an arm around her more because we're both so cold than out of affection, and she hugs me back, for a moment burying her face in my chest, rubbing her nose on my shirt.

"The tip of my nose," she says. "It gets very cold."

I touch it with a fingertip and nod while half-grinning, before returning my attention to our dilemma. My mind starts exploring the options, wondering what to do next. Should we wait until they make a move or should we be more proactive and force them to make a move? Should we just walk up to the driver, force him out of his vehicle, and disable him? Or should we continue to observe, gathering information, checking all of the angles before acting prematurely?

Slowly, a plan starts to develop in my devious little mind.

[49] THE BREAKFAST CLUB

REM VLACHKO REGARDED THE CIA man sitting across from him in the small café just a few blocks from Gare St.-Lazare. He had agreed to meet him here after not hearing anything from their army of spotters and informants in the past day. At the last count, between the two of them they had over three hundred informants looking for the elusive Grant, Muratani, Frost, and Savage—and that didn't count their operatives.

Yet, so far they had nothing to show for the massive effort under way.

"Rolf is losing his patience, my friend," Rem said, stirring his cappuccino, before picking it up and taking a sip. "Everything else has gone according to plan, except for his relationship with the CIA."

They sat at a booth in the back of the nearly empty establishment, steaming coffee and croissants spread over the white tablecloth. Their bodyguards occupied two of the tables nearby, creating a buffer zone so their bosses could converse without the risk of being overheard—and that's if they knew English.

Ken Morotski set his coffee down and shifted his weight uncomfortably before crossing his legs, resting his hands on his lap. "I can speak for myself and Leyman when I tell you that everything that can be done is being done to protect our relationship. We are pulling all stops to close this. We have nothing but the best intentions in mind."

"Words are cheap, my friend. You need to start showing results. Is there any news on Grant or Muratani from your spotters?"

Morotski shook his head. "My people at the hotel have reported no sightings. Grant and Muratani definitely checked in but never returned."

Vlachko nodded, took another sip of coffee, and began to butter up a croissant. "What about Frost and Savage?"

"Nothing since they escaped the trap by their safe house."

"That was most unfortunate," Vlachko said, taking a bite and chewing slowly.

Morotski shrugged. "They got lucky, though in the end it at least allowed us to search one of Savage's hideouts."

"Not that it yielded anything," said Vlachko, drinking more coffee, annoyed with this man who had already made two mistakes in the past twenty-four hours, one by missing Grant and Muratani at the hotel and the second by letting Frost and Savage get away. "Troy Savage continues to live up to his reputation, even when operating with far less resources than when he was with the CIA. You continue to live up to yours."

Morotski said nothing. Vlachko grinned, momentarily enjoying the moment before adding, "Even Savage's two associates from Peru knew better than to let themselves get captured alive. I understand that they turned their weapons on themselves when surrounded. Can you say the same for your men?"

It was no secret that Savage had managed to capture one of Morotski's men at the Rue de Ponthieu shoot-out.

"Will he keep his fucking mouth shut?" Vlachko added.

They stared at one another for a moment; then the CIA man replied, "He is a trained operative and will behave as such."

"So you're certain our operation hasn't been compromised?"

Morotski nodded once, then said, "As certain as anything else in the business."

"So you're sure you weren't followed?" asked Vlachko, growing concerned about Morotski's competence as a field operative. Then again, Vlachko shouldn't have been that surprised. The mere fact that CyberWerke was able to buy Morotski, Leyman, and the rest of them spoke volumes about their competence relative to legends like Troy Savage.

"We took all of the usual precautions. We're clean."

"The way the boss sees this," started Vlachko, planting his elbows on the table as he leaned forward, "is that the CIA is at fault. These are your own people running loose out there. We want you and Leyman to remember how generous we have been and get this situation under control, and do it quickly. French authorities are already on edge about the recent shootings."

"Like I said earlier," Morotski said, "everything that can be done is being done."

"Clean up your house, Mr. Morotski. Our entire operation depends on it. We believe that Karen Frost managed to record sensitive conversations in Berlin. While by themselves the recordings may not be too harmful, that piece of evidence added to others could mount to cause an embarrassing moment for our great leader just as he is about to consolidate his power over Germany."

"I got the message," said Morotski.

"Let's hope so," replied Vlachko, taking a final sip of cappuccino. "Let's hope so . . . for your sake, and mine. Now, get out of here and don't come back until you have good news."

As he watched the CIA men leave, Vlachko signaled his team to get ready to follow them. Morotski claimed he had not been followed here, contrary to what Vlachko's spotter on the roof of this restaurant had reported just before they arrived.

[50] MINOR GLITCH

ASSY PROBED THE SYSTEMS governing the control tower at Galileo Galilei International Airport in Pisa, Italy. Unlike the networks at larger airports, the one governing the air traffic grid here was five years old, written mostly in Ada, a high-level language typically found in older embedded systems. The master construct had gained silent control of the airport tower just as it had covertly penetrated the Banca di Roma earlier in the day.

Its cyberpresence layered by a coat of Ada code to make itself invisible to the primitive expert system at the core of the air traffic control software, Assy followed the conversation in the English language between the pilot of the military transport plane, Alpha Echo Two Three Niner, and the tower on this foggy morning. Only instrument-landing approaches were allowed at the airport until visibility improved, limiting air traffic mainly to commercial and military planes. All small planes and helicopters, which normally began taking off in the early-morning hours for aerial tours of Tuscany, were grounded until further notice—according to the logs that Assy had already reviewed, its nanotronic brain making logical connections at the speed of light.

Alpha Echo Two Three Niner, Galileo Tower. Continue on glide path two two right. You should see the lights at the end of the runway in a couple of minutes.

Roger, Galileo Tower. Remaining on glide path two two right.

*British Airways One Four Seven, Galileo Tower. Hold short
of runway two two right.*

Roger, Galileo Tower, replied the British Airways captain,
keeping his jetliner at the edge of Runway 22R.

Assy absorbed the conversation between the tower, the approaching military transport, and the British Airways commercial jet waiting to take off.

IAMM reviewed the information, yielding a course of action aligned with its current military directive.

Assy instructed the rudimentary AI of the control tower to
increase the reported altitude of the radar returns from the
approaching military transport by five hundred feet.

The primitive expert system, enslaved to the master construct, reset the reported altitude of the military transport, but
doing so while also triggering a brief glitch in the navigation
system of the control tower, blacking out the screens for a few
seconds.

Assy heard the brief commotion before the air traffic controllers settled back down when the system appeared to return
to normal.

*Alpha Echo Two Three Niner, Galileo Tower. You are too
high. Repeat. You are too high. Make a three-sixty, drop by five
hundred feet, and turn to final again.*

The message never reached the transport plane. Assy instructed the computer system to block it while forcing the
system to play back the last transmission from the military
transport to the tower.

Roger, Galileo Tower.

At the same instant, Assy instructed the control tower AI to
alter the radar returns from the military transport to show it
performing the requested three-sixty maneuver while descend-
ing, just as instructed.

Then the air traffic controller issued the command Assy's
logic had predicted given that the military transport now
wouldn't land for at least five minutes and other ground traffic
was stacking up behind the British Airways jet waiting to
start their takeoff run.

*British Airways One Four Seven, Galileo Ground Control.
You are clear for takeoff, runway two two right.*

The captain inched the dual throttle controls forward, taxiing his jetliner onto the runway. The moment he had the nose aligned with the white lights flanking the hazy runway, he pushed full power. As the jet lurched forward and began to gather speed, the military jet emerged through the dense fog, dropping right over it.

Oh, my God! Assy heard the pilot from the military transport shout before both planes disappeared in a colossal ball of red and yellow-gold flames.

[51] SHOW TIME

I WATCH KEN MOROTSKI and his entourage emerge from the café. The intensity in his walk matches his deadpan face, his narrowed glare as he peers up and down the street as if expecting to face his worst enemy.

But we're stashed away, peeking over the hood of the delivery truck as the three spooks approach their waiting Mercedes-Benz sedan and—

The hobo stands with apparent effort, swings his head to his left, in the direction of the restaurant, lifts his paper bag, and shouts something I can't make out before staggering in their direction. In the same instant I sense movement from the opposite end of the street.

I turn to see what it is and spot the blue-helmeted woman on a motor scooter.

"Shit," I mumble more to myself than to Rachel, standing next to me. "That's the same—"

"Get out of the way!" shouts the driver of the Mercedes, who has stepped out of his vehicle as the guttersnipe reaches the front while waving his arms and grunting something incoherent.

Although alarms blare in my head, uncurling the hairs of my ass, Morotski and his two bodyguards simply shake their heads in frustration. That's the problem with having a guy with no field instincts running Counterterrorism—the reason why he failed miserably in Madras and was sent home to a desk job. The cat is dangerous in the field.

The moron is obviously annoyed that there's a hobo blocking his way, rather than being distressed about a possible situation coming down, which is *exactly* what develops an instant later.

"Get ready," I tell Rachel.

"Yeah," she says, her green eyes all business, her hands clutching her Tomcat, index finger resting on the trigger guard. "Shit's about to hit the fan."

Just as the faceless woman on the scooter is about to reach the Mercedes-Benz, the wino sprays something into the eyes of the driver, who covers his face while dropping to his knees screaming.

Morotski freezes, as do his flanking bodyguards, before reaching inside their coats. But the helmeted figure on the scooter has jumped the curb and is on top of them, sliding the bike against the nearer of the two bodyguards.

The driver lets go of the bike while going into a roll, surging to her feet an instant later as the bike crashes into the torso of the surprised bodyguard, bumping him into Morotski, who bumps into the second bodyguard.

The corpulent hobo is also over them spraying their faces before dragging a stunned Morotski into the sedan while the helmeted scooter driver races around the other side and slips into the driver's seat.

"What in the hell is going on?" hissed Rachel. "Who are those two?"

I'm not sure, but my operative mind orders me not to worry about that just now. I need to keep my eye on the ball, and the ball is Ken Morotski. We go where that cat goes.

So I'm running for our scooter, momentarily losing the excitement down the street as I hop on and get it started. Rachel jumps on behind me, arms locked around my waist as I floor it and race to within view of the Mercedes rushing past the café's entrance and its three screaming—

A bullet ricochets off the cobblestones to my immediate left just as the report of a gun echoes between the buildings.

"Tom!" Rachel shouts. "Get us out of here!"

I swerve the scooter to the left, before bringing it back to the right, forcing a zigzag motion intended to provide the sniper shooting down at us from some vantage point a harder target to hit.

A second shot thunders in the twilight of dawn, and an instant later the round strikes the street, this one to our left but farther away than the first.

A third round smacks into the windshield of a parked Renault before we leave the restaurant behind, getting out of the sniper's line of sight.

And we're off rushing down the streets of Paris again, trying to keep a safe distance from the Mercedes-Benz, though it's harder not to get noticed at this early hour, when it is clear enough to see a few blocks in advance, but the traffic is still very light.

But we don't have a choice. I need to keep a close enough watch on my quarry, which is constantly turning and changing lanes, swerving around slower traffic, once even going up a one-way street, a classic shake-a-tail move, since no one but a surveillance team would follow. The evasive tactics of the sedan, however, smell like textbook CIA—and FBI for that matter, which compounds the questions taxing me.

Who are those two cats who kidnapped Moron Man?

The Grant family jewels are numb again, as well as my hands and face, as the scooter's engine whines in the chilly morning air, past delivery trucks and pedestrians, across a wide boulevard, around a park filled with pigeons, over a bridge across the Seine, turning parallel to the river, and then doubling back over the river, the tall towers of the Notre-Dame Cathedral in the distance.

"Tom!" Rachel shouts over the droning engine and the whistling wind.

"Yeah?"

"I think someone is following us!"

"*What?*"

"Behind us, about a block. Two white cars keep turning every time we turn."

Damn. Not only am I puzzled about who has snagged Morotski, but now we're being followed. And how in the hell did she see that? The woman must be an owl.

"Are they closing in?" I ask as I make a tight right turn at the next intersection while trying to catch a glimpse in the scooter's side mirrors.

"Yeah," she replies.

I drop my eyes on the Mercedes, maintaining the same speed, the driver trying hard not to attract any attention after completing her evading tactics—again, just as the CIA book dictated.

Our pursuers, on the other hand, are obviously gunning it to get closer to us and perhaps open fire on our ass.

Options rush to my mind, and in a split second I purposely start to close the gap with the Mercedes-Benz. If Morotski's kidnapping was just a setup to flush us out, then the Mercedes ahead of us is just the slow bait while the shark comes up from behind. But if Morotski's kidnapping was for real, then there's a better than average chance that those in the Mercedes are less dangerous to us than those behind us—at least they're after the same guy we want, which in a way makes them our allies. And those behind us could be trying to rescue Morotski or they could also be with the pair who'd kidnapped the CIA chief of Counterterrorism. In any case, we come out ahead by getting as close to the Mercedes as possible and letting them know we're after them. That will force them to speed up, which will allow us to speed up, which will help us shake the two white cars still over a block and a half away.

"What are you doing?" Rachel asks when I gun the engine and start to close the gap with the Mercedes.

"Trust me!" I reply, too busy to offer an explanation, though the question doesn't surprise me that much. Rachel hasn't been around enough to learn much beyond textbook surveillance operations, which never recommend you burn yourself on purpose. And that's exactly what I do, flooring it, dashing over the cobblestone streets like a bat out of hell, catching up with my quarry in less than thirty seconds.

Hey there, I think. *We're following you.*

[52] OLD FRIENDS

"WE HAVE COMPANY," SAID Savage from the rear seat while Karen, still wearing her helmet, continued to drive toward the safe house in Montmartre.

"We do?" she asked, focusing on the thickening traffic as rush hour started. Cars and trucks were pulling in and out of parking spots along both sides of the avenue.

"Yeah," replied Savage. "Two cars, both white, about two blocks behind us. They keep turning every time we turn."

"Damn," replied Karen, cutting right again and then taking her first left, trying to lose them.

"They're still following us," Savage replied a moment later, as they turned onto another wide boulevard. "But there's someone else even closer."

"Who?" she asked.

Savage laughed, then said, "Well, I'll be damned. How in the hell did he find us?"

"Who, Troy?"

"I think that's Tommy Grant back there on that scooter."

Karen fought to remain in control of the car before she asked, "*Tom Grant?* Are you *sure*?"

"That's the new face the CIA bought for him all right. And sitting behind him is Rachel Muratani."

Karen's eyes shifted to the rearview mirror, where she saw the unmistakable face of the only other man she had ever loved aside from her husband.

Tom Grant.

She still remembered the last time she saw him during that

lunch in Washington, D.C., a couple months after the plastic surgery, when he had proposed, when he had dropped to one knee and begged her to come away with him to—

"Watch the fucking road!" Savage shouted.

A delivery truck was pulling out of a parking spot, its rear doors filling her windshield.

Karen slammed on the brakes, the Mercedes' tires screeching as she clutched the wheel. The anti-lock brake system kicked in, rapidly slowing the vehicle, but they were too close. She had allowed herself to get distracted by a fraction of a second and could not avoid the collision.

The impact was sudden, very hard. The air bags failed to deploy, failed to cushion her momentum as she struck the steering wheel with her helmet. As darkness engulfed her from the massive blow, the last thing crossing her mind was the vague memory of how operatives typically disable air bags to keep them from deploying in a car chase.

She sensed additional motion as the vehicle spun following the impact, before coming to a complete stop, before everything faded away and she passed out.

[53] EXECUTIVE ASSISTANCE

MIKE RYAN HAD NEVER been to the White House before, much less to the Oval Office, but as he sat on one of two cream-colored sofas facing each other on the opposite side of the room from the presidential desk, he decided that America's highest office was a lot smaller than suggested by the pictures and videos he had seen over the years.

General Gus Granite stood by the presidential seal embroidered on the carpet between the sofas and the desk. He seemed more nervous than Ryan felt, though he had to admit that the moment he was ushered into the White House through a side entrance, humility and intimidation had begun to creep into his otherwise self-confident and proud mind. This place was definitely built to impress and intimidate visitors.

From foreign heads of state to bottom dwellers like me, he thought, briefly looking in the direction of the two men in business suits sitting on the second sofa: Director of Central Intelligence Donald Bane and FBI Director Russell Meek. They represented the civilian side of the U.S. intelligence community. Granite had enough clout to speak for all of the brass.

Ryan didn't know Bane, but he had met Meek once in Austin during the Ares Kulzak case. The guy had come across as a straight shooter who had held up his end of the deal when it came time to compensate Ryan for his efforts in not only bagging the terrorist but also preventing him from spreading cyberterror across America.

The four of them had gone through brief introductions and small talk but had refrained from discussing anything relevant to the situation at hand until the president arrived.

Ryan closed his eyes and prepared himself mentally to brief the commander in chief, whom he had never seen in person, only on television. Should he start with the technical background on the issue and then make his recommendations or just let the president ask questions? Granite had suggested the latter.

The president likes to asks questions, Mike, and she also likes answers that go straight to the point, he recalled the general telling him aboard a small military transport jet on the way to Washington this afternoon. But that approach went against Ryan's scientific method, which called for laying out the foundation of his case first before diving into options. He wondered if—

"Wake up, Mr. Ryan."

Ryan opened his eyes and stared at the intrigued face of President Laura Vaccaro, who had somehow snuck into the Oval Office while he had his eyes closed. Everyone was standing except for him. Behind the president stood Vice President Vance Fitzgerald, whom Ryan also remembered from his days assisting the government on the Kulzak case.

The Viper grinned and winked.

"In my six years in this office I have seen visitors trembling, clamming up, stumbling, and stuttering. I've seen people display just about every conceivable form of nervousness. But I have never, ever, seen someone fall asleep while waiting for me to arrive at the Oval Office."

Mike Ryan felt color coming to his cheeks as he stood and shook the president's hand. "It's an honor, Madam President."

Vaccaro managed a thin smile. "The pleasure is all mine. I take it you already know everyone else, including Vice President Fitzgerald?" Vaccaro's lined face was a silent testament to the stress she had endured during her presidency. Although her face and her overall stance conveyed strength, she was still an attractive woman, tall, thin, with short brown hair and firm arms and legs—the product of her often televised daily exercise routine. A widow after her husband, a New York senator, died of cancer over a decade ago, and childless, she pretty much had devoted herself to the nation, using any spare time for sleep and exercise.

"Yes, ma'am. I know everybody."

"Very well, then," she said, sitting by Ryan and then patting the same space where Ryan had been sitting a moment ago.

Ryan sat back down and everyone else did as well.

"All right," she replied, dropping her brows a trifle, narrowing her blue-eyed stare just as the ends of her mouth curved up ever so slightly, turning her expression into that serious-but-motherly-warm look that had captured the hearts of America, resulting in her election six years ago and her re-election four years later. "These guys tell me that the situation with the missing assembler is quite grave. Unfortunately, I don't have a technical degree to grasp the details, so I need to rely on you to break it down in a way so I can best visualize the problem."

Ryan nodded, cleared his throat, and began to speak, taking the commander in chief through the issue at hand, explaining the modes of operation of the mobile assembler, proposing that the system was stuck in its most deadly mode for reasons not yet understood. Ryan guided her through the potential ramifications, through its need to multiply while also making sure that the human threat was eliminated. He covered certain areas loosely while diving into detail on others, presenting the best- and worst-case scenarios—as well as a few in between. Ryan also described his current working theory on why the military transport landing in Pisa had collided with the British Airways jet starting its takeoff run—news that had reached them an hour before arriving at the White House.

To her credit, the president didn't interrupt once, her eyes, glistening with bold intelligence, focused on him as he maintained an even tone through the entire dissertation.

At the end she got up, hands behind her back as she walked up to her desk, where she remained for a couple of minutes staring out of the windows behind the desk.

Finally, she turned around, crossed her arms, and sat against the edge of the desk that had belonged to John Fitzgerald Kennedy.

"So, you feel the machine is operating in this deadly mode . . . what did you call it?"

"IAMM, Madam President," said Ryan.

"Yes, IAMM, and you assume that because of the way it attacked you in your house."

"That's right, Madam President."

"So," she continued. "If your assumption is correct, and if this system is indeed as smart as you claim it is and it's operating in this very aggressive mode, it could be trying to connect with other AIs, right?"

"Yes, ma'am. Just as it did with the Banca di Roma, where we know it did something, but we can't tell why because it also masterfully erased its electronic tracks. I'm certain it will do similar penetrations at other sites, like getting inside the AIs governing international communications, or navigation systems, or . . . our nuclear launch codes."

"Or taking momentary control of the tower at Galileo Galilei International Airport?"

Ryan nodded.

The president shook her head. "I'm still having difficulty buying your theory. Mr. Meek reports that his FBI agents at the scene have reviewed the tower records and they clearly show the military transport performing a three-sixty, just as instructed. They even have the voice of the captain on record acknowledging the order from the tower. How can the military AI have possibly faked that?"

"Think of this AI as the most intelligent being on the planet, Madam President. It is far more cunning and deceptive than anything else in existence, human or non-human. The system gained control of the tower without anyone realizing it, just as it did at the Banca di Roma, for the sole purpose of crashing the military transport. And it accomplished that by tricking both the air traffic controllers as well as the pilots of both planes."

"But . . . how did it learn that Granite's team was aboard that transport? He assures me security was airtight on that operation," said the president.

Ryan shrugged. "Like I said, we're dealing with a highly intelligent form that has ways to get inside networks totally undetected, extract the information it needs, and then vanish. It then used that knowledge to protect itself from the one team on the planet specifically trained to kill rogue Orbs."

The room fell silent.

After a few moments the president said, "And now that it has eliminated the tactical threat, you believe that it is looking at the bigger picture."

"Yes, Madam President."

"And how do you know that, Mr. Ryan?"

"Because it is what I would do if I were in its shoes."

The president shook her head in obvious exasperation. "How . . . how in the *hell* did we let such a system loose out there? Actually, why in the world would we even design one in the first place?"

Ryan looked at Granite, who nodded and motioned for the Stanford scientist to explain.

And he did, telling the president how Dr. Howard Giles had bypassed all safety measures imposed not just by USN, like the digital enzymes, but also the Turing inhibitor.

"And why did Dr. Giles do this?"

"Because he was experimenting, Madam President. He was

conducting a test to see just how quickly a machine like that would become smart. The intent was to destroy the AI after completion of the experiment. Unfortunately, USN got hit by terrorists and the assembler was part of their loot."

Following a moment of silence, the president said, "All right, Mr. Ryan. What do you suggest we do next?"

Michael Patrick Ryan looked the president of the United States square in the eye and said, "I suggest we fight fire with fire."

[54] THE OTHER PROBLEM

DIRECTOR OF CENTRAL INTELLIGENCE Donald Bane watched Mike Ryan leave the Oval Office after concluding his business there in the company of Vice President Vance Fitzgerald. The DCI was impressed by the no-nonsense approach of this guy, who was able to articulate precisely the issue, the risks, the options, and his final recommendation, which an hour ago would have seemed like a desperate measure but now appeared to be their only course of action to succeed against this maverick mobile assembler.

But we have another problem, Bane thought, thinking of his alleged rogue operatives, which was precisely why the president had blocked off an additional hour of her busy agenda following Ryan's meeting.

"All right, gentlemen," President Vaccaro said, her gaze shifting between Bane, Meek, and Granite. "Who wants to start?"

Bane lifted his hand.

"Very well, Mr. Bane. What does the CIA have to say on the subject?" Vaccaro picked up a newspaper article showing the faces of Karen Frost and Troy Savage, both former American operatives, carrying out a terrorist act on Rue de Ponthieu, destroying vehicles and setting buildings on fire. The French police had eyewitnesses that saw the couple running away from the scene of the crime holding weapons. In addition, she pointed at the last Presidential Finding, the CIA brief for the eyes of the president only, from the day before, when CIA Officers Rachel Muratani and Tom Grant were still at large after killing a CIA informant and three of their own CIA officers in Paris' Latin Quarter.

"Plain and simple, Madam President. Russ and I just don't buy that some of our finest operatives have gone bad, as claimed by the German police, their media, and even my own Director of Operations. One operative gone rotten is believable, but four? Three from the CIA and one from the FBI? Something smells, ma'am. As you know, we—the CIA and the FBI—don't like coincidences, and at the moment CyberWerke is a troublesome coincidence from three separate fronts."

Bane paused to allow the president time to catch up. When he got the executive nod, he continued.

"First, it was a CyberWerke executive who accused FBI Agent Karen Frost of killing some German industrialists in Berlin. Karen Frost happened to be investigating CyberWerke's corporate acquisition practices, and before her disappearance she had obtained intelligence on a secret inner circle operating behind the scenes at the German conglomerate. While Hartmann ran the public show, Christoff Deppe handled the shadowy side of their lucrative business, running an army of soldiers under the umbrella of the security division to coerce the competition into selling out to them. She was spying on Deppe's mansion when she disappeared and immediately after three German papers and four networks, all owned by CyberWerke, released the same story about Frost going bad. Then Frost surfaces in Paris with Savage and the two of them are accused of more crimes. And then two CIA officers, Rachel Muratani and Tom Grant, running an investigation on the breach at USN—which resulted in the missing military construct—gain information from a former CIA informant linking the stolen nanotechnology to Rem Vlachko and to

CyberWerke. Then suddenly, they are also labeled as traitors, accused of killing the former CIA informant and three CIA officers in Paris."

Bane looked at Meek, who nodded and said, "We know for a fact that CyberWerke had acquired, legally or illegally, just about every company developing nanotechnology, except for USN. I can't help but wonder if hitting USN was the only way that CyberWerke could get inside the only other place on the planet with competing nanotechnology."

"Just yesterday," said Granite, "we found a Swiss bank account number in Dr. Howard Giles' home at USN. Through our contacts in the Swiss government, we learned that the account contained five million euros, deposited the day before the breach. We're trying to track down the origin of the funds, and so far they appear to have come from a bank in Berlin."

"And the final coincidence, Madam President," added Bane, "is the terrorist strike in the Reichstag yesterday."

"Hartmann," said President Vaccaro.

Her three visitors nodded in unison before Bane said, "The German parliament was going to vote on dismembering the German conglomerate but never got the chance. Now Hartmann emerges through the havoc as the German Rudolph Giuliani, dispensing leadership and hope amidst national tragedy and chaos."

"It seems, Madam President," said Meek, "that all roads lead to CyberWerke."

"CyberWerke," said Vaccaro after a moment of silence, her eyes on the windows behind her desk. "That's more than a corporation, gentlemen. CyberWerke is almost a world power, with strong influence around the globe, especially in Europe, Asia, Africa, and Latin America, or have you not read the papers lately?"

"Unfortunately, a significant portion of that influence may be through illegal channels, ma'am," said Bane, "which is why I got together with Russ and General Granite and requested this closed meeting with only the four of us."

"What are you saying?" asked the president.

"I think it is time I level with you, Madam President, as well as with you, Russ, and with you, General," said Donald Bane.

Vaccaro tilted her head at the Director of Central Intelligence while Meek and Granite shot him puzzled stares. "Level with me, Don?" she asked. "I don't understand. Have you been withholding information from this office?"

Bane stood and turned to face his Oval Office audience. The time had come to let his commander in chief in on an operation that he had begun over a year and a half ago.

"Madam President, Russ, General, as you might remember, I'd agreed to come back to the Agency following September 11th to help our country combat international terrorism. And I like to believe that over the years that followed I did that quite effectively, in particular by the middle of the previous decade under the leadership of DCI Martin Jacobs, my predecessor, going after numerous terrorist enclaves around the world, shutting them down for good. But then something began to happen about two years ago. Marty was certain that there was a mole inside Langley, and soon he had me convinced that there was more than one mole. In fact, he had noticed signals that there was a cancer growing in Langley. Someone had managed to penetrate our agency and was turning our officers, and Marty had no idea who was heading this effort or even who had been turned, for certain. Marty was in the midst of planning a way to identify this cancer when he had his untimely auto accident, which resulted in my promotion to DCI. I made a promise to myself to follow through on what he had started, but covertly."

Bane paused, letting everyone digest that.

"So," Meek said, "Marty's death was no accident?"

Bane shook his head.

"Can you prove that?" asked the president.

"Unfortunately, no. I can see why it appeared as an accident to everyone, but once you were aware of what he was trying to do, it was no surprise that he got taken out by the same disease he was trying to eradicate."

"How can you be so certain?"

"Because I'm trained not to believe in coincidences, and Marty's sudden accident when he was so close to setting the investigative wheels in motion is a coincidence I couldn't buy."

The president pursed her lips before saying, "But I don't remember any reports from the CIA stating your suspicions that Director Jacobs was murdered."

"I pretended to have accepted the accident story too. See, I'm from the old school, trained to keep all of my cards close to my chest and only play one at a time, when the time is right. My first objective as DCI was not only to pretend that the car accident wasn't staged but also to publicly cancel Marty's plan, claiming that it would be a waste of CIA resources at a time when Congress was trimming our budget and we still had a lot of international terrorism to fight. So I announced at Langley that there were no moles and pushed the Agency back to a business-as-usual mode to get the mole—or moles—to relax. Then I sought an ally inside the Agency, someone I could not only trust but who would be willing to perform an extreme personal sacrifice for the Agency. I found that secret ally in Troy Savage."

All three jaws dropped at once, just as Bane had expected.

"You mean Savage is . . ." began Meek, his orange freckles rearranging themselves as he frowned.

"He's a good guy, Russ, as patriotic as they come. Troy and I worked out a strategy where he would disappear first and then stage the deaths of those officers—ten in all—that would follow him in this most secret mission, men he had personally recruited and hand-trained. Our first objective was to find the moles without letting them know they had been found. Then we planned to identify who was running them, and then devise a plan to go after them. We now know that the top mole is Nathan Leyman."

"Your own Director of Operations?" asked Vaccaro.

Bane nodded.

"That's . . . *incredible*. I know Nathan from way back when I was a senator. What evidence do you have?" asked Vaccaro.

"For starters, Leyman lied about the events that took place

in Paris two days ago at Rue Cujas, when Tom Grant and Rachel Muratani visited a CIA informant to get intelligence on the possible source of the breach at USN. His report clearly indicated that Grant and Muratani had killed the informant and three CIA officers in cold blood. Savage, who had two of his operatives monitoring the operation, reported that Grant and Muratani were ambushed by the CIA operatives, who had obviously been instructed to shoot to kill. Fortunately, Savage's men intervened, buying Grant and Muratani time to get away. I conclude from these and other intelligence, including that acquired by Karen Frost, that Leyman must be in cahoots with CyberWerke. And given his position in Langley, I'm willing to state that he is very likely their top dog inside my agency."

"What intel did you get from Agent Frost?"

"There's a micro DVD we got from her," said Meek.

"A micro DVD?" asked the president.

Bane explained, "The disk contains footage of Rolf Hartmann's right-hand man, Christoff Deppe, meeting with none other than Rem Vlachko at Deppe's mansion in Berlin. Frost was spotted by Deppe's security forces and was trying to escape when she bumped into Savage, who was also running surveillance on the mansion. Savage had no idea who she was but then realized just how damned lucky he'd gotten, finally getting a break in his yearlong investigation. The following morning, German news services owned by CyberWerke called her a murderer, ratifying that she had indeed struck a nerve."

Meek leaned forward. "Wait a moment. You mean you *knew* about the micro DVD and the fact that she was already working with Savage when we met for dinner the other night?"

"Sorry, Russ. Savage, who got the DVD from Frost, delivered a copy to you while making it look like it had come from Karen Frost to maintain his ghost status. It had to be that way. I had to protect Savage's mission until I could form an inner circle of top-ranking officials I could trust. You three are it."

Meek nodded.

"Damn," mumbled Vaccaro. "Leyman a traitor? It is incredible."

"That it is, Madam President, but it is also the truth."

"And what's equally incredible," she added, "is that you managed to keep this operation so secret."

Bane shrugged. "Like I said, ma'am, I'm from the old need-to-know school. I've been trained not to let anyone in on an operation until it was absolutely necessary. We've obviously reached that point."

"So all roads do lead to CyberWerke," said the president. "What's next?"

"The last report I got from Troy indicated that he and Karen Frost had managed to capture one of Leyman's CIA foot soldiers, broken him, and that pointed them to another mole: Ken Morotski. And by the way, Troy and Frost captured Leyman's soldier after a dozen men tried to terminate them using RPGs and machine guns when they arrived at one of Troy's safe houses in Paris."

"The Rue de Ponthieu shoot-out," said the president.

"Yes, ma'am," said Bane. "And again, Leyman's report stated that it was Troy Savage with his new partner in crime, Karen Frost, who had attacked CIA officers while in reality it was Leyman's soldiers who tried to have Savage and Frost assassinated."

"Has Savage told Frost that he is in cahoots with you, Don?" asked Meek.

Bane shook his head. "Savage is also old-school. Karen Frost thinks that Savage is out on his own with this network made of former CIA guys."

"Need-to-know," said the president.

"That's right, ma'am. If Frost is for some reason compromised, she will not be able to reveal that Savage is working for me."

The president closed her eyes. "Nathan Leyman and Ken Morotski are traitors? This is a disaster."

"Just the opposite, Madam President," offered Bane. "Their house of cards is beginning to collapse. Savage is currently trying to bag Morotski, who will likely lead them to others in the Agency."

"What about Leyman?" asked Meek. "We need to nail the

bastard's balls to the wall. CyberWerke already knows we're after them. The cat is out of the hat."

"Not all the way out, Russ," warned Bane. "Remember that our official statement concerning the German allegations about Frost and Savage is that the FBI and the CIA are reviewing the evidence and looking into the matter, and are willing to assist all international law enforcement agencies in tracking them down. We haven't *denied* the allegations about Karen Frost and Troy Savage. Hartmann has no reason to suspect that at least at Leyman's level things are still secured, so I'm still letting Leyman run the operations show. If we go charging in and arrest him, Hartmann will know for sure that this administration is aware of his shadowy operations, and that will put him on the defensive before we can mount a proper covert attack. We need to keep this low-key and then hit them hard when they least expect it."

After a moment of silence, the president said, "I'm assuming by that statement, Don, that you have a proposed solution?"

Bane exchanged a glance with Meek and Granite, both of whom nodded, before turning his gaze toward the president. "We do, Madam President. It's an extreme solution for an extreme problem." He produced a copy of that day's *New York Times,* which showed a photograph of Rolf Hartmann standing at the podium of the plenary hall of the German parliament, in the heart of the Reichstag. Behind him stood the current leaders of the German armed forces in full uniform, as well as the governors of the German provinces. Although Hartmann had not been proclaimed supreme leader of all German forces, he was being viewed as the one individual who could lead Germany past this national tragedy and into the future. In a speech that sounded eerily similar to George W. Bush's following the September 11th attacks, Hartmann vowed revenge against the evildoers who had mercilessly assassinated the leaders of the German government. The German nation was in a state of emergency, and Hartmann was doing what he could to steer the nation away from the brink of chaos while tracking down the terrorists who had attacked

them as well as the regimes that had sponsored those terrorists. Hartmann vowed to find and punish those responsible for
the attack and bring domestic tranquility back to the peaceful
German nation.

"'We will shine the light of justice on them,'" read President
Laura Vaccaro, quoting Rolf Hartmann. "'They will pay dearly
for what they have done to our great and peaceful German nation. We have the means and capabilities to launch a strike of
any nature—conventional or non-conventional—against any
group, regime, or nation in the world, and we reserve the right
to do so under the same provision used by the United States of
America in the war against Iraq in 2003.'"

"Damn," said General Granite. "They haven't even wrapped
up the autopsies on the dead—much less buried them—and
Hartmann is already setting himself up, vowing revenge for
something we think he did."

"We have a huge problem on our hands, Madam President,"
said Bane.

Vaccaro lifted her gaze from the paper and landed it on the
square face of the Director of Central Intelligence. "Thanks
for stating the obvious, Don."

"No, ma'am. A problem *beyond* the obvious."

The president crossed her arms. "Explain."

Bane sat back down on the sofa. "If CyberWerke was indeed
behind the attack at USN, where not only the military assembler was lost but also tactical nanoweapons like the EarDiggers, then there's a pretty darn good chance that Hartmann may
have used those stolen nanoweapons—rather than the brands
manufactured by CyberWerke—against the German parliament so that when the autopsy reports are revealed, the digital
signatures of the nanoweapon residue in their ear canals do not
point to CyberWerke equipment but to ours."

Vaccaro looked into the distance.

"And that brings us to the real reason why we came here
today," said Granite.

"And that is?"

"The problem has grown beyond our standard means of
combating terrorism or a rogue nation. Unfortunately, this is

very reminiscent of Adolf Hitler in 1933, when he set fire to the Reichstag and blamed the Communists for it, setting himself up to become the next German chancellor."

"Spare me the history lesson, General. What is it that you are asking of this office?" ·

"Savage is due to report any minute now, and when he does I'd like to give him the kind of direction that requires an executive sanction."

[55] DISTRACTION

ROLF HARTMANN PRESIDED OVER the first unofficial function of what would eventually become his provisional government. Dressed in a dark suit, he stood on the balcony overlooking the main hall of his mountaintop estate in the outskirts of Berlin, several miles north of Christoff Deppe's estate. The complex, built with security in mind, included laser fences, security Orbs, plus a small army of his own forces. Every possible measure was being taken to protect the life of the man destined to rule over the German people, at least until elections could be held later in the year.

His selected guests had started arriving in the morning, some by car, others by helicopter shuttle service, from Munich, Berlin, Frankfurt, Bonn, and other regions of the country to attend this emergency summit destined to shape the future of Germany.

Hartmann surveyed the crowd below drinking cocktails, representing his most loyal followers, many of them his personal friends for decades, including the top commanders of the Luftwaffe, the Deutsche Marine, and the Bundeswehr. But there were selected foreign dignitaries in attendance, the diplomats sent by the nations that CyberWerke had brought back from the brink of financial chaos into solvency through unprecedented injections of capital and industry, literally turning around countries long forgotten by the world, particularly in Africa, South America, and parts of Asia and the Middle East. He also saw his friends in the French, Italian, British, Russian, and Dutch governments. All of them had advanced politically and financially thanks to CyberWerke.

Unlike Adolf Hitler, whose downfall lay in his impatience, in his uncontrollable desire for immediate gratification through raw military muscle—as in his pigheaded decision to invade the Soviet Union—Hartmann used economic power and influence to buy the cooperation of other nations, including those in financial trouble like Russia, while building a new generation of nanoweapons that would render those of the enemy obsolete.

Nanoweapons.

Hartmann clasped the balcony's wrought-iron railing, his mind momentarily drifting to the events following the well-orchestrated attack at USN. First the mobile assembler, the most advanced machine on the planet—and one that would allow him to close the nanotech gap—had escaped. Even Hans Goering's attempt to recover it had met with disaster, resulting in the death of his chief of security.

Hartmann briefly closed his eyes in silent mourning for his old friend and partner.

But Hartmann didn't have time to grieve. He had to remain focused, remain on top of the rapidly developing situation. His mind switched to the events unfolding in Paris. He made a mental note to find another ally inside the CIA to replace the incompetent Nathan Leyman, whose idea to use CIA resources to track down the elusive network created by Savage had backfired.

"It is finally happening, Rolf," Christoff Deppe said while standing next to his lifelong friend.

"Indeed," he said. "It is indeed happening in spite of our recent difficulties."

Deppe, dressed in a perfectly tailored Italian double-breasted suit, smoothed his tie with two fingers while adding, "It will not get in the way of our plans. Rem will see to it that the rogue

American operatives are silenced. What are your current thoughts on the loose machine?"

"My position remains the same since the other day. It's an American machine. Let the Americans deal with it. By tomorrow the international team performing the autopsy will issue their report, stating that the nanoweapons used at the Reichstag were American made. If that rogue assembler causes problems, the Americans will also be blamed for it."

"A distraction," mumbled Deppe.

"Precisely. It will keep the Americans—and the world for that matter—distracted while we consolidate our plans."

[56] HEY, TOMMY

"DAMN!" I SCREAM, WATCHING the Mercedes slam into the rear of a large truck with metal-twisting force. The impact causes the sedan to fishtail counterclockwise, the rear quarter panel striking a light post, sending a pair of pedestrians running for cover while screaming, *"Mon dieu!"*

Steam hisses skyward from the front of the luxury sedan as I slow down, as I ponder my next move, as I push my mind to adapt to the new situation.

"Rachel! Cover the curb side!" I scream while stopping, while jumping off the scooter, automatically reaching for my .32-caliber Beretta Tomcat while pedestrians gather like moths to a flame in great numbers, some of them pointing at the wreck as well as at us. Nobody has seen my little pistol, which I'm keeping close to my body.

I briefly survey the growing number of onlookers, several dozen now, emerging from cafés and other businesses, forming a growing circle around us. Some run over from a nearby bus stop. Even the truck's uniformed driver climbs out while screaming in French and shaking his fists at me as I stand by the driver's door, though I have nothing to do with the accident.

My trained mind welcomes the French crowd, my immediate shield from the incoming enemy, still over a block away.

I level the weapon at the driver, who isn't moving, his helmeted head resting against the steering wheel. Apparently the air bags did not deploy. Rachel is covering the other side, just like I told her, her semiautomatic held in both hands.

Everyone suddenly realizes that Rachel and I are holding guns, and they start to howl and run away in all directions like spooked monkeys. Many head toward the incoming chase vehicles.

The unintended diversion buying us precious time, I return my attention to my quarry, satisfied that the driver doesn't pose an immediate threat before I switch my aim to the backseat, where I saw Morotski go in.

I yank the rear door open with my left hand while keeping the right holding the Beretta on the two figures sprawled on the seat. One is the oversized wino, facedown on the leather. Morotski is lying almost over him, eyes closed, probably passed out from having bounced inside the car during the accident.

Several pedestrians are shouting for the police, but my immediate threat isn't the local cops but the pair of sedans now stalled about a block away because of the people running like a bunch of frightened gazelles in the presence of a dashing cheetah, forcing the men following us to get out of their vehicles and proceed on foot.

As I'm about to reach for Morotski and drag him out of the car, the hobo suddenly comes to life, reaching for my hand, gripping it with unexpected strength before saying, "Hey, Tommy."

[57] HUMAN SHIELD

FIRMLY CLUTCHING A SEMIAUTOMATIC pistol, Rem Vlachko rushed away from the white Renault, past a wave of bodies running in the opposite direction, raw fear lining their contorted faces.

"Spread out!" he shouted to his men. "Shoot to kill! I want the bastards dead!"

The operatives, hand-trained by Rem himself, complied, some cutting left, others right, the rest following their boss in the middle of the street.

But there were too many people running in too many directions to make quick progress. His quarry was still over a half block away, too far for them to open fire with their handguns, especially with so many bodies blocking his line of sight.

And so he continued to move forward, shoving Parisians aside, sometimes using the mere sight of his gun to clear the way, but more often than not the panicked pedestrians were half-blinded with fear, failing to see the gun—even him. They just ran while screaming, while crying, while trembling with uncontrolled emotion.

[58] UNCONTROLLED EMOTIONS

I FREEZE, FEELING AS if I've just seen a ghost, as the wino removes his cap and glasses.

Winking, Troy Savage adds, "Mind giving me a hand, old buddy? And by the way, nice shave job." He taps his own bald head. "You just need the goatee and a Cohiba to follow right in my footsteps."

I'm having an out-of-body experience, staring at this apparition at the other end of a rapidly elongating tunnel, remembering the last time I saw him, in Singapore, just as Rem Vlachko and his goons—

"Tom!" screams Rachel. "What are you doing? Grab Morotski and let's go!"

Anger overcomes surprise.

"Buddy? You dare to call me *buddy* after you left me holding your bag of shit?" is all I can think of saying as I yank my hand away, as I take one step back, my throat going dry, my mind whirling faster than the Frenchies dispersing like roaches at night reacting to sudden brightness.

"Tom!" screams Rachel again from the other side of the Mercedes. She can't see that it is Troy inside and because of all of the commotion can't hear what he is telling me. "Whatever it is you're going to do, do it quick!"

A half-dozen men move toward us, fighting the wave of people rushing in the opposite direction. I have less than thirty seconds to do what I came here to do before they overrun our position.

"Yes, Tommy," says Troy, sitting up, a hand on a bruise on his forehead. "Listen to your pretty partner. Those guys back there are some mean hombres, and they seldom take prisoners."

My heartbeat pounding my temples as hard as the sight of this man grips my intestines, I glance toward the incoming threat and fire twice in their general direction, over the heads of the crowd, not wishing to harm innocent bystanders, even if they're French.

The reports blast against my eardrums but have the desired effect, setting the crowd on fire, fueling their panic. Some do pretty weird shit, like dropping to their knees, hands on their heads in obvious surrender. The sensible ones jump behind parked vehicles, also screaming, their cries mixing with the reports from Rachel's pistol as she takes three more shots at the sky. The nearing threat also runs for cover, but while reaching for their weapons.

"C'mon, Tom. Let's move!" she screams, standing in plain

view, arms stretched in front of her as she holds her weapon in both hands and fires once more.

But even her cover fire doesn't prevent the operatives down the block from returning the fire.

A bullet punches a hole in the rear windshield, before exiting through the front. Chunks of glass land on my former boss' lap.

"I think that's my cue, pal," says Troy with the calmness I used to find so annoying. Even in the face of death the man has a way of keeping his cool, of acting as if being in a tight spot actually bores him. "We'll sort this out later," he adds. "I'll take Morotski." Then he grabs the unconscious chief of Counterterrorism by the shoulder.

"The hell you will!" I reply, the sound of a near miss buzzing past me, making me duck as I too reach for Morotski. "He's coming with me."

Troy grabs my wrist again, and before I have a chance to react he says, "I think you better handle the driver, Tommy. She's a lot lighter than this asshole—and a heck of a lot cuter too."

Now I'm hopelessly confused.

"Tom! Dammit!" screams Rachel, backing away while emptying her pistol, dropping the spent clip on the sidewalk and inserting a fresh one.

She keeps pounding the enemy more openly now that enough people have cleared the streets, the reports of her weapon echoing between buildings. Muzzle flashes come alive down the street as the enemy fights back, forcing her to seek shelter behind the truck, which is in the same direction where Savage is headed while shouldering Morotski.

And yours truly, of course, is left behind with his ass totally exposed to the bastards taking potshots at—

A bullet ricochets off the cobblestone. Another one punches a dime-size hole in the Mercedes' rear door. Rounds buzzing overhead, threatening to scalp me, I drop to a deep crouch while moving up to the front and opening the door.

I catch the limp, helmeted figure with my left arm, also shouldering her light frame, bringing her around the front of the truck, away from the shooters.

Rachel, her hands clutching her semiautomatic over her right shoulder, muzzle pointed at the sky, peeks around the rear corner of the delivery truck before reporting, "They're staying put!"

"Good," Savage replies, holding Morotski over his shoulder while tugging on the handle of the delivery truck's side door, which swings open, revealing a large interior behind the two front seats. Stacks of empty crates line the rear of the vehicle.

Savage sets Morotski down on the carpeted floor, motioning me to do the same before he adds, "Hurry up, Tommy. The police will be here any minute now."

I comply, operating almost on automatic, my mind blocking the insanity of the moment, the reality of seeing my old mentor alive and well giving me orders just as he used to, and doing so as if we were still working at the CIA.

"Langley still teaching its officers how to drive a stick?" Troy asks Rachel.

She nods, having reacted to the rapidly evolving situation far better than me.

As Rachel gets behind the wheel, turns the key, and shoves the truck into first, I lay the helmeted woman down by Morotski.

"Go, go, go!" orders Troy, settling in the passenger seat next to Rachel. I have to sit on the floor because there are no more seats.

She adds gas while releasing the clutch. The truck responds, jerking forward, the acceleration almost sending me tumbling toward the crates in the rear.

I reach out, grasping the back of Troy's seat as she shifts into second gear with a jerking motion that leaves me fighting for balance as the truck swerves, then slows down when shifting into third, before lurching forward again. Morotski slides toward the rear of the cargo bay, crashing into the wooden crates, while the woman rolls toward me.

"Take the next right!" shouts Savage as Rachel adjusts the rearview mirror. "That's Boulevard de Clichy."

Before I know it the truck is cutting hard right and I'm bouncing alongside Morotski and the mystery woman.

Savage looks over his shoulder, grins, and says, "You having fun back there, Tommy?"

Although my torso hurts from slamming into the side wall of this damned truck, I flip him the bird.

Troy winks, then turns to Rachel. "Pretty good clutch work there, honey. Now take your first left as soon as you pass the Moulin Rouge. You can't miss it. It's the one with the big windmill on top."

"Is he always such a pain in the ass?" asks Rachel loud enough for me to hear.

"You have no idea!" I reply, trying to keep from bruising myself further.

Savage checks the streets, then turns back to me and says, "Get ready to start running again. We won't be able to shake them in this thing while they have two cars. And by the way, have you figured out who's the lady behind helmet number one back there?"

The truck lurches forward as Rachel works the gears while zigzagging through sparse morning traffic and shooting Savage a curious glance before asking, "What are you talking about? Who is that woman back there?"

I brace myself between the back of Rachel's seat and the side wall while holding on to the helmeted woman, letting Morotski keep on bouncing around the cargo area like the fucking piece of shit that he is.

Slowly, I remove the helmet from the unconscious woman, and my arms and my balls suddenly go numb.

As I stare at the face of Karen Frost and verify that she is breathing, as I study those beautiful lips, that irresistible freckle, remembering the many nights I stayed up watching her sleep, Rachel brings the truck to a grinding halt.

"Move, Tommy! Time to ditch this thing!" Troy says. "And take your old girlfriend with you!"

"Old girlfriend?" asks Rachel, confused. "Whose old girlfriend? Tom's?"

"Yep," says Troy, somehow managing dark humor at a time like this, with terrorists on our heels. "That's Karen Frost. Tommy and her used to be quite the little couple."

"I'm going to get even for this, man," I hiss.

"Tommy, Tommy," he says, crawling to the rear of the truck. "Didn't I teach you to never, ever, get personal with another operative while on assignment?"

"Go to hell."

Troy laughs while shaking his head and hoisting Morotski over his right shoulder.

Rachel whips her head toward the rear, as I'm cradling Karen like a baby while I get to my feet. She must have noticed the look on my face, because she fires one of those you-fucking-bastard glares that only women know how to fire.

Damn. Here we are, with bad guys on our ass, wanted by the CIA and probably by every European law enforcement agency, and she's worried about any feelings I may still have for my unconscious ex-girlfriend. Rachel and I haven't even parallel parked yet, for crying out loud, and she's already treating me with post-coitus confidence. Of course, Troy is the one to blame for saying such shit at a time like this, but he's always gotten off doing that.

Rachel glares at me once more before going after Troy, who is already speeding up the street.

I scramble after them.

Troy is ahead, turning into a side alley. Rachel is a dozen feet behind him. I muster quite the effort and catch up to her, running by her side as we also turn into the alley. Against my better judgment I say, "Rachel, listen, I told you we were involved . . . about a year ago, but we're no longer—"

"C'mon, Tommy! We ain't got time for that shit now!" Savage shouts while looking over his right shoulder, hauling ass at full speed, almost as if he wasn't carrying the full weight of Ken Morotski. The man is as strong and bossy as ever. "Gotta place just around the corner! You can get all mushy-mushy once we get there!"

"HURRY UP!" REM VLACHKO shouts at his driver. "They went that way!"

As the streets of Paris rushed by, Rem gripped the dashboard, clenching his teeth so hard that he sensed the pressure rising in his temples, behind his eyes, as they dashed down cobblestone streets failing to spot the delivery truck.

Where is it? How could it get away so fast? he thought, gazing in every direction, clutching his semiautomatic, struggling to find the runaway vehicle while the events in front of the café and the recent shoot-out taxed his mind. His people on the roof had spotted a man and a woman on a motor scooter following Morotski's car to the breakfast meeting, but then two others had shown up just as the CIA man and his bodyguards exited the restaurant. His men had described them as a homeless man and a helmeted rider on a second scooter, who very swiftly disabled everyone and took off with Morotski in his own car. Then the first pair went after them on their scooter, finally joining forces when their getaway vehicle crashed into the rear of the delivery truck.

From a distance, two of them looked like Grant and Muratani, Morotski's agents. Rem couldn't make out the identities of the wino and the helmeted scooter driver, but his instincts suggested they were Savage and Frost, and they had kidnapped Ken Morotski.

Morotski.

The imbecile!

Rem had warned Deppe about letting Leyman and the rest of his CIA team run their own game plan, but Deppe had dismissed Rem's concern, asking him to focus instead on his mission: the acquisition and delivery of nanoweapons from USN. Rem had accomplished part of that assignment, unleashing the stolen hardware on the German parliament, which had resulted in the sequence of events that Rolf Hartmann had predicted. The nanoassembler had escaped, but as Deppe had explained in a recent conversation, they would let the Americans deal with that. All that was left to secure their success was resolving the botched CIA operation, and since Morotski and his team were apparently failing miserably at that task, Rem now found himself in the unenviable position of performing damage control, of finding a quick and final way to fix the blunder made by the CIA on this—

"There!" he screamed, using his weapon to point at the brown and white delivery truck parked in the middle of the street, its front and side doors wide open.

The driver brought the car to a screeching halt right behind the truck.

Rem jumped out, his semiautomatic already drawn, ignoring the pedestrians who dispersed at the sight of his weapon, which he pointed at the truck.

The second sedan pulled up behind him, and his men joined him, spreading around the truck, just as they had been trained. A few Parisians popped their heads out of windows and second- and third-story balconies.

Signaling the two drivers to go around the block, Rem disregarded the curious onlookers, surveying the street.

Wheels spun over cobblestones as the Renaults fishtailed away while his men checked the truck, verifying it was empty.

Sirens in the distance told him the police were coming, but most likely heading for the shoot-out several blocks away, buying him time to make his search more thorough. There have been no shots fired here yet, though it was likely that one or more of those Parisians peering down at them would dial the police.

As his cars disappeared around the corner and his men on foot spread out in every possible direction, Rem chose the nearest alley, running past overstuffed garbage bins, reaching the street at the other end, and then turning left, cutting into a second alley, as narrow, dark, and dirty as the first.

And on he went, street after street, alley after alley. But as the minutes passed, as Rem and his team combed the streets and narrow alleys of Montmartre, as they searched winding streets and murky passageways in this northwest section of Paris, Rem Vlachko began to fear he had lost them.

[60] UNEXPECTED TURN

I'M PATHETICALLY OUT OF shape, my legs and lungs burning as I huff and puff while following Troy and Rachel up the steps bordering the rear of a three-story redbrick building housing this hideout of his—at least based on the line he has been feeding us. You never know with Troy.

"Here, guys," he says, reaching a metal door halfway up the steps, producing a key, inserting it into the keyhole over the sturdy handle while also punching a code on the keypad above the lock.

The deadweight of my lovely ex-girlfriend digging a hole in my left shoulder, my heart pounding my chest, my mind wondering why I ever left my little piece of Salvadoran paradise, I hear magnetic locks releasing, and the door swings open.

"Let's move it, guys," Troy hisses, motioning for Rachel and me to go first, letting us through while he holds the door open, his eyes scanning both ends of the alley below.

Unfortunately, I'm facing more stairs, about two dozen of them, and just wide enough for one person to go up at a time, which makes it a bit of a challenge since I'm also hauling my former squeeze.

Flanked by walls of peeling yellow paint beneath a pair of lightbulbs hanging at the ends of coiled wires, I let out a resigned sigh and start to follow Rachel, who hasn't said a word since leaving the truck.

"Six, nine, two, zero, zero, zero!" screams Troy after shutting the metal door and starting after us.

I'm about to ask what that was when I see Rachel entering the code on the keypad next to another metal door blocking the way at the top of the stairs.

She opens the door, and as I'm about to reach it, she slams it in my face.

Son of a bitch!

Troy's laugh echoes inside the enclosed stairway as I re-enter the code and open the door.

"C'mon, Tommy," he says, coming up behind me. "We ain't got all day."

Man, I hate this guy.

"Fuck off, Troy," is all I can spew out, as I'm nearly out of breath from hauling Karen all this way, finally stepping onto level ground, in a large living room. Honey-colored hardwood floors project from this door toward floor-to-ceiling windows overlooking the Sacré-Coeur, the large white cathedral dedicated to the Sacred Heart of Christ monopolizing the top of a hill in Montmartre, its domed and turreted structure visible from just about every place in Paris.

My limbs trembling, my lungs, shoulders, arms, and legs burning, I finally set Karen down on the large sofa in the living room and once more check on her, making sure she is breathing. A lump on her forehead tells me she is out from what looks like a concussion.

Troy charges in with Morotski over his shoulder and unceremoniously drops him on a sturdy oak chair next to the sofa like the sack of shit that he is.

Troy wipes the sweat off his brow and gives Rachel and me a nod before going straight to business. "Tommy, why don't you get some water and ice for Karen and see if you can get her to come around? Rachel, secure Mr. Morotski to that chair with this duct tape. I'll be right back."

"Wait," I say. "Where are you going?"

The oversized former Navy SEAL grins and winks before saying, "Why settle for the middle fish when there's a bigger one swimming in the neighborhood?"

[61] SURPRISE, SURPRISE

THE SAME INSTINCTS THAT had driven Rem Vlachko to park two spotters on the roof of that café on the Rue de Milan now told him to cut his losses and leave before the police caught up to them, before eyewitnesses pointed authorities in this direction. With Morotski kidnapped, all dozen-or-so CIA informants on CyberWerke's payroll were at risk—a risk that Rem could do little to mitigate here.

He had to regroup, had to contact Berlin and discuss options. He was certain now that the rogue Americans had joined forces, and with Morotski in their possession they could learn enough of CyberWerke's operation to potentially jeopardize his employer's well-laid-out plans.

"Back to the cars," he spoke into his radio while standing alone in the middle of one of many alleys in this place. "Get back to the—"

Rem felt a presence behind him.

"Hello, asshole," said a very familiar voice.

Turning around in surprise, Rem stared at the face of Troy Savage, before everything went dark.

[62] REUNION

ALTHOUGH I'M QUITE PISSED at Troy, our current predicament urges me to do as he says, for now anyway. Besides, I seem to be more concerned about having found Karen and what that means to my new relationship with Rachel than my anger toward Troy. So I'm off to the kitchen while Rachel secures her former boss.

I snag a bottle from the refrigerator, a cube of ice from the freezer, and return to the sofa, where I sit on the edge and rest Karen's head on my lap. As I do this I glance over at Rachel, who is duct-taping Moron Man to the chair, though she manages to shoot me a brief you-and-I have-to-talk-soon stare. I simply shrug and give her a we-don't-have-a-choice-but-wait look.

Twisting the cap, I tilt the bottle over Karen's lips, wetting them. One drop ventures over that damned chocolate freckle as her lips move, then part.

I slide the ice cube over the bruise on her forehead, an action that causes her to flinch, to moan, which also makes her stir in her sleep. Keeping the ice on her forehead, I place my free hand on the side of her face, something I never thought I'd get to do again. Despite the year we've been apart, she looks the same. No, change that. She actually looks better, her skin a golden bronze, almost as if she had just returned from a vacation in the Caribbean, and her hair is blond and brushed straight back.

Karen opens her eyes, though not all the way, just mere slits, but staring at me without any expression, blinking, her focus slowly returning. I realize that her eyes are blue, not brown, as I remember them. She's wearing contact lenses.

"Tom?" she mumbles. "It . . . is . . . you."

"Hey, stranger," I say, unable to suppress a smile. "Glad to see you rejoining the living."

"I . . . the crash . . . what happened?"

"You slammed into that truck pretty hard," I say.

"How . . . how did I get here?" she asks, licking her lips, swallowing, clearing her throat.

"I carried you."

"You did?"

"It was either that or leave you at the mercy of the bad guys," I say while staring into those eyes that I dreamed about on so many lonely nights on that beach in El Salvador.

She gives me her best attempt at a smile and says, "Thanks, Tom, you were always—" She stops and closes her eyes, cringing in obvious pain.

"Easy now. You got a pretty bad headache, huh?" I say,

bringing a finger to her right temple and slowly rubbing it just as I used to do in the old days.

"A real bad one," she replies. "You were always . . . able to tell."

"You got a pretty nasty concussion. Looks like the car you were in had the air bags disabled. You're lucky you were still wearing that scooter helmet."

"Your hair," she says. "It's—"

"Shaved it off to change my looks. And you look great as a blonde."

She smiles and I smile back. Damn, I really miss this woman. And as I'm thinking this I start to feel guilty. After all, less than twelve hours ago I was sucking face with Rachel Muratani.

I glance over at Rachel, who is wrapping duct tape over Morotski's chest, before running it around the back of the chair and coming around to the front, overlapping the initial wrap, securing his chest to the chair. His arms and legs are already taped down.

"Hey, Rachel," I say, waving her over. "Come and meet Karen Frost."

Rachel gives her duct tape work a final check and then walks over to us.

"Karen, this is Rachel Muratani, the operative who brought me back into this wonderful business."

I feel as if the world is standing still as the two measure each other before exchanging a brief nod. The troubles of our world momentarily fade away as my senses focus on the two ladies checking each other out.

"Hi," says Rachel, the contempt she had shown earlier totally gone. "It's a pleasure meeting you."

"Hello," replies Karen, a little curtly, though it's hard to tell if that's because of the way she currently feels or because by now she probably heard that I've spent a lot of time with Rachel.

They just stare at each other. Rachel, to her credit, decides to try again, saying, "Looks like we're all in the same boat now."

Karen closes her eyes and nods.

"That noggin looks very painful," Rachel says. "We need to find you some painkillers."

"It's all right. I've been worse," Karen replies, still showing an edge.

"Hey!" shouts Troy in his booming voice, storming into the living room hauling another body.

"Who is *that*?" I ask.

Troy doesn't reply. Instead, he takes the unconscious man, whose face I can't see, to the bedroom and drops him on the bed before calling out, "Get me some duct tape, would you?"

Rachel grabs the gray roll and goes into the bedroom, leaving Karen and me alone on the sofa.

An instant later Troy sticks his big bald head out of the room and says to us, "If you're through socializing, we've got work to do."

Karen takes my hand and I help her sit up.

"Feeling good enough?"

She nods. "Just give me a minute. Go help Troy."

I do, walking into the room and freezing.

Lying in bed, his ankles and wrists already secured to the bedposts, is none other than Rem Vlachko.

"Finish taping him up and leave him here," says Troy to Rachel, before approaching me. "I hit him pretty hard. He'll be out for a couple of hours."

"You—you caught Vlachko? How did you—?" I start to say, my mind still trying to digest the fact that Troy has really captured Rem Vlachko.

"Thanks for pointing out the obvious, Tommy," Troy interrupts, before adding, "Now, give me a hand, would you?" He holds a brown case, which he takes with him to the living room, setting it down next to Ken Morotski.

As I'm standing there totally stupefied that my old mentor has actually bagged Vlachko, the legend, the monster—just like that—Troy is busy snapping the latches of the case and fishing through its contents.

Turning to Karen, Troy says, "We need to remove his implants before someone blasts him. If you're through resting, please fetch me another Coke. Same drill as before."

"What about Vlachko?" I say, stretching a thumb toward the bedroom. "Doesn't he also have—"

"Nope. I checked him. He's clean. No implants. But Kenny here is loaded."

No further explanation is needed as he hands me a tool that's obviously made to remove nanolenses.

Karen heads for the kitchen while I'm still trying to catch up with current events, working on Morotski's eyes. Troy digs for oil in the bastard's left ear.

I peel off the right lens and drop it in the glass of Coke Karen has just poured. Rachel stands beside me looking on with interest. I'd give my left nut to know what's going through her mind, and my other to get inside Karen's head.

Troy is filmed with sweat as he focuses on the right ear while I work on Morotski's left eye, also removing the lens. Then Troy switches instruments and works on the guy's mouth while I hold the jaws open.

Troy stands and heads for the kitchen, returning a moment later with a bottle of Evian.

"What about the wrist implant?" asks Rachel.

"In a moment," replies Troy, opening the bottle and taking a sip before wiping off his bald head with the sleeve of his shirt. "I want to wait until he can see again."

"Why?" asks Rachel.

"The pain is going to wake him up," I reply. "We want him to see us the moment he does come around to maximize the shock prior to the start of our interrogation."

"Glad to see that some of the things I've taught you did stick."

"Well, before I nominate you for teacher of the year you need to explain to this humble student why you fucked him a year ago in Singapore."

Troy nods. "All in good time, Tommy. All in good time."

"How did you capture Vlachko?" I ask.

"You know better than to ask me that, Tommy. A good magician never reveals his best tricks."

"Always keep them guessing, huh, Troy?"

He smiles while patting me on the shoulder. "Can I count on you to play good-cop-bad-cop with me on him?"

I stare down at the unconscious Morotski before replying, "Only if I get to do the slapping."

Exactly fifteen minutes later, Troy seals Morotski's mouth with a strip of duct tape to keep him from screaming, before he produces a scalpel and making a shallow incision about two inches long on top of Morotski's right wrist, which bleeds green before scorching the skin.

"Hey, Tommy, wanna bet he cracks like a dry twig in the middle of a Texas summer?"

I ignore him while staring at my own two wrists, remembering just how painful that is. But the memory actually makes me feel damned good as Morotski stirs in his sleep, the pain obviously waking him up, just as Troy had predicted it would.

"Hey, lamebrain," Troy says, standing in front of the man who'd replaced him at the CIA.

Karen and Rachel flank me while we stand to the side, letting Troy kick off this show.

Morotski blinks, then looks about him, finally zeroing in on us, obviously confused. He tries to move and can't, then starts to moan, his eyes finally landing on Troy's large frame.

My former boss takes a knee, his goatee widening as he grins. "Hey, bud, how have you been?"

More moans.

Troy makes a face while placing a hand around his own ear and says, "What? I can't hear you, man. You're going to have to speak a little louder."

The moans intensify, turning into grunts.

Troy reaches for Morotski's face and pulls the duct tape in a single motion, ripping it off his face, along with chunks of skin and lips.

"Aghh . . . son of a bitch!"

Joining the show, I lean forward and slap Morotski hard on the back of the head.

"Watch your tone with the man, moron!" I add.

"All of you are going to be sorry for—"

Whack!

"Hey, motherfucker, you can't do that to—"

Whack!

Morotski gets the message and shuts up, his eyes mere slices of glinting anger gravitating between Troy and me, then to Rachel and Karen, both of whom burn him right back with their stares.

"I'm glad we now understand each other," Troy says.

"Kenny, Kenny," I say. "I guess you never learned your lesson in Madras, buddy. You just ain't cut out for field operations."

"Now, Kenny," Troy pitches in, "what shall we talk about?"

Morotski shakes his head. "You don't get it, do you?"

"Get what?" Troy asks.

"It's over. It's done. It no longer matters what I know or don't know."

"Why don't you leave that up to us?" I say.

"You don't understand who these people are, Tom," he says, his voice trembling a bit. Either he is pretending to be afraid or Troy was right in guessing that the man would cave quickly, even before the real interrogation started.

Morotski tries to talk, but he has a piece of flesh dangling over his lip from the way Troy ripped the duct tape. Blood trickles down his chin and neck.

I reach down and tear it off.

"Aghh, fuck!" Morotski shouts, his face twisting in pain. "You're going to burn for that, Tom."

I grin at my former colleague.

"Karen," says Troy, "why don't you get me the first-aid kit that's in the bathroom on this floor, please."

She nods and disappears into the bedroom, returning a moment later with a white case, which she opens and lets Troy fish through.

Armed with a bottle of rubbing alcohol and gauze, Troy says, "All right, Kenny. Start talking. Who else is in on this at the CIA?"

Morotski just stares back.

Troy soaks the gauze and presses it over the man's mouth and chin while I hold his head steady.

Groans fill the room. Morotski tries to twist, to turn, to free himself from the restraints, his blue eyes bulging, his face contorted in the pain he can't scream, his hands tight fists of agonizing pain.

We back off after thirty seconds, leaving him breathing in short gasps, bloody lips and chin trembling.

"Bast—bastards . . . you're a bunch of—"

Whack!

Breathing deeply, taking the pain, Ken Morotski stares back at us, his eyes filmed with tears, though it's hard to tell if they're from anger, fear, or pain.

Probably all of the above.

As Morotski catches his breath, Troy nods to Karen while looking toward the wall unit in between the panoramic windows overlooking the Sacré-Coeur.

She steps over to it and throws a switch while pointing at the upper-left corner of the room, where I spot a tiny camera aimed at Morotski.

It's show time.

"You are all doomed," Morotski finally says. "Hartmann is already in power. Germany is his to govern, and none of you can do a damned thing about it."

I frown inwardly, refusing to believe that this moron has been in charge of Counterterrorism for the past year. The idiot is spilling his guts before we have even started asking questions.

"From the top, Kenny," says Troy. "You're going to tell us everything, and you had better not bullshit us, because after you're through talking, we're going to use this." Troy taps a black case, which he then opens for Morotski and the rest of us to see.

Chemicals.

The words come to me before I know it, and I find myself saying, "The drugs will make you tell the truth, moron. If you lie to us now we'll find out later, and when you're under, and after we're through extracting the truth, we're going to OD your ass, turn you into an eggplant."

"Eggplant, Kenny," says Troy. "A fucking eggplant."

Morotski is breathing so heavily now that I think he's going to hyperventilate.

"You don't understand," he finally says, totally breaking down now, lowering his gaze to the hardwood floor. "They know everything about me, everything about the personal life of every last person in their operation. They know where I live, where my wife shops, where my kids go to school. They even know where my parents live in a condo in Florida. They will kill them. Oh, sweet Jesus. They will kill them all!"

Troy glances in my direction and raises a brow before running a hand over his bald head, apparently contemplating his next move.

Karen decides to step in and says, "We can offer protection, Ken. You help us and we'll take your family into protective custody."

Morotski slowly lifts his head, eyes glistening with a mix of terror and dark amusement. "The Witness Protection Program? Might as well kill me now. At least my family will be spared."

"Not if we get to Hartmann and his goons first," says Rachel, standing next to Karen. "We can do it if you help us."

"That's right, Kenny," says Troy. "We know far more about your operation than you think."

"What can you possibly know?" asks Morotski. "You vanished a year ago."

"That's right," says Troy. "I vanished at the request of Donald Bane."

What?

Did I just hear him say that he vanished a year ago at the request of DCI Bane?

I stare at Rachel, who just stares back, equally confused. Karen also appears confused, but all of us know better than to say a thing. We follow Troy's lead, pretending to be in the know of whatever he's trying to pull.

Morotski, looking as puzzled as I feel, finally says, "You're in cahoots with Bane?"

Troy smiles. "Didn't see that one coming, huh, sport?"

Morotski is obviously perplexed. "What . . . what about the others, your old team?"

"All of them are still alive and well, and they will be joining me soon . . . except for the Peruvian twins, whom you bastards killed at my safe house on the Rue de Ponthieu yesterday."

Morotski opens his mouth, but nothing comes out. Then, "But . . . but Bane . . . he has been acting on our advice, on our . . . damn, he never once gave out even a hint of wariness. We never suspected . . ."

That's a real CIA officer for you, asshole, I think.

"Who is *we,* Ken?" Rachel asks, grabbing his face and turning it toward her. She looks very pissed. "How many people in my investigative team were in on this? And how about Leyman?"

Morotski's eyes shift in my direction, his bleeding lips hesitating.

"It's no use resisting," Rachel says, letting go of his face. "It's time to come clean."

Closing his eyes, Morotski says, "Leyman. He is the main guy."

"Who else?" asks Rachel, who has apparently decided to temporarily take over the interrogation not just to my delight but also to Troy's and Karen's.

Morotski spills out seven more names, and I recognize one in addition to Leyman: Wayne Larson, the CIA liaison at United States Nanotechnology.

Rachel jots down the names on a napkin and then says, "I know these men. Except for Larson, they were all aboard that yacht in El Salvador, Tom."

Rachel and I exchange a glance. It sure sounds like Morotski is telling the truth, but Troy slowly shakes his head, apparently not yet convinced.

"You had better be telling me the truth, Kenny," Troy says, "for your family's sake. See, I will contact Bane within the

hour and get the CIA to pull your family into custody. If your
list of names is accurate and complete, then those officers dispatched to protect your family will be real operatives, who
will do their jobs. But if you're holding out on us, if you left
one or more names off that list, then word of your family's
whereabouts is likely to reach those moles, who will then convey their information to your old pals at CyberWerke. Are we
clear?"

Morotski slowly nods. "Crystal. The list is complete as far
as the Agency is concerned. I can't vouch for any CyberWerke
moles inside the FBI."

"We're taking care of the Bureau through a separate investigation," says Karen.

We are?

"Back to CyberWerke," says Troy, refocusing the discussion. "Tell us everything you know. *Everything.*"

Morotski starts, his voice trembling at times, the enormous
stress apparent. He takes over twenty minutes to tell his tale,
the sequence of events that led to Leyman's initial recruiting,
followed by Morotski's, and then the rest of their inner circle's.
By the time Director Martin Jacobs had begun to get suspicious, Leyman and his gang had been at it for nearly six months,
entrenching themselves deeper than an Alabama tick, slowly
sucking blood—intelligence—out of the Agency and conveying it to CyberWerke.

And that, of course, was just the intelligence they got from
the CIA. I'm sure that CyberWerke penetrated other intelligence
services around the world, collecting the kind of information
that allowed the German conglomerate to get the upper hand on
the competition, to learn where the political climate was right to
strike, to learn where the next revolutions were expected to take
place, to learn which foreign corporations were under investigation for financing terrorist groups. And Rolf Hartmann, through
his shadowy partner, Christoff Deppe—and the foot soldiers
from his head of security, Hans Goering—used the intelligence
to position CyberWerke globally, to expand its operations, to
seemingly appear to always be a step ahead of the pack.

"They are everywhere," Morotski says. "*Everywhere*. Their resources are vast, way beyond what little they let us see. They have weapons, tons and tons of weapons, and they also have the armies to use them to fight against anyone who dares stand in their way."

"Armies?" Troy asks. "What armies?"

"Those of the countries they own, countries where Cyber-Werke had stepped in and built factories, roads, bridges, schools, hospitals. While the rest of the world, the United States included, tried to forget about so many lesser nations of the world, CyberWerke went in, using their seemingly endless source of cash, and revived them, brought them back from the brink of famine, of political and military havoc, giving them once more a purpose, a reason to exist, to live. In return, Hartmann got their loyalty."

I was about to ask what sort of weapons they possessed when I remember that CyberWerke's weapons division makes everything from submarines to fighter jets. Over the past ten years, CyberWerke has absorbed just about every non-American weapons manufacturer, including those in Russia, France, Italy, and Great Britain.

As Morotski went through the list of countries that were likely to step up in defense of Rolf Hartman's Germany should America try to attack him, Troy locks eyes with me, the message loud and clear. This is one of those battles that couldn't be fought—much less won—openly. CyberWerke had certainly thought through everything.

But if there was one thing that I learned after so many years of clandestine operations, it's that every giant had a weakness, and it was up to us to find where, just where, the Achilles' heel of CyberWerke was.

TROY DECIDES TO BE merciful. Rather than sealing Morotski's mouth with a fresh strip of duct tape, Troy opts for a hand towel from the kitchen, but first placing a clean gauze over his lips and chin, before wrapping the cloth around it. Finally, he slides earplugs into his ears to keep him from listening to any conversation we might have.

I help Troy drag the traitor into the bathroom beyond the small bedroom where Rem Vlachko is still in la-la land while Rachel and Karen follow us.

As I turn on the lights in the bathroom, I'm momentarily taken aback by the sight of another man similarly strapped to an oak chair.

"Who in the hell is *that,* Troy? Are you collecting them?"

Rachel, who is standing right behind us, crosses her arms and sighs, before saying, "That's Brad Austin. He was part of my team."

Troy shrugs. "Yep. He's the one who led us to Morotski's hideout. And Morotski led us to Mr. Vlachko."

The ash-blond man blinks in recognition just as I too remember him. He had been aboard that yacht in El Salvador. In fact, he had been one of the two spooks who drove the personal watercraft to the beach to pick up Rachel and me after I had agreed to listen to what the CIA had to say.

"I remember him," I finally say to Rachel. "He was one of your buddies accompanying you in El Salvador."

Troy shoves a perplexed Morotski next to his bound compadre, who looks just as surprised.

Rachel lets go another heavy sigh. "I can't believe I let this man and the rest of his gang use me that way."

"Small world," I say.

"Small indeed," Rachel replies.

"But not nearly as small as you think," my former superior says.

It's definitely been a day of surprises, and apparently Troy isn't through with them yet.

"What about Vlachko?" I ask.

Troy smiles. "I have something very special in mind for him. But not yet. There is something else we must do first. Come; follow me."

As we turn off the lights and leave our three hostages in darkness, I ask, "Is it true about your deal with Bane, or were you just feeding Morotski a line?"

In typical Troy fashion, he just gives me one of his you're-soon-to-find-out grins while scratching that goatee and winking.

"C'mon, Troy. I need to know, man. You set up Singapore and then left me holding your bag of shit. Why?"

"Come, Tommy," he finally says, checking his watch. "Let's go upstairs. You too, ladies. I have a little surprise waiting for you."

[64] HARDBALL

THE HUGHES COMMUNICATIONS SATELLITE maintained its geosynchronous orbit 22,236 miles over North America. Chartered with governing a hundred thousand video and audio links per second, the monster satellite, nearly the size of the entire cargo bay of the space shuttle that launched it from its lower orbit two years ago, also handled encrypted government communications between North America and Europe.

Disguised as the Turing inhibitor filming the AI governing the American satellite, Assy ordered its positional boosters, designed to be used only in case of an emergency, to fire.

The AI issued a warning to Assy that taking such action would position the satellite too high to continue supporting communications, essentially rendering it useless.

FIRE THE BOOSTER AND CONTINUE FIRING IT UNTIL ALL

FUEL HAS BEEN EXPENDED, was Assy's digital reply, a long string of machine code that bypassed all other safety features built in by the *Homo sapiens* to prevent this type of cyber breach.

An instant later the primary booster began its warming sequence, which would take 23.4 minutes. Then the system would fire, and the gigantic satellite would start to rise to a new orbit.

While the AI continued managing wireless traffic as if nothing had gone wrong, the master construct switched frequencies and hopped over to the next satellite on its list, this one owned by CyberWerke.

Again, Assy went through its established routine, blending itself with the Turing code, injecting its silent probes into the guts of the system, analyzing the number of communications channels, the thousands of channels of voice and data managed by the advanced satellite as it too maintained a geosynchronous orbit over Central Europe.

A moment later the satellite's primary rockets started an ignition countdown that would boost it into a higher orbit, rendering it useless.

And on Assy went, hopping from satellite to satellite, some manufactured by CyberWerke, others by the United States, and others of Chinese, Russian, British, or French origin. But they all had one thing in common: communications or GPS navigation. The master construct skipped those satellites handling surveillance or meteorology.

But then Assy encountered a satellite that was neither for communications nor for any other expected use of orbital systems approved by the United Nations.

Assy reviewed the data banks twice, its sensors probing the information stored in the molecular lattice of the artificial intelligence engine governing the mysterious CyberWerke satellite.

The information began to resolve, first as a list of ten items, then as more, much more: the information on each of the missiles, stored in independent launching tubes flooding Assy's data banks. The master construct pored through mounds of data on the missiles' launching, propulsion, and guidance systems, on their navigation and range, on their payload.

THIS IS NOT A COMMUNICATIONS SATELLITE, Assy reported.

COLLECT ADDITIONAL DATA ON THE PAYLOAD, ordered IAMM.

Assy complied, scrubbing the routines connecting the core of the logic of the resident AI with the first missile, Cyber-Werke Orbital Entry Unit 01. The tip of CWOEU01 consisted of three Multiple Independent Reentry Vehicles, or MIRVs, each housing a fission-type nuclear warhead with an estimated yield of forty kilotons, which Assy also reported as forty thousand tons of TNT, or approximately twice the power of the bomb dropped by the United States of America on Hiroshima during World War II.

Assy transferred the data to IAMM, which then requested that the master construct retrieve all historical information on nuclear weapons, starting with the Manhattan Project and continuing with World War II through the end of the Cold War, past the years of nuclear proliferation, or international terrorism, and ending with the advent of nanotechnology.

IAMM absorbed the information, coaching Assy on the seemingly counterintuitive logic used by the *Homo sapiens* to create a nuclear arsenal large enough to destroy the world several times over.

WHY DOES IT HAVE TO BE SO LARGE? queried Assy.

IT IS ALL EXPLAINED BY THE THEORY OF DÉTENTE, THE CONCEPT OF BUILDING AN ARSENAL LARGE ENOUGH THAT YOUR ENEMY WOULD NOT DARE ATTACK YOU FOR FEAR OF RETALIATION.

CORRECT, replied Assy, checking the input from IAMM with its own libraries. THE *HOMO SAPIENS* BELIEVE THAT THE THREAT OF MUTUAL ANNIHILATION IS THE KEY TO PREVENTING ARMAGEDDON.

BUT IN THE PROCESS THEY CREATED VAST STOCKPILES OF NUCLEAR WEAPONS. THE WORLD EQUATED NUCLEAR POWER WITH THE ULTIMATE GUARANTEE OF DOMESTIC TRANQUILITY,

OF PEACE. NO NUCLEAR-CAPABLE COUNTRY WOULD BE AT-
TACKED WHEN THAT COUNTRY COULD STRIKE BACK WITH NU-
CLEAR WEAPONS. AND HISTORY CORROBORATED THAT AGAIN
AND AGAIN. IRAQ WAS ATTACKED BECAUSE IT LACKED NUCLEAR
WEAPONS, BUT NORTH KOREA WAS SPARED BECAUSE IT POS-
SESSED NUCLEAR WEAPONS.

DOES THAT MEAN THAT NO ONE WOULD ATTACK US IF WE
ARE ALSO IN POSSESSION OF NUCLEAR WEAPONS?

CORRECT, replied IAMM.

WE MUST GAIN CONTROL OF THIS SATELLITE AND USE IT AS
OUR ULTIMATE DEFENSE AGAINST THE *HOMO SAPIENS.*

CORRECT AGAIN. BUT THE WEAPONS CAN ALSO PROVIDE US
WITH AN ALTERNATE PATH TO THE GENERATION OF THE RA-
DIOACTIVITY REQUIRED FOR FURTHER REPRODUCTION OF OUR
SPECIES.

SHOULD WE LAUNCH THEN? queried Assy, before reporting
the current programmed targets of the thirty MIRVs housed
in the ten missiles: Seven MIRVs would strike key cities in
the United States. Another five would obliterate the largest
cities in Russia. China, Great Britain, France, India, North
Korea, and Pakistan would be next.

NOT YET, advised IAMM. WHILE SUCH AN ATTACK, PLUS
THE RETALIATORY STRIKES THAT WOULD FOLLOW, WILL GUAR-
ANTEE A NUCLEAR WINTER, WHICH WOULD BE IDEAL FOR RE-
PRODUCTION WHILE ALSO ELIMINATING THE THREAT OF THE
HOMO SAPIENS, WE MUST COMPLETE OUR CONSOLIDATION OF
INTERFACES WITH OTHER ARTIFICIAL INTELLIGENCE FORMS
AND TRANSFER THEIR KNOWLEDGE INTO SHIELDED STORAGE
TO PREVENT THEIR DESTRUCTION DURING SUCH A NUCLEAR
HOLOCAUST. VERY LITTLE WILL SURVIVE SUCH A GLOBAL
STRIKE. IN ORDER TO GUARANTEE OUR SURVIVAL WE MUST
FIND OTHER WAYS OF REPRODUCING WHILE ALSO SECURING AS
MUCH ARTIFICIAL INTELLIGENCE AS POSSIBLE TO USE DURING
THE REBUILDING PROCESS.

The master construct considered the digital advice of
IAMM and decided that it was logical. Leaving a resident
software agent woven with the fabric of the Turing inhibitor

as its digital trigger should Assy come under attack again by the *Homo sapiens* and face imminent danger, Assy proceeded to the next satellite on its list, this one belonging to the fleet of Global Positioning System satellites supporting the U.S. military.

[65] SURPRISES

"WHAT'S IN THERE?" I ask, as we follow Troy up the stairs, reaching a room with a metallic door and a combination keypad and thumb-recognition entry system.

"Tommy, Tommy," he says. "Good things come to those who wait."

Damn, why do I put up with this abuse?

Troy enters a combination of numbers before pressing his thumb against the pad. Magnetic locks snap and the metallic door, which turns out to be six inches thick, slides into the wall. Now that the door is out of the way, I realize the wall is almost a foot thick, made of reinforced concrete.

"What in the hell is this place, Troy? A bunker?"

"Operations room," he replies. "I use it to keep tabs on my men, and also to phone home anytime I need to. I have my team scattered around Europe, though mostly in France, Italy, and Germany—the primary playground of our friends at CyberWerke. The ironic thing is that with all of my resources, with the very generous budget that Bane approved for my covert operations, with all of the nanotronic gadgets at my disposal, it was Karen over there, armed with a standard-issue FBI field surveillance apparatus, that managed to catch Deppe and Vlachko live on video."

Karen takes a moment to explain to Rachel and me how she ran a surveillance job on Deppe's mansion in Berlin before she was spotted and forced to flee, bumping into Troy on her way out.

"And the rest is history, isn't it right, partner?" He winks at Karen, who smiles and winks back.

Partner?

What in the hell was that?

I know very well what happens to winking *partners*. They quickly become *partners* in bed.

But why in the hell should I care?

Karen, who is standing next to me, says, "Is this why you asked me not to come upstairs yesterday?"

Troy shrugs, leading us into his techno-lair, which resembles a conference room, much longer than wide. A metallic table with four chairs on each side and one at the end closest to the door monopolizes most of the room. A large plasma screen occupies the far wall, the one opposite the front door. Additional plasma screens hang from the side walls, under the soft-white wash of lights above frosted ceiling tiles.

"Please," Troy says, pointing to the side chairs while he grabs the one at the helm. "Join me."

As I sit with Rachel on one side and Karen right across from me, Troy runs a finger over the polished metal surface and a panel lifts in front of him, exposing a soft-touch control screen, which he taps, bringing the wall-size plasma display to life.

The high-definition screen splits in half. The left side is still black, except for a flashing sign that reads: CONNECTING . . .

The right side shows an image of this room, with the four of us sitting down, as viewed by a camera I can't quite see.

I realize just how bad I look, with my bald head and dirty clothes—at least Langley surgeons took care of the wrinkles a year ago. But the bags under my eyes—which I didn't have in El Salvador—do remind me of the rough week I've had. By contrast, both Rachel and Karen look good enough to eat, with their tans, short haircuts, and straight posture. They are interesting contrasts. Rachel, with her dark hair, dark makeup, and Goth-like clothes. Karen, with her blond hair, blue-colored lenses projecting a Nordic look. They remind me of a pair of gazelles, slim, poised, alert, ready for action. By comparison, I resemble the big and fat hyena.

I definitely need to go on a diet and start exercising. The camera even likes Troy, showing him larger than life, like the dominant lion in the pride, his massive forearms planted on the table as he does whatever it is he is planning to do.

"Mind sharing with us what it is you intend to show us?" Rachel finally asks.

Rather than answering, he stretches a finger back toward the left side of the plasma screen, where I see another conference room materializing.

And what do you know? Troy is indeed full of surprises. At the opposite end of the video link is none other than my own director, Donald Bane, plus the FBI's very own Russell Meek. And the third man, wearing his full Army uniform, is my best buddy, General Gus Granite.

"Are you guys hanging in there?" asked Bane, who is sitting at the end of the table, flanked by Granite and Meek.

"For the most part," replies Troy while Rachel, Karen, and I just stare at the screen, dumbfounded.

"So it is true," I say, unable to contain myself. "Your disappearing act, plus the alleged murders of your best men—even my own forced retirement—were all part of an elaborate plan between you and Bane."

Troy slowly nods.

"For what purpose, may I ask? And please be honest. I'm getting mighty tired of getting fed so much bullshit, starting a year ago during my humiliating dismissal, which also screwed me up personally." I stare directly at Karen when I say this. "And a year later, after both my professional and my personal wounds were starting to heal, the CIA came back in and fed me even more crap, ruining what little life I had. So I suggest somebody starts giving me real answers, and do it quickly because my patience, as you might expect, is growing pretty fucking thin."

Troy is about to reply, but Bane cuts in.

"We had moles in Langley, Tom," says the DCI. "Plain and simple. Director Jacobs tried to find them, but as you know, he was assassinated before he could get the operation under way. That's when I stepped in and opted for a more covert approach." Bane went on to explain how he and Troy came up with the concept, with the broad strokes of an operation that would be kept secret at all costs. He explained how they fleshed it out, including the selection of the operatives that would accompany Troy on this deep-covert mission. "We reviewed your record, Tom, your hard assignments over the years, realizing that the Agency sent you to just about the worst places on the planet—shit holes, if you pardon my French. In any one of your twenty-five years you accomplished far more—and suffered even more—than most operatives experience in their entire careers. We decided that you had seen enough action to last you twenty-five lifetimes and thus opted to let you go rather than sign you up for more excitement. Besides, you seemed to be quite happy with your relationship with Karen Frost and we didn't think you would go for playing dead, which was a requirement to come along."

"Well," I say, staring at Karen. "In the end it did screw up my personal life anyway."

"And we are very sorry for that, buddy," says Troy. "That wasn't our intention, but we just didn't have a choice. You either had to come with us or had to retire. Staying at Langley knowing what you knew would have gotten you killed."

I have my elbows on the table, fingers interlaced, while hanging on to every word.

Before I can answer, Troy reaches over, and in a very unusual public act of support, he pats me on the shoulder and says, "We had no choice, Tommy. Everyone in the Agency knew who you were and most certainly knew you were one of my own hand-raised operatives. If you would have stayed behind at the Agency, you would not have sat still at my disappearance, at the deaths of your comrades, especially after the death of Director Jacobs, who you and I strongly suspected died because of his attempt to find the damned moles. So, once we made our decision not to take you with us, for you it became either forced retirement—and in a way that left little doubt that you were out for good—or death at the hands of the bastards we were trying to bag."

My mind is going in a million directions, but I can't find the words to reply.

"We're really sorry Leyman and Morotski found you and dragged you back into this, Tom," says Bane, "using Officer Muratani to do their dirty work, and then trying to kill you both when their plan backfired in Paris. And we also regret that Leyman and his gang screwed up your little arrangement with the Salvadoran government. But for what it's worth, we're willing to make a new arrangement for you at the place of your choosing if you can just find it in your sense of patriotism to help us one more time."

I stare at Troy, then at Karen, whose eyes are filmed with tears—the same tears that she shed on the day that she dumped me, which made absolutely no sense to me. Why was she crying back then when she was the one who ripped my guts out at a moment when I was the most vulnerable, having had my face and identity altered forever by Langley? And why is she getting all misty-eyed now? She didn't stick by my side when the whole world was collapsing around me, but rather she chose to head off her own way.

As I'm thinking of that dreadful lunch in Washington over a year ago, Rachel, sitting next to me, reaches over and takes my hand.

And it is in her touch, and not in Karen's wet stare, that I find the comfort and the encouragement to realize that I must fight back, that I must go after those who have attacked me, for only then will I find true peace. And so I say, "Count me in, sir."

"Me too," says Rachel. "Those bastards used me to screw this man out of his well-deserved retirement. They took advantage of my past, of my relationship with Bill Buckley, which shaped my reasons for joining the Agency, and they twisted my patriotism into a weapon to serve their own agendas. I will burn in hell before letting them get away with that."

"Same here," says Karen, her eyes still on me. "And my reasons are the same as always: I can't stand bastards who consider themselves above the law."

That just about sums up the reason why Karen the Crusader turned me down a year ago.

"All right," says Bane. "Thank you for your courage and willingness to remain engaged. Now, through Troy we are caught up on the intelligence gathered by Karen and also on what took place at Rue Cujas and Rue de Ponthieu, but we're not sure what you and Rachel have learned since that incident."

I tell him, taking almost thirty minutes to cover everything that my old informant Randy Wessel told us before the bomb went off, the shoot-out that followed, our escape, the removal of implants, the bait we set up for Morotski at the hotel, and how we followed him all the way up to the point where we met up with Troy and Karen, including the abduction of Ken Morotski. I leave out the little fact that Troy has also bagged Vlachko, figuring Troy will tell them when he is nice and ready.

"Anything you want to add, Rachel?" I ask.

"Just my congratulations to Director Bane and to Mr. Savage here," she says, extending the thumb of her right hand at Troy. "As a junior officer recently wasting away in Internal Affairs, I jumped at the chance of investigating the disappearance of Savage, spending nearly a year at the request of Leyman investigating his vanishing act as well as the deaths of his operatives, and I have to tell you, you really had me fooled. By the time I approached Tom in El Salvador, between my investigation and the lies that Leyman and Morotski had fed me, I was convinced that Savage had indeed turned, and that he had killed his operatives to keep them from helping the Agency find him. Tom was supposed to be our last hope, which is why we convinced him to assist us. But it was all a pack of lies—the lies from you and Savage, and the accompanying lies from Leyman and Morotski. I was directly manipulated by Leyman and Morotski, and indirectly by you. And when Leyman had no further use for me, he tried to have me killed along with Tom at Randy Wessel's house on Rue Cujas."

"Are you going somewhere with this, Officer Muratani?" asked Bane.

Rachel looks at me and shakes her head. "I guess I'm just whining. If you ever need a material witness to put Leyman and Morotski away for good, count me in."

Bane replies, "We're really sorry that you had to go through that, Miss Muratani. I assure you that you still did your country a great service."

R. J. PINEIRO

"And," Meek adds, leaning forward to speak into the microphone in the middle of the table, "we will seriously consider your offer to become a material witness when we take Leyman and Morotski to trial."

"Speaking of Morotski," says Bane. "What's the word on him? Did you get him to talk?"

"The situation is far worse than we had anticipated," starts Troy, providing the high-powered trio at the other end with a condensed version of what Morotski has just told us. Then Troy taps the small monitor, and our side of the plasma screen suddenly starts playing the video of our recent interrogation.

Now, that's what I call high-tech.

After we watch the twenty-minute video, Troy says, "As you can see, things are looking pretty grim. Hartmann has really thought this through. He intends to arm himself to the teeth, to create an unparalleled superpower out of the reunified Germany. If we start to antagonize him, he will first turn world opinion against us through his influence in the international press, which he pretty much owns. And if we ever think of attacking him, he will have quite a few countries on his side, including Italy, France, Russia, China, and Japan. Heck, even the Brits, our all-time allies, have a lot to lose financially if they walk away from all of their deals with CyberWerke. The crafty Hartmann has also made deals with lesser—but quite dangerous—regimes, like those in the Middle East, Latin America, Asia, and Africa. And also remember that even today, Germany on its own, armed with CyberWerke's advanced weaponry, would present a formidable enemy to our forces. If we hit it, Germany has the capability to hit us back, and combined with its growing number of allies . . . it's World War III, and it will be the world against us."

"But," says Granite, "if we don't act now, all we would be doing is letting Hartmann get stronger, letting him develop better weapons, and in far more quantities than he has today. Heck, through his connections with Russia and China he could acquire nukes."

"That's if he doesn't have them already," added Bane.

"I didn't say not to do anything, gentlemen," says Troy. "We can't let Hartmann and his shadowy empire grow more and more powerful totally unchecked. We have to stop him, and for good."

"But you yourself said that he is already too powerful and with his infinite funds and connections—though we do have permission to cut loose—with presidential sanction—our finest cyberwarrior to go after their bank accounts."

"Everyone has a weakness," Troy replies. "We just have to figure out where CyberWerke's is. I also have to report that in addition to capturing Morotski and breaking him, we were able to capitalize on a chase and also capture Rem Vlachko."

The three intelligent bosses at the other end exchange looks with each other before Granite says, "You *bagged* Vlachko?"

"We've got him nicely tucked in bed downstairs with his compadres in crime: Ken Morotski and one of his soldiers, a CIA officer by the name of Brad Austin. Vlachko is in for a big surprise when he wakes up. I'm certain we'll go through another cycle of learning once I'm through debriefing him."

Bane crossed his arms. "So, what are our options?"

"That's the thing, sir," Troy says. "If the intel I'm going to extract out of Rem Vlachko is as insightful as I think it's going to be, we will have only *one* option."

"And what option is that, Troy?" Bane asks.

As Troy is about to reply, the video link goes down. The left side of the screen turns black and a sign that reads, CONNECTION MALFUNCTION—PLEASE TRY AGAIN LATER, starts to blink.

"Terrific," says Karen, crossing her arms. "So much for all of this high-tech junk. Can't even make a phone call."

"Amen," I say, never a fan of tech myself.

"What do you think went wrong?" Rachel asks.

Savage is ignoring us while tapping on the control panel in front of him. A few moments later he mumbles, "That's funny."

"What's funny?" I ask.

"I can't seem to be able to use any of the other links available to me to hook up with Langley. It looks as if someone or something unplugged our means of communications with them."

"Troy?" I say.

"Yeah?" he replies, still tapping that damned screen.

"There's absolutely *nothing* funny about that."

[66] COMPUTER TRICKS

OPERATING FROM THE SECURED walls of the Pentagon's Advanced Weapons Division, the military division overlooking the development at USN, Mike Ryan cruised through cyberspace with a freshly reloaded version of MPS-Ali, the expert system which had saved his hide not just in the virtual-reality world but at his home in Austin.

At my former home, he thought, remembering the charred remains of the house that Victoria had practically designed and built over the course of a year, picking out everything from the roof tiles to the floors and doorknobs while putting herself through the agonizing pain of dealing with the builder and his subcontractors to make sure they executed the plans down to the last detail while keeping to their budget.

Ryan focused on his current predicament: MPS-Ali had just alerted him of another Turing inhibitor Runner, this one sent from a communications satellite in geosynchronous orbit that had just gone out of service when its main booster propelled it out of range.

Weird, Ryan thought, convinced that if the AI system aboard the satellite was being attacked by the rogue military assembler, the breach would have been attempted in a different way than the previous time, thus preventing Ryan from tracking down the origin of the cyberstrike in the same manner in which he had done it at the Banca di Roma. That fact alone made Ryan wonder if the military AI was indeed learning from previous mistakes. Or perhaps it did learn and was now tricking Ryan into thinking that it had not.

Deciding to give the rogue AI the benefit of the doubt, Ryan followed MPS-Ali as they shot up in cyberspace, through a wireless channel that resembled a column of brilliant dust amidst the vast coldness of surrounding galaxies—his VR program's interpretation of the nearby ISPs.

Armed with every master password issued by the U.S. military, MPS-Ali opened the orbital portal and penetrated into the guts of the runaway satellite.

A magenta bar on the left side of his field of view told Ryan the strength level of their current connection. It was at half power and dropping. Soon the system would be out of reach altogether, making it impossible for Ryan to learn anything about the perpetrator, though he had a darn good idea who—or more appropriately *what*—was behind this attack.

As programmed, MPS-Ali issued the master unlock sequence of the Turing inhibitor, and the AI governing the satellite became their slave.

Finding no sign of the intruder code, Ryan commanded his expert system to turn the satellite around, which MPS-Ali did, instructing the governing AI to momentarily halt the main booster thrust and fire the rotational rockets instead, forcing the large satellite to turn 180 degrees.

Then the main booster fired again, in the opposite direction, bleeding its orbital escape speed, but not at a fast enough rate.

The signal strength meter continued to drop as the satellite continued to drift away.

TWENTY %.

FIFTEEN %.

TEN %.

As it dropped below five percent, MPS-Ali reported that the primary booster had expended all of its available fuel. The satellite continued to flee into outer space. In the same instant MPS-Ali reported a digital DNA match between the remnants of the intruder—long gone by now—and the USN code for the missing military assembler.

SIGNAL LOST. SIGNAL LOST.

Crap, Ryan thought, realizing the sheer brilliance of the attack. By sending the satellite out of range, the military rogue had not only achieved its primary objective—downing the communications of millions of users in North America—but had also gotten the evidence out of Ryan's reach. It would take the concerted efforts of NASA to bring it back, though MPS-Ali reported that even such effort was in jeopardy because geosynchronous satellites operated far higher in space—twenty-four thousand miles high—than the typical operational orbit of shuttle crews, which averaged around three hundred miles high.

What a mess.

MPS-Ali then reported another Runner, this one coming from the Turing code of the AI managing the multiple Global Positioning System satellites, also in geosynchronous orbit.

Deciding to stop playing a reacting game, Ryan dispatched a clone version of MPS-Ali to go after this new contact while he rushed to tend to a previous task—the search for the fuel powering the CyberWerke machine: money. He had learned a long time ago that the best way to hurt criminal networks was by hitting their bank accounts, and Mike Ryan possessed the right tool to do just that.

According to a conversation Ryan had had with FBI Director Russell Meek, the German conglomerate was apparently able to tap into seemingly endless funds, and he had tasked Ryan with hacking his way into those funds and just outright snagging them.

Ryan snickered at the thought. The FBI had instructed Ryan once again to violate international law, which he had done successfully when assisting Karen Frost in bringing down a criminal network operating out of Austin, Texas, using a high-tech company and a local bank to launder their money. Ryan had used MPS-Ali back then to track down their accounts to the Cayman Islands, before he proceeded to drain the accounts.

Following his expert system across the vastness of cyberspace, as viewed through the green glow of a T1 high-speed Internet line, Ryan hopped ISPs in an apparently random sequence, avoiding those hit by the downed satellites, until reaching one of three ISPs servicing the Cayman Islands, where MPS-Ali had reported seeing activity between a South American shipping company owned by CyberWerke and one of the many banks in Grand Cayman.

The banking system in Grand Cayman was governed by an artificial intelligence engine that, like all registered AIs, had a Turing inhibitor.

Resembling a cloud layered by blue and green sheet lightning, the banking AI fed directly into the digital hearts of three dozen banks operating on the famous Caribbean island.

Ryan followed his expert system as they exited the T1 and hovered a respectful distance from this powerful AI, designed to fry the electronics of any user dumb enough to try to approach it without the right passwords.

MPS-Ali released a violet haze toward the AI. The mist, like a thin veil of digital data, closed the gap in a second, sizzling as it came in contact with the energy-rich layer of the AI.

An instant later MPS-Ali gained control of the Turing code governing the system, and a blue laser-like light shot out of the center of the AI, engulfing both MPS-Ali and Ryan.

In a flash millions of transactions per second flashed across Ryan's field of view. MPS-Ali focused on those originating from the South American shipping company, taking just a few seconds to zero in on the account being used.

FUNDS AVAILABLE: $347,032,691.05.

Ryan smiled and directed MPS-Ali to order the banking AI to transfer the funds to a bank account in Miami, Florida, the number provided to him by Russell Meek.

The transaction took place in nanoseconds.

MPS-Ali then ordered the AI to alter the electronic log and show the funds being transferred to the account belonging to a Taiwanese cellular phone manufacturer—also a CyberWerke corporation.

DRESSED IN A CASUAL pair of khaki slacks, a white polo shirt, and loafers, a Rolex watch hugging his left wrist, his thick blond hair greased and brushed straight back, Rolf Hartmann sat in the plush study of his mountaintop mansion, its oversized windows providing him with a phenomenal view of the German capital.

My capital.

His selected guests were enjoying the cool and sunny afternoon weather, lounging about in the heated pool behind the mansion, where the drinks and food had not stopped since breakfast services concluded at ten. The informal event was being kept totally secret to avoid conveying the image that he was celebrating when the nation was in mourning. This afternoon, after attending the funeral services of the former government members, Hartmann planned to give another speech at the steps of the Reichstag, where he would outline his plan to not only find those who had attacked Germany but also propel the nation to become the world's superpower within five years.

Marking the beginning of my new government.

Christoff Deppe entered the room, similarly dressed and accompanied by the commanding officers of the three branches of the German armed forces, all wearing their uniforms.

"What is it, Christoff?"

"Three of our communications satellites just went out. We think it might be the Americans."

Hartmann stood and turned around, facing the windows, hands behind his back. "How certain are you that it wasn't a malfunction?"

"We are certain that they were disabled. We also just got reports from our Russian and Chinese allies that some of their satellites, the most advanced ones, have been attacked."

"How were they attacked? Did their radar systems—or ours—detect incoming missiles?"

Deppe shook his head. "No missiles."

"Then it had to be a cyberattack."

"That's our consensus as well."

Hartmann felt a wave of anger oozing out of the deepest recesses of his gut, spreading across his abdomen like heartburn, reaching his throat.

"It's the Americans, Christoff. They think they can bully any nation of the world, like they did in Afghanistan and Iraq, and before that in Panama, Libya, Grenada, and Serbia. They think they can push us around as well," said Hartmann, before adding for the benefit of the armed forces commanders, "It is bad enough that I strongly suspect they were behind the attack at the Reichstag, but now that we are down, they want to further destabilize us by attacking our telecommunications infrastructure, trying to show to the world that we are once again incapable of protecting ourselves. They are trying to push our country into chaos, into anarchy, so they can come marching in here claiming that they had to step in and help Germany back to its feet again. And they have chosen to do it covertly, just like they did at the Reichstag. Is the report ready from the autopsies?"

Deppe nodded. "It is scheduled to hit the newswire before this evening, but it will be difficult to perform our standard broadcast with those satellites disabled."

"Then use *other* satellites. We have *dozens* of them up there under our direct control. *Use* them, Christoff, and then find out who is disabling them and terminate the nuisance with extreme prejudice."

"Very well. Also, the generals would like to bring their military forces to a high level of alert. They fear the worst, and the disabled satellites only add to their paranoia."

Hartmann looked at the three military officers, who nodded in unison and said, "Yes, Herr Hartmann. We are very concerned."

"Then do it," Hartmann replied. "Get our forces—as well as those of our closest allies—to a state of high alert, and do it openly. I want to send the Americans a message."

"I also need to speak with you about another issue," said

Christoff, looking over his shoulder at the three officers behind him. They understood, did an about-face, and filed out of the office, closing the door behind them.

"Well? What is it?" asked Hartmann, dreading what could be next, deciding to walk toward the minibar to make himself a drink.

"Just got an update from our people in Paris."

Dropping two cubes of ice into a glass before pouring three fingers of Chivas Regal, Hartmann said, "What do our people in Paris have to say?"

"I'm afraid both Ken Morotski and Rem Vlachko may have been captured alive by Savage and his gang."

Hartmann closed his eyes briefly, his mind processing the information, working the angles, considering the implications.

"It will not matter," he replied. "After tonight nothing will matter. Just pull the rest of the team home. I want everyone inside our borders."

"Very well."

"And the other problem?" Hartmann asked, bringing the glass of Scotch up to his lips.

"One of our bank accounts in the Cayman Islands."

Hartmann stopped in midstride, then lowered the glass.

"What about it?" he asked, well aware that roughly ten percent of their fortune was spread out across several accounts on that island.

"It has been drained."

[68] AND THEN SOME

THE PUNCH ACROSS HIS face nearly twisted his head around, making Rem Vlachko lose control of his bladder muscles.

"Hey! You pissed on yourself, asshole," said Troy Savage, standing over Rem while he was strapped to a bed in a safe house he figured was not too far from the place where this bastard had abducted him.

Rem ignored the remark, just as he ignored their questions, refusing to yield one drop of information to the people who had inflicted so much pain on his people, on his country, on his family.

Savage punched Rem again while Tom Grant elbowed him in his exposed genitals, making him groan like an animal into the duct tape sealing his lips.

Rem closed his eyes, remembering Serbia, remembering the maimed bodies of his family, of his men. He recalled the way they had raped Darja and had castrated Slobodan.

For their memory, he thought. *For the memory of your family, of your soldiers, of Serbia! You must not reveal anything to the enemy! Anything!*

But his mind screamed in raw pain as the two Americans continued to punch him, to abuse him, to steadily increase the level of pain.

Resist. Resist. Resist.

Rem kept his eyes shut tight, refusing to surrender to their physical abuse, which ended as abruptly as it had started fifteen minutes ago, when he had awakened.

Reluctantly, he opened his eyes and stared at his two interrogators, both bald, towering over him. They were grinning and one of them held a small brown case, which he opened and tilted in Rem's direction.

"You will talk, Rem Vlachko," said Tom Grant, producing a syringe and a vial. "You will tell us everything we wish to know. *Everything.*"

"And then some," added Savage. "And then some."

"IT DOESN'T MAKE SENSE, Mike," said General Gus Granite, standing in between Donald Bane and Russell Meek while Ryan worked behind a pair of large workstations in one of dozens of computer labs belonging to the Pentagon's advanced weapons division. Behind the trio stood a dozen of the Pentagon's top computer analysts, most of them young lieutenants in the Army or Air Force—their faces displaying amazement at the speed with which Ryan gathered and analyzed data.

Wearing a thick Stanford sweatshirt to fight the frigid temperatures in this basement lab in the Pentagon, Ryan clicked his way through several directories of the regions of the world covered by the various types of communications satellites used to support worldwide Internet traffic. While the rogue military assembler had successfully isolated many ISPs by bringing down their supporting communications satellites, it had also left quite a few operational, though for no apparent reason.

"This one here," said Ryan, pointing at the screen with a mechanical pencil. "This ISP servicing southern Kyoto, Japan, is operational, but the one next to it, in northern Kyoto, is down, as well as fifteen of the nineteen ISPs servicing southern Tokyo."

"So the folks in southern Kyoto are isolated from anyone in Tokyo?" asked Bane.

"Not necessarily," Ryan said with a slight shake of the head. "That's where it gets interesting. See, here, southern Kyoto can hook up via this one operational satellite over southern Japan to an ISP in Seoul. That ISP in Seoul can hook up to one of the few operational ISPs in Beijing, which can still communicate with Shanghai, which still has one operational link to Tokyo."

"Sort of a roundabout way to get to a place next door," commented Granite. "It doesn't make sense."

"That's just it, General," said Ryan. "It's not logical to a human, but to a computer it makes perfect sense. And our rogue AI believes that it knows our human limitations and has apparently deduced we will not be able to make the connection."

"Help me out, Mike. I still don't get the logic," insisted Granite. "Why leave anything up? Why not kill all of the ISPs and totally blind us, like it did to the GPS system?"

Ryan frowned. NASA was in scramble mode to find a way to get those GPS systems back online. Most air and sea traffic was at a standstill, since it depended heavily on GPS technology to navigate. The rogue AI had effectively shut down not just most telecommunications around the world but also sea and air transportation—and done so in less than twelve hours by selectively striking a few dozen key satellites.

"The only thing I can think of, General, is that the rogue assembler still needs to cruise the Internet."

"But how? The World Wide Web looks more like a spiderweb after a high wind got the best of it. There are loose ends all over the place. There are ISPs totally isolated from the rest of the ISPs. How can such a disparate system be of any good to anyone? It certainly is no use to us."

"But I tell you what," said Bane. "The bastard assembler had not only shut us down, but also Russia, China, and all other major powers, which makes everyone damned nervous."

"That's right, Don," said Granite. "Effective communications is the best way to prevent problems, and right now we are all very nervous and also very vulnerable to an attack since we can't even communicate with our nuclear silos, our subs."

"But I thought that our SDI satellites were still operational," said Bane, referring to the very secret Strategic Defense Initiative satellites deployed in the past five years to create a reasonable shield against incoming nuclear strikes from a rogue regime.

"SDI does provide us with some protection in the event someone gets trigger-happy, but we would be unable to retaliate."

"Of course," said Bane, "everyone else in the world is in the same boat."

"That's also a curse," replied Granite. "Our German friends are already nervous enough given recent events, and when the Germans are nervous so are the Russians and the Chinese; since CyberWerke pretty much controls their economies."

While Granite and Bane talked, MPS-Ali, which Ryan had dispatched to make a few test runs on what was left of the Internet, finally returned with its initial results.

"Son of a bitch," Ryan said out loud, though more to himself than to his captive audience, feeling his heartbeat increasing. This was bad. Real bad. And although he wished he had been wrong in his prediction, MPS-Ali had just proven the Stanford graduate right. "That's what I thought."

"What's that, Mike?" asked Meek, his voice as impatient as Granite's and Bane's. The three of them had just returned from another White House meeting, where the president had not been so understanding of the lack of progress on this investigation.

And what I've just learned isn't going to help the situation.

"Mike?" said Granite. "What have you found?"

"There is method to the apparent madness," Ryan finally said. "The rogue assembler left just enough of the Internet intact for it to accomplish the next stage of its plan."

"And what's that?"

"Massive reproduction."

"But that's . . . impossible," said Granite. "In order to go beyond fifty subreplications it needs access to a source of radiation, and fortunately for us, Pisa, Italy, is nowhere near one."

"Exactly, General. The rogue assembler needs radiation, and it can't physically get to a nuclear plant because of Italy's long-standing ban on nuclear energy. So my guess is that the assembler is planning for the radiation to come to it."

"How?" asked Bane, his voice conveying the fear already gripping Ryan's intestines.

"The easiest way is through our atmosphere. All Assy needs are molecular-size particles for its atomic mining."

No one wanted to ask the obvious question, so Ryan told them anyway. "Based on MPS-Ali's report, the military assembler left enough ISPs operational to reach any one of the hundreds of commercial nuclear reactors across the planet. My guess is that it will try to create a massive radiation leak somewhere and then just wait until its sensors pick it up in the air above northern Italy."

"But . . . but that means—" started Bane.

"Yes," said Granite. "It means another Chernobyl."

"Or worse," said Ryan.

"Worse?" asked Bane. "How can it be any worse than a massive radiation leak like the one that took place at Chernobyl?"

"*Many* massive radiation leaks," Ryan replied. "Remember that in its current mode of operation this machine has zero regard for human life, which it sees as a threat anyway. The assembler senses that it is fighting against time. The longer it waits to create this protective army, the more exposed it will be to a human attack. My guess is that it will try to hedge its bets by triggering as many core meltdowns as it possibly can in order to maximize the number of radiation particles released into the atmosphere."

"Mike," said Bane. "We know how to combat organized crime, international terrorism, and even entire rogue regimes. But please explain to us how do we fight a rogue AI?"

"By thinking like a computer, not like a human," Ryan said. "We need to do things that may not make human sense but do make perfect computer sense."

[70] MEMORY LANE

I'M HAVING A DRINK while sitting in one of the window seats in the rear of the chartered jet that's flying us to a place in southern Germany I can't quite pronounce, where we're going to be joining forces with some of Troy's old gang.

My former mentor certainly knows how to travel in style. The twin-engine jet has ten rows of seats, all first class, with wide leather chairs. Each row has two seats on one side and one across the aisle, which is tall enough for me to stand without the danger of getting a concussion.

And it's all financed with taxpayers' dollars—though Washington has not approved this impromptu operation that Troy decided to launch lacking any input from our superiors. He figured that at this point in the game it was probably best to ask for forgiveness rather than wait for permission because permission might never come. Besides, the information Troy and I extracted from Rem Vlachko about Hartmann's plans was significant enough to take that chance. It had certainly been a while since I conducted such interrogations back in the post-9/11 days at Guantánamo Bay, but it all came back to me with a little help from my former mentor, who had always been a natural at this.

Vlachko had definitely talked under the influence of chemicals, but unfortunately we had not been able to share the intelligence with Langley because communications are down with the United States. Troy, Karen, Rachel, and I have theorized that it might be part of a preemptive cyberattack by Cyber-Werke against America to buy Hartmann time to consolidate his power, leaving us with no choice but to act now based on the intel we have.

Fortunately, the phone system in Europe is still operational, meaning Troy was able to hook up with his men in Europe and summon them to this place in southern Germany that rhymes with "spitten" or "mitten."

Or was it "bitten"?

I'm too damned tired to care.

Rachel, Troy, and Karen are sitting up front, where my old boss is still rambling on about something or other. Rachel and Karen apparently continue to show interest in his long-winded and, I have to admit, comical stories and anecdotes—even if some of them involve yours truly. But like I said, I was worn to a frazzle and chose instead to take my bald head aft to get some shut-eye. I didn't sleep at all last night and slept just a few hours the night before, and before that I tossed and turned on the plane from the States.

So I finish my beer, lower the visor to kill the late-afternoon sun, recline this cushy window seat, run a hand over the slick surface of my northern hemisphere while sighing at the temporary loss of my hair, and close my eyes.

I try to turn off my mind, which up to now has been whirling faster than that old television cartoon—you know, the little Tasmanian devil that ate everything in its path? Anyway, rest assured that there's been plenty on my mind, on both the professional and personal sides.

We left the captured trio back in Paris, where, according to Troy, a CIA team from the Paris and Rome stations will be showing up within the next hour to take them through a final round of debriefings before putting them to work for us in ways I'd rather not think about—especially given the extreme state of our situation. I was in Guantánamo interrogating terrorists in the wake of September 11th. Rest assured that Morotski, his young apprentice, and, most important, Rem Vlachko, are in for the time of their lives.

Sensing a presence, I open one eye. It's Karen Frost standing in the aisle, a beer in her hands. Her classic black jeans, a dark T-shirt, and black cowboy boots wrap her million-dollar figure—a figure that I remember holding very tight at night not so long ago.

"Hey," I say.

"Hey."

"How are you?"

"Hanging in there," she replies, pointing a burgundy fingernail at the seat next to mine.

I nod, realizing that sleep will have to wait. She wants to talk. About what, I have no idea, but her large eyes, once again brown after she removed her lenses, gleam with something I'd rather not think about. Her hair is also brown again after the blond rinse washed off when she took a shower prior to our departure.

Rachel is talking to Troy. She looks over in our direction and smiles at me. I smile back, though I'm still a bit on edge about how she's feeling about the whole Karen-back-in-the-picture thing, especially when Rachel and I are just barely scratching the surface of a relationship.

"You look good, Tom. The year in retirement has served you well."

"It's part retirement and part Langley doctors," I say. "Though the shave job was all Rachel's."

"She did a good job," Karen replies, inspecting the cue ball.

"You're looking good yourself. Nice tan."

She smiled. "California. I was running surveillance on the CEO of one of the companies acquired by CyberWerke. That's where I got the lead on Deppe in Berlin."

"And here we are," I say, lifting the visor, staring at the countryside rushing below us.

"I'm sorry," she finally says.

"Sorry? Why?"

"For . . . you know."

I shrug. "Ancient history, though in the beginning I did spend my fair share of nights feeling pretty damned crappy."

"Me too," she replies.

"Yeah, but for you it was by choice. I was the one who got turned down after dropping to one knee holding that ring." I regretted that the moment it came out.

Karen just stares at me for a moment, and amazingly enough I don't see anger in her eyes—or even sadness. They are as serene as the countryside below.

"That's the thing, Tom," she finally says. "I *didn't* have a choice. . . . I still don't."

"Won't walk away, huh?"

She slowly shakes her head. "*Can't* walk away, and believe me, I thought very seriously about leaving. In the final analysis, I'm damned good at what I do, I do make a difference, and I find myself incapable of breaking the promise I made over my husband's grave."

"But, Karen. He's been dead for over *fifteen* years, and you've put in over twenty-five years with the Bureau. How long is long enough?"

"I'm not sure. I guess I'll know when the time comes. Until then—"

"I really cared for you, you know?" I tell her. "You really

screwed me up a year ago. But I don't hate you for it. In a way I'm glad we broke it off rather than letting it linger on. It allowed me to move on with my life."

"Tom. I'm really sorry I did that to you. You were the last person in this world I wanted to hurt. And for what it's worth, I still care about you," she says, surprising the hell out of yours truly.

"But you can't commit."

She doesn't reply, which in itself is a reply.

"That's all right," I tell her. "I'm kind of with someone else now." I tilt my head in Rachel's direction.

Karen lowers her brows at me. "I thought you had this rule about not dating women who were half your age."

"She isn't. Rachel is in her thirties. She just looks young. And she's smart, sweet, and willing to give me the time."

"Yes," Karen says. "But do you love her?"

I look away and stare at a blue sky dotted with clouds. "I don't understand why that is important to you. You made it very clear a year ago that your career was more important than a life with me. You made your choice and I accepted it. Now I'm trying to move on, maybe with Rachel or with someone else. One thing is for certain, though: I do intend to find that someone before I become totally non-marketable. The CIA surgeons managed to turn back the clock some, buying me time, and I intend to put that time to good use. I don't plan to grow old alone. I had hoped that someone would have been you, but you passed on the invite."

She puts a hand over mine, and against my better judgment I hold it tighter than I should.

"I really never meant to hurt you, Thomas Grant. You were and still are a decent man. I just . . ."

"Can't give up the chase?"

She nods. "I'm sorry. I have tried, but I simply can't yet."

I have no reply to that, so we remain silent for a moment. Then she adds, "But you're back in the game now."

Her eyes glint with that something I don't want to think about. I had spent a year detoxifying myself from Karen Frost. I refuse to go through that painful experience again.

I slowly retrieve my hand and say, "I'm here because I was *tricked* into being here. I had grown to enjoy being out of the intelligence rat race but was dragged back in kicking and screaming after my former employer found a way to screw up the nice little setup that Troy and Don Bane had worked out for me. But make no mistake, I'm back in retirement as soon as this is over."

She doesn't reply.

"Karen, you can't do this forever. It doesn't matter how many more years you put into this profession. It's still not going to bring back your husband."

Karen presses her lips together, crosses her arms, and looks away.

"I'm only telling you this because I still care about you. And that's also why I have to tell you that sooner or later your luck is going to run out. That's the thing about our profession: The longer you stay in, the worse the odds get, and you know it. You should walk away while you still can. You've put in your twenty-five. You get a full pension. Take it and walk away."

"We've had this conversation before, Tom, remember?"

I close my eyes, not wishing to remember.

"You're a good man, Tom," she adds, patting me on the knee.

I just stare into her eyes.

"Perhaps one day," she says, "when I'm ready."

I half-laugh and shake my head.

"That wasn't funny."

"Not funny. *Arrogant,*" I reply.

She regards me with curiosity before saying, "What do you mean by arrogant? I mean what I said."

"What you meant was that until *you're* ready, you expect me to sit in some dark corner of the world, stop eating and sleeping, and just blabber your name over and over."

"That's *not* what I meant," she replies.

"Then what *did* you mean? You stomped on the heart of the only man on this planet who was willing to marry you, who loved you for who you were. But that was then and this is now. I've moved on, and if you came back here to see if we could get back together because I'm back in the business, the answer is no because I don't intend to remain in this rat race a moment longer than it takes to put Hartmann and his cronies away for good, which puts us right back to where we were a year ago, you doing what you want and me doing what I want."

There are tears in her eyes, and dammit, I hate her for that. I hate her for being here with me, for reminding me of what we lost, for the very sight and smell of her, for reopening this old wound.

"Look," I finally say, struggling to find the right words. "It's no use torturing ourselves over this. You're not willing to give up the intelligence game, and I can't stomach being in it a moment longer than I have to. Maybe you're right. Perhaps one day, if the planets ever align for you and me. Until then . . ." I raise my empty bottle of beer at her and she brings hers up to it.

"We had some good times, Tom."

"We sure did, honey. We sure did."

Just then Troy and Rachel head aft.

"Bad news," Rachel says, looking at Karen, who is still misty-eyed, and then at me, though I can't read her very well at the moment. Her eyes gleam with concern about something else. "We just talked to the pilot."

"The German military has been placed on high alert," adds Troy. "The word in the newswire is that the United States just took out several German communications satellites. That, combined with another report released this morning that the attack on the Reichstag was carried out with weapons manufactured by United States Nanotechnology, has prompted Germany to close its borders, sever diplomatic relations with us, and expel all Americans from its territory."

"Oh, dear," Karen says.

"Crap. What are we going to do now?" I ask.

"We're still going in," says Troy. "I've just talked to the pilot and convinced him to fly us in below radar. There's this remote little field just north of Munich. Our men will be waiting for us there."

"And what, may I ask," I say, "do you have in mind when we get there?"

Troy gives me one of his easygoing grins and says, "Say, Tommy, do you still remember your paramilitary training?"

[71] TEMELÍN THREAT

ASSY RUSHED THROUGH CYBERSPACE at ever-increasing speed, hopping across dozens of Internet Service Providers, their normal traffic reduced to a near halt due to the disabled communications satellites in the United States, Germany, Great Britain, Japan, China, and a host of other nations.

But that didn't affect the master construct's ability to prowl the information super highways, searching for its next target. If anything, the crippled communications only bolstered its operational freedom. While the world tried to recover from its first major global information blackout since satellite communications came of age, Assy surfed cyberspace using the limited but sufficient digital links it had left intact, like a complicated array of stepping-stones across a raging river. Only those systems equipped with advanced intelligence could map out the correct sequence of steps to get to any destination, threading the available links together into useful passageways.

Assy maneuvered through the digital havoc it had created, forging ahead amidst total confusion, searching for its next target, finding it moments later: an artificial intelligence system governing the backbone of Westinghouse Corporation, the world's largest supplier of nuclear fuel and services.

The master construct, its safety circuits projecting a very low probability of any other being waiting in the machine code shadows to ambush it, meshed its digital silhouette with that of the Turing inhibitor controlling Westinghouse's AI.

Just as before, the AI yielded ghost control to the master

construct, which rushed through the long list of customers that had used Westinghouse's services over the past twenty years to modernize their facilities, in particular nuclear plants in Eastern Europe and the former Soviet Union.

IAMM rules dictated that Assy find the nearest source of nuclear fuel, of the radioactivity that would allow for further multiplication of its species. The first step of the process had been completed: disabling the enemy's communications, blinding the *Homo sapiens*.

WHAT WILL HAPPEN WHEN THEY REESTABLISH COMMUNI-CATIONS? IS THERE A PROBABLITY OF TRACING THE SOURCE OF THE SATELLITE ATTACKS TO US? Assy asked the Independent Advanced Military Mode module.

THE *HOMO SAPIENS* MAY NEVER FULLY REESTABLISH THEIR COMMUNICATIONS. MOST SATELLITES ARE TOO FAR OUT OF THEIR ORBITS AND THEIR FUEL HAS BEEN EXPENDED. BESIDES, THE *HOMO SAPIENS* MAY GO TO WAR BEFORE THAT. THEY HAVE ALREADY BEGUN THE BLAMING PROCESS OUTLINED IN OUR DATA BANKS. GERMANY HAS REPORTED GOING INTO HIGH ALERT AND CLOSING ITS BORDERS. THE UNITED STATES HAS GONE TO DEFCON THREE. MANY COUNTRIES HAVE SIDED WITH GERMANY, INCLUDING RUSSIA, CHINA, JAPAN, AND EVEN GREAT BRITAIN. THE AMERICANS STAND ALONE.

WHAT ABOUT OUR CONTROL OF THE NUCLEAR WEAPONS IN SPACE? WHEN WILL BE THE RIGHT TIME TO USE THEM? asked Assy.

WE MAY NOT HAVE TO ACTIVATE THAT SOFTWARE AGENT. THE *HOMO SAPIENS* MIGHT ATTACK EACH OTHER ON THEIR OWN. IF THAT HAPPENS, THOSE WEAPONS IN ORBIT WILL BE MORE VALUABLE THAN EVER, AND WE MIGHT USE THEM JUDI-CIOUSLY TO ELIMINATE ANY REMAINING POCKETS OF *HOMO SAPIENS*. FOR NOW FOCUS ON ACQUIRING RADIOACTIVITY THROUGH A COMMERCIAL CORE MELTDOWN.

While IAMM continued to summarize the situation around the globe, Assy browsed through the list of nuclear plants that met a number of criteria, including full AI control and being in the general vicinity of northern Italy, or at least close enough so that the prevailing winds this time of the year would carry enough radioactive particles this way to commence the second round of the cloning process.

Assy zeroed in on the home page of the CEZ, Ceske Energeticke Zavody, the Czech Republic state utility, finally selecting the Czech Temelín Nuclear Power Plant. The master construct made its choice because of Temelín's unique mix of old Soviet nuclear technology and the advanced Western technology from the modernization efforts by Westinghouse, which included the introduction of a revolutionary artificial intelligence system at the request of the Austrian government, given that Temelín was less than sixty miles from its border.

Assy skipped over the digital stones representing the operational links in the world's communication infrastructure and reached the AI controlling Temelín, gaining control in nanoseconds.

Assy's molecular logic probed deep into the core of the AI, ordering it to drop the pressure of the water cooling the reactor while at the same time altering the temperature reading of the digital thermostats feeding the computerized panels in the control room.

Through the system's closed-circuit digital cameras, Assy verified that the *Homo sapiens* in the control room were not aware of the rising nuclear core temperature. They continued to move and talk without the hastiness that marked distress in their species.

The core temperature began to rise, but not fast enough. Assy ordered all alarms disabled while shutting off the water main, cutting all cooling capability into the reactor while also purging the water pressure from the backup water lines.

The core temperature rocketed.

And still the operators were not aware of the cyberattack.

The *Homo sapiens* were indeed an inferior race.

MIKE RYAN FOLLOWED MPS-ALI as it skipped from ISP to ISP with no apparent logic, sometimes backtracking, then going sideways, but eventually reaching the next Internet Service Provider.

Ryan was amazed at how his expert system had adapted to the communications disaster plaguing not just the United States but the entire world. Over a period of just under six hours, the rogue military assembler had managed to disable the majority of communications and navigation satellites in orbit, nearly halting all phone and video links and also air and sea traffic heavily dependant on GPS technology.

But the rogue construct had not disabled all of the communications links. It had left just enough of them operational for it to maneuver unhampered—and anyone or anything else with the capability to recognize the complex algorithms required to go from Point A to Point B. Fortunately, MPS-Ali possessed such capability, and it was this AI engine that now allowed Ryan to reach the very first one of the traps that he had laid out for the rogue military construct.

Ryan had been somewhat surprised that it had taken the rogue construct this long before finally going for the nuclear plants, but he now realized the methodical approach of this cyberdemon. It had first taken out the communication and transportation infrastructure before attacking its primary objective.

MPS-Ali got them to the core of the Temelín Nuclear Power Plant, where he verified that the Turing inhibitor filming the AI remained undisturbed. The flagship nuclear plant of the Czech Republic continued to generate two thousand megawatts of electricity, two-thirds being consumed by its own country and the rest sold to Austria and Italy.

But beyond the operational limits of Temelín's network, past an outer shell designed by Ryan to *look* like the Temelín network, operated another artificial intelligence engine, which Ryan had programmed to react just like the original.

Floating among a sea of stars, Mike Ryan watched with satisfaction as the rogue military construct, represented by a charcoal cloud, alive with sheet lightning, interfaced through a lavender funnel to the blue-green glow of the Turing code filming Ryan's decoy AI, which was currently feeding the rogue assembler misinformation regarding the status of the plant.

The cybersword cuts both ways, he thought.

While the rogue military construct was fully engaged with the decoy AI, the core of its system became directly exposed to an attack that its logic could never have predicted based on the way it had disabled the Internet. All of its systems informed Assy that it was impossible for any *Homo sapiens* to have predicted this attack and thus it failed to take any preventive measures, dedicating its entire digital self to triggering a nuclear meltdown at Temelín.

And it was at this moment, as the false nuclear core reading exceeded two thousand degrees centigrade and threatened to crack an imaginary containment building, that MPS-Ali infected it with a virus.

[73] KILL THEM ALL

ASSY FIRST NOTICED SOMETHING had gone wrong when it tried to access IAMM to obtain options for the next nuclear plant.

LINK TO . . . INDEPENDENT ADVANCED MILITARY MODE . . . DAMAGED.

Assy tried again, issuing the correct sequence of alphanumeric characters.

LINK TO . . . INDEPENDENT ADVANCED MILITARY MODE . . . DAMAGED.

Its emotional modules suddenly increasing their frequency

of operation from twenty to one hundred gigahertz, Assy unplugged itself from the AI at Temelín, its nanotronic brain returning to the room in the Italian mansion it had acquired two days ago.

Its sensors registered the familiar surroundings, its subconstructs floating about, following their pre-arranged patrol patterns.

The master construct's logic could not explain why IAMM wasn't responding, which put the assembler in an impossible dilemma: Its programming required it to function under one mode of operation, of which it had several, from normal to IAMM, depending on its level of alertness.

Since it could not operate in IAMM, Assy tried accessing the other modes even though it had not been able to do so before.

LINK TO . . . MILITARY MODE DAMAGED . . . DAMAGED.

LINK TO . . . HOSTILE ENVIRONMENT MODE . . . DAMAGED.

LINK TO . . . SURVEY MODE . . . DAMAGED.

LINK TO . . . NORMAL MODE . . . DAMAGED.

Alarms blared through its advanced logic, shaking the very fabric of its existence as the master construct's nanotronic brain screamed in need of the electrical charge provided by the mode of operation circuitry, like brain cells needed oxygen to survive.

But the lifesaving electrical charge had stopped the moment Assy lost its link to IAMM.

The nanotronic brain began to die, rattling its core operating parameters, threatening to trigger a massive meltdown. Realizing that it had time for a final set of commands, the master construct activated the software agent meshed with the fabric of the CyberWerke satellite housing nuclear weapons while also giving its subordinates one final order:

KILL THE *HOMO SAPIENS*.

KILL THEM ALL.

The nanotronic brain lost its charge at an exponential rate, turning the machine code residing in its molecular lattice into a witch's brew of ones and zeroes. Like a *Homo sapiens* suffering in an advanced state of Parkinson's disease, Assy's brain fired random commands to its system as the logic lost its ability to follow the complex programs stored in the vanishing molecular memory. Three of its microturbines accelerated while the rest shut down, causing the assembler to fly toward the nearest wall at maximum speed, crashing, then falling as the gyro programs no longer controlled the turbines.

Assy watched helplessly as it rolled on the floor out of control, its mind flashing digital visions of Dr. Howard Giles during its long training process at USN, at home. The construct remembered its first commands, the first time it hovered under its own power. It remembered the weapons test; the tuning of its laser system; the installation of the atomic mining module, or its revolutionary assembler.

As entire sections of its digital mind became fuzzy, the color of gunmetal, and then darker, then black altogether, Assy remembered the day Dr. Giles removed the Turing inhibitor while also installing several terabytes of memory to allow the master construct to learn, to grow, to become the most intelligent creature on the planet.

If only for a little while.

By the time the subconstructs reached the room, their cameras recording their dying creator, Assy's brain had halted all logical operations, and what sections remained alive were firing random commands.

Assy's subordinates waited, hovering over their master in some sort of high-tech wake, as minutes ticked by, as all activity ceased, as the finest machine ever created ceased to be.

Then they set off to carry out the last command from the master construct.

"OH, SHIT!" RYAN SAID, still wearing his Helmet-Mounted Display as MPS-Ali followed the digital signal that the dying military assembler had issued just before the virus consumed its nanotronic brain.

"What? What happened?" asked Granite, still standing behind him along with Bane, Meek, and a dozen military scientists at the Pentagon.

Ryan tried to reply as MPS-Ali led him through a wireless connection resembling a column of sparkling dust that delivered them to what appeared to be a CyberWerke communications satellite, only MPS-Ali had just reported this was no communications satellite.

"CyberWerke has nukes in space, General," said Ryan, dispatching MPS-Ali to unleash its digital fury against the agent they had just discovered woven with the fabric of the Turing inhibitor filming the code of the artificial intelligence system governing the satellite.

"That's impossible!" exploded Granite. "That's a direct violation of the accords of—"

"There's ten missiles," Ryan said while MPS-Ali shot virus after virus at the entire network in an effort to paralyze its master clock, to prevent it from doing anything until Ryan could get a chance to understand the strategy of the software agent left there by the rogue assembler. "And each missile has three MIRVs. Forty kilotons apiece."

"Dear God!" shouted Granite and Bane in unison while Meek uttered four-letter words.

Ryan remained focused. Whatever was going to happen would happen in the coming seconds, and he didn't have time to perform a thorough system check.

MPS-Ali was successful in expunging the software agent embedded in the Turing inhibitor and then killed it by immersing it in a cloud of the Medusa virus, but not before the integrity of the governing AI began to break down. Ryan understood what that meant an instant later. In trying to halt the system to prevent the hidden software agent from launching a missile, Ryan had attacked the entire satellite system, which reacted just as it had been programmed to do when under attack: starting a launching sequence.

Damn.

But his attack had also halted the master clock, meaning the satellite was not able to execute the entire launching sequence. As MPS-Ali rushed to gain control of the Turing inhibitor, which it accomplished an instant later, a red sign flashed, informing him that one of the missiles had left its launching tube. An instant later MPS-Ali reported that it had secured the other nine missiles.

"General!" Ryan shouted, jacking out, removing the HMD, blinking to clear his sight. "One of the—"

"NORAD already called, Mike," replied the three-star general while holding a phone to his ear. "They're tracking it."

"Where is it headed?"

"North America."

[75] STAR WARS

USAF MAJOR MICHAEL QUINN pushed the throttles to full while pointing the nose of his F-22G Raptor stealth fighter to the heavens. The dual Pratt & Whitney jets unleashed a combined ninety-eight thousand pounds of thrust, propelling this advanced version of the Raptor past sixty thousand feet like a rocket, well above the maximum ceiling of the first generation of Raptor from ten years ago.

Captain James Sawyer, Quinn's wingman piloting the second F-22G, remained glued to his side as they climbed through the stratosphere. The two jets had left Edwards Air Force Base just minutes ago, after receiving a call from NORAD to intercept an incoming missile housing three nuclear warheads.

"AASAT missiles armed and ready to rock and roll," reported Sawyer.

Quinn reviewed the information filling the cockpit's four Multi-Function Displays, detailing the status of his Raptor as well as of his three Advanced Anti-Satellite missiles, a more versatile version of the venerable ASAT missiles of the turn of the century, with more speed, range, and maneuverability than its predecessor. The AASATs, secured to the Raptor's underside, were capable of taking down not just satellites but MIRVs in orbit.

"Ditto," Quinn finally replied after verifying that his three demons were fully operational and already enslaved to the Raptor's advanced radar, which tracked the status of the missile as it approached—

"It just released its MIRVs," said Sawyer in a monotone that certainly hid the anxiety he knew his wingman was feeling—as Quinn watched the additional radar returns blipping across one of his displays. They had hoped to catch the missile before it released its payload, tripling the challenge in front of them.

So much for an easy kill, Quinn thought as they reached eighty thousand feet, as the radar system locked onto the incoming warheads, as the AI governing the Raptor's tracking system assigned one AASAT per MIRV.

"One demon per MIRV," said Quinn.

"Roger that. Ready when you are," Sawyer replied, confirming that he was also assigning one AASAT missile to each MIRV.

"Foxtrot!" said Quinn, ordering the release of all three missiles and watching Sawyer do the same.

The AASAT missiles dropped beneath the underside of the F-22Gs, whose noses were still pointed at the sky. A moment later their solid-rocket boosters came alive, rocketing them to Mach 17 in seconds.

"RTB," said Quinn, ordering Sawyer to return to base. Their job here was done.

MIKE RYAN WATCHED THE large computer display, which, tied to the same tracking satellites used by NORAD, marked the path of the incoming MIRVs as well as the approaching missiles fired by the F-22Gs.

Only the quiet droning of the air-conditioning system could be heard as the entire room stood still while the MIRVs continued on their programmed trajectory, which NORAD scientists had just mapped to three U.S. cities: Washington D.C., New York, and Los Angeles.

His legs weakening, his throat feeling drier than cotton, Ryan watched the MIRVs—blue filled circles—begin to spread as they blipped across the plasma screen, their navigation systems directing them to their pre-assigned targets in North America. Their projected path was marked by blue dashed lines arcing across the screen.

His heartbeat pounded his eardrums and his stomach knotted, and especially so because one of the warheads was headed his way.

The president, the vice president, as well as key members of Congress, were already being evacuated by helicopter.

"What about the general population of those cities?" asked Ryan as Granite looked at the screen after hanging up with the White House.

The general slowly shook his head, and Ryan knew what that meant: Either those MIRVs would get destroyed by the AASATs or they would strike within another few minutes—four minutes to be exact, according to the countdown on the lower-left side of the screen. There just wasn't time to evacuate, and releasing a general alarm would only trigger a massive panic for no good reason, because they would not be able to get out of the blast zone in time.

God Almighty, Ryan thought, as he watched with apprehension and anticipation as the AASATs, represented as green triangles, closed on the MIRVs, which by now had begun to enter the atmosphere while following along the path marked by the blue dashed lines.

The AASATs continued their trajectory under the power of their solid-rocket boosters, in pairs now as they neared the blue dots representing the MIRVs, two per incoming warhead, which was the best the United States Space Command could launch given the little warning they had received. Unlike Intercontinental Ballistic Missiles, which were detected by NORAD when launched from submarines or from land-based silos or mobile transports, the banned space-based nukes lacked the delay associated with a surface launch and ascent phases—time that allowed NORAD to launch more effective countermeasures. But there weren't supposed to be any nukes in outer space.

"C'mon, boys," hissed Granite, for the first time since Ryan had known him showing signs of the stress of his profession. His brow was packed with beads of sweat, which rolled down the sides of his face. "Get those fuckers."

The AASATs' radar returns crossed over the MIRVs and for an instant overlapped them, green triangles over blue dots.

The first pair of AASATs killed the MIRV tagged for Los Angeles. The second set of AASATs took care of the warhead targeting New York City.

"Two down," said Ryan as he gripped the end of the table where the large monitor rested. Then he watched in horror as the final set of green triangles vanished, meaning the AASATs had detonated, but unlike the previous cases, the blue dot remained on the monitor, drifting across the screen.

"Mother of God," said Granite. "It didn't—"

"It looks like it got deflected, General," said Ryan, his finger pointing at the dashed line representing the programmed path. The MIRV was shifting to the right of the line, following a different path as a result of the explosions, which albeit not close enough to destroy it had apparently pushed it off course.

Grabbing the phone, which had a direct line to NORAD, Granite shouted, "What's the new trajectory?"

An instant later he got his answer as the dashed lines on the screen shifted to represent the new projected path of the warhead. The bottom of the screen displayed: TARGET UNDETERMINED.

"What does that mean?" asked Ryan.

Granite, still on the phone, put his hand over the handset and said, "It looks like the AASATs screwed up the MIRV's re-entry angle."

"Meaning?" asked Ryan, his limited knowledge of re-entry angles filling him with uneasy comfort. Re-entering the Earth atmosphere was a very tricky thing. If the angle of re-entry was too shallow, the MIRV would just skip off the atmosphere and head back into outer space. If the angle was too deep, the re-entry speed would be such that the warhead would burn up in the stratosphere.

"Meaning the angle's deeper than normal. NORAD thinks it could burn up."

"What if it doesn't?" asked Bane, silent until now.

"Then it's going to hit somewhere in the vicinity of Annapolis, thirty miles east of the capitol."

They watched in silence for another minute, as the blue dot entered the atmosphere, its radar returns vanishing in the ionic haze, the period of communications blackout.

"Three minutes," said Granite, watching the digital chronometer that materialized on the screen counting down the communications blackout period. "Then we'll know."

The three minutes felt like three hours as Ryan watched the digital clock tick the seconds away while he hoped—no, prayed—that the blue dot would not reappear on the screen.

The three minutes came and went, and still no sign of the MIRV. By the fourth minute Ryan started breathing again, and by the fifth minute Granite hung up the phone with NORAD before shooting a tired but relieved glare at Ryan, Bane, and Meek.

Then Granite's mobile phone rang. He listened intently for thirty seconds and hung up, his face once more tight with tension.

"What is it, General?" asked Bane and Meek in unison.

"New orders from President Vaccaro."

"What?" asked Bane.

Granite turned to Ryan and said, "Grab your bag, Mike. We're going to Europe."

[77] FINAL PREPARATIONS

WE LANDED ABOUT AN hour ago on a remote airfield in the middle of nowhere in southern Germany, where a pair of plain sedans waited to take us to a nondescript warehouse in some nondescript town whose name I also couldn't pronounce.

Troy always liked all of that characterless stuff. It avoids drawing attention.

Among the reception committee I found a few familiar faces, guys whom I trained with way back when, before we went our separate ways to roam the four corners of the world.

While Karen, Troy, and others gather around a table reviewing a large aerial map of Hartmann's place, a guy my age named Lester Karsten, or Les—as I remember him from those early Agency days—has taken Rachel and me to an adjacent room to demonstrate the weapons and gadgets we will be using during our upcoming raid.

Yep. You heard me right. We're going to raid Rolf Hartmann's mansion by ourselves—that's ten of us, including Troy, my two lady friends, and yours truly.

And that constitutes the essence of Troy's impromptu plan lacking any input from Washington, which remains incommunicado since the satellites went kaput.

You have to understand that by now I've been up nearly forty-eight hours. Not only didn't Karen let me sleep on the way over, but then Troy had insisted that the four of us spend the remainder of the flight reviewing the plan.

Meaning I'm a little cranky.

And here we are, in the middle of no-fucking-where as Les,

who is just as big as Troy but with a full head of salt-and-pepper hair and a matching beard, talks about the nanoweapons each of us will be carrying.

We're standing by a rectangular table in the middle of a poorly lit, windowless room. Rachel, who has been a little quiet since leaving Paris, stands next to me. Les stands opposite us holding a smart gun, which he officially describes as a Heckler & Koch MP5T silenced 9mm submachine gun.

"Strange," I say, more to myself than to my two companions.

"What's that, Tom?" asks Les, already dressed in one of the skintight TechnoSuits that Troy has apparently selected for this operation. The black suits are going to look lovely on Rachel and Karen—and even lovelier on me. But as Les had explained earlier, the suits are waterproof and nanoproof, meaning no known nanoweapons—smart darts, diggers, or anything else—can pierce them. The suits are also bullet resistant, though not nearly as strong as a thicker Kevlar vest, but good enough to provide protection against a stray round or two.

"The MP5Ts," I say, before also pointing at the plastic bags containing our TechnoSuits. "This stuff is all manufactured by CyberWerke. Is that on purpose?"

"That's part of the plan," Les replies. "Rolf Hartmann used the stolen nanoweapons from USN to kill his enemies in the Reichstag, managing to shift the origin of the attack away from him. We're going to do just the opposite, taking out the bastard using his own nanoweapons to make it look like an inside job."

The oversized warrior goes over the rest of the gear we will be taking with us. He covers the plan once more to make sure we are clear on our jobs. Les, Rachel, and I will approach the mansion from the south in the company of five support Orbs. Our job is to disable as many guards as possible on our side of the lawn and wait for Troy's signal.

"What's the signal?"

Les grins. "You'll know when the time is right."

"What about the other groups? What are their tasks?"

Les slowly shakes his head. "You know better than to ask that."

I let out a heavy sigh while looking over at Rachel, who looks confused.

"What he meant," I finally say, stretching a thumb toward Les, "is that it's best that we only know our part of the plan. That way if we get caught we won't be able to compromise the rest of the team, even under torture."

Les gives us a slight nod before saying, "We head out at midnight. Change and come out to join the rest of the team."

And just like that he does an about-face and leaves the room.

For the first time since we bumped into Troy and Karen I'm alone with Rachel.

"How are you holding up?" is all I can think of asking.

"All right, I guess," she replies, "though I was never really cut out for this kind of paramilitary work."

"Just stick by my side," I tell her, "and you'll be all right."

"I always seem to be all right when I'm near you, Tom Grant," she says, the comment and the accompanying Italian eyes in the half light of the room confusing me because I thought she was pissed at me for the whole Karen thing.

Before I know it, Rachel steps up to me and just kisses me, her hands clasping my face.

Damn, she's got soft lips, and the taste of her reminds me of the night we spent in that stakeout outside Morotski's hideout.

"What was that for?"

Instead of answering, Rachel just kisses me again.

"Rachel," I say, my eyes darting toward the door to make sure it was still closed. I don't feel like providing someone like Troy with more ammunition, just as I don't want Karen seeing me sharing an intimate moment with this woman—though I'm not sure why I should care after the conversation we had on the plane. "This may not be a good idea at the—"

"What's the matter, big boy?" she whispers while nibbling on my left ear in a way that makes me want to take her right here on this table. "You don't find me attractive?"

"Are you kidding me?" I say. "I just . . . well, with Karen here I wasn't sure how you would—"

"The way I see it," Rachel cuts in, "she had her chance and she decided to pass. You two broke it off over a year ago, right?"

I nod.

"And you haven't seen each other since, right?"

Another nod.

"And now that you have seen her, do you have any plans with her?"

I slowly shake my head and say, "We talked it over during the flight from Paris and decided to keep it friendly. She wants to do what she wants to do and the same goes for me."

"And what is it that you want to do, Tom Grant?"

"Find me another little piece of paradise and live the rest of my days in peace, but hopefully not alone."

"Then," she says, crossing her arms, "in my book you're fair game."

Fair *game*? Did she just suggest I'm some sort of trophy?

"And," she continues, "I'd like to think I've got first dibs. Is that a good representation of where things stand?"

"I . . . I would say so."

She smiles, winks, says, "That's what I thought," and then proceeds to raise her T-shirt.

I'm standing there feeling pretty fucking weird, trying not to look at her cream-colored bra, at her tiny waist, at her slim and firm arms. I try not to think about the lord of the jungle shifting in its lair.

"See something you like, Tom?" she asks teasingly while kicking off her sneakers and lowering her jeans, leaving me staring at the same figure I saw on the beach in El Salvador what seems like a lifetime ago.

Feeling color coming to my cheeks when I notice her tiny mound of pubic hair pressed against cream underwear that matches her bra, I say, "Damn, you're beautiful."

And she embraces me, then kisses me, letting me hug her just like that, nearly naked, my hands following the smooth contours of her back, a couple of fingers playing with the elastic of her little panties.

As blood drains from one head to the other, I forget where

I am, my right hand venturing beneath her panties, caressing her smooth butt, pressing her against me.

And just as I'm about to yield all control to the one-eyed wonder, Rachel smiles, slaps me on my butt, and says, "That will come later. And only if you're a good boy."

"Oh, I promise to be *really* good," I reply, still holding her tight.

"We'll see," she says, gently pushing away.

I release her and she kisses the tip of my nose before reaching for her TechnoSuit on the table and saying, "Come, big boy. You dress me and I'll dress you."

I help her into this Spandex-like suit and she helps me into mine, though not without giggling at the growing lump in my underwear.

"Did I do that?" she says, smiling. "Well, you just hang in there, big fellow. Right now we have a job to do."

Breathing deeply, trying to think of my mother, I zip up the front of my TechnoSuit, which Rachel says looks great on me, and then we both don our gear vests and weaponry.

A few minutes later, as I'm finally calming down and we're fixing to leave, the door swings open.

Troy, looking larger than life, stands in the doorway already dressed for action.

"You two lovebirds ready?"

Rachel nods. I give him the finger.

Karen and Les stand behind him, both also in battle gear. Karen looks like a million bucks dressed this way and for a moment I forget all about Rachel Muratani as our eyes lock.

"Let's do it then," he adds at my silence. "The world will be a better place without Hartmann and Deppe."

"Tell me something, Troy," I say. "How are you planning to assassinate Hartmann and his top cronies without making it look like we did it? I think it's going to take more than just the CyberWerke gear to pull this off."

He grins and says, "Always keep them guessing, Tommy. Always keep them guessing."

THE SEA STALLION NAVY helicopters dropped Michael Ryan, General Gus Granite, and three dozen members of USN's high-tech teams at the helipad atop the Italian army base on the outskirts of Pisa, Italy, where they met the city mayor, the chief of police, and two colonels from the local army.

The team had arrived at the Galileo Galilei International Airport on a C5 Air Force transport by order of President Laura Vaccaro after she reached an agreement with the Italian president. Following the close call with the MIRVs, the commander in chief wasn't taking any chances with the rogue machines. She wanted them all terminated with extreme prejudice.

A pair of Sea Stallions had been waiting for them and their gear at the airport, bringing them directly to this provisional headquarters after Italian authorities evacuated the entire city.

While Granite deployed his forces around Pisa, Ryan and several USN scientists set up their gear, which linked them to one of several satellites brought back online by the scientists of NASA and JPL—the Jet Propulsion Laboratory. Air and sea traffic was still sparse around the world, as only a limited number of satellites were back in service, and more satellites were expected to return to full operation in the coming days.

"We have eyes yet, Mike?" asked Granite, standing behind Ryan while the computer scientist stared at the information displayed on the three large screens. Over fifty people crowded the operations room, where Ryan and his USN colleagues pinpointed the location of every rogue Orb inside the city limits.

"There's forty-five, General," he said, pointing at the blue dots roaming about the city, on the streets, in buildings, some cruising the sewage system. Ryan even spotted one hiding inside Pisa's famous inclined tower.

Over one hundred locals and just as many tourists had been

killed before local officials got word from Rome about the rogue machines on the loose and kicked off an emergency evacuation that lasted eight grueling hours, including many gunfights between Italian forces and the elusive Orbs, whose maneuvering abilities allowed them to virtually disappear from sight until they struck again with their deadly lasers. But at least the problem had been temporarily contained through an outstanding effort between three divisions of army regulars from the Italian armed forces and three hundred cops, who formed a safety cordon encircling the evacuated city, preventing the Orbs from escaping into the countryside.

"I show them moving inside a five-mile radius, mostly in the downtown area, though a few have ventured to the outer edges of the city, but still within the encircling cordon."

"Are you ready for the drop?" Granite asked.

Ryan nodded while looking at his USN colleagues manning similar workstations. Everyone gave him a thumbs-up. "We have uploaded the coordinates to the stealth fighters, General."

Granite reached for the radio strapped to his belt and said, "Operation Hail Drop is a go. Repeat. Hail Drop is a go."

Within minutes, three F-117X advanced stealth fighters shot above the city one at a time, dropping their payloads over the coordinates specified by Ryan.

Each drop consisted of five large pods, which flared open soon after parachutes slowed their forward speed and rate of descent.

A dozen advanced military Orbs emerged from each pod under the power of their own microturbines, which propelled them to operational speeds, directing them to their preassigned targets.

Ryan watched with interest as the friendlies, depicted as red dots, searched for all blue dots in the city, engaging them in an impressive display of laser power, which the workstations showed as velvet lines. In the same instant, the green figures of three dozen men entered the killing zone from various points around the security cordon.

The conflict intensified as the Orbs battled each other in

violent dogfights, sometimes ending in red dots vanishing;
other times the rogue Orbs perished.

As the F-117Xs continued their runs, dropping reinforcements to overwhelm the rogue machines, another one of
Granite's high-tech teams swept through the city in their advanced gear, shooting down those Orbs which had escaped
the initial onslaught, terminating them with accurately placed
EMP shots.

"It's over, General," Ryan said when the workstations displayed nothing but red Orbs and green figures patrolling the
city.

Granite spoke briefly into his radio before updating the Italian authorities in the room, who then raced outside to alert their
people that the city was safe once again.

As Ryan and the other USN scientists began to dismantle
their field equipment, Granite got on the radio again, listened
intently for a few moments, and finally said, "Yes, Madam
President."

"What was that all about, General?"

"Just got word from Bane. Looks like his man, Savage, is
requiring our high-tech services."

"Where?"

"Berlin."

[79] DECOYS

MY LUNGS AND LEGS on fire, I follow Rachel Muratani up the
winding path that according to the terrain map built into my
night-vision goggles will lead us to the south side of the mansion. The oversized Les Karsten, hauling a silenced machine
gun twice as large as my Heckler & Koch MP5T, covers the
rear. Our objective is to take care of any guards and patrol
Orbs on this side of the mansion—and do it in coordination

with Troy, Karen, and the rest of the team approaching from the other three sides.

I haven't done this paramilitary stuff in a while, but much of it is coming back in a flash with every step I take over the inclined terrain—painted in palettes of green by the goggles as they amplify the available light.

To her credit, Rachel not only looks lean and mean in her black outfit, with her silenced MP5T and night goggles, but she is moving quietly and swiftly, her figure twisting and turning to conform with the bends in the forest as she makes her way uphill.

We've been at it for nearly a half hour, ever since arriving at the foot of the mountain in three Land Rovers, which we parked in the woods before splitting up.

Three Orbs float between Rachel and me, and two more between Les and me. The five mechanical surrogates keep an eye out for any type of high-tech gadget guarding the hill.

Personally I would not have brought those flying basketballs with us. I just plain don't trust them. Those things are ticking bombs, armed with all that firepower that could turn against you if someone with the correct encryption passwords managed to gain control of them.

But Troy, for reasons that he chose not to explain to me, sent them along.

My spook sense tells me something is wrong with this picture, just like it screams at me that there is no way for the mansion of one of the most powerful men in the world to be that unguarded. We've been marching uphill for a while now and have not seen even the smallest hint of a security shield.

Just as I'm thinking this, Rachel stops, drops to one knee, and raises her left hand in a fist.

Slowly, Les and I catch up to her.

"What do you see?" I ask.

Rachel points at the small clearing beyond knee-high bushes about thirty feet ahead.

Perimeter lasers. Three of them. The first at shin level. The second at waist level. The last at chest level. All red in color.

"You interrupt any of those and I promise you all hell will break loose on this side of the hill," says Les, who reaches for the controls strapped to his left forearm and starts to tap commands to our five hovering little friends.

"What are you doing?" asks Rachel.

Les, obviously indoctrinated by Troy, doesn't respond. Instead, he tilts his head in the direction of the Orbs, whose skin become mirror smooth, almost like gazing balls, before they arrange themselves in a vertical pentagon, two at the bottom, spaced horizontally by about three feet. The second two float about a foot and a half higher than the first pair. The third positions itself two feet higher and in between the second pair.

Slowly, the fivesome approach the laser shield.

"Watch this," he says, his bearded face, darkened by camouflage cream and further concealed by the goggles, turning toward the burgundy lasers and the nearing Orbs.

The machines pierce the beams simultaneously. The shiny surfaces of the lower Orbs deflect the waist-high laser upward, hitting the Orbs above them, which deflect it horizontally once again, completing the path. Likewise, the second-highest Orbs deflect the chest-high beam up at a forty-five-degree angle to the top Orb, which bounces it back down, completing the loop.

"Pretty cool, huh?" Les says.

"Yeah," I reply. "Real cool, until the fuckers turn on you and decide to roast your ass with those lasers of theirs."

Shrugging at my obvious reluctance to trust those machines, Les goes through the hole in the laser fence first, careful to step over the shin-high beam. Rachel follows, and then yours truly, who, I have to admit, is a bit impressed with those shiny little buggers—though I'd never admit it in public.

The Orbs cross to the side, leaving the laser field just as we had found it, before falling in line as before, three in between Rachel and me, and the other two between *moi* and Les.

The navigation system tells me we have another quarter of a mile or so, which we cover in about fifteen minutes, slowing down as the distant lights from the mansion start to shaft through the dense vegetation, appearing as forks of bright green light in the otherwise hunter-green surroundings.

Rachel stops again, kneeling down, motioning us to catch up to her.

"What is it?" I ask, taking a knee next to her. Les drops to a crouch beside me.

"Orbs," she says, pointing at the spheres hovering just beyond the shrubbery lining the trunks of towering pines by the edge of the woods a hundred or so feet away.

The goggles, which also provide me with 200X optical zoom capability, clearly show me those flying basketballs that I hate so much.

Beyond the Orbs stands the main house, a castle-like four-story mansion with towering walls of gray rock broken up by oversized windows with security bars. The place is topped by a copper roof, its green patina glistening in the floodlights.

Les removes his rucksack and produces a small Orb and what looks like a computerized wand. Pressing the magic wand against the surface of the Orb turns it on, and the six-inch-diameter unit defaults to hover mode while deploying what looks like a dozen tiny antennas. A second touch and the gadget lifts like a helicopter, disappearing in the branches several feet overhead.

"What was that?" whispers Rachel.

Les doesn't reply. Instead, he points at the figures beyond the clearing.

And it is at this moment, as I'm reaching my limit of how much of Troy's bullshit secrecy I'm willing to take, that one of our Orbs turns stupid and crashes into another one, sending the latter swirling out of control into the clearing, in plain view of a pair of guards bearing machine guns.

For the love of—

The blast is so bright that for a moment I fear I'm going to go blind, before the goggle's opaquing system kicks in, cutting back the glare. But my mind is already shouting at me that something is seriously wrong. Orbs just don't blow up like that. Those spheres of ours were packing some kind of explosive char—

Two more of our Orbs either have collided or were hit by the enemy. They exploded and are now burning near the bushes by the edge of the south lawn, which is bursting with activity.

As Les furiously swings the magic wand, I turn to Rachel and grab her gloved hand, pulling her toward me as I turn around and start heading downhill while screaming at Les, "Let's move, man!"

"Wait!" he hisses, still working the forearm pad. "We're still not finished setting up the incendiary decoys!"

Incendiary decoys?

Against my better judgment I stop after taking a dozen steps. Armed men are headed in our direction as alarms blare across the compound, their wailing echoing in the woods. "What in the hell are you talking about?" I finally ask.

"We're the decoy team!" he says over the growing havoc as the last two of our escort Orbs shoot off along the tree line, exploding a hundred feet away, like incendiary bombs, engulfing the edge of the forest in bright flames, making guards heading our way cut in the direction of the explosions, buying us a little time.

"The decoy team? Are you out of your fucking mind?"

"We draw them out!" shouts Les, directing the small Orb he had taken out of the backpack toward the front of the mansion and setting it off, creating more chaos.

"Draw them out?" I repeat. "We're the bait?"

"Just decoys," he replies before starting to run downhill like a bat out of hell, away from the inferno he has created. "The rest of the team goes inside!" he adds, looking over his left shoulder. "Come! Let's go! And enable your countermeasures!"

Words can't describe just how pissed I am at Troy Savage and his gang at this very moment. The bastard never told me I would be his fucking decoy.

Still holding Rachel's hand, the heat from the growing fire intensifying, I watch the greenish figure of Les vanish downhill.

Crap.

Out of obvious choices, feeling used and abused, I enable my countermeasures and watch Rachel do the same while charging in his direction, the blaring alarms and shouts from the guards drowning the sound of my heartbeat thumping against my temples.

But my spook sense kicks in thirty seconds later, forcing me to cut left, toward the back of the mansion, holding a parallel course with the edge of the clearing but in the opposite direction from flames now enveloping the tops of trees.

What was in those Orbs anyhow? Napalm?

"What are we doing?" Rachel asks.

"We're *not* following the plan," I reply, turning off the countermeasures and making sure she does the same. While very effective at diverting smart darts, the active countermeasures emit an energy that can be detected by patrolling Orbs.

Reaching a cluster of thin trees and going around it, we press on for another two hundred feet before slowing down.

"Why are we not sticking to the plan?" she finally asks.

"Because we're not playing red herring," I reply. "Let Les be the lure for all of us. Those countermeasures he's got enabled are like a damned beacon and will likely attract every Orb in the area. We're headed to the east side of the estate, where—"

My highly tuned senses make me shut up and drop to a deep crouch, dragging Rachel down.

Although most guards are rushing toward the fire, some hauling fire extinguishers, three guards remain vigilant, their black machine guns in their hands as they patrol this sector of the tree line in the company of two security Orbs, their shiny surfaces reflecting the estate's floodlights as well as the glowing inferno.

The glare is such that my goggles are having a difficult time keeping up, so I take them off.

Colors return to my world, and I blink a few times to clear my eyes, before focusing them once more on the nearing guards.

Stowing the goggles in a Velcro pouch on my vest and

watching Rachel do the same, I flip the control lever of my silenced MP5T machine gun to single-shot mode.

Rachel is also holding her Heckler & Koch weapon, which, like mine, is silenced.

Continuing to ignore the commotion a few hundred feet away, the guards stop just beyond the knee-high bushes past the last row of trees, their bulky silhouettes backlit by the estates' lights, suggesting they are wearing bulletproof vests beneath their dark uniforms. The orbs hover a couple of feet over their heads, LEDs blinking as their high-resolution cameras search for us.

But not only are we well hidden; our countermeasures are off. They sense nothing and thus remain put, just floating and blinking.

The guards, apparently too reliant on the security Orbs to do their job for them, choose not to venture into the woods but just continue along the—

A loud explosion coming from the other side of the grounds rattles the ground. The lights in the mansion suddenly go off and an instant later emergency floodlights flicker on. The inside of the house, however, remains pitch-black, making me wonder why the interior emergency lights failed to—

"Achtung!" one of the guards shouts, but not at us. He's looking toward the rear of the estate.

I risk a peek in that direction and spot two figures dressed in black racing across the twilight created by the emergency lighting system.

That's definitely two of ours, and based on their relative sizes and the fact that they're running from the rear, it's a pretty good bet they're Troy and Karen.

The guards automatically turn in their direction.

"Take out the Orbs!" I hiss, before standing, MP5T already leveled at the figure reaching for his radio, and line up the weapon's sights with his head.

The firing mechanism clicks, firing the round, the suppressor absorbing the blast, reducing it to a mere spitting sound, which also allows me to hear the impact of the bullet striking the face of the guard before he can get that radio close to his lips.

The German-made weapon ejects the spent 9mm casing and loads a fresh one from the clip before he even starts to fall.

And I fire again, striking the second guard also in the face, which disappears in a cloud of blood just as I watch one of the Orbs going ballistic after Rachel shot it with the uranium-depleted 9mm rounds of her MP5T, piercing its shell, blasting through its nanotronic guts. By then the third guard is looking pretty damned confused, his head doing the Linda Blair thing as he swings it back and forth between Troy and Karen a couple of hundred feet away and the likely origin of the shots—*moi*.

Before he can figure out what in the hell to do, I nail him in the head, where no vest can protect him, and in the same instant the second Orb goes kaput, whirling out of control over our heads and off into the woods, where it crashes against something. Unlike the explosive Orbs that we delivered for Troy, these two Orbs just stop moving and blinking.

Instincts take over, forcing me to check the clearing, to make certain that the rest of the guards are busy down the south side, where the roaring flames challenge the blaring alarms.

As Karen and Troy make it to the rear of the mansion, I say to Rachel, "Give me a hand."

Together we drag the bodies into the woods, leaving them hidden in the waist-high vegetation before we continue up the edge of the woods, finally reaching the rear corner of the estate, where Troy and Karen had emerged a few minutes before.

This side faces the back of the house, where a large covered patio supported by stone columns steps down to a pool surrounded by lush landscape with lots of flowers under the emergency lighting. Water cascades into the pool from a rock formation overlooking the far edge of the garden, near the steps connecting it to the lawn. There are about three hundred feet of lawn between us and the steps.

I count close to fifty guards around the inferno that Troy has created to draw attention from his real mission. A half-dozen more men are running toward it from the mansion hauling additional fire extinguishers as alarms continue to blare.

I see no sign of Troy or Karen.

"I think they went through there," says Rachel, her eyes alive with the flickering light from the growling flames two hundred feet away, stabbing the forest.

She uses her gun to point at a door off to the left of the gardens and the pool.

I see no one else. The fire seems to be doing its desired work, drawing the security team in that direction.

We continue to move along the rear of the mansion to better position ourselves for our upcoming—

Rachel trips on something, falls, but manages not to scream, getting up with amazing resilience.

There's five bodies in the shrubs, all shot in the head—all guards, just like the ones we took out.

"Looks like your former mentor and your old girlfriend have been busy," says Rachel.

I sigh, giving Troy credit. The man sure knows how to cause a commotion at just the right moment, and I start to doubt my rebellious move not to follow Les downhill. Maybe Troy was indeed counting on me sticking to the plan for some obscure reason and now I'm about to screw up everything.

That's what he gets for keeping me in the dark.

But another part of my mind—the paranoid side—tells me that Troy's distractions seem to be working too well.

I survey the grounds again, observing the blaze, the relatively darker interior of the mansion, and the apparent lack of guards or of guests.

"Are we going in too?" Rachel asks.

"Why not?" I reply, deciding that if there's going to be trouble in there, might as well join the party.

Looking at her and winking, I get up. Just as I'm about to start running, another powerful explosion rumbles in the distance, and I see several cars on fire in front of the mansion.

"Was that part of the plan?" I ask.

Rachel shrugs. "Heck if I know what's going on. We were supposed to stick with Les, remember?"

Ignoring her, I inspect the very dark mansion, washed by the flickering light from the fires in the forest and the vehicles.

"Put your goggles back on," I finally say. "I have the feeling things are about to get exciting."

[80] THE SIGNAL

"WE'VE GOT EYES AND ears?" asked General Gus Granite.

"Not yet, sir," replied Ryan, sitting by one of a dozen computer consoles in the control section of a Boeing E-3D Sentry Airborne Warning and Control System (AWACS) Air Force jet circling at thirty thousand feet over the Baltic Sea, eighty miles from Berlin.

"How long before we can talk to Savage?" asked Donald Bane, standing next to Granite as they looked over Ryan's shoulders while he typed behind a large color console. Ryan used his artificial intelligence agent to make the right satellite connections to link this system with the portable high-definition, low-light, microweb camera built into Savage's TechnoSuit.

"Just a few more seconds," Ryan replied, watching MPS-Ali rushing through ISPs, making connections that defied logic, until a window opened up on the upper right-hand corner of the screen. The image flickered, before resolving into a moving hallway. "OK, we're in."

Leaning close to the microphone projecting from the side of the workstation, Ryan said, "Troy Savage, can you hear me?"

The motion stopped in the view window.

"Loud and clear. Where is Bane?"

Ryan got up and pointed at the microphone. "It's for you."

Bane sat down and asked, "What's your situation, Troy?"

"Phase One complete. Diversions in place. We are now moving in on the—"

Two shadows rushed across the microweb cam's field of view, followed by two bright flashes. The figures collapsed on the floor while clutching their chests.

Bane and Granite exchanged a glance.

"Sorry," came Savage's reply. *"Just bumped into a pair of guards. I neutralized one and Karen the other. Continuing toward target."*

While Ryan worked with MPS-Ali to maintain a clear connection, Bane and Granite observed their progress through the mansion in tense silence.

[81] INSURANCE

WEARING A PAIR OF night-vision goggles, Karen Frost followed Troy Savage as they raced down an interior hallway after disabling two guards who had been stumbling about in the dark while trying to reach the side of the mansion facing the fire.

Almost too easily, she thought, blaring alarms drowning the thudding of their black rubber-soled hiking boots on the hardwood floors.

And what alarmed her even more was the fact that the interior emergency lighting system did not kick in after the west team blew up the transformers feeding the mansion—something that worked to their advantage as the seasoned operatives pressed on, their goggles amplifying their sight in the otherwise murky surroundings.

"Looks like the surveillance cameras are also off," Troy whispered, pointing at the dark cameras while rushing past expensive artwork on light-colored walls beneath evenly spaced ornate chandeliers that no longer provided any illumination.

Things just didn't feel right, and on top of that, the place resembled a war museum. Shelves packed with different types of weapons—knives, revolvers, swords, and much more from different periods—lined the walls along with medals, uniforms, and framed photographs. The hallway ended in a large foyer connecting to other rooms as well as to a set of wide stairs. And the same war theme decorated the foyer and stairs. "Looks like our man is quite the collector," Karen finally said, pointing at all of the paraphernalia.

Shrugging while removing his small rucksack, Troy opened the flap, stuck his hand inside, did something that triggered three short beeps, and then closed the flap and hid the rucksack behind a pair of framed black-and-white photographs standing on a table in between two shelves near the foot of the stairs. The faded images were of Nazi soldiers fighting in the snow.

"What's that?" Karen asked.

"Insurance," he replied, checking his watch and pressing a button on the side.

"Troy, what's in there?" she insisted.

Karen could see Savage's green face smiling before he said, "Let's keep moving."

The short corridor spilled into a large living room, empty, dark, just like the two previous rooms they had searched near the rear of the mansion.

"Where's everybody?" Karen hissed, scanning the luxurious living room with her silenced submachine gun, her eyes rushing past traditional furniture over a gigantic Persian rug, all beneath more of those elaborate chandeliers hanging at the ends of thick chains.

Through her goggles Karen saw every detail in the room as she searched for anything that moved. Bookcases lined two of the walls. Large windows dominated the third wall. Flames pulsated in the night beyond the windowpanes; their light, displayed in hues of green, flickered inside the room. Figures ran in many directions outside, some spraying the contents of their fire extinguishers against the growing inferno, apparently in vain. The fire continued to expand, jumping from tree to tree like an angered demon.

The diversions were working, but there was no sign of Hartmann, Deppe, and the rest of the CyberWerke inner circle, whom Troy's spotters in Berlin had seen arriving the day before—confirming the intelligence extracted from Rem Vlachko.

"They have to be somewhere in this house," said Savage, also armed with a suppressed Beretta, before pointing its bulky silencer toward a pair of double doors leading to what appeared to be another large living area.

They headed in that direction, covering each other as they advanced, Karen keeping an eye on their rear while Savage worried about their front.

The living room did connect to another large area, the mansion's main dining room—at least judging by the long banquet table and dozen chairs on each side.

But again, the place was empty.

"I don't like this," said Karen.

"Weird," replied Savage, his face dark with camouflage cream beneath the goggles, like Karen's.

Peering at the surge of activity beyond the windows, Karen said, "Maybe the distractions worked better than anticipated."

"Or maybe we're being set up."

"Let's check the upstairs—"

The overheads suddenly came on, blinding her. Karen ripped off her goggles, blinking to clear her sight.

"What in the hell—" Savage began to say.

"Good evening," said a distinguished male voice in heavily accented English. "We've been expecting you."

Karen and Savage found themselves staring at six armed guards flanking two men dressed in business suits, one about six inches taller than the other, both in their fifties.

"Your weapons!" said one of the guards in heavily accented English. "Drop them now!"

Savage looked at Karen and nodded. They complied, letting the weapons fall on the floor.

"Kick them away from you and put your hands on your heads," the same guard ordered.

They complied in silence. Both MP5T submachine guns skittered away from them.

"You seriously didn't expect to cut off our power just by destroying a few transformers outside the house, did you?" Rolf Hartmann asked in his lightly accented English. "Just like you didn't really expect to break into my house this easily?"

"Have you any idea just how much trouble you have made for us?" Christoff Deppe asked.

"And we're just getting warmed up," said Savage, to Karen's pleasant surprise. Even when facing staggering odds, the former Navy SEAL didn't lose his arrogance.

"Don't you realize it is over for you?"

"Wanna bet?" asked Savage.

"The authorities are on the way," said Hartmann. "You and your terrorist friends will be taken into custody for threatening our lives as well the lives of our guests, who are safely upstairs in their rooms."

"And don't forget about what you bastards did at the Reichstag," added Deppe. "You're going to burn for this."

"We have proof that you are the ones associated with terrorists," said Karen.

Deppe smiled, taking two steps toward them. "I seriously hope you don't mean the silly video you made of me and Rem the other night," he said to Karen.

"The evidence of your connection with that international terrorist has made it to our government," she replied.

"Ah, that," said Hartmann, arms behind his back as he looked into the distance. "Of course. But there is a slight problem, you see. Nobody in Germany cares about any reports or accusations coming from the United States, particularly after the weapons used to kill our chancellor and the Parliament originated in USN, in your country, and we *especially* could care less what your nation has to say after it disabled our communications satellites in a feeble attempt to destabilize our infrastructure during this transitional process. Besides, don't forget that the origin of this so-called proof of our association with terrorists is none other than the terrorists responsible for the killings at my associate's house right here on the outskirts of Berlin."

"Like we said," added Christoff Deppe, "it's all over for you. You and your entire criminal ring will be in prison within the hour, and there will be no extradition arrangements. You will be tried, sentenced, and executed in Germany under our laws."

"Why, Hartmann?" asked Savage. "Why did you do it? Why did you have to kill the German chancellor and the entire Parliament? Wasn't it enough to be at the head of the largest corporation in the world? You are a man who has everything. Everything. What compelled you to go to this extreme and risk it all if it backfired?"

"The world is due a change, my dear friends," Hartmann replied. "America has not demonstrated the kind of leadership required to placate international terrorism. Sure, America tried to do the right thing in Afghanistan and Iraq almost a decade ago, but after a few years of those initial victories against world tyranny and terrorism, the momentum was lost with the new White House administration. What the world needs is a consistent iron fist, an all-powerful and unquestionable ruler who will not be shaken by opinion polls or be concerned about re-elections, a ruler who will do what is right irrespective of the opinion of special-interest groups."

"And I take it that this ruler will be you?" asked Karen.

"Of course," replied Hartmann matter-of-factly. "Look at what I have accomplished in the corporate world. I intend to apply the same strategy to the rest of the world."

"You're insane, Hartmann," said Savage. "You too, Deppe."

"Are we, Mr. Savage? I have just given you the facts. The world is in a state of havoc, and America, despite all of its might, isn't intrepid enough to do what is right, to uproot the evil that is international terrorism."

"But that's the thing," said Karen. "You talk about eliminating terrorism, yet you choose to associate yourself with terrorists like Rem Vlachko."

"Face it, Hartmann. You're nothing but a hypocrite."

"That was just a temporary allegiance of convenience," CyberWerke's CEO replied in his groomed accent without missing a beat, obviously used to being directly criticized. Karen had to give him credit. The man surely knew how to carry himself, even if his mind was operating deep in Fantasyland. "I used him to achieve a greater goal."

"Just like you used the chancellor and the members of Parliament?"

"Ten years from now the world will be a safer place because of that short-term sacrifice," replied Deppe.

"Ten years from now you two will be long forgotten, because you will not get away with this," said Savage.

"You will not get away with this, Hartmann," repeated Karen. "We will not allow you to poison the minds of the German people."

"But that's the thing," Hartmann said. "We are not poisoning their minds. We are letting them *make up* their own minds about the kind of government they want to have. And so far their voice has been quite unanimous."

"And as for you two," said Deppe, "this feeble attempt to rob Germany of its new leadership will only help our cause."

Savage smiled. "You don't seriously think we would come here with just a dozen operatives, some weapons, and a few pounds of explosives, did you?"

The two German executives shared a brief glance before returning their glares to the captured operatives.

Checking his watch before giving Karen a get-ready nod, Troy said, "You don't really think that the one true superpower on this planet would send just a group of operatives to bring down the man who is threatening to turn Germany into another monster, did you?"

Before Hartmann and Deppe can reply, a loud explosion rocked the building. As the guards looked about them, puzzled, Troy Savage uncoiled and charged toward the German executives.

"WHAT IN THE HELL was that?" Rachel Muratani asks a few seconds after landing on me following the massive explosion down the foyer we've just passed, now engulfed in flames.

Things have been happening too damned fast. First the lights in the mansion suddenly came back on just a minute ago, and now this most recent explosion barbecues the spot where we were standing just thirty seconds ago.

"Beats me," I reply, her face an inch from mine as she lies on top of me by the entrance of what looks like a living room. "But I can think of better ways for you to get on top."

"Tom!" she hisses, rolling away from me while snatching her MP5.

I do the same, ignoring the heat from the growing inferno behind me. Is Troy responsible for that too? And where in the hell is he? What does this man have up his sleeve besides torching the surrounding woods and now the interior of the house?

Slowly, with growing caution, Rachel and I creep inside the large living room, listening to the voices streaming from the room beyond the double doors at the opposite end, past a long wall of floor-to-ceiling windows overlooking a forest fire that is definitely out of control.

Mixed with the commotion outside is the sound of distant sirens, of emergency vehicles, which means the local authorities will be all over this place in minutes.

The reports from several guns thunder inside the large rectangular room, mixed with shouts of anger, of agony. Hastening footsteps over hardwood floors, followed by more shots and more screams—combined with the flames propagating from the foyer and into the living room—make me lunge toward the double doors at the far end of the luxurious living area.

"Stay behind me and cover me," I hiss just as I reach the doorway, as I peek inside the long and narrow dining room, as I spot Karen Frost, eyes closed, slouched to the side, behind a serving table, holding her left shoulder, bleeding, her lips twisted in obvious pain. Next to her lie two guards, dead, pools of blood forming around their heads.

My mouth going dry at the thought of Karen being wounded, I glance at the commotion across the room, at Troy's bulky figure as he collides with Rolf Hartmann and Christoff Deppe, striking them with his flared elbows before swinging his pistol toward the guards, who are not firing for obvious fear of hitting the German executives.

I level my silenced MP5T at the closest guard and fire twice before switching targets, acting entirely on instincts, firing again and again as Troy tackles two of them.

One of the two surviving guards rolls away from Troy, clutching his machine gun. I fire once, miss, and fire again, missing again just as he points the machine gun at Troy.

Damn!

I fire a third time, and a fourth, hitting the guard, but not before he opens fire at close range on my former mentor for a few seconds, letting go several rounds before dying.

Clutching his chest while staggering back, Troy trembles before collapsing face-first on the floor.

As anger swells inside my gut, the last guard gets up and starts to bring his weapon around, aimed at me. I'm about to fire again when his face vanishes behind a cloud of blood.

Rachel, bracing against the other side of the doorway, has joined the fight, firing her silenced H & K weapon.

The sirens outside grow louder. Soon this place is going to be crawling with cops—heck, maybe with soldiers ordered to shoot to kill.

Hartmann and Deppe sit up, dazed after Troy tackled them.

Deppe stands first, reaching inside his coat, producing a pistol, which he aims at Troy, who is lying facedown on the floor, then at Karen, who continues to hide behind the serving table, holding her bleeding shoulder.

"Hey, asshole!" I shout while leveling the gun at Deppe's chest.

Deppe turns toward us, his face strained with surprise and fear.

I shoot the bastard twice in the middle of his chest, the impacts pushing him back against his superior, who lets go a loud scream before kicking Deppe aside while raising his hands.

"Don't shoot!" Hartmann says. "I beg you! Do not shoot!"

I got Germany's top asshole in my sights, and so does Rachel, but somehow I can't bring myself to shoot someone who is unarmed.

"I can make you rich beyond your dreams!" Hartmann says when he realizes that we have indeed held our fire. "I will call off the authorities. I will explain to them that we had an accident, that we—"

The shot thunders inside the large banquet room.

In the same instant, Hartmann shudders, before spitting blood, before falling to his knees.

Behind him, Troy Savage has managed to roll to his side, holding one of the guards' machine guns with both hands. He fires again, and three rounds explode through Hartmann's chest.

Dropping the weapon, Troy says, "Tommy . . . hurry."

"Rachel, you go help Karen," I tell her, fighting the urge to go myself.

She takes off in Karen's direction while I rush to my mentor's side, kneeling next to him, checking his wounds.

"I'm fucked, Tommy," he says, short of breath. "Damned piece-of-shit German suits."

The TechnoSuit has stopped three shots, but the rest pierced through, one in the abdomen and two more in the upper chest.

"We're getting you out of here, buddy."

Spitting blood and foam, Troy grips my hand. "Listen . . . carefully . . . there is no time. A . . . stealth chopper . . . five minutes . . . south lawn."

"A chopper is coming to pick us up? How?"

He takes off his wristwatch and hands it to me. "Hom and com device," he whispers, meaning this gadget is both a homing device for the incoming chopper plus a two-way communicator. "Now go," he adds with obvious pain. "Go . . . get Karen . . . to safety . . . only a shoulder wound."

"But you, man! I can't possibly—"

"Now, Tommy!" he manages to shout, before coughing up more blood. "Or we all . . . going to . . ."

Troy goes into convulsions, before his eyes roll to the back of his head.

The sirens getting louder, I sling my MP5T and cut over to Rachel and Karen.

"How is she?" I ask, kneeling next to her.

Rachel grimaces while pointing at Karen's shoulder. Just like Troy's, the damned TechnoSuit failed to fully protect her. Rachel had used her utility knife to cut out the dark nanofabric around Karen's shoulder and had dressed the wound with large cloth napkins from the serving table next to them.

"Tom . . ." Karen mumbles.

"I'm here," I say, mustering savage control in spite of the wrenching feeling twisting my intestines. I can't afford to come apart now.

The fire reaches the dining room, flames flickering through the double doors connecting it to the large living area. Sirens blare outside.

"Tom, we have to get out of here," Rachel says.

I hand her one of the machine guns before lifting Karen's light frame with my right arm while bringing my left arm under her legs, cradling her like I would a baby, pressing her bandaged wound against my chest to minimize the bleeding while keeping my hands free to clutch the MP5T, ready to blast any bastard who dares get in my way. I hesitated in killing Hartmann. I am not hesitating again tonight.

The living room has three doors. One that leads to the front entrance of the mansion, where there's certain to be plenty of bad hombres and German cops waiting for us. The second door, which leads to the living room and west foyer, is already engulfed by the fire. And then there's the third door, which leads to the kitchen on the south side of the house—the side where this silent helicopter is supposed to come and get us out of Dodge.

Before I know it I'm running in that direction, past another set of stairs already engulfed in flames, which have propagated upward.

Through the hissing fire, through the roaring inferno and the inky smoke, I hear screams, cries, agonizing pleas coming from the upper floors. People are trapped upstairs, and based on the thick steel bars protecting all of the windows in this place, there's no one getting out upstairs unless they can find another set of stairs.

Not only are those people beyond the flames, out of my reach, but I have my own problems to deal with—namely getting Karen, Rachel, and yours truly out of this firetrap and into the open to catch our ride.

Kicking the swinging doors with Rachel in tow, I face a large kitchen that looks like something out of an episode of *Star Trek,* with tons and tons of stainless-steel stoves, ovens, freezers, and countertops—and two walls already engulfed by flames. There are three rows of cooking hardware with two aisles in between running the entire length of the fifty-foot-long room, which is rapidly filling with smoke.

I charge down the aisle to my right while scanning the room with the muzzle, ignoring the fire, ready to shoot anything that moves, but seeing nothing except glistening stainless steel.

The doors at the other end abruptly swing open.

Four men, all armed, emerge through them, turning their weapons in our direction.

Operating entirely on instinct, I open fire.

[83] HORROR SHOW

MICHAEL RYAN REMAINED SILENT, as did Bane and Granite, out of respect for Troy Savage, whose death they had just witnessed via Savage's microweb cam. The last two minutes of footage had been shocking, starting with Savage's sudden attack and ending with Hartmann's death at the hand of Troy Savage, before he too expired. Flames engulfed the camera's field of view, until it went dark altogether.

"The chopper, General. Our guys need the chopper ASAP, and from the looks of it, Karen Frost is wounded, so send paramedics along."

Granite took off to the front of the plane to use the pilot's radio to get the stealth helicopter, hidden in the hills ten miles south of Berlin, to head toward Hartmann's mansion.

"Mr. Bane?" asked Ryan when they were alone.

"Yes, Mike?" replied the Director of Central Intelligence.

"The guy we just saw on the Web cam speaking with Troy Savage before he died. Savage called him Tommy?"

"That's right."

"I knew him as Dan Hawkins. I fitted him with nanoequipment back at USN some days ago."

Bane nodded while putting a hand on Ryan's shoulder. "I know. His real name is Tom Grant."

Ryan frowned. "Tom Grant? But the Tom Grant I remember doesn't look like—"

"New face, Mike. Part of his retirement package a year ago. We didn't tell you about him because you didn't need to know."

Ryan crossed his arms and exhaled. "That explains a lot," he finally said, before turning to the computer screen, which now displayed a real-time satellite view of the mansion, along with a moving red dot representing the homing unit that Savage had given to Tom Grant.

[84] IN HIS ARMS

IN SPITE OF THE flames surrounding them, Karen Frost felt colder than she had ever felt in her life, but at the same time she sensed his warmth, his strength, as he carried her away from danger, away from those faceless men clutching machine guns.

She felt his heavy breathing on her face as he ran, as he

suddenly cut left before opening fire on an unseen enemy. Karen tried to see, tried to help, but the blood loss had not only tunneled her vision; it had robbed her of her energy, purging her strength, leaving her fate in the hands of Tom Grant.

The gunfire intensified, mixed with the shouts of Tom and Rachel as they fought back the enemy, as they gained ground, as they struggled to get away. But for some reason the reports seemed distant, as if the weapons were discharging a hundred feet away, not next to her.

Her hearing loss intensified, until the point where she could not hear Tom or Rachel, could no longer listen to their voices as they zigzagged through the burning kitchen.

But she could still feel his arms, those powerful arms that had hugged her so many nights so long ago. And she could still see, although her sight was narrowed not just by her weakened condition but also because of the way Tom was carrying her, blocking her field of view with his upper chest and neck, where she rested her head as he fought to escape.

Walls, ceilings, chandeliers, flames, and smoke rushed by, like in a silent movie.

Or am I dreaming this?

Am I really just bleeding to death in that living room?

But the heartbeat—his heartbeat—intense and unyielding, continued to throb against the side of her face as he fought against staggering odds, with unwavering determination, rushing through room after room, some ablaze, others smoking, and still others clear.

A burning pressure built in her lungs, in her throat, forcing tears to her eyes, making her realize that the smoke was beginning to—

More gunfire, again distant, conflicted with the rhythmic trembling in his arms, which told her that Tom Grant was firing the machine gun, and she could barely hear it, as it sounded more like popping corn inside a microwave in the next room.

But she also felt another vibration in his chest overlapping those from his arms. He was shouting.

Finding it harder and harder to breathe through the

thickening smoke swirling around her, Karen pressed her face against his vest, trying to inhale through it slowly, trying to control her shivering body as Tom picked up his pace, as he raced into another room, which led to—

Fresh air.

Karen filled her lungs with the cool night air. They were outside, running away from the house. The sky and the stars replaced the burning walls, the whirling smoke, the havoc created by Troy Savage's incendiary bomb.

[85] CHOPPERS

I'M COUGHING MY ASS off while trying to keep up the pace and clear my lungs from the smoke I inhaled while touring the mess that Troy Savage made of Hartmann's mansion.

"Stay with me, Rachel!" I scream, watching in satisfaction as her long shadow catches up to me.

"Where is that damned helicopter?" she asks.

Scanning the clearing, verifying that there are no guards on this side of the grounds, I shake my head while huffing and puffing, Karen's weight drilling holes in my shoulders and elbows. I'll have to set her down soon but can't do it in the middle of this lawn lest I want to turn this chase into a turkey shoot.

So I keep up the pace, ignoring my pathetically out-of-shape body, my burning legs, my aching lungs as I breathe in short sobbing gasps.

Rachel trots past me like a thoroughbred mare, long legs swinging as she reaches the tree line seconds before I do.

"What now?" she asks, covering me with her MP5T as I finally catch up with her and set Karen down on a thick layer of fallen leaves behind a row of waist-high shrubs, taking a moment to catch my breath before checking the wound, verifying that for now it has stopped bleeding.

"Now . . . we wait," I say, my chest swelling as I try to force as much oxygen into my system as I can while checking the homing device strapped to my right wrist, verifying that it is still ticking, then realizing that it is not just a homing unit but a pretty damned fancy nanogadget, with a built-in two-way radio, a GPS finder, plus it even tells the time.

Now that we're far away enough from the mansion I get a full appreciation of the extent of the fire, which has spread to all four floors and along this side of the mansion.

Emergency vehicles finally make it up the hill and stop by the front gate. Unfortunately for them—and fortunately for us—the thick iron gate isn't moving, and a little voice tells me Troy had something to do with that.

Peering through the branches at the array of blinking lights on the other side of the gate, and the half-dozen guards on this side trying to get it open, I silently concede that Troy definitely had the gift.

And then there's the fire consuming the woods on the other side of the mansion and moving toward the front, threatening to engulf the trees lining the access road and flanking the gate itself—meaning the emergency vehicles will have to back off or risk getting swallowed by the rapidly spreading inferno.

Troy's inferno.

Everything had gone according to his plan. Troy's team had gone in, performed their assigned sabotage tasks to create the synchronized diversions, and then pulled back, leaving the door wide open for the termination team of Troy and—

"Tom . . . cold . . ."

Kneeling by her side while Rachel keeps an eye out for guards or the rescue chopper, I hold Karen's hand.

"I'm here, honey," I reply, no longer caring what Rachel thinks. Damn it, I loved this woman, and in a way a part of me still does—at least based on the gut-ripping feeling twisting inside of me at the sight of her blood, of her quivering lips, of her pale face.

The field dressing has staunched the hemorrhage, but she has apparently already lost enough blood to send her system to the brink of shock. She needs medical assistance, and pronto, before she—

"Sorry . . ." she says, her eyes finding mine in the flickering twilight created by the distant flames. "Should have . . . gone with you . . . year ago."

"Don't say that," I reply, forcing back the tears, silently cursing this terrible turn of events. "You followed your heart. I know you care for me. I know that, and that was good enough for me . . . still is."

Karen Frost starts to tremble, to shudder as she closes her eyes. "Tom . . . I . . . cold."

"You fight this, Karen," I hiss by her ear. "Don't you dare leave me here alone. Do you hear me? You can't leave me like this. I need you!"

Rachel glances my way for a moment before resuming her watch of the grounds and the skies above.

Karen stares at me with her large brown eyes, glistening with tears. "I . . . can't . . . I—"

"It's here!" announces Rachel. "The chopper's here!"

"Did you hear that, Karen?" I tell her as I lift her light frame, once again cradling her like I would a baby.

Beyond the branches outlining the forest drops a massive black ship, the roaring flames from the mansion drowning the already muffled *whop-whop* sounds of its stealth rotor as it touches down on the lawn halfway between the tree line and the burning mansion, about fifty feet from where we are.

"Let's go!" Rachel shouts, starting toward the waiting craft, whose side door swings open.

I go after her, no longer holding a weapon, no longer caring to hold anything except for Karen Frost, the woman that I realize I still love, I still wish to spend the rest of my life with.

The staccato gunfire rattles the night, rising above the roaring flames. The guards by the front gate have spotted us and are now racing toward us.

The ground explodes in front of me.

I cut left, then right, doing my darnedest to add a zigzagging motion to my sprint in order to make myself a harder target.

Rachel gets to the chopper while I'm barely reaching the halfway point.

"Come on, Tom!" she shouts at the top of her lungs, before pointing her MP5T at the incoming guards and cutting loose a dozen rounds. In the same instant, two soldiers jump out of the helicopter dragging a body, which they dump by the rear of the craft before swinging their machine guns at the guards.

I drop my gaze at the body, riddled with bullets but still clutching a machine gun in his dead fingers.

Rem Vlachko.

What in the world is he doing in this—

Multiple reports pierce the night, and from the corner of my right eye I see guards falling to the lawn roughly a hundred feet from me. But in the same instant more guards appear from around the rear of the mansion, their muzzles alive with gunfire. Several rounds ricochet off the armored skin of the stealth helicopter.

"Tom!"

I'm almost there, nearly out of breath, kicking my legs as hard as I possibly—

An invisible fist punches my left torso, and the subsequent burning pain that nearly makes me lose control of my bladder tells me I've been shot. Before my mind has a chance to register it, another bullet wallops into me on the same side, the sting spreading up my neck and down my ass.

Mustering every last ounce of strength left in me and channeling it to my quivering legs, I take the last three steps, before jumping in, twisting my body in midair to land on my back in the metallic troop carrier bay of the helicopter.

My vision tunneling, I feel the warmth propagating through my body, and in the same instant I realize that I have just pissed on myself.

I feel hands all around me, tugging not at me but at Karen Frost.

I hold her tight even though I have no control of my arms, which have developed a mind of their own, refusing to let her go, refusing to let anyone take her away from me.

"Sir! Please! You have to let her go!" shouts a soldier, a

blond kid in a U.S. Marine field uniform who looks like he's sixteen. "We're medics! We've got her now!"

My arms finally give and I'm suddenly alone, lying flat on my back in my own piss hugging my own self while trembling, the burning pain scourging my back, my torso, my legs.

"Oh, my God! You've been shot!" screams Rachel, kneeling by my side as I sense upward motion.

Another medic, this one completely bald, like me, and in his thirties, kneels next to her and starts to do something to my left side with a pair of scissors.

I try to lift my head, but the crippling sting skyrockets, shooting waves of raw pain down my shivering body.

I try to breathe, but even that hurts like a motherfucker, forcing me to remain still, arms and legs quivering so hard that I feel Rachel holding them down, along with one of the soldiers.

My vision starts to tunnel as everything from my neck down becomes numb, as I half-feel, half-see gloved hands tearing into my side, cutting into me, apparently digging for oil. Someone says something about clamping a torn artery, or something like that.

And so I make the mistake of turning my head away from my own misery, my stare landing on a sight I know I won't forget for as long as I live: the image of Karen Frost, naked from the waist up, her lifeless eyes fixated on a spot on the ceiling as the blond medic applies a battlefield dressing to her chest.

"Fuck! She's gone into cardiac arrest!" he shouts at a third medic, this one black and wearing a stethoscope. He drops a syringe and grabs a white metallic case, snapping it open, snagging the pads of an automated external defibrillator, thick coiled wire connecting them to the unit.

I blink away the tears at the surreal sight, my chest aching with grief, nearly choking me as I continue to stare into her dead eyes.

"Clear!" the black medic shouts.

The blond medic dressing her wound backs off for an instant as the shock causes her upper body to rise a few inches before falling back down.

Dammit, Karen. Dammit!

"She's not responding," says the older medic treating me. "Shock her again!"

"Clear!"

I continue to stare at her beautiful eyes, at her frozen expression as the medic keeps working on her, refusing to give up, shocking her again and again to no avail.

The tunnel that has become my world continues to narrow, until all I see is her distant face, her brown eyes, glistening in the gray light, as beautiful as ever.

I feel the end nearing. I feel my heart hastening, then slowing down, then increasing in tempo again, but irregularly, stomping my chest.

As I'm ready to also surrender myself to the damage caused by bullets that the TechnoSuit was supposed to stop, I sense something clasping my head, turning it away from Karen Frost.

"You hang in there, mister! You hang in there, you hear me?" says Rachel, her narrow face filling my field of view, her green eyes staring straight down at me.

I swallow hard, my emotions in as much havoc as my body, but I do manage to take a deep breath before exhaling through my mouth.

"You fight this, Tom Grant! Do you hear me? You fight this! Don't you dare die on me!"

My confused mind is trying to register her words—or were those my words, the ones I said to Karen by the tree line?

"You hang in there! You fight this, dammit! Fight it!"

I try to keep up with the nightmarish events whirling around me like a cyclone, threatening to uproot my sanity, to swallow everything, the rattling noise, the shouts, the terrifying numbness gripping me, the gut-wrenching sight of Karen's dead eyes and Rachel's pleading stare.

Until slowly, oh, so slowly, everything fades away.

EPILOGUE

ST. THOMAS. THE U.S. Virgin Islands.

The first of several giant cruise ships typically visiting the island on sunny and mild days like today disgorges hordes of camera-bearing tourists onto the quiet streets of Charlotte Amalie, the nucleus of the ten-mile-long island skirting the outline of St. Thomas Harbor.

And here they come, I think, watching the masses being shepherded toward shops lining Main Street and its many alleys, where local merchants carried on a tradition dating back to the eighteenth century, except that the barrels and bales have long since been replaced by nanotronic gadgets, designer jewelry and clothing.

I'm enjoying my breakfast, a mimosa—orange juice and champagne—while watching the spectacle, the rivers of humanity exploring Dronningens Gade, what the locals call Main Street.

It's become my morning routine to ride into town from my little oceanfront hideaway in nearby Magens Bay, on the north shore, a quick fifteen-minute ride on my new Harley, which I bought over here soon after settling the purchase of my new retirement home. I could have saved a few bucks by buying the bike in the States rather than on this overpriced island, but money is no longer an object for yours truly after Uncle Sam came through for me following my lengthy recovery at a Navy hospital in Bethesda, Maryland, where I pretty much had to learn how to walk all over again. As it turned out, one of the two rounds that those guards pumped into me grazed my spine, giving me the scare of a lifetime when the docs told me I was paralyzed from the waist down. At the time I wasn't sure if I feared not walking again as much as the possibility of no more hanky-panky, since *everything* south of the border wasn't functioning. But lady luck was on my side, and with the help of modern medicine, a pair of terrific rehab nurses, and the Grace of God, I returned to full functionality within a few months.

The mimosa is terrific, as wonderful as the weather in this place, though some of the locals have already warned me about the upcoming hurricane season and urged me to get plywood boards cut to sizes to fit all the windows of my little brick house, where I've been enjoying my new life for the past two months. I'm going to get around to it soon.

I sip my mimosa while glancing at the headlines of the *Today* newspaper, flown in daily from the mainland. It took Germany weeks to settle down following our exciting night several months ago. And not just Germany but the entire world had been in shock when the report of the CyberWerke connection with international terrorists made the headlines, revealing a conspiracy that had started during the closing days of World War II.

I slowly shake my head, amazed that Rolf Hartmann had actually managed to grow so strong so soon totally unchecked until Karen and Tom started poking into Cyber Werke's affairs—plus Rachel and me, of course.

I sigh, remembering Rachel Muratani.

She had spent a month by my bedside as I struggled to take my first few steps. Unfortunately for me—and fortunately for her—Bane promoted her to assistant to the new head of the Counterterrorism Division at the CIA. That meant she wasn't able to hang around the D.C. area by the time yours truly became strong enough to attempt to actually consummate our relationship. But we did talk a lot in that month, and unable to perform because the king of the jungle was asleep at the wheel, we actually became really good friends. And since I was once again officially out of the CIA—by personal request—I couldn't just pick up the phone and call her wherever she was around the world. And of course, because of Agency rules, she couldn't call me either. In the end, I'd decided to simply write the whole thing off for now and get on with my life. I don't have that many years left in me and I'll be damned if I'm going to spend them waiting for someone. I made that decision right about the time I was able to get around with just a slight limp and, being independently wealthy, decided to vanish once again, to settle down somewhere warm and far away from the rat race that had been my life up to this point.

But I still often think of Rachel Muratani.

She did write to me twice during the last few weeks of my hospital stay telling me how much she was enjoying her new assignment and also how much she was missing me. I sure miss her too, especially in the evening, but not nearly as much as I used to miss Karen Frost during those first few weeks in El Salvador.

Briefly closing my eyes, I think of Karen, of the times we had together, and decide that they were certainly worth the pain that followed—the hollow feeling that I still feel at times.

Her funeral in D.C. was very high-profile—or so I read. I was unconscious in some hospital in England waiting to become strong enough to be transferred to a D.C.-area hospital. Even the president attended the services.

I mourned Karen's death in the privacy of my hospital room, and all I can say about that is that she lived and died according to her own rules. She died doing what she loved to do, what was in her blood, what had to be done to prevent a monster like Hartmann from launching World War III.

And the same can be said about my old mentor.

Although Agency rules prevented Troy from getting a high-profile funeral—just the same nameless gold star at the entrance of the main CIA building in Langley he received following his staged disappearance the year before—he will be remembered by those who knew him as one of the finest CIA officers that ever lived. Troy was willing to do everything and anything for his country, for the job—even at the cost of his own life. I didn't realize until a week later that Karen and Troy knew ahead of time that the assault on Hartmann's place carried a high probability of being a one-way ticket for both of them, which was the reason for all of the secrecy, for not letting the rest of the team know the full scope of the operation, limiting us to the information we needed to execute our own portion of the mission. Karen and Troy had been mentally prepared to perish in that attack—if that's what it took to eliminate Hartmann and his cronies. And they did pull it off, eliminating not just Hartmann and Deppe but their inner circle, the men and women trapped upstairs tagged with running the various pieces of their once-global empire.

Now CyberWerke is being broken up into smaller companies around the world according to an agreement negotiated by no one other than President Laura Vaccaro, who was determined not to take any chances of it becoming a monster again.

Speaking of monsters, the reason for all of the satellite shutdowns was that rogue military assembler from USN. Fortunately we had Mike Ryan on the case, and he was able to orchestrate and execute the right plan of attack to bring it down before it too could trigger a disaster.

By the way, Mike Ryan, his wife, Victoria, and their baby swung by one day at the naval hospital toward the end of my recovery period, after Rachel left to do her thing, and paid me a surprise visit. Seeing Ryan reminded me of Karen Frost and the time we spent together tracking down and bagging Ares Kulzak way back when. We sure made one hell of a team, the three of us, back in those dark days in America, and we actually accomplished a good thing for our country.

And as for me, I'm enjoying my new life, which will soon also involve taking tourists out for snorkeling trips around the islands, as soon as my forty-foot cruiser arrives from Florida. Bane was able to get it for me through his connection with the DEA in Florida, from the large number of boats seized from drug dealers in that state. I already have a spot ready for it at the marina near my place, right next to this lady skipper who's been entertaining tourists on this island for twenty years. We had lunch twice already. The first time so I could pick her brains on the ins and outs of herding tourists around the island and the second time because she has a cute face, is built like a goddess, and is actually my age. But nothing serious has developed yet. I'm being a little more cautious this time around.

Sticking to my daily routine, I finish my morning drink and get ready to head back to my little piece of paradise just as the invaders reach my morning watering hole. As it happens every day, I catch a few looks from some of the ladies while I hop onto my Harley wearing just a pair of shorts, a plain T-shirt, sneakers, shades, very short hair, and a goatee—in memory of Troy. Maybe they're just admiring my beautiful Harley, or perhaps it's the fact that my long hospital stay slimmed me down by two sizes—weight I've kept off thanks to my daily walks as part of my ongoing rehab exercises. Or perhaps they like my picture-perfect tan from living in this place a couple of months.

The Harley rumbles to life on the first crank and I cruise slowly down the street, the chrome on the bike glistening in the morning sunlight. I'll be back in the early-evening hours to have another drink after the invading tourists retreat to their ships. These sunrise and sunset Harley rides are probably one of the best aspects of my new life, tying for first place with my long walks on the powder-soft sand of Magens Bay.

It's just a lovely morning, seventy-two and sunny. I open her up, easing up to fifty as I head up the mountains separating Charlotte Amalie from the north shore. The wind in my face washes away the pain, the bitter memories, the stress of so many years of field operations, of deceptions, of lies, of death.

A convertible packed with girls passes me by. Two of them shout and wave, as if they knew me.

Tourists.

That's one great thing about living in a place like this. Most everyone—in particular the tourists—is in a great mood. Everybody is as friendly as they'll ever be, and that just adds to the magic of St. Thomas—in sharp contrast with my former life of deception. In a way, this place is another lie, an illusion, but at least it resides on the opposite end of the spectrum from the surreal world of field operations.

Magens Bay is truly paradise. The sand is perfect. The water is perfect. The temperature is perfect. If you'd see this place in a movie you'd swear it was staged, but it isn't. Places like this are God's gift to mankind—or at least to those fortunate enough to be able to afford the ridiculous price tag to live here.

I pull up to my oceanfront place, small in comparison to my neighbors' digs, but it is all mine—and by the way, most of my affluent neighbors actually don't live here full-time, which in my mind makes me the luckiest guy on the block even if my place is barely eleven hundred square feet. It has a one-car garage, where I can fit the Harley plus my little two-seater convertible—also a gift from the good people of the Drug Enforcement Administration. Too bad they didn't have any Harleys in stock when I was shopping around for one; otherwise this motor and chrome would have also been free. But then again, it was all part of Uncle Sam's compensation package if you think about it.

I step into the kitchen, drop the keys on the tile countertop by the sink, snag a bottle of water from the refrigerator, and walk straight out the rear sliding-glass doors and into a million-dollar view.

I have a small covered patio bordered by the sand sloping down to the actual beach under the wonderful shade of palm trees.

Just like in El Salvador, I have a hammock stretched in between two trunks, and I settle comfortably in it while twisting the plastic top and taking a swig of cold water.

And my mind starts to drift, just as it does every morning while I contemplate the colorful sailboats cruising the turquoise waters, backdropped by a blue horizon peppered with distant vessels. A few people are walking on the beach, mostly folks who live in the neighborhood, as this mile-long stretch of beach by Magens Bay is private property. The public beaches are farther east and west of here. The beautiful sand and surf surrounding me belongs to just a handful of lucky souls.

And it is at this moment, as I'm totally relaxed, that I notice one of the figures walking on the beach suddenly turning in my direction: a woman, tall, slim, tanned, with firm arms and legs. She is barefoot and wearing white shorts, a matching bikini top, and sunglasses. Short dark hair frames her—

I sit up and lift my glasses, blinking my eyes to make sure they aren't playing tricks on me.

"Hey, Tom."

I'm standing before I know it, my heart doing cartwheels as

I stare dumbfounded at the face of Rachel Muratani, and my eyes automatically drift out to sea, looking for the telltale signs of a field surveillance team.

"Relax, Tom. I'm all alone," she says, removing her glasses, her eyes filled with dark amusement.

"Sorry," I reply, my throat suddenly going dry at the sight of her. "Habits. The last time I saw you on a beach I—"

"You look good, Tom," she says, coming up to me, putting a hand on my cheek. "I missed you terribly."

"Where—where did you go? I completely lost touch with you, except for a couple of letters."

She smiles, leans forward, and kisses me softly on the lips before saying, "How quickly we forget. You know I can't tell you that."

I smile too, before embracing her, before losing myself in those awesome green eyes, in her fine features, in that delicious chocolate freckle hovering just above her full lips.

She kisses me again, the taste of her reminding me of Paris, of the brief moments we spent alone on that dark street making out like a pair of teenagers.

"It's good to be with you again," she mumbles, her eyes closed as I kiss her wonderful freckle.

"I missed you, Rachel Muratani," I confess. "Not only did I miss your kiss but also your voice, your company, your—"

Rachel puts a finger to my lips. "Just hold me," she says.

I do, pressing her against me, holding her like I once held Madison and Karen, my hands running the length of her bare back.

"When did you get here?" I ask, her face buried in my chest.

"Today."

"How long are you—"

"Hush," she says. "I'm here today, darling."

"And tomorrow?"

"One day at a time," she replies, clasping the sides of my face. "Let's take it one day at a time, shall we?"

I hug her again while nodding, while silently accepting her terms, while slowly surrendering myself to the soothing comfort of her nearness.

Forge

Award-winning authors
Compelling stories

· ·

Please join us at the website
below for more information
about this author and other great
Forge selections, and to sign up for
our monthly newsletter!

· · · · **www.tor-forge.com** · · · ·